Rave Reviews for Virginia Rich's Mouth-watering Whodunits!:

"For midnight readers and eaters."

—*Daily News* (New York)

"A case of delicious homicide."

—*House & Garden*

"A rich concoction of culinary expertise and homicidal horrors."

—*Booklist*

"Virginia Rich has a keen sense of social satire and an ability to evoke the precise character of life in a small New England town. But what I enjoyed most was eavesdropping on Mrs. Potter's culinary ruminations. Good food . . . an inquisitive mind, and a keen appreciation of how eating well contributes to the quality of life."

—Richard Sax, *Cuisine*

The Nantucket Diet Murders

Virginia Rich

A DELL BOOK

Published by
Dell Publishing
a division of
Bantam Doubleday Dell Publishing Group, Inc.
1540 Broadway
New York, New York 10036

The trademark Dell® is registered in the U.S. Patent and Trademark Office.

ISBN: 0-440-16264-5

Reprinted by arrangement with Delacorte Press

Printed in the United States of America

April 1986

10   9

RAD

The island, the town, and some of the houses are real. The Scrimshaw Inn and the characters are real only to the author. The recipes on the book's last page and inside back cover are deliciously real.

To the Sandwich Girls of Nantucket
and the Tight Little Group of Chestnut Hill, Philadelphia;
to several special others in both places;
to some of their mothers
and all of their daughters.

I

Oscar deBevereaux painfully eased his sagging flesh, his aching bones, into the high old-fashioned tub.

"Hell of a way to end the day," he said to himself, thinking of long-ago late afternoon parties on Long Island, when Bunny had been alive, of tea dancing at the Plaza in even earlier happy days.

Then, as he knew they would, came memories even more painful than the torment of his arthritic hips and knees. He thought, as he knew he would, of Marthé, his plump and beautiful little Marthé, riding her fat pony in late afternoon Long Island sunshine. Then, of an older Marthé playing tennis with laughing, long-legged boys on the tennis courts in the lower garden, of a white-aproned maid carrying great trays of milk and lemonade and sandwiches and cakes to hungry young friends, their golden arms and legs glowing in the light.

He thought of his daughter, as round and sleek as a young seal, making her neat trim dives into the pool beyond the house. He saw her joining her schoolmates in field hockey. *"Yea, Martie!"* he heard girls in school uniforms cheering from the sidelines.

Again he could hear her say, at first cheerfully, and then in later times plaintively, "But I'm just too *revoltingly* fat!"

He and Bunny had remonstrated, he remembered, and he could still see Marthé's firmly set, square little jaw. She was still saying the same words when her emaciated body had to be carried upstairs for the last time to her girlhood room in the big Long Island house. *"Too revoltingly fat."*

How light the burden of that coffin must have been, Oscar deBevereaux thought again, as it carried the wraith, the caricature, of that once beautiful, sturdy little body.

The sorrow was as new as it had been that day, and so was the rage that had been its companion for all these years. Soon, he told himself grimly, he would be able to act. At long last he was now building a case, in the eyes of the law he served and respected, that would begin to avenge his daughter's death, although a case that involved another child and a tragedy of a different kind.

He groaned, perhaps from the slight relief of the hot water as he soaked his aching joints. Was that someone at the kitchen door downstairs? He heard a woman's voice, the words unintelligible, then the door's closing. Never mind, he told himself, he could never have got there in time anyway, and what deuced difference could it make? People were always coming in and out his back door, and one reason it was left unlocked was so he wouldn't have to disturb himself coming up and down stairs. His bath, his bedroom, his comfortable living room, were on the second floor of his Nantucket house, a remodeled small barn in the center of town. The kitchen, a small guest room and bath, and the large dining room that doubled as a downstairs sitting room were on the first.

Half dozing now in the cooling water, he roused at the thought that for a second time the kitchen door downstairs had been opened and closed, but this time he heard no call of greeting.

Maybe it was Edie, with something from the office. He'd given her the afternoon off for some kind of softball girls' do at the Scrimshaw. She'd told him it was her birthday; it seemed only three months since her last one, he thought irritably. Anyway, he'd see her in the morning, whenever he managed to get down. Today, with no secretary in the office, he had taken the afternoon off himself, had removed the phone from the hook and settled down with a book in front of the upstairs fireplace.

About to turn on a fresh stream of hot water, he reconsidered. Slowly he hoisted his now waterlogged and wrinkled body out of the high, claw-footed tub. Awkwardly he toweled his softened skin and eased his arms and shoulders into a gray flannel bathrobe. He'd go down to the kitchen and make himself a cup of tea, at least, even if he didn't feel much like dinner. Maybe, if it was there, he'd even try some of that comfort-comfrey stuff, whatever it was called, that Beth Higginson had said she'd leave for him, see if *that* would help this damned arthritis.

A tin canister on the kitchen table next to the back door was neatly labeled *Comfrey Tea* in Beth's familiar hand. The wilted clumps of half-green leaves it contained looked unpromising, but he told himself Beth was the authority on herbs, not he. He boiled water in a saucepan, added a small handful, and let it simmer for a minute or two, a procedure that seemed vaguely suitable for extracting its virtues, if any.

The resulting pale liquid seemed too anemic in color and aroma to suggest it would be an effective remedy for anything at all. He decided to let it simmer a little longer while he looked for a possible message from a second caller. Finding none, he decided he had only imagined the second opening and closing of the kitchen door.

When he thought the tea must be sufficiently brewed (it was no darker and no more aromatic now), he filled his big tea mug. Then, neat as always in his bachelor kitchen, he rinsed the sodden leaves into the garbage disposer in the sink. As they flushed away, he rinsed and dried and put away the saucepan.

With mug in hand, he made his way back upstairs to his big chair in front of the fire. It was only good manners to try the stuff, and its taste was not too disagreeably grassy. After all, an old friend had gone to the trouble of bringing it to him. He'd drink it now before it got cold, then call to thank her in the morning. Tell her he felt better, whether he did or not.

The grip of sudden pain in his chest, when it came, made him forget his aching bones, even the sharper hurt of old memories. His head was splitting, and so, in a great revulsion of nausea, were his stomach and bowels, a red flood of pain engulfing him in continually increasing rhythm.

Through glazed eyes, Oscar deBevereaux saw the curl of surf on his own beach on the Long Island shore, each crest flaming in the sun, a red ebb and flow commanding his entire attention. Finally there was no pain, but the ebb and flow of each crested wave continued, now blue in the fading light. Then, at the last, there were only soft murmurs of gray water and white spindrift along the sand.

2

"You're all so gorgeously *thin!*"

These, Mrs. Potter's first words of greeting to a reunion of old friends, were spoken only minutes after her return to the island of Nantucket and less than nine hours before Oscar deBevereaux's death. It was to be nearly twenty hours before she would learn this sad news of yet another old friend of her many years on the island, and perhaps twenty-one before she began to feel uneasy about the cause of his death.

This day, a Wednesday, at noon, her smile embraced all of the seven women gathered at the round luncheon table. At that early hour theirs was the only party in a room that in summer would have been crowded with tables and the murmur of well-bred voices. Today the pine-paneled room was quiet, warm and welcoming, filled with good smells, with growing plants, with masses of pink poinsettias left from the holidays just past. The bay window enclosing the round table was bright with moving patches of January sunlight. A small fire sputtered gently in the old center fireplace.

"How do you do it?" she asked. "We all went on the same diets, off and on for years, without really changing very much. And now *look* at you!"

Mrs. Potter's hostess, one of her dearest and oldest friends
and the reason for this return visit to the island, was first to
answer. "Oh, I haven't lost much yet," Gussie told her, with
an affectionate squeeze of her arm. "Less than ten pounds.
The others started earlier—aren't they wonderful?"

Gussie's smile was as bright and engaging as it had been
forty years ago. With no pretense of being younger than she
and Mrs. Potter both were, her face showing light lines of
both laughter and sorrow, Gussie seemed even more radi-
antly beautiful now than she had been at eighteen.

"Speaking for myself, I weigh exactly what I did when I last
saw you, and thirty years before *that,*" Dee said, at Mrs.
Potter's right, with a shrug of her elegant shoulders. "You
look pretty marvelous yourself with that Arizona tan. Particularly since your hair is as much gray—let's say *silver*—as
blond now. Nice effect." The last was spoken with careful and
professional approval. "We look good because you're glad to
be back."

"I'm serious," Mrs. Potter persisted. "Of course I'm
overjoyed to be back with Les Girls, and you always look
wonderful, Countess. So does Bethie. You two are unchanged, which is perfect. But the rest of you—what *are* you
all doing to yourselves?"

Mrs. Potter's gaze went around the table. First there was
Dee, Countess Ferencz, the youngest and newest member of
the group, whom she had proclaimed unchanged. Mrs. Potter did not quite remember when or why Dee had come to
the island, but she gradually had become part of the group in
the past ten years. Nearly six feet tall, showing more strong
bones and white teeth in her face than the others, Dee was
wearing her familiar trademark hat: firm, straight-brimmed,
dark brown, placed squarely on her head over dark, ungray-
ing hair pulled back into a great braided chignon. Her heavy
gold-and-silver earrings, so large they would have overpow-
ered any other face around the table, were the same ones
Mrs. Potter remembered. Dee needed no change. She
looked like what she was—a former fashion editor, one who
had early learned her own style.

Next to Dee was Bethie—Beth Higginson—whose solid plump comfort, an exception to the new and remarkable thinness of the others, had a beauty of its own order. Beth's pleasant, quizzical brown eyes beamed back at Mrs. Potter from a firm and rosy face, framed in a wreath of nicely cut curly white hair. Her Tyrolean hat was scarlet, with an extravagant cockade of feathers.

"Now don't look at *me*," Beth implored. "I'm going to make an appointment with the man next week or the week after that, I promise you all. Only you've got to agree I can't possibly start a diet this minute. I made a dilled fish mousse yesterday, and there's that to finish. Then I *can't* throw out the last of the Christmas fruitcake little Mary Bee sent me— she made it herself from Grandmother Higginson's old recipe. Or was it little Beth Ann Cox who made it? Anyway, before I start any new diet I have to finish up the last few of my holiday burnt sugar almonds—they're lovely chopped and sprinkled on vanilla ice cream. I remember you used to like them, Genia, and there's a little box of them waiting for you at Gussie's.

"Speaking of dieting," Beth went on, before Mrs. Potter could do more than smile appreciatively in reply, "I have to tell you about a marvelously light cranberry dessert I just remembered. Jim used to love it. You put raw cranberries and some chopped apple and pecans in the blender until they're sort of a mush, then you fold in some marshmallows and whipped cream. It's just a froth, really, and *so* refreshing. You all must try it for your diets as soon as I locate the recipe again."

"Your idea of light food and diets is fantastic, Beth," Gussie said. "I suppose there's whipped cream in that light fish mousse of yours, too?"

Another voice spoke from across the table. "I happen to *know* you think crème brulée made with light cream instead of heavy is a real Weight Watchers special."

"I've been spoiled," Beth admitted happily. "Jim wasn't a very big man, as you all remember." (Mrs. Potter thought of Jim Higginson—compact, dark, tough and feisty, a good newspaperman.) "In spite of not being very big himself, Jim said he liked having a wife who was what he called 'a fine figure of a woman.' And now the only other man's opinion that counts with me is Arnold Sallanger's. He says my health is superb, but I do think he made a little point of having his nurse weigh me a second time, with him watching, on my last checkup."

She paused and shook her head, with a flourish of the feather cockade, her smile rueful. "So I really am going to make that appointment, honestly, I promise. Next week. By the end of January at the latest."

Mrs. Potter's regard continued around the table. It was actually of the other four that her wonderment had been spoken. Like Beth, they were women who had known each other for many years.

Their friendship, that of the original core of the group, had begun in long-past Nantucket summers. In those years they came to the island for a month or a season, and most of their husbands commuted for weekends from city offices elsewhere.

With one exception, their children had grown up together, learned to sail together, to drive cars, to play tennis, and had in a few instances become briefly but inconclusively engaged to be married. They and their families had picnicked and birthday-partied together, had eaten and drunk at each other's houses for years. As the years went on, these women had shared the sorrow of their husbands' deaths, two of these within the last year. Through all of this time they had kept up an informal getting together, in a way that eventually evolved into a weekly lunching event. They knew and accepted each other's foibles, they worked together for the community good, and they were proud of each other's accomplishments.

She could not remember when they had begun to call themselves "Les Girls." Over noontime sandwiches at the Yacht Club, she thought, when some of them—those beyond bicycling range—were still chauffeuring their young to their days on the courts or the harbor. With a few inevitable dropouts over the years, with the return to the fold of Helen Latham after several years' absence, and with the more recent addition of Dee, the group had remained remarkably cohesive—even more so now that they all, in spite of punitive Massachusetts state income tax laws, had declared the island their year-round home.

Mrs. Potter felt herself quite as much of the group as ever, even though the ranch in Arizona and the cottage in Maine had taken the place of the Philadelphia and Nantucket houses that had been home before that. They had all kept more or less in touch through phone calls and letters, and regularly so in her own case with Gussie, whose friendship antedated even their early summerings on the island.

Now, after her absence of nearly two years, although Dee and Beth seemed unchanged (and to Mrs. Potter, Gussie was changeless), four of these old friends appeared almost like tiny strangers.

Leah, next to Beth, kissed her fingertips in a graceful wave, a gesture of thanks for the implied compliment of Mrs. Potter's questions. "Do we really look all that much better?" she asked, her rings and bracelets jingling musically. The lift of her eyebrows said she was confident of the answer.

Mrs. Potter looked at Leah's small pointed face and the pale fluff of hair above it. Memory showed a certain roundness, below a heavy fringe of bangs—once brown, then streakily buff. After Leah's widowhood several years ago, this fringe had been maintained at a sober, unrelieved shade of oxford gray by Larry, Les Girls' favorite island hairdresser. Now the newly soft bangs were almost platinum above Leah's green eyes, which she did not remember as being slightly slanted. The green reflected the vivid green of Leah's sleek wool sweater and trousers. Her fine-boned hands were smooth, her small bright nails were well shaped. Mrs. Potter definitely remembered Leah's hands as being forever work-worn in the years after her husband's death—in no way of necessity, but by what seemed constant and compulsive polishing of silver and furniture and washing of windows in slavish dedication to the big house in which she had been widowed.

What had happened to about twenty pounds of Leah Carpenter? And how had a rather nondescript gray tabby—a good woman dedicated to perfect widowhood, a woman whose only dramatics had been occasional indulgence in self-chosen martyrdom—become this small purring kitten?

"You *know* you look completely different, Leah," Mrs. Potter told her, "and you've got to tell me the secret."

Mary Lynne, next to Leah, replied instead, her honey-smooth voice making every sentence end in a soft, deferential question mark. "Genia, honey, hasn't Gussie told you? That the *most* marvelous man has come to the island? Not that we all don't have more than enough men to go around these days, which has to be a pure miracle from heaven in a place with so many of us widows. Isn't it amazing? Right here in town as many unattached men as women?"

Mary Lynne's soft southern voice was familiar. The sharp cheekbones were not, nor the flat planes under Mary Lynne's long strand of pearls, under her loose-fitting beige jersey and matching pants. Mary Lynne's statuesque beauty had been trimmed to the bone. Suddenly Mrs. Potter saw the Tennessee homecoming queen, lithe, active, auburn-haired, confident, yet by ingrained tradition claiming an air of helplessness they all knew was totally unmerited.

"Oh, we have *men*, Mary Lynne, such as they are," Dee said, with a touch of acidity. "Our old lawyer, our old doctor, our old lush of a stockbroker, our nonwriting author-in-residence, our pet poodle retired clergyman. And of course Peter, here at the Scrim." Dee lowered her voice. "Peter is the exception, as you well know. The rest of them are pretty much on their last legs, if you ask me."

"Dee, honey, the *health* of our dear boys is not the *point,*" Mary Lynne went on. "It's just how *many* of them there are." Her voice never lost its tentative, questioning lilt. "Most places there aren't half as many men as women our age, don't you know, Dee? Lordy, back in Chattanooga there are never enough to go around, my friends write me, of any age or state of debility whatsoever."

"Get back to the new man, Mary Lynne. I know the old ones," Mrs. Potter prompted. "And what does he have to do with how thin you all are? I can't believe you're all wasting away in unrequited love, at our age, at least not all for the same man."

There was a perceptible pause, and then Leah spoke, the pale fluff of her hair still a shock, as was the green sparkle of her slanted eyes. "It's unbelievable, Genia," she said. "Everything's different since Tony came. That was last June, and now he's staying all winter. It's a miracle."

"Leah calls him the *Master,*" another member of the group put in unexpectedly. Mittie's clear, slightly nasal New England voice was flat and self-assured. "She says she's joking, but she really *does*. I think that's sacrilegious, and incidentally, Leah, so does George Enderbridge. The Altar Guild was a little bit shocked, too, to hear you'd said that, and I think you should know."

"Don't be silly," Leah said. "Until I began to call him Tony, I just said 'Doctor.' He prefers that to his real title, he told me so."

"Oh, a new *doctor,*" Mrs. Potter said. "How does dear Arnold feel about that? What does he say about a new man coming in and taking over his patients? Or is Arnold ready to retire?"

"Tony isn't a *doctor* doctor," Mittie assured her quickly. "He's frank with me about this, naturally, knowing of Daddy's former standing in the academic world. Tony's degree is Ph.D., and he studied at Heidelberg. Anyway, you don't go to him for the flu or a broken leg. His field is health and beauty."

Mittie's light brown hair was smoothly turned under in the same pageboy style she had worn for years. The bright pink scarf, high on her throat above her pastel-striped wool pullover, exactly matched the pink of her well-fitted wool pants, both garments looking exactly like those—except for being much smaller—Mrs. Potter thought Mittie might have worn two years ago, when she last saw her.

Mittie, like the others, had never been really fat (although Mary Lynne had been close to it, Mrs. Potter recalled), but her gently settling shape had been that of one who had given up the sports of her proper New England upbringing—tennis, sailing, skiing, swimming—for bird-watching and needlework. Her love for gardening was in landscape design, not in stooping and bending and digging. While her life had become more sedentary, the years of outdoor sports, of sun and wind, had left their mark on Mittie's fair skin, etching it with a network of fine lines, which now seemed more deeply wrinkled.

Mary Lynne's soft, questioning voice continued her place in the talk. "You *know*, Genia, honey," she said seriously, "that we've all tried pretty much to keep ourselves up to the mark?" Mrs. Potter nodded expected agreement. "The thing is, now we have someone giving *direction* to our lives."

"This is absolute rubbish," Dee, Countess Ferencz, whispered into Mrs. Potter's right ear.

Helen Latham's clear midwestern voice, used to authority, now took firm command. "What everyone is trying to tell you, Genia, is that a remarkable man has come to the island, and I can't imagine why Gussie hasn't told you all about him. I met him first—he came here visiting old New York friends at the start of last summer—and he insisted on taking a personal interest in my case from the start. I see a great future for him here."

"Whatever he's doing, you're the thinnest of all," Mrs. Potter said. She remembered Helen's undefined and unremarkable square shape, her somewhat heavy jaw and features, her stiffly set dark hair. Presiding at a committee meeting, Helen always made Mrs. Potter think of a Roman emperor. No, better yet, of Mussolini, one hand upraised to command instant silence and attention.

Helen today was a tiny, rigid doll whose dark fluff of hair seemed a—chocolate? no, *cocoa*—version of the pale lemon-vanilla cotton candy on Leah's head, or Mary Lynne's of spun maple syrup. Cotton candy, fragile and full of air. Larry was clearly outdoing himself with his newly and fashionably thin year-round regulars.

Mary Lynne's soft voice again regained the floor. "You can see we're all learning so *much*, Genia, darling," she said. Mrs. Potter nodded expectantly. Her friends smiled back at her.

Impatiently, she broke the silence. "I can't stand this any longer," she told them. "Gussie, you're responsible for my being back on Nantucket. If you expect me to unpack my bags at your house after lunch, tell me. *What's going on with you all?*"

Mrs. Potter's hostess squirmed. "I was going to give you the full rundown later," she said, "but since you've brought us this far, with your usual nose-poking"—and she gave Mrs. Potter's arm another affectionate squeeze—"you might as well hear the whole story about our wonderful new celebrity on the island. I can't wait for you to meet him."

"Celebrity, my foot," Dee said flatly. "Resident, yes, and you all think you have a wonderful new magic man, and yes, you're all certainly *thin*. What Genia has to know is that the miracle man is Count Valerian Mikai Alexander Antonescu Ferencz, no less. It's Tony, Genia, *my* Tony. At least he was my Tony for two years, which was exactly twenty-three months too long. We got married just when I landed the job as editor of *Éclat* and Tony was beginning to make a name for himself in the diet and beauty racket."

Dee looked steadily around the table, her gaze level beneath the stiff dark brim of her hat. "I'm not saying he doesn't know his business, my dears, and apparently he's learned a few more tricks since he started out. All I want Genia to know is what I should have warned you all as soon as he set foot on the island. Tony Ferencz is a complete and unmitigated *bastard*, and you'll all be sorry before this is over."

3

The table was silent. Lips were closed in resolute smiles. Eyes glanced about the room in a bright, polite way, indicating that there would be no unseemly disagreements among friends. Quickly, with her usual composure and grace, Gussie spoke up. "Shall we think about lunch? Genia just got in on the late morning plane from Boston, remember, and we came directly here to the Scrim from the airport. I'm sure she's starved."

As she spoke, a light babble of voices came from the doorway of a private dining room, open to the main room in which Les Girls of Nantucket were seated. Occasionally a high shriek of feminine laughter broke the ripple of sound.

A stout middle-aged waitress came in from the kitchen bearing a heavy tray of drinks and disappeared into the doorway. Moments later she was back in the main room and at Mrs. Potter's side, giving her a familiar and friendly pat on the shoulder. "Glad to see you back," she said. "Seems like old times to have all you gals together again. A real reunion. What'll it be, ladies?"

"I'm ready to order, Jadine," Beth answered promptly. "The Yankee bean soup, please, and then I think the individual chicken pot pie and the fresh fruit salad plate with cream cheese dressing. I'll decide about dessert later. I see your Scrimshaw Rum Pie is on the menu, but this might be a good day for a hot mocha fudge sundae."

She faced the others apologetically. "I played paddle tennis on the outdoor court most of the morning," she explained, "and I'm planning to walk the beach at Eel Point after lunch. I need my strength."

Dee set the handwritten menu aside with a brisk, dismissing gesture. "Just a pot of tea for me, please, Jadine." Turning to Mrs. Potter, she spoke beneath her breath. "You wait and see about Tony."

"I'll order for the rest of us," Helen Latham said decisively, her glance around the table apparently assuring her that she was, as usual, to be the voice of the group. She spoke to the waitress. "We'll choose our lunch from the salad bar, Jadine. No roll basket or butter on the table. And we'll begin with a glass of freshly squeezed vegetable juice—whatever Peter has them turning out in the kitchen today."

Turning to Mrs. Potter, she continued. "And you'll go along with us, I'm sure, Genia?" The brisk tone, which had settled the issues—usually wisely—at so many island committee meetings, was still commanding. It surprised Mrs. Potter to hear it coming from this new and tiny doll. With affectionate amusement, she realized that Il Duce was still running the show.

A murmur came from Beth. She believed she *would* have just a small basket of the small hot breads with her lunch, and were there any little cinnamon rolls today?

A second murmur, and Mrs. Potter suggested another slight change. "The salad bar sounds perfect, Helen, and I can see from here how tempting it looks," Mrs. Potter assured her, "but a January day needs more than vegetable juice to celebrate a reunion lunch, to my mind. Please change that to a dry martini—on the rocks with a twist of lemon, right, Gussie?—for me and Mrs. Van Vleeck, Jadine. And what for the rest of you? Drinks are my treat today."

"Oh, no, Genia. You have one—not for me, thanks." Gussie's voice was half regretful, but certain.

Helen spoke promptly. "We all know what Tony says about liquor." The slightly heavy jaw and forehead, a bit too large now in the small face, were still forceful.

The others were in instant agreement. "We just couldn't," Mittie explained. "We're *committed.*"

"I'm not committed," Beth put in cheerfully. "I'd like a frozen daiquiri. Not too sour please, Jadine. Peter knows how I like it. A drink is just what we need to celebrate Genia's return to the fold."

Mrs. Potter, who without Beth's acceptance would have withdrawn her suggestion, now turned to Dee. "You'll join us?"

Dee's acceptance was as prompt as Beth's had been, but Mrs. Potter felt slightly awkward in the face of the others' stand. "It's a cold day," she said apologetically, realizing that it was actually rather warmer than usual for the season.

Leah's small kitten face was downcast, as something seemed to prompt her to take up a familiar refrain. "These January days *are* gloomy," she said. "I just can't get used to going home to a big empty house without darling Fanwell there." Her lips pursed and her rings and bracelets were silent.

Gussie glanced sideways at Leah with less than her usual ready compassion. She herself had been most recently widowed, and for a third time. All of the women at the table would be returning to houses in which they lived alone. Leah's claim to special circumstances was, except for Gussie's glance, rather blankly ignored.

Of all of them, only Helen Latham had a child at home, an only daughter in her mid-thirties, of whom, Mrs. Potter remembered, Lew used to say that she had an utterly forgettable face. She always had to prompt her husband with the name, and she herself often had to struggle to remember, not always quickly enough, that Laura Latham, Lolly, somewhat vague and seeming not overly bright, nearly invisible in her mother's admirable and forceful presence, was Helen's daughter.

Of the entire group, Gussie Van Vleeck was the only one to have even temporary company at the moment—that of her old friend, Mrs. Potter. And Mrs. Potter, widowed herself since her days as a regular member of the lunching group, also lived alone, most of the time in a sprawling ranch house miles from her nearest neighbors.

Gussie's regard of Leah softened as she caught a glimmer of amusement in the eyes of her guest, and she quickly suppressed a smile. As Mary Augusta Baines of Rye, New York, and Eugenia Andrews, fresh out of Harrington, Iowa, they had found the same small things funny from the day they had met in the halls of their freshman dormitory. Among these shared amusements—sometimes rueful ones—was the opinion that Leah was out to win the title of World's Most Bereft Widow. There was the accord of concealed glee now in observing that Leah was still competing, still winning, even though she was out of mourning clothes at last and again wearing her pretty rings and bracelets.

A louder burst of laughter now came from the adjacent room. There was a brief round of clapping and more high-pitched shrieks of laughter.

"Softball girls in there, really whooping it up," the waitress announced as she brought the drinks Mrs. Potter had ordered, and glasses of pale liquid, its color vaguely orange, for the rest. Another crescendo of laughter came from the private dining room.

"Jadine, didn't you forget something?" Dee asked, with a flash of smile. "You know Peter likes to send a little pot of his special cheese with the cocktails."

Nodding with apparent satisfaction at being reminded, the waitress rushed back with the complimentary specialty. Mrs. Potter watched Dee Ferencz top a crisp rye cracker with a quick, neat, and generous mound of the cheese-rum mixture. Dee's entire lunch today, she realized, would be these cheese-spread crackers and probably several small hot breads from Beth's luncheon roll basket, along with the pot of tea she originally ordered.

As she sipped her own drink, Mrs. Potter tried to keep up with the surface play of conversation. She found that, being alone as much as she was now—and happily so, for the most part—she found it exhausting to follow so much talk at one time. Her mind sifted out snatches, much of it news Gussie had previously relayed by letter or telephone, hoping that her facial muscles were making appropriate responses and wondering vaguely why Gussie had not told her about this new diet celebrity who had come to the island. Her friends' voices seemed higher in pitch, their speech more rapid, than she recalled.

". . . died while we were sailing," Mary Lynne was saying.

". . . a heroine," the others chorused proudly, "bringing in the boat all alone . . . too late, of course . . ."

This, she knew, was the story of Bo Heidecker's fatal heart attack the previous summer.

". . . naturally Mummy's furniture has to be kept heated," Mittie was explaining, "and the Shimmo house could be drained and closed . . ."

This meant Mittie must be living for the winter in the old family house on Main Street, above Gussie's.

"Cottage Hospital . . . new president of the board . . ." That was Helen, Mussolini now reduced to a china doll. The others beamed.

". . . plans for the Daffodil Festival in April . . ." That, it seemed, was again Mary Lynne. The others beamed again. "We're so proud of her for not giving up the chairmanship after Bo's death," someone said.

". . . have to say about six names—Paula, Clare, Ginny, Tricia, Annabel—before I remember which one . . ."

This apparently was part of a report on Higginson daughters and daughters-in-law, and there was a groan of sympathetic laughter.

". . . told her we'd learn to bake Portuguese bread . . ."

That had been part of Gussie's telephoned invitation, which had brought Mrs. Potter back for this midwinter visit.

The death of Gussie's third husband, in late fall, had perhaps come as a liberation to them both—to Gordon from querulous invalidhood and to Gussie from several years of being tyrannized by his bad-tempered illness—the invitation had not been based on need for sympathy or support.

Years ago, Mrs. Potter had flown to Gussie's side at the moment she learned that Gussie's first husband, who was also Mrs. Potter's favorite cousin, had been killed in a hunting accident. She had done so as well when Gussie's second husband died of a heart attack in New York, sharing Gussie's grief at the loss of the good man she had loved so greatly for so many years, and the father of her two children. Just as Gussie had come to be with her when Lew died.

This time they both—she and Gussie—had known without saying that it had not been necessary for her to come back to Nantucket when Gordon died, and that this January visit was purely for the pleasure of continuing their old friendship.

The mention of bread-baking had apparently caught Beth's attention, and her response brought Mrs. Potter back from her thoughts. "Portuguese bread—marvelous!" Beth was saying, enthusiastically, then adding a note of doubt. "But Manny said he wouldn't be back until May. I put a dozen loaves in the freezer before he closed, of course. I always do."

The old town bakery was closed for the winter, everyone said. There was no way they could learn to make Portuguese bread, they said, and besides, who eats *bread?*

Mrs. Potter smiled. "I do," she said, "and you all know I've been trying to bake real Portuguese bread for years. I trust Gussie. If she says we're going to make Portuguese bread, we *are.*"

Thus, ignoring the rising decibels of laughter from the doorway of the private dining room, talk continued at the round table in the bay window.

". . . so many things we share." This was Leah's voice, trailing into a familiar plaintive note. "Most of us past garden club presidents, nearly all of our husbands once commodores

of the Yacht Club . . . some happy memories, some tragic
. . ."

There were husbands then, Mrs. Potter reflected. On Nantucket it was always summer then, and summer was always weekends. The harbor was always blue at midday, dotted with racing sails. The nights were always starlit, the surf always music on wide clean beaches.

There were picnics then, parents languorous by the firelight after a day in the sun; teen-agers clustering around a portable radio just out of range of the light, scuffling sand with bare feet as they taught each other the twist and the frug, dances they hadn't learned at their proper off-island winter dancing classes.

There were husbands then. An album of snapshots flashed through her mind. Jules Berner, basking in Gussie's admiration, shaking himself like a slightly grizzled water dog after swimming the harbor from Coatue to Abram's Point. Bo Heidecker awarding bright pennants to prizewinning juniors at the Yacht Club. Les Latham, pale, plump, and serious, cackling in unwonted hilarity in a bright-flowered shirt at a beach club luau. Ab Leland with Mittie and their two blond sons at St. Paul's, their voices clear and true, the music and words so familiar—a tribute to compulsory chapel at the best prep schools—that they scarcely glanced down at their hymnals.

There was Fan Carpenter, the night Gussie gave him the nickname, from then on known to everyone except Leah as "Fannypatter." There was Jim Higginson whirling and pivoting Beth on the dance floor in a spirited foxtrot that turned into an unabashed tour de force jitterbug finale. Beer and Bloody Marys and gin and tonic; husbands, weekends, and laughter. Lew, with one arm thrown across her shoulder, driving home in the honeysuckle-scented darkness, in the old blue convertible.

Mrs. Potter roused herself as Leah repeated her words, "So many memories . . ."

"We know, Leah," Dee reminded her briskly. "We're all

women alone. Only some of us are more alone than others, aren't we?"

Gentle interior rumbling, reminder of the hours since her early breakfast, directed Mrs. Potter's attention to the salad bar. Taking up one long wall of the paneled, low-ceilinged room, it was flanked on both sides with plant stands and hanging baskets bearing a profusion of exuberantly thriving green plants. Philodendrons, ivies of many kinds, many-hued begonias, peperomias, dieffenbachias, sansevierias, bright pots of impatiens and nasturtiums, plus the soft pink and strong green foliage of the holiday poinsettias, all glowing under softly focused light.

As she gazed, the owner of the inn came toward them from the kitchen and bent quickly to kiss her cheek. "Potter, old dear, how wonderful to have you back!" Peter Benson exclaimed. "We've missed you! I adore my girls—how would I exist without you all?—and now the circle is complete again! How long will you be here?"

Before she could answer, he continued rapidly. "Now let's see, may I give a little dinner for you soon? No, let's make it a Sunday breakfast at the beach shack instead, shall we? You love picnics, Potter, and winter ones are the best. No sand, no bugs, everything cozy by the fire." He turned to the others. "Now all of you promise to come help celebrate Potter's return. You hear me, guys? Nobody says no to this party!"

"Nobody ever says *no* to any of your invitations, Peter," Mrs. Potter said. "Are we free Sunday, Gussie? I'd love it."

Gussie's assent seemed to be taken for granted as Peter spun Mrs. Potter around to a view of the dining room.

"Did you see what we're doing?" he demanded. "Those are fresh herbs growing in that hydroponic tank by the salad bar—can you believe it? Even in the restaurant on top of the World Trade Center in New York there isn't anything better. Some good places grow their own herbs this way in the kitchen, or so they tell you, but mine are right out here where you can feast your eyes as well as your greedy little tummies. Edible decor, my darlings!"

"You know Tony really inspired the idea," Leah put in.

"Now, Carpenter," Peter replied promptly, "Tony is staying here at the inn for the winter, as you all well know, and I'm the most loyal fan he's got around here, but nobody knows what's good for you better than old Uncle Peter. I spent more than two thousand dollars for that herb garden tank, and the idea was mine."

He turned to Gussie. "So what do you say, Van Vleeck? Is it a party for Sunday, say one o'clock at the shack?"

As Peter bent, affectionate, brotherly, to kiss Mrs. Potter a second time, she thought, as she often had before, that Peter treated them all like little boys—like eager, active little schoolboys, to be gently teased and chivied and ordered about. It was his special magic that he only ordered them to do those things that would prove to be fun (and often good for them as well), and he went to a great deal of trouble to arrange his amusements for them.

Peter left to return to the kitchen, but his path was momentarily blocked by a plump, scurrying figure in a tan gabardine raincoat and matching small-brimmed round hat, carrying a large shapeless bag over one shoulder. The pair made an awkward two-step, dodging from left to right, until Peter stepped firmly aside, propelling the newcomer gently into the private dining room, where the shrieks of laughter and applause were steadily increasing.

"Was that Lolly?" Mrs. Potter asked. "I haven't seen her for so long I couldn't be sure."

Helen Latham replied. "I don't know why she couldn't have come over to speak properly to her own mother, and certainly she should have greeted *you* properly, Genia. Sometimes I give up."

"I'm sure she was in a hurry to join her party," Gussie explained good-naturedly. "I saw her with Edie Rosborough the other day and they were so busy talking they didn't even see me."

"Oh, *Edie,*" Helen said carelessly. "I suppose I should be glad she seems to have found a girl friend at last—you know Lolly never really *has* fit in with people we all know. Since she met the girl, it seemed they asked her to join this little softball group, and she even got her first job a while back. She's a volunteer assistant at the science library. Not much of a job, but it's something for her to do."

Mary Lynne's conciliatory voice quickly tried to cover up Helen's disparagement of her daughter. "When the playing season is over, these girls are all too busy with their jobs around town for a celebration, Linda Peaseley told me. So they save up their dues and wait until now, when things are a little slack. The natural science library is closed today, I think, and the Peaseley travel agency where Linda works for her father has got everybody scheduled for whatever winter trips they're taking. Not that any of *us* is considering such a thing right now. Lord love a duck, Genia, you couldn't pay any of us to leave now that Tony's here."

"Ozzie told me things are quiet in his law office now, before he starts on our tax returns, so I suppose this is a good time for Edie to take the afternoon off," Mittie added. "Besides, I think someone said it was her birthday."

"Listen to them!" Mary Lynne marveled. "Did you ever hear such a-whooping and a-hollering? They're having themselves a high old time today."

On a fresh wave of laughter the team members burst into the dining room. Lolly Latham waved uncertainly toward their table, following the young woman Mrs. Potter now remembered from past visits to Ozzie deBevereaux's law office, where she had for some years run his affairs with single-handed competence. Mrs. Potter remembered other familiar faces—a teller from the Pacific Bank; a perky and pretty librarian from the Atheneum; a dependable alto in the choir at church. Others were new to her. All were attractive, fresh-faced young women in their twenties and thirties. Their laughter abated slightly as they straggled into a semblance of a line.

Among them was a tall girl with an oval face, biscuit-colored skin, and softly rounded features, her black hair in a single braid down the back, wearing a bright head scarf tied Indian fashion. She waved energetically at Gussie.

As she waved back amiably, Gussie leaned toward her

houseguest. "Tell you about her later," she whispered. "She's our secret weapon."

As members of the team surveyed choices of salad greens, of cheese and chicken and beef and vegetables, of ham and bacon and croutons, of condiments and salad dressings, Peter Benson appeared at the side of the hydroponic tank at the end of the long table.

With small shining scissors in hand, he seemed ready to harvest a sprig of one or another of the green herbs as a final, fresh-snipped salad topping. Mrs. Potter could hear him reciting the choices—salad burnet, lemon thyme, chervil, basil, tarragon, chives—identifying as he spoke, charming each guest with his attention.

With this group, Mrs. Potter saw that Peter's attitude was quite different from the affectionate and irreverent chaffing he accorded her own friends. To the softball girls he offered the flattering attention of a respectful courtier. They responded with sudden grace, becoming for a moment a pageant of young queens. Even Lolly Latham, lumpy and graceless, seemed to glow as he spoke to her.

"I wish she'd find a boyfriend her own age," her mother said forcefully to her own group. "Every time an older man like Peter pays any attention to her, she acts like an idiot. You should see her when Tony comes to the house! I can't tell her they're only being nice to her on my account."

Helen's sigh seemed more exasperated than sorrowful. "I keep hoping this new friend of hers, Edie Rosborough—she's Ozzie's secretary, you know—will find her somebody more suitable. One of the locals, if there *are* any single ones. You know I've never gotten her to snap out of it since Lester's death."

Mrs. Potter suddenly remembered the shocking story that must have shaped the life of Lolly the child. Helen's plump pale husband had died a suicide, almost twenty-five years ago, in Chicago. The ten-year-old Lolly, she now recalled, had been the one to be awakened by the gunshot, and had been the one to find her father's dying body on the living room sofa. It was no wonder Lolly Latham was shy and retiring. Walter and Elna, Helen's cook and butler of many years, had once begun to describe the scene for Mrs. Potter, until she had firmly changed the subject. Unbidden, the picture came back to her now—the shattered skull, the warm wet blood still flowing on the cushions—the picture that might still be seen in unspeakable horror behind Lolly's light blue eyes.

She looked again now to see Peter Benson drape a casually affectionate arm over Lolly's shoulders and to see Lolly's upward glance, nearly smiling, almost trustful. Peter's tact and kindness were unfailing, as always, in any group.

Then another gentle rumble beneath her cashmere sweater and her soft tweed travel suit reminded Mrs. Potter that her airport breakfast at Logan had been a long time ago. She looked around to see if anyone else at the table was as ready as she to have lunch. Peter's shining scissors were beckoning.

As she prepared to suggest following the young women in quest of food, a soft gasp came from several throats at her own table.

"There he is," Leah breathed. "There's Tony."

"Now you'll see what we're talking about," Gussie said softly in Mrs. Potter's left ear.

"Now you'll see what I mean," hissed Dee at her right.

4

The young queens of the softball league became giggling schoolgirls, stumbling and bumping each other's elbows, and Lolly Latham's face seemed deeply flushed, far beyond the faint pinkness Mrs. Potter had noticed when Peter Benson was speaking with her.

The group at the round table sat erect, stomachs pulled in and chests lifted. Then, following Helen Latham's lead, they rose and propelled Mrs. Potter toward the center of the room.

"Tony, you must meet the new girl in town," Gussie said as the tall man strode across the room toward them and raised her hand to his lips. "I told you that my dearest old friend was coming, and here she is. Genia, this is Tony, Count Ferencz."

Tony was enchanted to meet the dear Eugénie of whom he had heard so much. Mrs. Potter was enchanted, although she did not say so, to have her hand kissed with an air of admiring respect that at the same time held a hint of challenge. There were very few men who kissed one's hand at the ranch, and she adored being called Eugénie.

Each hand in the group was kissed in turn—Leah's small pointed fingers, almost clawlike in her new thinness, bejeweled, in constant flashing motion; Helen's hands, like her heavy features, seeming a little too big for her thin arms; Mary Lynn's fingers, creamy, square-tipped, and firm, their obvious competence belying the soft languor of her speech; Mittie's hands, small, tanned, childlike; finally Beth's, each as plump and smooth as a dove.

Each face in turn seemed to shine with new light, reflecting the flattering intensity of the gray eyes and the moment of undivided attention.

Only Dee had remained at the lunch table, where she was spreading another cracker with cheese, she and her former husband apparently disregarding each other's presence. This must create a continuing social problem, Mrs. Potter thought, since Dee was firmly a part of the group that now appeared to acclaim Tony as—what had Mary Lynne said?— "someone to give direction to their lives."

As the softball girls fluttered around the edge of the small circle of Mrs. Potter's friends, newly animated, centering about Count Ferencz, as Peter waved and beckoned them on to the salad bar with his silver scissors, the room seemed very full and confused. Her friends seemed to be competing for the tall man's attention, and he, with effortless grace, seemed to be managing a special smile or special word for each one.

"Simply marvelous, Gussie," she was close enough to hear him say. "You're a star pupil and I've decided you're about ready for the next step. Very soon."

Then he bent to hear some question of Leah's, the words lost in the voices around them and in the sudden jingle of Leah's bracelets. Mrs. Potter's thoughts took a wild leap into what she knew of fencing terms: *swordsman, rapier, thrust and parry*. The lean, flat-muscled body moved with a fencer's grace. The slightly hooded gray eyes, the narrow lips, the controlled, sharply modeled features, even the high, domed forehead above a slightly receding hairline, all appeared to her as a kind of guard, a fencer's mask.

"Tony, can you give me a hand?" she heard Peter Benson call from his station at the hydroponic garden. "Something I have to see to in the kitchen."

The softball bevy milled together in happy confusion as the swordsman's figure crossed to the salad bar. Only Lolly Latham remained on the sidelines, awkward and apart, until one of the girls pulled her into the circle. "My dear young ladies," Mrs. Potter heard him say, "do give me the honor of prescribing the right herb for each of you. I must observe you closely to do this. Let me begin with this charming person. Your name, *chérie?*"

Edith Rosborough, the birthday girl, flushed with pleasure.

"And what is it that you do, besides playing the ball game and decorating our day?" the count inquired. "Ah, law secretary, is it? I must look at your eyes now, and the palms of the two lovely hands that do this law typewriting."

After considerable time, when the softball group had disappeared into the private dining room with full plates and in a state of ecstasy, Mrs. Potter's party proceeded to the buffet. Peter Benson had returned to the dining room, relieving his guest from his temporary post at the herb garden, and the two stood side by side. "I'll let you take over with the small fry," Mrs. Potter heard Peter say, "but I'm not sure I trust you with my guys." Peter's square and solid bulk, his open face and ready smile, seemed to exaggerate the tall elegance beside him, and his slightly baggy tweed jacket and flannel trousers were equal contrast with Tony's closely fitted continental tailoring.

When it came time to make her own lunch selection, Mrs. Potter was happily deliberate, even as she realized that she appeared embarrassingly greedy as judged by the restrained choices of her friends.

The enticements were many. From them Mrs. Potter assembled for herself a bed of buttery Boston lettuce with a few pale spears of endive, both of these a treat often unobtainable at her nearest Arizona market. She added a few sprigs of dark green native watercress, which she felt sure had come from watery beds in Quaise, east of town. For color she added some crisp radish slices and several wedges of bright (but undoubtedly tasteless, she knew) Florida tomatoes. Then, even though she saw that her friends were forgo-

ing the heartier items, she decided not to feel guilty about
her level of near starvation. She served herself generously
with julienne strips of rare roast beef. She added a few neat
matchsticks of Swiss cheese. With a rueful grimace at Gussie,
her hostess, she added several rings of crisp red onion. Then,
with a mental apology to all doctors of diet and health and
beauty, she topped the whole thing with a good spoonful of
rich blue cheese dressing.

"Now, Peter, what does this call for?" she asked her restaurant host. "I'm embarrassed at what an enormous plateful I
have and how hungry I am—but doesn't it look *wonderful?*"

"Couldn't be improved," Peter told her, "except for this
snip of fresh basil to give flavor to the tomatoes. Pitch in now,
Potter, and I'll have Jadine bring some rye bread for you.
That's all it needs."

When Mrs. Potter returned to the window table, Beth was
eating her even heartier fare with untroubled enjoyment.
Dee was drinking tea, and Beth's roll basket was being steadily depleted.

"Did you notice if Peter has any lovage up there?" Beth
asked as she surveyed the fresh fruit plate she had ordered
along with her hot chicken pie. "This has a good cream
cheese dressing, but it needs a little something. One thing I
added to my own herb garden last year was lovage, and it's
awfully nice with fruit. I think I'll just go up and take a look."

The others at the table were slowly, almost painfully so, it
seemed to Mrs. Potter, squeezing wedges of fresh lemon
over salad greens, over cucumber and raw mushroom slices,
over chopped raw zucchini and cauliflower. They had
elected a variety of herb choices, including that of fresh
nasturtium blossoms on Mary Lynne's leafy platter. No one
else had succumbed to the lure of an oily dressing.

Her own group had barely begun before various softball
girls were returning for second platefuls. Jadine was rushing
about, moving between the guests with fresh plates and re-
plenishments for the long table.

Mrs. Potter remembered later, when it seemed necessary
to do so, that Peter had called, "Higginson, could you or

somebody spell me for a minute? Tony's taking a breather and I'm needed for a jiffy in the kitchen. You guys know as much about herbs as I do anyway." They had all, except for herself and Dee, briefly served a turn at the hydroponic garden. It seemed Peter's way of honoring their garden club expertise and of involving them all in the ritual, one of his ways of keeping them all entertained and amused.

When Beth took her turn, she had turned to Mrs. Potter in explanation. "Peter knows I'm an herb gardener," she said. "Most of us are, actually. Anyway, he knows I've suggested comfrey tea to Ozzie deBevereaux for his arthritis, and he says at least it won't hurt him." Then, spotting Edie at the buffet, she called out, "How *is* the boss today? Taking the day off too? I'll stop in with the comfrey and say hello before dinner."

The return of Count Ferencz caused new excitement, she recalled, and whoever was then in charge relinquished the herb-cutting scissors. After that she only remembered Beth's decision about dessert, which proved to be the rum pie, after all. It had been, she said again apologetically, a favorite of Jim's.

"That's ridiculous, Beth," Helen told her. *"Everybody's* husband loved desserts. Order the pie if you want to, for heaven's sake, but don't blame it on Jim."

Mary Lynne's voice was placating. "Bless their dear little old hearts, they *did* love desserts, didn't they? Bo's mother copied out a whole book of his favorites for me as a present when we got engaged. And I swear to goodness, her darling boy could tell, forty years later, if I changed anything by a quarter of a teaspoon."

There was sympathetic laughter, and conversation continued at the round table. In the next room there was clearly speechmaking, punctuated by bursts of laughter and loud applause.

Both groups were momentarily stilled when Jadine came in bearing a tray with a large decorated cake, slowing as she went through the door of the private dining room to shield the flame of its single tall pink candle. Then the expected chorus of feminine voices began, most of them singing in lower register to lend strength to the sentiment.

The chorus grew stronger as one key was agreed upon. *"Happy birthday to you . . ."*

The singing continued, then wavered, faltered. As the words *dear Eeeee-dy* were reached, it dwindled from a few uncertain voices to total silence, a silence far louder than all of the laughter and clapping and shrieking of the preceding hour.

The thud of an overturned chair broke the silence, and there was a small clatter of china, as Linda Peaseley appeared in the doorway, her napkin still clutched in her hand. "Get Mr. Benson," she said loudly. "Edie's choking. She can't get her breath."

Before anyone could speak or move, the girl with the smoothly rounded face and the long braid appeared beside Linda. "Does anybody here know the Heimlich maneuver?" she called sharply. "One of the girls is choking on a last bite of salad or something. She can't get her breath."

Gussie jumped to her feet. "I've practiced it," she said. "I'll try, if no one else knows. Get Mr. Benson, Jadine."

Peter was out from the kitchen and into the private dining room before Gussie could get there. Edie, unable to speak, stood before her place at the table beside her overturned chair her eyes wide in a frantic gaze, pointing helplessly toward the pink-lipsticked circle of her open mouth.

Peter approached her quickly from behind as Mrs. Potter's party crowded into the doorway. The softball girls, except for Linda and the girl with the braid, still sat in their places at the table, staring in disbelief.

"No, pound her back first," Gussie called out. "That's the first thing, the Red Cross says."

Peter had already encircled Edie's waist and clasped his hands above her midsection. He administered a convulsive squeeze. "I learned it this way," he grunted. "Doesn't waste time."

Edie's eyes grew even wider. An incoherent, almost sound-less appeal came from the roof of her straining mouth. The young women at the table and the group in the doorway watched in horror as her face grew red, then purple. Peter repeated his firm, sudden squeeze.

He released her quickly; his deft, square fingers explored the open mouth. "No chunk of food," he said abruptly. "Can't get my fingers in her gullet, but her tongue's not turned back."

He grasped the girl's stiff body again in a spasmodic embrace and, as he did, shouted over his shoulder, "Call the hospital, Jadine."

Helen Latham was already at the telephone in the front hallway. "The ambulance is on its way," she told them calmly. "Don't worry, she'll be fine."

"Shall I get her coat and things?" Lolly asked timidly.

"Hurry up, then," her mother said. "I'm going to follow the ambulance in the station wagon to be sure everything's under control, and you might as well come along."

"She didn't get a chance to make her birthday wish," Jadine said as, seconds later, they heard the approaching siren. "Look, will you, the candle's still burning."

5

"Want to turn on the local news while I do something about our dinner?" Gussie called from the kitchen.

Mrs. Potter struggled to her feet from the depths of a soft old leather sofa in the library, where she and her old friend had, for the past hour, continued their catching up on family news.

Earlier she had unpacked her bags with Gussie's assistance, in the casual intimacy of former roommates. As they moved together putting things away for what was to be a stay of several weeks, Gussie came to the bottom of one bag and let out a shout. "Yellow pads! Does *this* take me back! Are you still making lists and notes and settling all the problems of the world with these things?"

Not bothering to reply, Mrs. Potter took the small stack of lined yellow legal pads and set them on a small desk before a window. She looked down happily at the small part of the garden at the side of the house, admiring the now rusty brown clusters of hydrangea on a bush she had long loved in its blue-violet summers.

"I remember all the nutty things you used to write down," Gussie continued. "Dates, of course, and notes about exam schedules, and even things no one in her right mind would *have* to write down, like *wash hair, write home, study library*. I always thought you were going to write *get up* or *go to bed*. As far as I could see, you never looked at the lists again and they were all things you'd have remembered just as well without them."

"I did too look at them," Mrs. Potter replied with dignity. "I crossed those things off when they were done. Besides, I always find I can think better, about lots of things, if I write them down."

"I know—they weren't all just reminder lists, even then," Gussie said. "Who was that beau of yours from MIT—you know, the one you fell in love with our sophomore year?"

Mrs. Potter resented the fact that her face was suddenly warm, and she turned again to the window to look at the hydrangea. "Well, yes," she admitted. "I think I fell in love with his Boston accent, actually, on our first date. It sounded so elegant, so *classy*."

"What I remember is your deciding how you felt about him by writing down a whole list of his good points and his not-so-good ones," Gussie persisted.

"I cannot believe you read my private notes," Mrs. Potter retorted. "That's disgusting. Anyway, even if you did, or if I showed them to you, I'm certain neither of us can remember what went in which column, except for that wonderful accent. I would simply *melt* when he'd say things like 'pa'k the ca' behind the apa'tment.'"

Suddenly she, too, was laughing. "How many years since I've seen him, I wonder?" she said, although something told her she could add that number rather quickly if she chose to do so. "He's probably a cranky, arthritic old scientist somewhere, married to a proper Vincent Club Boston woman who takes that absolutely swoon-making accent of his quite for granted."

The unpacking accomplished, at Gussie's insistence Mrs. Potter had gratefully agreed to a nap in the big four-poster bed, suddenly too sleepy to accord more than a brief glimpse of admiration at the handworked crewel of the canopy over her head. Later, further refreshed by a bath in the huge, claw-footed tub, and comfortable in a long jade-green wool caftan, she had joined her hostess in the library.

They had not spoken of the day's lunch party. Mrs. Potter had once voiced her concern about the secretary's bout of choking, but Gussie, with her usual practical common sense, had quickly reassured her. "Someone would have called us if she weren't quite all right," she had said. "Now tell me, is Benjie still in San Francisco? And what's new with the girls?" She named and inquired for each of them and for each of Mrs. Potter's precocious and beautiful grandchildren. She reported on her own daughter's new job as a volunteer lawyer for Legal Aid. She told of her son Scott's internship with the Santa Fe Opera, after his late return to college and his recent graduation with a master's degree in performing arts administration.

Mrs. Potter hadn't known there was such a thing, although it sounded reasonable enough. "I hope he majored in fundraising," she said. "If not, he could take a few lessons right here on the island from Helen. She's superb at it. Isn't it interesting that people always seem to give more to a rich solicitor? I suppose they hate to look cheap in front of their rich friends but can think of lots of excuses to make to their poor ones. Anyway, the move sounds perfect for Scott, and I'm sure Louisa and her husband know all about it."

The two Berner and three Potter children had known each other nearly all their lives. In their growing-up years they had turned up at each other's family dinner tables without notice, and they still saw each other often. Scott was a godfather for one of the children of Louisa, Mrs. Potter's eldest. Marilyn, the lawyer, and her husband were friends and now neighbors of her younger daughter, Emily, in Philadelphia.

Now, in answer to Gussie's suggestion, Mrs. Potter snapped on the local island TV station. The reception seemed a bit fuzzy and the hand-lettered local advertisements, endearingly amateurish, reminded her of those flashed on the screen in the old movie house of her Iowa youth, shown between the news of the world and the comedy, and again before the main feature.

"What's this new shop that's opening Friday?" she called to Gussie through the open kitchen door. "They keep showing a picture of a lot of noses. And who's Mary Rezendes?"

"Tell you later," Gussie shouted back. "It's part of my secret!"

"Fog tonight, maybe light snow by morning," she called in turn as the Nantucket weather station report followed. "Good thing I got in today before Logan weathered in. Of course, I could have taken the bus to Woods Hole and then the boat, unless the fog was impossible, but this way I got back in time for our lunch at the Scrim. I can't tell you how good it is to see everyone again, and everyone looking so *great!*"

Gússie returned to the library and pointed toward the open doorway leading to the front hall, which in turn opened into large connecting parlors on the other side of the house. "Want a drink?" she asked. "You remember where the liquor closet is in the back parlor—I'm sure there's everything there."

"I'll get myself a light Scotch and water," Mrs. Potter declared promptly as she rose to cross the hallway. "As long as you aren't letting me help in the kitchen tonight, this will give me a chance for a real look at the other side of the house while I'm getting it. I know you've bought some new paintings since I was here last."

The two rooms, each with its high ceiling centered by white plaster garlands and whorls and rosettes, each with its white marble-faced fireplace, above which hung a great gold-framed mirror, each with tall windows with white interior wooden shutters folded back into deep window recesses, were open as one. The sliding double doors, their hardware of heavy silver, as were those of the window shutters, were seldom closed, and the rooms were carpeted as one with thick pale gold.

Heavy off-white damask covered big chairs and comfortable sofas, further softened with needlepoint-covered pillows of Gussie's own design and execution. The white walls were covered with framed paintings, large ones alone or smaller ones grouped together, some modern, chiefly French Impressionist. The warmth of their colors, with that of the needlepoint, gave the long double room vitality and warmth.

Certain familiar objects reminded Mrs. Potter of how long she and Gussie had been friends. First of all, there was the house itself. Soon after their college graduation Gussie's first marriage had been to Mrs. Potter's favorite cousin, Theo Andrews, and it was he, to celebrate his sudden success in business, who had bought the big Main Street mansion. There, the two had happily planned a lifetime of summers together.

The grand piano had been Jules Berner's, Mrs. Potter remembered, and it was there that he used to entertain them all with wild and brilliant improvisations. By then Gussie, a richly adored young wife, had married Jules, a successful New York investment banker. It was through the years of their summers here that the two families, the Berners and the Potters, had maintained their long friendship.

A stiff, but bright and engaging, painting of Dutch burgher houses caught her eye. This had been her and Lew's third wedding present to Gussie as a bride. A year after Jules's fatal heart attack four years ago, Gussie had again remarried, this time to Gordon Van Vleeck, a Nantucket-summering bachelor from Schenectady. They knew that Gordon was inordinately proud of his Dutch ancestry, and hoped that the small painting would please them both.

She and Lew had not really liked Gordon, and had done everything they tactfully could do to discourage Gussie's remarriage after what seemed to them such a short time.

"I think our Gussie's a gal who just has to be married," she remembered Lew's saying. "She's not as independent as you might be, Genia. . . ." Lew then could not have known how independent she was going to have to prove herself. It was a help at times to remember his confidence in her.

There was nothing to be gained now by wishing that they had been able to talk Gussie out of what had been an unfortunate third marriage. And she certainly had not come to Nantucket now to share any further mourning over Gordon's death. She went to Jules's piano and dashed off a quick double-time version of Chopsticks, just to let Gussie, presumably still busy in the kitchen, know how glad she was to be back on the island.

Drink in hand, she returned to the library to find her sitting comfortably in a wing chair with a glass of soda water. "I think it's great you aren't drinking," Mrs. Potter told her. "Calling it Health Week after the holidays, are you?"

Ignoring the television set in the corner, the two began to recall all those times in their shared past when they had declared Health Week. Early to bed for a week, they would vow (it never took more than one night, actually, to catch up then), after the red-rimmed eyes and exhaustion of exams or after a particularly strenuous weekend. No desserts for a week, they would decree, as penance for an after-hours orgy of ice cream and pretzels and sardines. No smoking for a month, just to be sure they weren't getting the habit. They now agreed that the no-smoking times had become more and more difficult in the years that followed.

"Matter of fact, I never did entirely quit until last fall," Gussie admitted, "but Tony says it's terribly aging to the skin."

"Your skin looks great," Mrs. Potter told her. "I'm not sure that quitting has done that much for mine, even though I stopped years ago. Anyway, it's wonderful to know that the insides of lungs do really restore themselves after a few years, and it's great not to cough, and of course to be able to really smell things. Nice things, at least."

"Like fresh-baked bread," Gussie added. They smiled at each other across Mrs. Potter's glass of Scotch and Gussie's of Perrier.

"Again, it's Tony," Gussie said diffidently, returning to the subject of liquor. "I suppose you *could* call it Health Week, only it's much more than that. What he's doing for me is *so* wonderful. Part of it, of course, is his diet. He prescribes this for each of us individually. There's lots more to his program than that, only I haven't progressed that far yet. Leah and Helen are much more advanced. So far I'm just doing his diet plan for me, and he's very firm about not drinking, not for any of us."

"Which brings me back to why haven't you told me about Tony before," Mrs. Potter began, when the continuing voice from the television altered in pitch and volume, announcing the start of the local island news.

"Edith Rosborough, secretary to the well-known Nantucket attorney Mr. Oscar deBevereaux, died early this afternoon at the Nantucket Cottage Hospital," the voice told them as the picture on the screen showed a large white building.

"Miss Rosborough celebrated a birthday lunch today in company with members of the Nantucket Ladies Softball League, of which she is president. Apparently choking on a morsel of food, she was rushed unconscious to the hospital from the Scrimshaw Inn, where the birthday luncheon took place. A hospital spokesperson says that an allergic reaction may have caused the strangulation."

The two women stared at the blurred screen, then at each other, in compassionate and shocked disbelief. "Oh *no,*" Gussie exclaimed. "They were having *such* a wonderful time, the bunch of them."

"Ozzie will be shattered," Mrs. Potter thought to say. "Shouldn't we call him? Or shall we go over? It's just a step."

"Let's wait until morning," Gussie decided. "The poor guy is in terrible shape these days. Let's just hope he's sitting in his hot bath now, as he says he always does at the end of the day to ease his joints, and then popping into his warm bed, poor old dear."

6

Mrs. Potter awoke, on the first day of her return to Nantucket, rested and happy. She stretched, catlike, in the canopied bed. Faint light in the windows told her that January dawn was approaching the island, and the muffled sound of an early truck on the cobblestones told her it had snowed in the night. She snuggled down again in smooth, fragrant old linen sheets, beneath a silk-covered down comforter.

At last she reached with a toe for the slippers beside her bed and slid out of the luxurious cocoon of the guest room bed. She crossed the room, her step soundless on the old oriental scatter rugs spaced on the polished, wide-planked floor. She splashed water on her face and brushed her teeth at the enormous marble washstand in the big bathroom and put on a warm pink robe.

Quietly she descended the wide stairway, its cushioned carpeting soundless under her feet, one hand on the smooth mahogany stair rail to assure her safe passage toward the pale light showing through heavy leaded-glass sidelights flanking the big solid front door.

Familiar with every inch of her old friend's house, Mrs. Potter now doubled back past the long low chest in the hall, glad to see that it still bore the huge Chinese vase and the heavy brass candlesticks she remembered, as she headed for the kitchen at the back of the house.

Outside in front, Mrs. Potter knew, was an imposing facade, presenting a double set of granite steps to the cobblestoned street. Their twin curves of iron railing ended in shining globes of polished brass, matching the gleam of the heavy knocker on the door above.

She also knew that Gussie's first question on interviewing a prospective new cleaning woman was "How do you feel about brass?" Once a week, summer and winter, someone had to polish these glories of an earlier age. Gussie occasionally had to remind a reluctant helper, "It has to be done; there are just you and me; you might as well know which of us I elect for the job." It would have been unthinkable for Gussie to let the brasses, indoors or out, become dull and neglected, even if she herself sometimes proved to be the only one to do the polishing.

"I shouldn't be allowed to live in this house if I don't intend to keep it up," Gussie always said. "I love it, and also it's kind of a public trust, in a funny way. Theo felt the same way about it from the first, and we decided that if we couldn't afford to take care of the place, we shouldn't buy it."

Gussie had continued to live in the house in her days as Mrs. Jules Berner. It had been their summer home for the thirty years of their marriage, alternating with winter city headquarters in a ten-room duplex apartment high above the East River.

During those years, Mrs. Potter and Lew had occasionally stayed in the same elegant old guest room when their own house on 'Sacacha Pond was not yet open for the summer. They and their children had come there over the years to dinner parties and breakfasts and lunches and holiday gatherings, just as Gussie and Jules and Marilyn and Scott had come to Quidnet. As parents they had shared numberless cups of tea or coffee in the big old kitchen, either in the sunny corner looking out onto the big garden in the back, or cozy in soft chairs in front of the kitchen fireplace. Their children knew in both houses where to find Nabiscos or peanut butter, and in later years where they were expected, on occasion, to find a bed and, if necessary, the sheets for it. She knew her way to the pantry, the liquor closet, the garden, the books in the library.

This morning she was sure she made no sound as she came to the old swinging doors at the back of the hallway leading to the kitchen. It was wonderful, she thought, to be visiting in a house where she felt free to get up at her usual ranch hour, knowing she could make her early morning tea without wakening or inconveniencing the household.

The kitchen was dim, as had been the front hall as she slipped through the quiet door, but a light from the big pantry, off at her left, made her stop short.

"Caught you!" Her hostess appeared in the lighted doorway. "Thought you'd sneak down for your tea, did you? Didn't know I get up early these days too? Well, you'll know when you learn more about Tony's program. I was expecting you—the kettle's just ready to boil.

"Cranberry muffins sound good?" she continued as Mrs. Potter was making the tea. "I wish I could toast some Portuguese bread for you, but for now you'll have to make do with these, hotted up from the freezer. I made them before I began Tony's diet."

Slightly surprised to know that Gussie's own breakfast was to be only the glass of pale juice she had carried in from the pantry, Mrs. Potter assured her that homemade cranberry muffins would be a great treat. The two were still sitting comfortably in bathrobes and slippers when they heard a light stamping of snow boots at the kitchen door opening to the side porch of the house.

"You're out early, Bethie!" Gussie exclaimed. "How about a hot muffin? I'll make you a cup of coffee—I know you prefer it in the morning, but Genia likes her tea and Tony has ruled out coffee for me, so I'm afraid it will have to be instant."

Instant suited Beth very nicely, and she'd love a cranberry muffin. From the pocket of her coat she produced a small vial holding artificial sweetener. "Aren't you proud of me?" she asked. "I'm really going to get serious about this diet idea, and I thought I'd begin right away, even before I go to see your miracle man." She was out for a morning walk, something she and Jim had always done together, even back in his Boston newspaper days.

"Not a soul out yet in this lovely light snow when I came down India Street," she said. "I don't know when it started. It hadn't begun when I walked down to Ozzie's at the end of the day yesterday, shortly after dark, right after I heard the TV news about Edie Rosborough. Isn't that *dreadful?* That poor girl—and I kept thinking of Helen's Lolly, too. Helen said she was Lolly's first real friend. She must feel *so* sad."

Beth sighed. "Anyway, after I heard the news I thought I'd try to cheer Ozzie up a little, or at least tell him how sorry I was, and then I remembered I was going to take him some of my dried comfrey. To make tea for his arthritis, you know, and for whatever else is ailing him."

She sighed again. "I couldn't rouse him, though. Maybe he was soaking in his tub, or he may have been at the hospital making arrangements about Edie, although there were lights on upstairs in his living room."

As she broke open a hot, crusty brown muffin and lavishly buttered the first morsel, she exclaimed with pleased surprise, momentarily forgetting Oscar deBevereaux and the comfrey. *"Whole* cranberries!" she marveled. "They're delicious—but I thought you always had to chop them up for muffins. I always do."

"Aren't they pretty?" Mrs. Potter agreed. "I haven't seen whole cranberries used like this since my Grandmother Andrews made individual steamed puddings with them."

"You might find them a bit tart," Gussie warned them, "except that the bran muffin part seems sweet enough to me to temper the bite. Probably your grandmother's puddings had a sweet sauce that did the same thing."

"A fluffy hard sauce, as I remember," Mrs. Potter said. "I can taste it now. Cool and rich, vanilla-flavored, with a sort of slippery feeling on the tongue."

"I'd love both recipes," Beth told them, buttering another

morsel of muffin. "Don't you adore cranberries! Do you think they're Nantucket's most special native food?"

Nothing more Nantuckety, they agreed. Cranberry sauce and cranberry conserve, lattice-topped cranberry pie ("Mock cherry, they used to call it," Gussie said), cranberry nut bread and molded cranberry salad and even cranberry dumplings.

"Cranberried sweet potatoes," Beth said yearningly, "cranberry cake, cranberry cobbler, cranberry pecan pie. And my cranberry fluff, if I can ever find that recipe."

"Would you believe cranberry soup?" Gussie asked. "It's delicious—sort of a cranberry borscht, with beets and chicken broth. It was in that New England cookbook Mary Allen Havemayer did, when they had the Book Corner, remember? She was a wonderful cook."

"How about Swamp Fires?" Mrs. Potter put in unexpectedly. "I'm not much for vodka myself, but it's a terrific party punch. We served it at our ranch Christmas parties—at first just with the thought of offering something new to our Arizona neighbors, and then after that almost by popular request. It got to be quite a ranch tradition. Cranberry juice, vodka, and champagne—that was the general idea of it."

"Trust you to think of Swamp Fires, Genia," Gussie said. "Always ready for a drink."

"Reformed characters are always so holy," Mrs. Potter retorted. "I'm sure we got that punch recipe from you. And I *know* we learned to make beach plum slivovitz right here in this very kitchen. You fill a quart jar with whole, washed beach plums, add a teaspoonful of sugar, and pour in good 151-proof rum to the top. Then you set it away and forget it for a year, at least. Am I right?"

Gussie rose, rather grandly, to put on the kettle for fresh tea and coffee. "Be that as it may," she said, "we're talking about whether cranberries are the food most people associate with Nantucket."

"No," Beth asserted positively. "Nor bay scallops, superb as they are, nor beach plums. There's only one food that's *really* Nantucket, and that's Portuguese bread."

Ignoring the truth that Cape Cod might make the same claim, or New Bedford, or other places on the coast where Portuguese sailors and fishermen had settled, the three nodded in complete agreement. Portuguese bread was, for most residents and visitors to the island, Nantucket's most special and memorable gastronomic delight. Pale and crusty on the outside, each small round loaf was unbelievably creamy and long-lasting within. Delicious fresh from Manny's ovens, it still tasted fresh for two days, if it ever lasted that long. After that, it became a new delight, sliced and toasted.

There had been a time when Mrs. Potter had worked hard at trying to duplicate, or even approximate, Manny's Portuguese bread, once the bakeshop was closed for the winter. She collected every recipe she could find for French bread, Cuban bread, Puerto Rican bread, all of which, the cookbooks assured her, were the same thing as Portuguese. They were not.

Those formally called Portuguese bread were invariably of the sweet, egg-bread, Easter-bread variety. Nice, but totally unrelated to the unprettied goodness of real Nantucket Portuguese bread.

Mrs. Potter had approached proper, black-clad Portuguese great-grandmothers on the island and on the Cape and had filled her notebooks with their claims to the one and only authentic recipe. (Younger Portuguese descendants denied any bread-making knowledge or interest.) Her friends had been periodically invited to lunch or dine to sample each latest attempt, then pressed into accepting foil-wrapped loaves for their freezers. Some of these breads were fair, some were awful, but even the best had never been Portuguese bread—not the bread Manny turned out in dozens and dozens of firm round blond loaves each day from late spring to late fall.

There came a day each November when Manny declared *bastante*. He pulled down the bakery blinds. He took himself off to his own condominium in Fort Lauderdale, where, as they all knew, he had genuine crystal chandeliers. There, everyone felt sure, he stuffed himself comfortably all winter with soggy pizza, stale hamburger buns, and soft white sandwich bread, with an occasional cold, hard bagel to exercise his *dentes*.

"But to go back to Ozzie," Beth reminded them, sighing. "I wonder how he's taking the news about Edie."

"Her death will be a terrible loss to him, I imagine," Mrs. Potter said. "Didn't she really run the office? And, just between the three of us, has Ozzie been completely on the ball as a lawyer for years?"

"Oh, yes, he's sharp enough, and we still all go to him," Gussie said. "He handles Mittie's affairs as a trustee, and Leah's. I don't know about Mary Lynne, since Bo's estate is still in probate in Tennessee. Dee goes to him for real estate contracts, and even Helen has him make out her tax returns, although she seems to be an absolute whiz at managing her own investments. I sometimes wonder if she wishes she were still running the company back in Chicago—she did for a while, you remember, after Lester's death. She's the only one of us, I guess, besides me, who doesn't have everything all neatly tucked away in a trust."

"My son Laurence takes care of everything for me," Beth said. "Such a help, and a saving, too. We try to keep everything in the family."

This seemed reasonable, since Beth's was a large tribe, most of them living within close range, in and around Providence. Among them they maintained several big Nantucket summer houses on Hurlbut Avenue, their sandy beaches adjoining. There all the Higginson grandchildren spent the summer, seemingly distributed impartially among whichever of the aunts and uncles were currently in residence. They all sailed, they all played tennis, the Yacht Club was their second home, and they all won prizes at everything they did, following the lead of their energetic and athletic grandmother.

The talk reverted to widowhood (as it often did, Mrs. Potter reflected) and to whether it was a comfort to have had one's husband arrange for a supposedly all-wise, permanent, fatherly trust department—a law firm or a bank—to be in charge of one's worldly goods.

"I always thought it was the slightest bit presumptuous of Lew," Mrs. Potter confessed. "I suppose it's good not to have to think about investments and the like, not that I have nearly as much to think about as Helen does, or as you do, Gussie. Still, it did irk me a little, and I asked him once, after reading some new wills he'd had drawn up for us, why there was a trust for me if he died first, but not for him if I did. He muttered something about 'women sometimes get carried away by their emotions, especially as they get older.' That, from Lew! And about *me!* I told him I thought he was just as likely to get wacky in his old age as I was."

"There have been times when I wished Theo and Jules had done that," Gussie confided. "Leave things for me in a trust, that is. But Theo and I were so young when he died, and he'd made so much money in a hurry with that invention of his, and then he was killed so suddenly . . ."

Mrs. Potter had a sharp recollection of the day she heard the news of the hunting accident in the Vermont woods. How awful it must have been for Gussie, she thought, as she had so many times since then. Each of them hunting alone—the four of them—Theo, Gussie, and another couple, the husband a friend with whom Theo had gone deer hunting since the two men's college days together. The stray shot from somewhere, never determined. Theo's body, bloody and already lifeless on the brown carpet of the woods floor before any of them had found him.

Gussie went on, after her brief pause. "You'd think that of all people Jules Berner would have set up a trust, wouldn't you? After handling other people's money all his life, and always having all we possibly needed ourselves? Jules was a wonderful husband, as you two both remember, but he couldn't bear the thought of being that much older than me. Remember how he always had to outplay everybody at tennis and outdance everybody on the floor and outswim everybody at the beach club? His lawyers told me after his death that he'd been putting them off, saying he'd get around to a proper trust in good time, that sort of thing. Through his partners I've always had wonderful people to advise me, and I usually do what they suggest, but actually I'm quite free to do as I like. I could set up a home for cross-eyed cats, if I wanted to."

Again, Gussie paused. "I guess everybody knew what was happening with Gordon. He lived on my money, and it was a good thing there was enough, considering his medical bills. There certainly wasn't anything for *him* to leave, or to set up any trust with."

"We all thought the Van Vleecks had oceans of money," Beth said, surprised. "He and his mother had come to the island starting with the year one, and they seemed very well off, I always thought."

"Mama Van Vleeck had it," Gussie said flatly, "but she certainly didn't part with any of it for Gordon when we got married. She was furious about that—do you remember?"

Mrs. Potter did indeed remember. "She was a holy terror, no doubt about it," she said. "And she'd counted on Gordon for so many years to be a darling and dutiful son that she probably felt deserted. Or maybe she just thought he didn't need it when he married you. After all, Gussie, no one ever thought that you had to worry about money, and she knew he'd be well taken care of."

All three women then agreed that, no matter how their financial futures were arranged, or even how apparently secure, inflation had made changes in their lives.

"That's one of the things different on the island," Beth told her. "Everybody feels the pinch a little if they live on a fixed income, even if it's quite a decent one, I suppose. None of us really lives extravagantly."

"I think Mittie may be a little pressed these days," Gussie said, "although she's too proud to admit it. And Dee, of course—it's crazy, but she always seems to be living on the brink of total poverty in spite of all her big real estate commissions and special discounts."

"Another change—we all lock our doors," Beth said. "We never used to. And I even have a big dog. Samson would make a terrible watchdog, but I hope nobody but me knows that. He's big, anyway, and he barks a lot. I left him at home to guard things now, even though I'm sure I left the door locked, too. I even went back to check when I was halfway down the block. Is *anybody* as forgetful as I am, I wonder?"

The other two assured her they were, out of politeness and also perhaps from awareness of the occasional blank drawn in place of a familiar word or name.

"So we all lock our doors, and Helen even has a security system that rings at the police building," Gussie said. "She wouldn't have a gun in the house, of course, after what happened to Les, but I think the rest of us all have one stuck away somewhere that we refuse to admit and would be afraid to shoot."

"Ozzie doesn't lock *his* doors," Beth remarked. "I told you I was there late yesterday afternoon? When he didn't come to the door, I just shouted upstairs to him from the kitchen and left the comfrey."

The telephone rang. "Answer it, will you, Genia?" Gussie asked. "I want to get this round of muffins out of the oven for you and Beth."

Helen Latham's voice was calm and controlled. "Oh, yes, *Genia.* Yes, I can speak with you just as well. You both must know by now about poor little Edie Rosborough, and I wanted you to know they were wonderful at the hospital. Arnold was called in at once, and he tells me the girl apparently had a violent allergic reaction to some sort of vegetable matter, possibly one of the herbs at the salad bar."

Mrs. Potter expressed dismay, but Helen cut her short. "What I really called about is that I'm here at the hospital again now for an early conference with the administrator, and there's even more shocking news. At least shocking to all of *us*. Ozzie deBevereaux died last night. At home. Apparently a sudden heart attack. Arnold stopped by his house about nine to tell him about their not being able to do anything for Edie. Of course, he thought Ozzie knew about her dying, and I expect he did, although I tried to phone him earlier and the line was always busy—phone probably off the hook. Anyway, Arnold found the lights on, went upstairs, and there he was, in his big chair in front of the fireplace. I suppose it wasn't entirely unexpected, in Ozzie's state of health, although the heart trouble hadn't shown up before. Terrible, isn't it?"

Beth declined a third muffin as soon as Mrs. Potter relayed the news to the two at the breakfast table. She rose decisively, retrieved her fur-collared storm coat and her bright wool hat from the coatrack in the back hallway, and pulled on her warm gloves.

"Maybe I was there when he was having the attack, maybe even when he was dying," she said sadly. "I wonder if he ever found my comfrey. I think I'll go by his house now and see if there's anything I can do."

"But Ozzie doesn't have any family," Gussie protested. "You know his wife died years ago, when they still lived on Long Island, and their daughter even before that—when she was in her early teens, I think. There won't be anything you can do, Bethie, or anybody in the house now. Have another cup of coffee."

Beth's firm round chin was resolute. "I'll just see," she said. "Maybe there's *something* I can do."

7

"I wonder if Beth remembers it's our day for Meals on Wheels?" Gussie said after she had left. "Too late to catch her —she'll be halfway to Ozzie's by now. If she forgets, you can do the rounds with me, Genia—it's a lot easier with two. Sometimes parking is almost impossible on some of the narrow little one-way streets, so we take turns, one to drive and the other to carry in."

"Love to," Mrs. Potter assured her. "Even if Beth shows up, as I'm sure she will—I don't think she's half as forgetful as she pretends to be—I'd like to go along for the ride, and maybe see some old friends. Is Jimmy Mattoon on your list? He used to be our old handyman, and I think he still lives alone, down on one of those little streets off Orange."

"Ozzie is one who *should* have been on our list," Gussie said soberly. "I expect he ate miserably, although of course not for lack of money. We accept donations now, you know, from people who can afford to pay, and it's surprising how many people are glad to pay for a good simple hot meal at noon and a cold one—sandwich and fruit, or whatever—for supper. It's prepared at the hospital, and of course Helen has it organized like a Swiss watch."

"I'll bet the prospect of a little visit with you or Bethie is as cheering as the food," Mrs. Potter remarked. "That darling round face of Beth's, and her crazy bright hats—if I were one of your customers, I'd consider Thursdays the red-letter day in my week."

"Oh, the whole crew all week is great for that kind of thing," Gussie said. "Beth probably *is* the most fun as a caller, because she's always so sunny and cheerful. Still, everybody tries to look bright and smartened up for the day of her rounds. Or *his*. We have men volunteers too, you know."

"I hope not Ted Frobisher," Mrs. Potter replied. "I'd hate to ride with *him* down all those little streets. As I remember, he'd be too befuddled by noon to find his way around town, or to remember who got what, if he's still drinking as much as he used to."

"I suppose he is," Gussie said, without great apparent concern. "Ted's always just a little bit stewed, but he's never really out of line. Always the same wonderful manners he learned at his mama's knee in Wellesley; always the same totally proper dress for every occasion—Jules used to call it 'elderly Yacht Club attire.' You know exactly what I mean. And he still putters around with his greenhouse. Ted hasn't completely lost his marbles, Genia. He still keeps his office up above the Pacific Club, right next to Ozzie's, and he has his connection with the same good Boston brokerage firm."

The thought of Ozzie had them both shaking their heads sadly. Poor Ozzie, they both said again, let's hope he just slipped away peacefully.

Then, brightening, Gussie crossed to the kitchen door and opened it to look out. Large, soft flakes of snow were falling, then melting in soft dark circles on the cobblestones. The neatly trimmed hedge of yew below the side porch was frosted with white, and the shrubbery beyond the garden in back was sharply outlined.

"Let's go down Main Street and see the Christmas trees one last time before they're taken down," she urged, "and enjoy the snow before it all melts and gets slushy. It's too warm for it to last."

She closed the door reluctantly. "Oh, and I haven't told you," she continued. "I've invited some people in, mostly old friends of yours, on Saturday afternoon. And Tony Ferencz, of course. Later, after we've had a walk we can take a look in the specialty places for party cheeses and things."

As they went up the wide front stairs to dress for the day, Gussie paused, one hand on the gleaming mahogany handrail. "It may seem heartless not to cancel my party because of Ozzie's death," she said. "Still, everyone is dying to see you."

Resuming her quick, light ascent, she added, "And I want you to have every possible opportunity to know Tony."

Mrs. Potter was suddenly reminded of Mary Augusta Baines, college freshman. "I've just met the most wonderful new man from Amherst," the young Gussie was saying, "and I can't wait for you to meet him." There had been a number of wonderful new men from a number of colleges, Mrs. Potter reflected, before cousin Theo came on the scene.

The two met again, shortly, in the upper hall at the top of the staircase, wearing wool trousers and warm sweaters. A large gilt-framed mirror reflected the meeting of the similarly clad figures—one with softly cut, slightly curling hair, lightly frosted in a way not so much disguising its gray as blending it into a new and becoming color; the other gray-blond, her hair smoothly pulled back into the same knot she had worn, although with a period of various changes in between, since their college years together.

Mrs. Potter drew back in momentary dismay. "I didn't realize I was getting so *fat!*" she exclaimed. "There must be something wrong with my scales. Every morning they tell me about the same thing, give or take a pound or two. *But look at me!* Standing beside you I look absolutely *gross.*"

Gussie's trousers and sweater, nicely fitted, as were Mrs. Potter's own, were clearly a size—could it be two sizes?—smaller. "You're not fat, Genia," she said comfortingly. "In fact you look pretty good by the standards we used to apply to ourselves ten or twenty years ago. I know you may think the fashion of being quite thin is only a fad, or purely vanity, but Tony has convinced me it's as much for health as for looks." As Gussie spoke, she turned to look at her full-length profile in the mirror.

"Don't *do* that!" Mrs. Potter begged her. "I can't bear the comparison!"

"If you're serious," Gussie said, "you may decide to join the club. You know I don't mean it's really a *club*. It's just that all of us—except Bethie and Dee—are totally committed to Tony Ferencz. His program is different for each of us—we all know that, and he's asked us not to discuss it with each other. All I can tell you is that all of us who are his regulars think that he's wonderful."

"I saw the change in all the others the minute we were together at lunch yesterday," Mrs. Potter told her. "I just hadn't realized how fat I look next to you! Frankly, it's rather a shock."

"Let me ask Tony what he thinks about taking on a new client," Gussie said doubtfully. "I think he really wants to stay with just the small group of us for individual counseling. He says he only wants people who are permanently on the island for now, although of course that will change once he establishes his foundation. And even that is confidential, so will you please forget I mentioned it? He's a wonderful man, but some things make him very angry, like discussing his plans, even anything about his methods, with outsiders."

Feeling fat, taken aback at the realization that she was now an outsider, at least to Tony Ferencz, in a place she had known and loved and been a part of for so long, Mrs. Potter flattened her stomach muscles, tucked under her behind, and followed Gussie's slim figure down the stairs.

Even as she wondered what Tony and his diet and his confidential methods could do for *her*, Mrs. Potter's thoughts veered sharply to the two deaths of the previous day. It seemed too much a coincidence that a secretary should die of an allergic seizure at a Wednesday lunch party and that her employer, Mrs. Potter's old friend, should die that same evening.

Nonsense, she told herself briskly. Ozzie was older than the rest of us, and in poor health. It was possible that news of

Edie's death had precipitated his fatal heart attack or whatever it was. The whole thing was simply chance—sad chance, for both of them.

However, the breakfast conversation had pointed out an uncomfortable fact. The two of them, Ozzie and his secretary, were equally privy to the affairs of all of her friends, it seemed, and probably to those of dozens of others of the island's winter population as well.

So it was, that perhaps twelve hours after Oscar deBevereaux's death, and less than an hour after she had learned of it, Mrs. Potter began to feel vaguely troubled.

8

Scarved, wool-capped, and storm-coated, the two women separated moments later to descend to the street by the twin stairs flanking Gussie's front door. Each brushed the snow from the round brass finial on her side of the stairway, and they smiled at each other in the sunshine.

Yesterday's uncertain January patchiness had become a new world of clear blue and white. The red brick of the great houses across the street, one of them Helen Latham's, showed sharp and clean against the white of small gardens; the heavy wood frame above each window held a ledge of soft white snow; snow-capped iron railings were cleanly defined.

"If we don't hurry, it will all melt before we get there to see the trees," Gussie urged as Mrs. Potter stood looking, unwilling to move. "Come *on!*"

"It's just that this place is *so* beautiful," Mrs. Potter said. "You forget, being away, just how perfect it all is, and how *real.*"

"It's real," Gussie said. "It never changed and it never had to be rebuilt, the way they did when they restored Williamsburg."

"Poor old Nantucketers," Mrs. Potter said. "The bottom dropped out of the whale oil market when somebody drilled an oil well out in Pennsylvania. They couldn't afford to modernize." She thought of what those modernizations would have been—fake English timbering and fancy shingle patterns—and how blessedly the island had been spared.

Suddenly she clutched her hostess's arm. "Gussie," she said quietly, "even if you've gone down this street a thousand times, you've never seen it like this."

From Orange Street to their right, the clock on the South Tower struck nine. A few tracks of early cars and trucks had left their marks in the snow on the wide cobblestone street leading down to a glimpse of the harbor, sparkling in the sunshine at the bottom of the hill. A few foot tracks showed on the broad sidewalks, but for the moment not a car was parked on the quiet, snowy street, not another person was in sight.

For the moment, the world between the big red-brick bank at the head of the street, and the smaller, older red brick of the Pacific Club at the foot was entirely their own, in unbelievable contrast to Mrs. Potter's summertime memories, when it was thronged with well-dressed strollers and shoppers, with people in shorts walking their bicycles on the sidewalk, with clusters of eager buyers circling bright flower stands or choosing fresh-picked local vegetables from the backs of parked trucks. Now tall Christmas trees marked the front of these two landmark buildings. Along each side of the street were a dozen or more smaller trees. Each of them, large or small, had this morning been returned to its forest beginnings by the magic of the snow.

"The lights and trimmings were taken down yesterday," Gussie said softly. "All of the holiday glitter is gone. It's just snow and trees."

As she spoke, a green town truck entered at the foot of the street and parked at the central corner, in front of what Mrs. Potter always called "the paper store." Two men in heavy jackets and dark, billed caps climbed out of the cab, lit cigarettes, and looked around slowly.

"We just made it in time," Gussie said. "They've come to take down the trees. Let's walk on down to Straight Wharf on our side of the street and pretend they aren't there."

The two walked slowly down the hill toward the harbor, scarcely glancing at the old brick storefronts and shopwindows—shops that had been filled with tanned and affluent summer customers the last time Mrs. Potter had seen them. Their displays of books and gifts and antiques and confections and beautiful textiles could wait. For her now, there was only the quiet and the snow and the reborn trees.

Mrs. Potter broke the silence as they passed the friendly old red bricks of the Pacific Club, discreetly peering in to see if any early morning cribbage players were already at their small tables in the back room. "Did it ever occur to you," she asked, "that it could have been the Nantucket Tea Party in the history books? Those three ships carrying the tea from England might have come in to Nantucket instead of Boston Harbor. They were owned here, remember? And by the same company that used to have headquarters in this building. Can you see the old Nantucketers painting themselves up like Wampanoags and dumping that tea in the harbor here, rather than pay the king's taxes?"

"Highly unlikely," Gussie assured her. "The ships—what were their names?—belonged to Mr. Rotch all right, and his office might have been up the stairs behind this door, up where Ted's and Ozzie's are now, but my guess is that those early Nantucketers were too good merchants to dump valuable tea overboard. Anyway, the island was always really more Tory than otherwise, although nobody talks about that now."

"Speaking of merchants," Mrs. Potter said, "is the Christmas Walk still going strong?"

This holiday event had begun only a year or two before Mrs. Potter's last wintertime stay on the island. The annual putting up of the trees on Main Street, their lighting and trimming, had been a tradition for many years before that. Then, sparked by whoever's bright idea the two could not remember, the merchants of the town had added an embellishment of their own. When the trees went up in December, they designated an evening for this special Christmas event. All of the stores and shops remained open until late in the evening. There was street entertainment with music and carols; there were special Christmas treats and prizes and good things to eat; the shops, bejeweled in their Christmas finery, were a part of a continuing round of small holiday parties, their owners for the evening more hosts than merchants. The Walk had become an off-season tourist attraction, a new tradition on an old cobblestone thoroughfare.

"Usually I have a cocktail party beforehand," Gussie said, "and then we all go to the Scrim or someplace for dinner after we've done the entire tour. This year, I just didn't feel like it. Partly because of Gordon's dying in October, and I hadn't really begun having people in. And then partly because I had just got such a good start with my program with Tony, and I didn't quite trust myself with all that liquor and fattening food in the house."

"But you're having people for cocktails Saturday on my account," Mrs. Potter pointed out. "Are you sure you want to? I mean, you really can't have a cocktail party without liquor and a lot of things to eat that aren't on *anybody's* diet."

"Yes, I do want to, and everybody's invited, but it's not a cocktail party," Gussie said. "To be honest, I expect everyone *does* think it is. That's the assumption when an invitation's for five o'clock. The fun of it is, I'm going to shock the socks off them—they're coming to a tea party."

Seeing the look of mild surprise on Mrs. Potter's face, Gussie elaborated. Tony was terribly tolerant, of course, except for his special clients, but he was adamant about no liquor for *them.* (Mrs. Potter had a guilty recollection of proposing drinks at yesterday's lunch party.) Gussie continued that all of them, all of Tony's "people," would find it so much easier if drinks weren't offered, and anyway she thought it was high time someone came up with an alternative to cocktails for casual hospitality.

"So nobody's going to worry about disobeying Tony," she went on. "We'll have tea and a lot of really good little things to eat for whoever isn't dieting, and this will be your coming-back party."

"It sounds wonderful," Mrs. Potter said. "Of course, I saw all of Les Girls yesterday, and Peter Benson. But there are the other men—I'm eager to see Arnold Sallanger, naturally. He'll always be my favorite doctor. Ted is fun, in a way, even if he always is a little tiddly. George Enderbridge is nice, if a bit worthy, but of course as a clergyman and retired head-master he can't help that. And I suppose Victor Sandys is coming? Is he writing anything these days, and has anybody persuaded him to get a hearing aid?"

"You forgot Ozzie," Gussie reminded her. "Poor Ozzie."

They walked onto the wharf that encircled one end of the marina, sending hundreds of starlings beneath the heavy planking into twittering panic. "The weather's been like fall, up to now," Gussie said. "They'll take off when it gets really cold. My perennial borders are still halfway green—did you notice?"

Broken shells crunched underfoot. A gull stalked away as they approached, a scallop shell in his beak, glaring back at them over his shoulder.

They looked out across the water, now a milky turquoise, toward the houses at Shimmo and Monomoy on the southern rim of the harbor.

"There's Mittie's house," Mrs. Potter observed. "What a view she has of the harbor from that hilltop of hers."

"I think she told you she's moved into town for the winter," Gussie said. "It's nice having her nearby, but I think she misses her gardens out there, and that beautiful house. The problem is money—we're afraid she may be having a little trouble."

Mrs. Potter remembered the Main Street house very well from visits when Mittie's parents had been alive. She could not help wondering if it also wasn't pretty expensive to keep up, maybe as much as the house at Shimmo. It undoubtedly cost a great deal to heat and a fortune to have repainted every few years.

"At least she has a nice stretch of lawn for an eventual

garden behind the house," Gussie said, "if she sells the Shimmo place. Her ace in the hole was going to be the rental of the apartment over the old carriage house in the back of the property. It's really charming, and it should bring a nice amount for a summer rental. The living room looks out over the lawn between it and her parents' house, remember? The property goes all the way through the block, so Mittie's on Main Street and Dee's at the back. The apartment is almost across from Ozzie's house—I'm sure you know the place."

Mrs. Potter remembered very well, but the reference to Dee was puzzling. "I thought Dee had a tiny place on Milk Street, or was it Vestal?" she said. "She's living in Mittie's carriage house? I can't see that's going to help Mittie's financial picture, Dee being as, well, hard up—I almost said penurious—as she always seems to be."

That was the problem, Gussie explained as the two walked around the marina. "Mittie has always taken having money as a matter of course, so when Dee had to leave her little rented place, she invited her to move in for the winter. And now I think she's embarrassed to suggest that Dee pay her any rent, and she has the expense of extra utilities, and she's probably agonizing over telling Dee that she wants to let the agents line up a good profitable summer rental for her."

"I can't believe it!" Mrs. Potter exclaimed. "Mittie is always so sure of herself. I can't imagine that she won't simply tell Dee the whole thing: that she can't afford to keep her on as a nonpaying guest, and that she needs and expects the several thousand dollars—four or five at the least, maybe ten, the way things are going now—that some nice summer people would pay for the place for the season."

"Mittie does seem totally assured, socially," Gussie said. "It's just that talking about money is something she can't do. Or maybe her pride keeps her from admitting she made a too hasty invitation and that she regrets it. To Mittie, that would be the worst possible manners."

The two had made their way around the pattern of the wharves of the marina. "Shall we step it out a little and go all the way to the circle?" Mrs. Potter asked. "There'll never be a prettier day, and we're both dressed for it."

They walked briskly, delighting in the blue of the harbor as the sun rose higher in its restricted southern arc of New England winter. Meanwhile, Mittie's move into town had reminded Gussie of another one of the group of women who lunched together weekly. "It's quite different for Helen, of course," she said. "In money problems, I mean. She's spent a fortune on that house and, recently, on her new garden-room addition. She and Lester used to come summers years ago to that big house they rented on the Cliff, remember? And then we were all so proud of her when she had gumption enough to buy one of the bricks and came here to stay on the island, a few years after he died." Gussie was musing now. "She was the first of us to be widowed."

"What a long time ago that was," Mrs. Potter mused. "I think Lolly was still very young when they came to stay, and Elna was more nurse than cook. Remember how surprised we all were when Helen let Lolly stay on in school here through high school? I suppose that's why she always seemed so much more a part of the town group, like the softball league yesterday, than, say, of the Yacht Club, even though she grew up in one of the grand brick mansions. She was always such a quiet little thing and I don't think any of our children ever knew her very well."

"She had reason to be a quiet little thing," Gussie replied. "We're all inclined to forget what it must have done to her to be the one to find her father after he'd shot himself. And after that, I really think Helen turned over the parents' job to Walter and Elna."

Mrs. Potter remembered Helen's plump, elderly cook and houseman very well. "I suppose Lolly was lucky that the two of them stayed on all these years," she said. "At least they knew what she'd gone through."

Gussie was thoughtful. "Walter once told me she used to wake up screaming for months afterward, and they tried to make things easier for her any way they could. That worried me—I thought maybe they'd given her paregoric or something of the sort to calm her down, but if so, it was apparently before they moved back here to stay. By then, which was a couple of years later, he said she was better."

"I think they may simply have let her overeat," Mrs. Potter said. "It would have been so easy for them to do, if it seemed to make her feel better. That might account for her being overweight now, and the reason she's always seemed, well, out of things. Instead of going out to play, I have an awful feeling she went to her room with a handful of cookies, and that maybe she's still doing it, in a manner of speaking."

"They've done the best they knew how," Gussie said. "At least Walter said she always came to the two of them with her troubles. That was something. But nothing could have made up for the shock of Lester's shooting himself and Helen's obvious indifference to the child after that. Maybe even *before* that, for all we know. Helen's not a very warm person and she's always had a very busy schedule. Poor little Lolly."

"Did you see how she seemed to respond to Peter yesterday?" Mrs. Potter asked. "I thought that was very nice."

"What I'd really like is to turn her over to Tony," Gussie said. "He could do wonders with her. Peter's a dear, of course, but Tony could work a miracle, at least with her looks, and that, as we all know, can make all the difference in the world in how we feel about ourselves."

"All right, we'll give her to Tony," Mrs. Potter said, "and then to Larry to do something about that frizzy home permanent—I'll bet Elna did that. While we're planning this great make-over, you can take her to that little woman of yours at Bergdorf's to find her some decent clothes. That old raincoat and hat yesterday were a disgrace."

Gussie was totally serious. "Helen said Edie Rosborough was her first real friend, and I wonder if maybe she wasn't her only real friend. Edie's dying that way, right beside her at the lunch table, must have been almost as much of a shock as her father's suicide was. I say it again, poor Lolly."

They continued walking steadily, occasionally pulling close to the edge of the path to avoid spattering slush from an oncoming car. Gussie continued talking. "Funny how all of us first came here as summer people and then stayed on, all but you, when the husbands died or retired."

The salt marshes at the edge of the harbor showed brilliant blue pools in the morning sunlight, suddenly almost as blue as in summer, when, rimmed with emerald grasses, they reflected warmer skies, of even deeper blue. The sight did not entirely block a disquieting thought, at the mention of husbands.

Again remembering a glowing and triumphant young Gussie, saying, "I've just met the most wonderful man!" Mrs. Potter resolved to find out immediately how serious this Tony thing was, starting with the question of why Gussie hadn't told her about him before.

Gussie looked slightly embarrassed. "First, I was too busy taking care of Gordon," she said, "and then when I began to realize that Tony was becoming important in my life, I thought it was just the diet, and how much better I was feeling. Now, I don't know. Anyway, I really do want you to get to know him too, while you're here."

Mrs. Potter knew her old friend to have been an unquestionably faithful and loving wife to her first two husbands, and at least a dutiful one to her third. Was Tony to become the fourth, and Gussie the second Countess Ferencz? She was not sure she liked the idea, without being at all sure of why.

"Being a widow isn't the worst fate in the world," she heard herself saying. "I know your Tony is terribly attractive, but will you promise me something, Mary Augusta?"

Gussie looked at her quizzically.

"Promise me," Mrs. Potter continued, "that if you ever do think of marrying again, you'll take plenty of time to learn all about the man in question, whoever he is."

Gussie smiled amiable agreement. "I'll let you help decide next time," she said. "Maybe. All right, *probably.*"

This sounded very much as if there might be a next time. Mrs. Potter decided she had said enough for the moment. She also decided she now *really* wanted to know what Dee Ferencz had been talking about when she said her former husband was—what was it?—an unmitigated bastard?

9

They walked as far as the traffic circle, from which the south road led to the airport and the Milestone Road started eastward toward 'Sconset. This, Mrs. Potter remembered clearly, branched northward along its way, leading to Monomoy, Shimmo, Shawkemo, Polpis, Pocomo Head, Wauwinet—that litany of Indian names on the southern rim of the harbor—all those now nearly deserted winter communities that would again be full of color and life in the summer season.

"Let's go back by way of Orange Street," Gussie said, "at least as far as Mary Lynne's. We might as well do the tour of where everyone's living now, so you'll really feel at home again."

Mrs. Potter was savoring every step of the way, a route as familiar to her as her daily Maine walks from the cottage to the post office in Northcutt's Harbor, as familiar as the two-mile ranch road from headquarters down to the RFD mailbox on the county road in Arizona.

Here, as a walker or bicycler or in a four-wheel car, she thought she knew almost every street, road, lane, pathway, or rutted road on the island. It's like an old and much-loved book, she thought to herself. Open it anyplace and you know what came before and what's going to follow. Put me down almost anyplace on Nantucket, she thought, on clean winter-bare pathways or on green shady streets dappled with sunshine, and my eyes and feet are going to know where they are.

As they passed Manny's bakery, she grimaced at the CLOSED sign in the window, then returned to her musings about the island's special enchantments. "After being away for a while, I just can't get over it," she told Gussie. "Other places have so many mixed-up styles—Spanish and Tudor and early-California bungalows and French Provincial suburban all in the same block. Here—well, there may be a few exceptions, but they're just that, *exceptions*. There's one clean pattern, and that's the stamp the old Quaker builders left behind them. Simple lines, center chimneys, those heavy board framings for windows that still have their ledge of snow now, like white eyebrows. Weathered shingles or white clapboards . . ."

"White trim on the shingled houses, or soft painted gray trim, like on Beth's perfect little old house on India Street," Gussie continued enthusiastically. "And don't you love the houses with raised foundations of brick or stone with basement windows where the old summer kitchens used to be?"

"I just realized what makes it so clean-looking," Mrs. Potter went on. "Most of the houses front directly on the street, with the gardens and outbuildings in the back. Having them all lined up together this way, you aren't looking at driveways with boat trailers parked in them, or at people's barbecue grills or clotheslines, if people have clotheslines anymore. You don't see any of the usual front yard *clutter*. All you see are the fronts of these incredibly lovely houses, big ones and little ones."

As she spoke, she knew it was not only the clean island architecture she loved, with its satisfying rightness of proportion and scale, but the delight of the vistas at each bend of the winding streets, down crooked lanes, up and down the gentle slopes of the village streets. There were unexpected little paved courts, lined with dollhouses. There were houses tucked behind other houses, houses set sidewise. There were tiny gardens, bright with massed color in summer, today clean and beautiful with the tinsel touch of melting snow and sun, to be glimpsed through high privet hedges, and great gardens hidden from view behind old brick walls covered with ivy.

Before they reached Mary Lynne's white-columned front door as they headed back home, they met Mary Lynne herself, slim and lithe in a fitted ski suit.

"Awful, isn't it, about Ozzie," she said as they met. "Helen just called me. The poor old dear dying alone that way. And then that poor girl yesterday at the Scrim. I know how Peter must feel that he wasn't able to save her."

She straightened her shoulders. "But don't you two look great!" she said, her voice determinedly cheerful. "Like a couple of sisters out in the snow! I *told* myself this would be a wonderful morning for walking, and you two are the living proof of it. Now you come right back to my kitchen with me for coffee and tell me where all you've been." She grasped each of them by the arm.

Before Mrs. Potter could reflect, somewhat wryly, on the present disparity of sisterly sizes, Mary Lynne was tugging them both toward her doorway. "The chairman of the antique auto parade isn't coming for at least a half hour—that's part of the Daffodil Festival, Genia—and he's always comfortably late anyway. Don't you just hate and despise people who are always on time? Come right back in with me now and meet my babies and we'll have a good visit!"

Gussie interrupted, pleasant but firm. "We'd love to, another day. Right now you get *your* walk while you can, before you get wrapped up in festival plans. We'll see you tomorrow at Larry's, if not before."

Mary Lynne, agreeing reluctantly, headed down the street as Mrs. Potter admired the slim shape in the ski suit, a shape she had never suspected was there beneath the former imposing façade of Mary Lynne Heidecker in the years she had known her.

"She's been wonderful since Bo's death," Gussie said as they went on. "She gets out and walks. She's got these two new little dogs—hear them yapping in the house now?—to keep her company. Lhasa apsos, a new breed to me. She's lost all that weight, and she's being a magnificent chairman for the festival. Mary Lynne is much tougher than she will admit."

"When you called me last summer, I realized that, if I hadn't before," Mrs. Potter said. "No wonder she felt sorry for Peter. It must have been terrible for her having Bo die out there in the sailboat and not be able to do anything to save him."

They had not yet encountered other friends as they walked. From time to time they had waved at passing cars or trucks—the garbage man, the plumber, a woman with a familiar face and a carful of small children. It was not until they neared the top of Orange Street that they were hailed with a genteel shout.

"Genia!" Ted Frobisher called out as he came down his front steps, just a little unsteadily. "I must say, you're looking great!"

Ted lived, as she knew, in one of four attached houses known as "the block," just as the big red-brick mansions on Main Street were known as "the bricks." Built in a style now said to be town houses, or before that, row houses, in Philadelphia and Baltimore, each was a generous and quite elegant dwelling. The shared wall of the long-ago construction had been planned, it was said, to conserve both heat and land space, and perhaps to afford comfort and company to the families of sea captains during the months or even years of long whaling voyages. Each had its beautiful front parlor, its elegant dining room just behind, its side hall and fine stairway leading to two upper floors of bedrooms.

Mrs. Potter remembered that Ted had once taken her down into what had been the old basement kitchen before a newer one had been added to the back of each house, long before he came there to live. High windows gave good light on the front, on the street side. The huge fireplace was dark and long unused. A rusting bicycle leaned against one wall.

Ted was using part of the long room for garden supplies, as

a potting room, he had told her that day, with a stairway leading up to a small attached greenhouse adjoining the present-day kitchen at ground level.

Her chief recollection of this long-ago tour was of cobwebs and old shelves laden with dusty canning jars and old bottles. That, and someone's—was it Lew's?—comment that the chief potting done on those premises was that which Ted did to himself.

As they now exchanged the greetings of old friends who have not seen each other for several years, Mrs. Potter reflected on how little real pleasure there is in hearing "You're looking great." She favored the opposite approach.

"Ted, it's marvelous to be back!" she told him, "and I'm so pleased at running into you this first morning. I hope you're well—you look a little pale, but perhaps that's because I always think of you with a deep summer tan."

Ted beamed, immediate proof of her theory that people prefer to be told they may not look too robust. Then the response can be that they're actually *fine*, with the implication that whatever they're suffering (everybody's suffering *something*), they're doing so gallantly, in noble silence. She liked this much better than hearing the opposite: You may think I look well enough, but let me *tell* you what I've been going through.

"I'm absolutely topnotch," he assured her jauntily. "See you Saturday, Gussie, at your house, cocktails at five, I remember. So good of you to include me."

He again raised his Irish tweed hat and, again somewhat unsteadily, turned to walk up the street in the direction of his office.

Then, as if remembering necessary courtesies, he inquired if they had heard about Ozzie. Too awfully sad, he told them, dying by himself that way. Must have been late at night, since he'd heard Ozzie in his office at maybe eleven, eleven thirty.

"You were working that late?" Gussie asked in surprise.

Well, some way he'd fallen asleep at his own desk after work. The admission clearly left him a little abashed, and he seemed relieved when Mrs. Potter asked if he was sure he wasn't working too hard.

"If we're going to go past everyone's houses without going all the way around by Main Street," she said after Ted had gone on, "let's take my shortcut."

This, apparently unknown even to Gussie, led them back a few doors down Orange Street, then along a nearly obscure path (really too close to someone's house for daytime use, Mrs. Potter realized, which meant she must have used it as a quick way to reach some Orange Street friend's house in the evening) through a small jagged break in a tall hedge and hence into the parking lot of St. Paul's, and from there out into Fair Street.

Gussie, while applauding the footwork, vetoed a second suggestion: that they stop at the church to admire the Tiffany windows. Instead, she led Mrs. Potter to the front of the church, where the lettered wooden sign proclaimed the hours of worship. "See anything different?" she asked.

It took only a moment for Mrs. Potter to see what was missing. "It used to say 'Enter, Rest, and Pray,' " she said, "and there was something about being open twenty-four hours."

"Beth told you you'd find changes," Gussie said.

As she spoke, a tap on the window in the adjoining parish hall caught their attention. "Come on in," mouthed the kitten face below the pale fluff of hair. She beckoned, then with difficulty pushed up the old wooden window sash.

"Terrible about Ozzie," Leah said, now audible. "Helen called. She's been trying to get Mary Lynne to tell her, too, but her phone was busy as usual. I wonder if she knows?"

Gussie and Mrs. Potter nodded emphatically.

"I'm about to demonstrate basic altar arrangements for our new members—want to watch?" Leah asked, drawing back from the window, her hands sheltering her hair from the breeze.

Gussie was pleasant but definite, as she had been with Mary Lynne. "Wish we could—haven't time," she called back. "Meals on Wheels day for me and Beth, remember?"

A bearded young man in a sweat shirt appeared at Leah's side and helped close the window, waving genially at Gussie as he did, and peering questioningly at Mrs. Potter.

"New rector," Gussie explained. "You'll meet him Sunday. About Leah—she's an expert on altar flowers, you remember. The new members of the Altar Guild are lucky to have her showing them how. It's a very special art. It was the one thing she did keep on doing, all these years she's been widowed, other than take care of that house of hers. Of course, you could see for yourself yesterday how she's changed since she started going to Tony."

"I agree with Beth about all the changes around here," Mrs. Potter said, "but at least the names of the streets are the same." They entered a small lane across from the church. "I love this one, 'Lucretia Mott.' One of the Coffins, wasn't she? Early feminist? Reformer? Anyway, a heroine. And now this darling little one-block lane named for her."

She began to laugh. "If they ever name one for you, it's going to have to be longer than this just for the street sign. How'd you like to be remembered for 'Mary Augusta Baines Andrews Berner Van Vleeck Street'?"

Gussie said she did not find this even slightly amusing. Instead, she pointed down the next street toward the old carriage house once belonging to Mittie's parents, now remodeled and presently occupied by Dee.

"I can't believe Dee's being so downright unpleasant and spiteful about Tony," she said. "Just because they couldn't make a go of their marriage when they were both young and had very demanding and separate careers, she's going out of her way now, it seems to me, to say horrid and belittling things about him. It isn't like her."

It also was not like Gussie to sound so critical. She knew, as well as Mrs. Potter did, that Dee—former fashion editor and now successful and independent in real estate sales—was adored by everyone on the island, from the greasiest garage mechanic to the starchiest summer headwaiter. She was beloved of every shop owner, every visiting artist and musician and actor. She was popular with several different sets of fashionable summer people as well as with the established winter and year-round society of which Les Girls were a part.

In fact, Mrs. Potter was tempted to remind Gussie of all this, simply by comparing Dee's position in the community with Helen Latham's. Helen's managerial skills were legendary, she was skilled at pointing wealthy donors in the direction of worthy causes, she carried her own impressive aura of wealth. Yet more people liked and trusted Dee.

At the same time, Mrs. Potter also privately wondered, as she often had in the past, not speaking her thoughts aloud for fear of adding fuel to Gussie's ire, why it was that this chic, well-dressed, successful woman—charming, talented—was what the Potter children would only have described as a *mooch?*

As they neared the carriage house, Mrs. Potter knew she must seize this chance for a talk with Dee. "Mind if I run up and see the place for a minute?" she asked. "Dee's little car is in the drive, so I expect she's home. I'll be home in—half an hour, all right?"

"Don't forget this was your getting-acquainted-again walk," Gussie reminded her. "Pay attention to Ozzie's house across the street when you leave Dee's, and then be sure to look down Pleasant Street at the Shrine." She pointed, with a glint of amusement, in the direction of Leah's big house. "Thank heaven she's letting up on dear sainted Fanwell. And you'll go by Mittie's house and Helen's as you come down Main Street. But be back by eleven thirty—you hear me?"

IO

"I should have called you first," Mrs. Potter apologized when Dee opened the door at the top of the outside stairway. "Do you want a morning visitor for about fifteen minutes?"

"Come in! Welcome to the new *chez* Ferencz," Dee said, with a wide flash of white teeth. "No, with Tony on the local scene, I can't say that. This is most definitely *chez moi* and *moi* alone. This is a great time, and I have a half hour before I show some property out beyond Dionis.

"And, yes, I know about Ozzie's heart attack," she continued. "Helen called me. I wish I'd run over last evening to check on him after I heard the evening news and knew his secretary had died. Anyway, come on in and see what you think of the place."

The apartment spoke more of Mittie the owner than of Dee the tenant. Its furnishing was a monument to the tastes and hobbies of Ab Leland, Mittie's late husband. Ab's collection of old wooden decoys was displayed on open shelves everywhere, or had been made into bases for table lamps. Ab's tennis trophies ranged on the living room mantel. Prints depicting ducks and geese in flight, hunting dogs, horses, and boats under full canvas covered the walls. A full-rigged ship's model topped the television set. A ship's sextant had its place among the decoys in the bookshelves, and a brass ship's clock was striking the hour.

"Six bells, eleven o'clock," Dee announced, with an air of resigned amusement. "Mittie furnished this place with a lot of Abbott's special treasures and she thinks it's perfect, of course. I sometimes wonder why she didn't make room for them in the ancestral house up front." She pointed across the stretch of lawn to the back of the old house.

"I think it's all quite perfect for what she first had in mind," Mrs. Potter said boldy. "Summer rental, wasn't it? It's charming for that, but I can see that it might be a bit much for really *living in,* and it doesn't seem your sort of place at all."

Dee shrugged. "I shouldn't complain. At least the price is right—*zilch.* Mittie asked me to use the place as a favor to her, you know. I think she's timid about being alone since Ab died, and it seems to be a help to her to have a friend in the apartment. I go across to have dinner with her every night I can—every night I'm home. She says it's easier to cook for two than for one, and my contribution is washing the dishes, since we all know I can hardly bóil water."

Varying viewpoints, Mrs. Potter reflected. A generous and now regretted invitation from Mittie, or Dee's generous concern for a possibly lonely friend?

In the case that Beth (or was it Gussie?) had been right about Mittie's need for money, Mrs. Potter ventured another comment. "You're so good at finding the right tenants for people," she said. "Maybe by summer Mittie won't need so much bolstering, and when you find a place that seems more like you, you can help her with renting this apartment."

Dee was silent. I've gone too far, Mrs. Potter thought abjectly. We all know Dee is a penny pincher and we love her in spite of it. Now I've appeared to accuse her of sponging, and that's not at all the reason I came to see her. I'm going to change the subject immediately, although what I'm asking may prove awkward too.

"Dee, remember the first day I was back?" she said, interrupting a perceptible moment of silence. "Everyone was singing the praises of your former husband, and you told them something I haven't been able to get out of my mind. 'You'll all be sorry,' you said, or something like that."

Dee's questioning eyebrows were her only response.

"Why do I want to know?" Mrs. Potter answered the eyebrows. "You've certainly seen that all of our friends have—what's the expression?—have flipped their wigs over your Tony."

"I told them, and I told you, Genia, not *my* Tony. We separated long before the two years we were married."

"I'm not prying just for gossip," Mrs. Potter persisted. "What worries me is that Gussie may be really falling for the man. She's a wonderful person, Dee—you know that. And she's awfully vulnerable. She *needs* being married, she needs someone to cherish and look after and look up to, all at once. It's what she was born for, and she was absolutely wonderful for all three of the men she was married to—Theo, then Jules, and finally even Gordon Van Vleeck."

"Who was a total disaster," Dee remarked. "He lived like a leech on Gussie's money, and he was a bore and a complainer and a terrible hypochondriac."

"She didn't know enough about him before they were married," Mrs. Potter said, meanwhile reminded by the word *leech* that Dee was, in spite of her disclaimer about being there for Mittie's sake, not only living rent free but apparently also as a freeloading nightly dinner guest.

"You want to know about Tony before Gussie gets in too deep?" Dee asked wryly. She paused. "There are a lot of things I could tell you, and one in particular I probably should, but won't. I think I'll just tell you a story about three beautiful people, quite a long time ago."

Mrs. Potter waited expectantly.

"Let's say there was a rising young lawyer and his beautiful wife and they lived in a beautiful house on its own beautiful beach on Long Island, and they were very rich. Everyone thought they had everything in the world to live for. And they thought so too, particularly since the third person was their beautiful daughter—cute as a button, bright and popular, and the joy of their lives."

Mrs. Potter felt a sudden cold lump in her midsection. This was not going to be a happy story.

Dee continued. "The rich young lawyer and his beautiful wife thought the sun rose and set on their beautiful child. She was blond and tanned and a natural athlete, but, as young teen-agers are likely to be, a little—shall we say, chunky? Not fat, mind you, except the way a puppy is fat, or maybe a young seal or a little bear."

Mrs. Potter's sense of foreboding increased.

"I did tell you that our rich young lawyer and his beautiful wife were fashionable people, didn't I? Their pictures were in the flossiest magazines, *Éclat* among them. They were trend setters, and also, I suppose, trend followers.

"About that time a young man arrived in New York. Tall, handsome, aristocratic. A touch of European accent. A way with women that had them all hanging on his every word, and a plan for getting rich by letting them listen to him. 'Do what I tell you, lovely ladies,' he said to them in effect, 'and I will make you more beautiful than you ever dreamed and I will keep you that way forever.'"

Mrs. Potter listened, seeing that tall young swordsman's figure.

"To make his plan successful, this young man—the newcomer with the air of an aristocrat, the appeal of a tomcat," Dee spat out the words, "this young man had to become known to the women of society. He had to make himself fashionable.

"And what was his road to acceptance? His picture must appear in the right magazines, he must be interviewed by the right people, he must be seen with the right people. And who could better help him with this than an ambitious young woman who had just been made editor of *Éclat?*"

Dee abandoned the role of storyteller. "Oh, damn it, Genia, I was insecure and lonely, and afraid somebody in New York would find out what a small-town hick I really was. I looked like a fashion editor ought to look—I was born with the right bones and my mother had been a dressmaker who made all my clothes and taught me how to wear them. I studied journalism in college and I learned something about the trade in a good department store, working summers. I'd written about fashions and women's features on my hometown newspaper. Most of all, I worked very hard. But inside, if you can believe it, I was still scared." She paused. "Now I've never told this to anyone else before . . ."

Mrs. Potter slowly nodded, the gesture her promise that Dee's confidence would be safe.

"What nobody knows," Dee went on, "is that five years before all this happened, I got on a plane in Altoona as Dora Stell Grumbley. After two free airline drinks I decided one thing. Dora Stell Grumbley wouldn't make it. When the plane got to La Guardia, it was Dee St. Germain who got off."

"Nice," was Mrs. Potter's comment. "I like that—it must have been fun."

"It helped," Dee admitted. "Still, even when I got the job at the magazine, and the top job five years later, I was still pretending to be a lot more assured than I felt. You can put together this part of the story pretty fast. Ambitious young foreign aristocrat on the make. Ambitious young editor just as much so. Dee St. Germain becomes Countess Ferencz, which gives her a real title and a feeling that she's at last part of the international high society her magazine is written for."

She went on. "Tony Ferencz is launched as a sensational, successful, world-famous authority on health and beauty. Society women are falling all over themselves to become his first American clients."

On the floor beside Dee's chair, on a spread newspaper, were two pairs of shoes, a tin of clear shoe wax, and a polishing cloth. She touched a shoe tentatively, found it dry, picked it up, and began to rub it briskly. Mrs. Potter knew instinctively that the plain dark leather pumps and the English walking shoes, clearly not new, were intended to remain in service for more years to come.

Dee continued as she polished each shoe in turn. "Sorry about the background soap opera," she said lightly. "I've never told anyone this before, except to say Tony and I were once married. The story I started to tell you was about the three beautiful people on Long Island—the young lawyer and his wife and their darling, but ever so slightly chubby, daughter Marthé."

Mrs. Potter found herself continuing the story. "Fashionable new young foreign authority attracts the attention of the young wife, along with her friends," she told Dee slowly. "Daughter persuades herself that, as her mother and her mother's friends say, 'you can't be too rich or too thin.' Am I right?"

"To put the most generous possible interpretation on it, Tony didn't know as much about diet then as he may know now," Dee said. "Maybe he wasn't aware of the fact that the child was actually ill—anorexia nervosa, of course. No matter how thin they get to be, young girls especially, they're convinced they're still overweight, even when they're down to matchsticks."

"Tony did that to Ozzie deBevereaux's daughter?" Mrs. Potter asked somberly.

"He *should* have known. Whether in stupid ignorance he killed her with a terrible diet, or whether he neglected proper treatment once she was really ill, I don't know. I don't imagine the distinction was important to Ozzie and Bunny once Marthé had passed the point of no return."

Mrs. Potter recalled Gussie's earlier words. Ozzie's wife and daughter had both died years ago.

Dee forestalled her question. "Bunny died of heartbreak, I think. She always felt it was her fault, just as I've always known it was partly mine, for having launched Tony in his career."

"And Ozzie—how did he feel?" Mrs. Potter asked. "About blame, that is?"

"There's no doubt about *that* part of the story," Dee said flatly. "In Ozzie's mind, Tony Ferencz was a murderer. First of his child, indirectly of his wife. It's just lucky for Tony that poor Ozzie is dead. Anyway—so now you know the story. It's just one of the reasons I say everybody is going to be sorry Tony ever came here.

"Now let me scrub my hands," she said, "and put away these shoes. I'll show you the kitchen and the rest of the apartment."

In Dee's small, rather bare kitchen Mrs. Potter saw the trademark dark brown felt hat on a newspaper, its brim covered with yellow granules. "Cleaning it with cornmeal, the way my mother taught me," Dee explained. "I'll have to brush it now, if you'll forgive me for going on with my various jobs. I do have to meet my clients soon. They're staying at the Jared Coffin and they've asked me to lunch there before we start looking at property."

Mrs. Potter made the expected quick tour of the rest of the apartment—two small bedrooms and a new and quite elegant bathroom. "It all looks exactly like Mittie," she remarked as she prepared to leave. "All her favorite colors, even to the bright pink of the towels and the pink-and-green-flowered shower curtain."

As she left hastily, to allow Dee time to make her appointment, she remembered that she had referred to yet another and perhaps even more disturbing story about her former husband. For now, there was no more time and she had enough to think about. If Ozzie and his secretary had died because of their knowledge of this past, unhappy secret—a preposterous thought—it was clear that Tony would be the prime suspect. Gussie was not going to like this at all.

As she left the carriage house, a less dreadful and yet long-perplexing question went through her mind. If Dee was reaping an occasional fat commission on real estate sales in Nantucket's ever-demanding market, why was she polishing those same old shoes—albeit very good old shoes—and cleaning with cornmeal that same old—albeit terrifically becoming—hat? Mrs. Potter thought she took care of her own basically classic wardrobe. However, there always comes a time when things must be replaced. Dee's reluctance to do so seemed an obsession.

II

On her way home, aware that she could meet Gussie's eleven-thirty deadline without hurrying, Mrs. Potter did as she'd been told.

Gussie had told her to look across the street to Ozzie's house. She faced the path leading to his kitchen door, the obvious and easy entrance to his house. According to Beth, this was the one door among those of her friends' houses that still was left unlocked.

She sighed. Now it seemed even the church doors were barred except for times of services. It used to be so comfortable when we all could run in and leave a note or a plate of cookies or a marked magazine article for each other, she thought. And once in a while it was so comforting to slip into the small side chapel of the church, softly lighted and still, at the end of a solitary walk late at night.

At least her uneasiness about Ozzie's death suggested no picture of a stealthy figure slipping through that unlocked kitchen door. A sudden heart attack, even if unexpected, was not the work of an intruder. At least not the work of a killer with knife or gun, weapons whose mark would have been unmistakable.

As she walked a few steps farther, she could look at the front of the house, to which access was only by way of a little-used white wooden gate in a high privet hedge. She saw that the snow had now melted, except for a shaded patch in the front doorway and some ragged white clumps held by heavy bare vines on their lattices, outlining the doorway and nearly covering the front of the quiet house.

At the corner, she looked left down the street to Leah's house, another ship owner's mansion of an earlier age. The Shrine, she smiled, using Gussie's name for it. Thank heaven, Gussie says she's letting up a little on dear sainted Fanwell. Someone said she even used to scrub the brick sidewalk in front, just to show the rest of us how a truly devoted widow should behave.

Then as Mrs. Potter found herself back on Main Street, she passed Mittie's present house, where there was no sign of activity. Peering down an opening between it and the next house, she could see the sweep of lawn dividing the main house from Dee's carriage-house apartment at the back of the block. It seemed weed-grown and neglected.

Renovating that lawn in itself is going to cost a fortune, she thought. It's all run to sand, which is really the chief part of Nantucket soil, and that means digging it all up and replacing the whole thing with fresh topsoil. Maybe Mittie ought to forget about cherishing Mummy's furniture and unload the place.

Then, glancing across the street, Mrs. Potter called to the plump, white-haired man polishing the big brass door knocker of Helen's great red-brick mansion. "Hi, Walter!" she shouted, crossing the cobblestones to speak to him. "How's Elna? You two keeping busy? Tell her I'll stop in to say hello someday soon when I come to see Mrs. Latham and admire your new garden room. I hear it's pretty splendid."

Helen was the only one of the group to have live-in help. She was congratulated on the gleaming perfection of the house, but, in spite of having a cook, Elna's nominal title, Helen set a poor table. Dinner at her house might be as uninspired as canned beef stew, although it would be presented handsomely by Walter in a huge silver dish. Helen ate without noticing what was set before her, Mrs. Potter remembered, in the same way she ate far better fare at the houses of her friends.

The thought of food made Mrs. Potter suddenly hungry after the long morning walk. As she returned to Gussie's doorway, flanked with the twin steps and the two gleaming brass globes, she wondered if Gussie, too, might not be famished, with only that glass of whatever it was, now long ago, for her breakfast.

"Could we split that last cranberry muffin?" she asked as she met Gussie in the hall. "Before we do anything else? I'll start this Tony diet of yours tomorrow, if you'll tell me about it, but I'm not ready for it today."

Gussie disregarded the question and her face seemed troubled as she reported a phone message from Beth. "We just hung up," she said. "She hadn't forgotten about Meals on Wheels, but she said she just didn't feel quite up to doing the rounds with me today, if you wouldn't mind standing in for her. I said of course, but Genia, do you ever in your life remember a time when Beth Higginson didn't feel up to anything and everything?"

Gussie continued, clearly puzzled. "She said she'd spent the morning at the science library, of all places, and that she'd probably go back this afternoon, and that Lolly Latham was being a lot of help to her. In fact, she said she thought we'd all underestimated Lolly."

Mrs. Potter decided that if Gussie wasn't going to eat the half muffin, perhaps she had better do so herself so that it wouldn't be wasted. From the look on Gussie's face, she felt a certain concern for Beth, and a shared curiosity about the science library visit, but at the same time she was wondering how and when to tell Gussie the story of the three beautiful people on Long Island. The last of the muffin was suddenly tasteless as yet another vexing thought crossed her mind.

"Tell me," she asked, "do you think Ted was a little squiffed, even this morning? It's plain enough to figure out that he'd been drinking at his office yesterday. He was embarrassed when he as much as admitted it, saying he'd fallen asleep at his desk and waked up late at night to hear Ozzie come in. Helen said Arnold found him at home, dead in his chair, at nine."

"It gets dark so early these days, I expect Ted just lost track of time," Gussie said charitably. "Come on now, time to take off if you're going to do the rounds with me in Bethie's place."

When they returned, after taking the food containers back to the hospital, cleaning and spraying them according to accepted procedure, Mrs. Potter settled with relief into a kitchen easy chair.

"That was fun, but it's quite a workout," she said. They had delivered twelve sets of meals—a small container of hot spaghetti and meat balls, a small salad, a slice of garlic toast, and an apple for midday dinner; an egg salad sandwich and chocolate pudding for supper—to twelve different people. "You're marvelous, Gussie, to find your way to all of them and to remember all the one-way streets and to whip up and down so many back stairs, and still manage a quick chat with each person."

"I ought to know my way—we've been doing it long enough," Gussie said. "Everybody missed Beth, though, couldn't you see? Let's call her later and insist on knowing what's the trouble. I've never known her to beg off on *anything,* all the years we've known her."

The two now sat at the round table in the kitchen, listening to reassuring sounds of a vacuum cleaner being run in the front parlor. Gussie had set out a bowl of red apples and a round provolone cheese for their own delayed lunch—delayed, at least, according to Mrs. Potter's usual inner timetable.

She took a grateful sip of the white wine poured for her, deciding as she did so to postpone further thoughts about Tony and the people in Dee's story until she was alone and could figure out the best way and time to tell Gussie about it. Somehow she felt there would be other stories told her—perhaps about less beautiful people, perhaps even about her own Nantucket friends—if she continued her attempt to protect Gussie from a too hasty fourth marriage. "I hate to think you opened that bottle just for me" was all she said.

"No problem," Gussie assured her. "It'll get drunk. You may want another glass now and some later in the day." She returned then, bearing a small beaker, from a quick trip to the big pantry from which Mrs. Potter had seen her emerge when she came down into the kitchen at first daylight.

"Carrot juice," she explained, in answer to Mrs. Potter's questioning eyebrows. "Want to try some? It's all I have for breakfast, maybe with a cup of tea, and sometimes again with my lunch."

Mrs. Potter accepted a small glassful, pronounced it delicious—who *doesn't* like the taste of sweet raw carrots?—and cut herself another wedge of cheese and apple. "Any little wheat crackers?" she asked, with the easy assurance of an old friend.

"Now let's talk about party food," Gussie said, after the cheese and apples and while Mrs. Potter sat nibbling a last crisp cracker with a second glass of wine. "I haven't given a tea party for years, if you want to know the truth, and I'm not quite sure where to begin."

Mrs. Potter admitted that, except for occasional callers to be given a casually offered afternoon cup of tea—with which one might produce a bit of toast or the odd cookie, if any such was on hand—it had been years since she, too, had connected the words *tea* and *party*.

"Anyway, Teresa's accomplished the first step this morning while we were walking," she said, admiring the gleaming silver tea service, freshly polished, on the kitchen sideboard. "The second one is simply having good tea, and we know how to do *that.*"

They agreed that the procedure was quite different when making tea for a lot of people, rather than for two or even six, and that they'd both learned this much from their mothers. One pot of very, very strong tea, which could be made in advance and kept warm, with refills waiting in the kitchen. One pot of very hot water, preferably freshly boiling. A bit of one and a lot of the other in each cup, as the tea pourer received requests for weak or strong, along with answers about sugar, milk, and lemon.

"That part's simple enough, then," Gussie said. "Let's make a list from here on."

From her large crewel bag in one of the big chairs in front of the fireplace, the bag she had placed there the previous day with her current needlepoint for possible future moments of stitchery, Mrs. Potter had already brought out a lined yellow pad. "Tea—Earl Grey, do you think? Check milk. Lemons. Cube sugar? How many are we having?"

"Oh, a couple of dozen," Gussie said. "Maybe thirty. As I said, all of the old crowd, plus Tony, of course, and a few others. I just asked people as I ran into them last week, either new people I thought you'd like, or various old buddies. Actually, I think all of them except Peter Benson assume it's for cocktails. I mentioned tea to him, because I thought he'd be amused seeing people's surprise. He looked a little doubtful at first, but then he promised he'd get away from the Scrim to be here, no matter what."

Gussie continued. "You'll pour, of course," she said. "What kind of flowers for the table, do you think? Anything specially good with whatever you'll be wearing?"

"What about some long-stemmed anemones if we can get them?" Mrs. Potter asked. "Sort of springlike and cheerful for this time of year. And I'll wear whatever you say. You saw what I brought."

Gussie voted for a banana-colored wool dress she had helped to unpack, saying that she had something rather like it—simple, but dressed-up enough for anything on the island short of a real dinner party.

Involuntarily, Mrs. Potter sighed. Gussie's dress, a size—two sizes?—smaller? She finished the last of the wine in her glass hastily, regretting the second glass as she did so, and the extra wedge of cheese, and all those crackers. "Let's get on with the list," she said.

No need to get out cookbooks for inspiration, they decided. They began to remember tea parties they'd given in the past, for various worthy causes, and the tea parties their mothers used to have.

Little sandwiches were an absolute must, they agreed. Very thin, crusts cut off, and no trouble to make with the very thin-sliced firm bread one could buy nowadays. Cucumber, naturally, and maybe tomato. "If we do tomato ones, we'll give them a good sprinkle of basil," Mrs. Potter suggested, "the way Peter did for my salad yesterday. Beth will have some dried from her garden, if you don't."

"How about watercress?" Gussie asked. "We can get that perfect cress right here on the island, and we'll make little rolled sandwiches with a nice sprig sticking out both ends."

Mrs. Potter was writing. "Butter—remember to soften. Mayonnaise, bread, watercress, cucumbers, tomatoes. Basil —Beth?" She laid down her pen. "What about using that great recipe of yours for a parsley dip as a sandwich filling?" she asked. "As a matter of fact, why not *have* some cocktail party food? How about those great little hot cheese things of yours? I know Teresa doesn't cook, for you, that is, but she can certainly get those in and out of the oven if we have them chilled and ready. And what about that stuff you do with chopped ripe olives and garlic?"

The list progressed to possible sweets. More sandwiches, they finally agreed, little open-faced half slices, lightly buttered, using Gussie's recipe for cranberry cheese bread for one kind. For a second, Mrs. Potter suggested her great-grandmother's orange bread, claiming she knew the recipe by heart, having made it for so many years.

"Write it down for me, will you?" Gussie asked, proffering a file card. "Seems to me you once said it had no shortening in it. Maybe some of the dieters will be glad to know."

Mrs. Potter wrote quickly, using abbreviations. *Peel of 2 oranges, cut in fine slivers. Cover with water, add 1/2 c. sugar, simmer till tender. Remove peel, cook liquid down to about 1/3 c. In mixing bowl comb. another 1/2 c. sugar, 2 c. flour, 3 t. baking powder, 1/2 t. salt. Add milk to orange syrup to make 2/3 c. and mix with 1 egg. Stir all tog. with orange peel. Greased loaf pan, 350, 45 min.*

"There!" she exclaimed, looking up. "That's clear enough. Grandmother Andrews would be proud of me. It was her mother's recipe, and one of the first things she taught me to make. We'd better bake it and your cranberry cheese bread on Friday, don't you think? They'll slice better the next day."

It was too soon after the holidays, they told each other, to even *think* about cookies. Gussie had one big leftover gift fruitcake she hadn't unwrapped. They'd have a plate of that, sliced very thin, just to make more of a show on the sweet side, and if it wasn't eaten, Gussie would send the whole thing home with Teresa, which is what she probably should have done with it in the first place. And there was the yet unopened box of burnt sugar almonds Beth had brought to welcome Mrs. Potter.

"Let's call her back and see how she is," Mrs. Potter suggested. There was no answer, although she let the phone ring a few extra times.

The yellow pad list seemed complete. Then, "just for *pretty,*" Mrs. Potter suggested that she might pick up a box of old-fashioned pastel bonbons when they went shopping later. "The little paper cups will look as if we'd gone to the proper amount of trouble," she said. She added this entry to her list, and then began to laugh.

"I was just remembering bridesmaids' dresses, and how absolutely sappy we looked in them. Tulle or chiffon or net of some kind, or even worse, taffeta, all in sweet bonbon colors. . . ."

Gussie protested. "I thought you looked very nice in that pale green with the matching horsehair picture hat as my maid of honor," she said. "Although I suppose it *was* all pretty saccharine, with ten bridesmaids in matching shell pink. How many of those dresses do you suppose we all bought—in colors we called 'peach' and 'seafoam' and 'aqua' and 'orchid'—before we got each other all married off?"

"And never wore again, although our mothers always expected us to," Mrs. Potter added. "All those bertha collars and little ruffled sleeve caps . . ."

"All those dyed-to-match satin pumps," Gussie reminded

her, "and how expensive we thought they were, at six dollars a pair including the dye-to-match. I seem to remember sometimes the bride's mother shelled out for those as well as buying the hats."

"What I seem to recall is that we were all a little bit fatter than girls are now," Mrs. Potter said. "Not *really* fat, but I think we'd look that way if our pictures were compared with a modern wedding party."

"What I seem to remember are *ushers,*" Gussie said dreamily. "Do you remember that absolutely wonderful man —from Dartmouth, I think he was? At Barbara's wedding in Montpelier?"

Mrs. Potter failed to remember that particular wonderful man from Dartmouth, and continued to think how unutterably dowdy she must have looked in seafoam green with a matching horsehair picture hat. She resolved not to stuff herself on tomorrow's cucumber sandwiches.

Gussie interrupted these mildly uncomfortable thoughts. "What time is it?" she shrieked. "Genia, don't bother with those lunch dishes, don't put your hair up again, or *anything.* Just jam on your hat—we've got to be *going! Teresa?* Remember you promised me Saturday, too, this week? Genia, let's *go!* You'll miss the surprise!"

12

"I can't remember—do I kiss you?"

The speaker, slight, fair-haired, his smile eternally boyish in an unlined face, greeted Mrs. Potter with vague cordiality as she and Gussie started down Main Street.

Mrs. Potter decided to give the question the deliberate consideration the speaker had not, perhaps, intended. "I don't remember either, George," she said at last. "Shall we just shake hands and decide what to do about it later?"

George's best clerical chuckle covered any possible lapse of memory. "Okay, I think you always used to, George," she told him forgivingly, "and I just now realized you've had to face that problem before. All those trustees' wives and students' mothers at your school, and before that all those women parishioners. It would have been dreadful to be kissing when you shouldn't and maybe even worse not kissing when you should. Yes, you kiss *me*, but just on one side."

"Turn around and walk back down Main Street with us, George," Gussie urged, with a tug at his elbow. "You can share the big surprise with Genia. *Come on*, shake a leg!"

Between the two women, each as tall as he, George Enderbridge seemed fragile and weightless, as smooth and dry as a leaf clinging to a winter branch. Gussie had taken for granted his willingness to join them, but with a surprising show of firmness he kept them from sweeping him along with them.

"I assume you know about Ozzie," he said, his voice deeper and more resonant than his small frame suggested. "I've just been at the parish house to inquire about arrangements for a memorial service. The rector insists the deBevereaux executor has other plans, specified by Ozzie a long time ago. There will be nothing here except a special prayer at morning worship on Sunday, and burial will be on Long Island. His body's already been flown off-island, and it seems the little charter plane is having a real workout. His secretary's body was taken home to Ossining, or wherever she came from, earlier this morning, with her brother here to accompany it." George sounded disappointed, even slightly affronted.

"We're very sad about both of them," Gussie told him. "We all were there, you know, at the Scrim when she had the start of her allergic seizure. Maybe when Ozzie had news of it the shock brought on his heart attack. About the services—I suppose their family ties off-island are the important thing. But I'm sorry, George, honestly, we can't stay now. Come on now, we've got to get *moving!*"

George had more resistance than Gussie had expected. He would not, he thought, join them for the surprise, whatever it was. He was expected at Mittie's to report on the funeral arrangements, or lack of them. Mittie took continuing interest in church matters, he said with approval, although she was no longer president of the Women of St. Paul's. He would, however, look forward to seeing them both again on Saturday at the cocktail party.

The sidewalks were now dry in the sunshine. The last of the Christmas trees were gone, with only a few fir sprigs here and there, not yet swept away, as a reminder of their morning splendor in the early snow. Mrs. Potter stopped short in her tracks.

"I smell fresh bread!" she exclaimed. "Gussie, stop rushing us! Slow down! *Gussie!*"

A broad, triumphant smile was Gussie's answer. She waved a theatrical arm toward a hanging sign in front of the tiny shop ahead, a sign Mrs. Potter felt sure had not been there on their morning walk down this same street, hanging above a shop she had not noticed then, nor remembered from the past.

" 'The Portuguese Bread Man,' " she read in tones of bewilderment. "There's no bakery on Main Street, Gussie. What's this all about?"

The air was filled with the fragrance of freshly baked bread. Around them a few people were pausing, as they were, sniffing the air. Others appeared, converging from all directions, as if drawn by a magnet. In the few steps it took the two women to reach the front of the small shop, they were surrounded by people—a dozen, two dozen, a growing throng.

The small-paned shopwindow displayed a large hand-lettered sign. FOLLOW YOUR NOSE TO THE PORTUGUESE BREAD MAN, it read. On the windowed door beside it—the entire shop no more than eight feet across—was a second sign, OPENING FRIDAY.

Pushed by the growing sidewalk crowd to a position in front of the closed door, Mrs. Potter mounted the single flat stone step and tried the handle. Shrugging, she turned. "Apparently they're not open," she explained, apologetically and unnecessarily. "Today's Thursday. Friday's tomorrow."

Feeling foolish at making such obvious announcements, she stepped down to Gussie's side. "Somebody's baking in there right now, and the smell of it's driving the whole town crazy. Why don't they just open up and start off with a great box-office smash right now?"

Gussie lifted a quick, gloved fingertip in a gesture of secrecy. "Let's go across the street," she said, "and I'll tell you all about it."

"Let's have a soda at the drugstore, then," Mrs. Potter proposed. "Actually, I'd love a ginger ice cream cone, if that isn't too much right after lunch."

They went into one of the two old-fashioned drugstores,

side by side and so nearly identical in their layout that Mrs. Potter never knew which one she was in without going back outside to see. Gussie took a stool at the short fountain counter, and as Mrs. Potter sat beside her, she ordered decisively for them both. "We'll have iced tea," she told the pair of plump, aproned girls behind the counter, interrupting their conversation.

Chastened, knowing that what she'd *really* intended to order had been a chocolate frappe (pronounced and often spelled "frap" in Massachusetts, known more prosaically in her Iowa youth as a chocolate ice cream milk shake), Mrs. Potter accepted what seemed to her the unseasonable glass of iced tea meekly. The girls behind the counter resumed their conversation and the store was empty, all of Nantucket's winter afternoon shoppers apparently still clustering about the front of the little shop across the street, drawn by the ineffable and irresistible fragrance of baking bread. Still, as if fearful of being overheard, Gussie lowered her voice to a whisper as she told the story of the new bakeshop.

To begin with, she explained, it began when Teresa's oldest granddaughter, Mary Rezendes, went off to Radcliffe, where she'd graduated, with honors, last June. While she was in Cambridge, she met a young man from St. Louis, Hans Muller, who graduated at the same time from the Harvard Business School. Hans followed her here to the island and spent the summer working for Teresa's brother.

Mrs. Potter interrupted. That same pretty girl with the long braid and the head scarf at the Scrimshaw with the softball league?

Gussie nodded, impatient of interruption. Hans's father had a chain of bakeries as well as a lot of other interests in St. Louis. He had been a baker's apprentice himself as a boy, and had insisted that Hans, in turn, learn the trade, as well as go to graduate school in business management, in order to take over the family enterprises later on.

"So what did he do for Teresa's brother, if that's part of the story?" Mrs. Potter asked.

"You mean you didn't know? Teresa's brother is *Manny!*"

"I guess it's coming clear, but not entirely. Mary Rezendes is home from Radcliffe, her Harvard B-school boyfriend spends last summer as a baker's helper for her uncle—I've got that straight. And now, presumably, he or she or they are setting up competition for poor Manny, while he's gone, in that tiny little hole-in-the-wall space across the street? I'm not sure I think this is exactly cricket. And besides, unless that building runs a whole lot deeper than I think it does, there can't be room for ovens and supplies and all those big mixers and cooling racks."

"Now you're getting the picture," Gussie assured her. "To begin with, they aren't competing with Manny. He's got a stake in the whole operation, and he taught Hans to make real honest-to-goodness Manny-style Portuguese bread, and Hans will begin baking it tonight or tomorrow morning or whenever it is that bakers bake bread. And he'll be doing it right there in Manny's kitchens in the back of Manny's regular bakeshop."

"I still don't get all of this," Mrs. Potter said. "I see we've got a couple of bright young people setting up in business and I'm glad it's with Manny's backing and blessing. I still can't figure out how the smell of *tomorrow's* bread, baking in ovens at least eight blocks away, is wafting out *today* right across the street from where we sit."

"You forgot what I told you about Mary Rezendes," Gussie reminded her. "Yes, she's pretty and smart and has her grandmother's lovely skin and oval face and black hair, and yes, she's Manny's grandniece. Besides all that she studied chemistry and neurology and she's a specialist in *olfactology*, if you know what that is. She knows all about things called odorants and pheromones. Believe it or not, she's a specialist in *smells*.

"After months of laboratory work," Gussie continued, "Mary has come up with an absolutely wonderful attar, made of artificial ingredients, that gives out the wonderful smell of yeast and browning crust and to-grandmother's-house-we-go!"

Gussie hugged her knees with delight. "The mechanics are

simple enough to put the smell out into the street, as the two of them explained it to me. The chemical mixture is warmed in a little heater she contrived, and she rigged up the reverse of an exhaust fan through a grill over the doorway of the shop, which pipes the lovely smell out to the street."

As she spoke, the sleek, biscuit-colored girl with the long dark braid came into the drugstore, followed by a young man, dark, rather stocky, wearing a three-piece suit. "It's working!" Mary Rezendes whispered as she took the next stool. "We thought we'd sneak out the back way and come out to hear what people were saying."

Gussie introduced the two, and at her signal the four heads drew together above the counter, their voices lowered. "Can you imagine what this is going to do when the streets are full of summer people?" Hans asked. "We'll have special carrying bags with the logo. Every day-tripper going back on the boat to Hyannis will be a walking ad for us. We'll ship airmail. We'll be famous all over the world. We'll have to enlarge the operation and install a computer system."

"Let's wander back on the street," Mary urged him. "I want to get a few good quotes for our next week's ads."

"I haven't forgotten," Hans said as they got up to leave. "Next week you'll have your first Portuguese bread lesson, and I'll show you the new plans for the bakery. We're programming the software ourselves in our spare time. Hey, Mary, wait up!"

"Finished your iced tea?" Gussie inquired. "It's exercise time. We didn't have time for it this morning and it makes me feel stuffy to miss a day! Tony says you have to listen to your body, Genia, let it tell you what it needs."

Somewhat bleakly, Mrs. Potter thought that what her body was telling her was that she needed that chocolate frappe, and that a BLT on toast wouldn't really be too much to go with it, after an apple and a bit of cheese for lunch, but she rose dutifully from the drugstore stool.

"All right," she agreed reluctantly, "but give me a minute first to buy those bonbons for the party. Then where to? I hope you do it at your house and not in some marvelous new little health gym you've got tucked away on a side street as another surprise."

That will come, Gussie assured her as they walked back up Main Street. "Tony has fabulous plans, but it won't be in any little exercise club. I can't tell you about it, or he'd be furious, but what he's planning will be the most important thing to come to the island since the days of the whaling ships."

Later, Gussie, in a long-sleeved purple leotard with matching tights, handed Mrs. Potter a pair of what she assumed were Jules's or Gordon's or perhaps young Scott's old balbriggan pajamas as an exercise suit. "We'll get you fixed up properly tomorrow," Gussie promised, "with a quick trip down street. Canary, geranium, or bluebell, madam? You can't have grape, because I bought that one."

Thus attired, the two spent an energetic half hour in a cleared third-floor bedroom. There were exercise mats on the floor, and in the corner an indefatigable record player exhorting them, in a voice sweet but adamant, to bend a little more, stretch a little higher, lift, push, touch inaccessible areas of the anatomy with other impossibly nontouching parts. To breathe, inhale, exhale. Raise, lower, and *reach*.

"That's enough," Mrs. Potter finally announced. "I still do my same old twenty-minute routine almost every day. Anyway, quite often when I have time, but this is just plain overdoing it." She stretched out on the thin mat, breathing deeply. After a few minutes, she went on. "I must say it's rather more fun to do a few new twists with a record to keep telling you how. I see new exercises in magazines and I clip them out, but they're too much trouble. I have to keep putting on my glasses to check again what to do on count three. The only new idea I've had recently is to do the old standbys while I'm watching the morning news."

"I tried several of those TV exercise classes," Gussie said, groaning pleasurably as she, too, stretched and relaxed. "Remember the yoga woman? I can still do the Archer and the Plough, I think, and maybe the Cat—or is it the Cobra I was pretty good at?—but I never mastered the ones with handstands."

"The meditation part gave me a lot of trouble," Mrs. Potter admitted. "I found myself planning meals or thinking of letters I ought to be writing. Anyway, that woman and the class members were simply too intimidating, especially the one with the white hair—there's always one with white hair and a great figure. She was always too much for me."

"I know that one," Gussie said. "She can breeze through aerobics that would leave the average twenty-year-old gasping."

"Remember we want to call Beth as soon as we're bathed and dressed," Mrs. Potter continued as the two rolled up their mats and left the back bedroom. "And then did you say we could have our before-dinner drinks in the cupola? I'd love to see the town again at dusk from that height."

Later, in the kitchen, Gussie relayed the substance of the just completed call. Beth said she was all right, but she sounded subdued and sort of far away. She *had* gone to Ozzie's house after she left them this morning, and they were right. There was no one there and nothing she could do, although she'd found a few ashtrays to empty and she'd washed up the mug she found upstairs by his big chair in his living room. She said she took her jar of comfrey home with her since she knew no one else would be using it there.

"Darling, practical, energetic Beth," Mrs. Potter said. "Trust her to be the one who'd find something useful to do, as a last good-bye to an old friend."

"What she did this afternoon didn't make much sense," Gussie continued. "She told me she went back and spent the afternoon at the science library, even after being there this morning. I asked her for heaven's sake *why*, and she really didn't say. Just repeated something about Lolly's being there, Lolly Latham. You remember Helen said she had a volunteer job there helping the librarian? And then she said again Lolly was very nice and a lot of help.

"In fact, she said Lolly even left work early and walked home with her, seeing she was upset—*think* of Beth's being upset!—and then came in and made her a cup of tea in her own kitchen and looked at her herb garden layout for next year and at her garden *workroom*. And she told me she didn't think any of us has ever given Lolly enough credit. She's always been in Helen's shadow, Beth said."

"This bothers me," Mrs. Potter said. "Not about Lolly— that sounds good. But Beth's no scholar. I can't imagine her spending the whole day indoors looking up anything, can you?"

"Something's wrong," Gussie answered. "If Beth's sick, that's odd enough in itself. She's never sick. But *if* she is, or at least what she's calling *upset*, why didn't she call one of us? Why wasn't she in bed today, for heaven's sake, instead of going in for all this library stuff?"

As she spoke, Gussie was putting a small covered container of ice into a large lightship basket, darkened and mellowed with age but still as sturdy as on the long-ago day it had been woven. She added a small squat bottle of mineral water, two stemmed glasses, then looked questioningly at her guest.

"Name your poison," she invited. They looked at each other in sudden surprise, but their raised eyebrows made the only comment.

13

Following this pause, Mrs. Potter, shrugging, poured gin and a few drops of vermouth into a small glass jar with a snug lid. "Enough for one martini," she said, feeling oddly apologetic. "Well, and maybe a small dividend while you finish that Perrier."

Both now wearing light wool pants and matching sweater tops, each carrying an extra cardigan, they climbed the broad stairway to the second floor; then the narrower one, enclosed, to the third. There were two other square, seldom used bedrooms, Mrs. Potter remembered, in addition to the one in which they had done their exercises. There was a big old-fashioned bathroom with a skylight instead of a window, and beyond it the storeroom.

She peered in to see the neatly stacked Chippendale dining room chairs she knew Gussie was saving for the time when Marilyn might find time for giving dinner parties as well as providing free legal services for the poor. There were cartons of books, racks of framed pictures and mirrors, old trunks that might hold costume treasures for Scott's future theatrical productions. There were accumulated treasures of

Gussie's past, and those left behind by former generations of occupants of the big white house as well.

From this level, the two ascended a third flight of stairs, still more narrow and steep, but open at the sides, leading directly into the cupola. There they found themselves high above the bare treetops, high above the streetlights in the late afternoon January dark.

The cupola room had six windows—two on the sides facing front and back of the house, one on each side. Its size always surprised Mrs. Potter, for seen from the street below it seemed a small, windowed cubicle. In actuality it held two full-length wide benches, one on either side of the open stairwell, their backs a continuation of either side of the wooden stair railing, with plenty of room on all sides to walk around easily.

Each bench mattress was covered with heavy old brocade in soft, faded colors. ("I used the old parlor curtains," Gussie explained. "Jules loved those colors so much we couldn't bear to part with them.") Each padded bench was firm, perhaps too hard to be comfortable as a bed, except for a group Mrs. Potter felt it was perfect for—a slumber party of pajamaed granddaughters. For sitting, Gussie had made each one comfortable with banks of soft pillows, their coverings also remnants of earlier glory. Flowered linen, silk and chintz and damask intermingled, from other downstairs origins and even from other houses. "You always were a saver," Mrs. Potter said. "I remember this pink-and-yellow-striped satin from the New York apartment."

Turning off the light to see better, and moving from one window to the other, the two had what Jules had once figured to be a 275-degree view of the town below. "In the winter, that is," Gussie added. "The trees cut off some of that in the summer, even though they're all below us."

Except for the lighted face of the clock on the South Tower, looming very large and near, Nantucket seemed to be at the small end of a telescope. Lights showed in tiny windows. Rooftops and chimneys were far below. A toy man and a toy dog, each wearing a doll-size sweater, appeared under a streetlight, then disappeared into the darkness of a side street. A couple, a man and woman thickly bundled in coats and hats, appeared, heading down toward Main Street, each of them carrying two large and obviously heavy suitcases. Mrs. Potter watched their slow, knee-bent progress.

The harbor was black to the east, ringed by tiny pinpoints of light at the marina. Brant Point light flashed a miniature beacon of red at the entrance of the harbor.

"I suppose the boat is on winter schedule," Mrs. Potter remarked, pointing to the row of overhead lights at the Steamship Authority building on the northernmost of the town piers.

Only one boat at this time of year, Gussie told her. It would be coming in about eight, in a couple of hours. Someday soon, she promised, they might walk down early in the morning and watch it leave.

They agreed that it was always an event, greeting either the arrival or departure of what they both still occasionally called "the steamer." The essential thing, when the boat was leaving, was to be at the Brant Point light, on the wooden walkway, waving and throwing kisses and waggling last frantic semaphores as the ship quickly turned and passed the point. Meanwhile, on shipboard, the departing ones were scrambling in purses and pockets for pennies to pitch overboard as the ship circled the small, squat lighthouse—an offering to the gods, in exchange for which one was promised a certain eventual safe return to the island.

The lighted spires of the churches attracted Mrs. Potter's bemused attention. Away to the north, that of the Congregational church, where the carillon was now ringing familiar vesper tunes. That of the Baptist church, nearby to the west, almost next door to Dee's carriage house. That of the Unitarian church, the South Tower, its lighted clock face a giant moon almost in the room with them.

When its weighty notes struck six, the two turned their gaze again to the houses below. There were lights in the front parlors of Helen's brick house across the street, and as they watched, lights came on above the front door. A figure emerged and headed up Main Street, in the opposite direction of the suitcase-burdened couple, then disappeared in the darkness. "I think that was Lolly," Mrs. Potter said. "That round tan hat and the tan raincoat. It certainly wasn't Helen."

The angle was wrong to see if Mittie's house was lighted. "I have a feeling she holes up in the back of the house these days to save on light bills," Gussie said. "Leah's house used to be dark at nights, but there are lights sometimes now, although we can't see them from here, now she's begun to perk herself up. Mary Lynne always draws her curtains at dusk. She says it's too easy for passersby to look in, walking or driving down Orange Street. And we can't see Beth's house from here, either—too many other buildings in the way. Hers always looks so cozy and inviting at night when you walk by—the little panes of the windows, and her lovely old pine paneling in the firelight."

Mrs. Potter pursued the subject of looking in windows after dark. "I used to do it quite shamelessly," she admitted. "Most Nantucket front rooms look as if they'd been set up for Act One in a period play, and in all my evenings of window-peeking I never saw a living soul. Nobody sitting reading, nobody walking across the room to poke the fire, so I really didn't feel I was intruding. All I saw were mantels with Staffordshire dogs on either side and a family portrait in between, and a lot of dried-flower arrangements and beautiful old picture frames. What I liked best were the wonderful colors of painted woodwork in some houses, mustard or gray-blue or gray-green, against nearly white walls. Although I had some favorite parlor wallpapers, too, deep reds and blues and golds."

"Clearly, you must have spent a lot of time at this Peeping Tom business," Gussie said severely. "I really don't know how I've put up with your dreadful habits all these years."

Mrs. Potter declined to answer. She sipped her drink and wondered vaguely what two people had been doing walking down Main Street in January with suitcases, with no boat leaving for the mainland until morning. A small-town mind, she told herself. You can't help thinking that everything is your business.

"I think it's too cold to go up on the roof walk, don't you?" Gussie asked. "Shall we save that for another time?"

Mrs. Potter nodded quick agreement. She remembered this final ascent on sunny days in the past. From the glassed-in security of the cupola room, a narrow flight of steps, scarcely more than a ladder with a knotted rope handrail, led still farther upward. There, a skylight could be raised to allow access to an open wooden platform on the very rooftop, a full five stories above the street.

In the January dark, the thought of being at that height, with only a low balustrade between watcher and wind, seemed not only too chilly but a little frightening. They were up quite far enough where they were, she declared.

Gussie sipped her iced mineral water; Mrs. Potter sipped her iced martini, wishing she had remembered to add a twist of lemon peel when she filled the covered jar. "Do you miss having a drink before dinner?" she suddenly asked. "I think I would—I usually do, have one, that is, even when I'm alone."

"After the first few days I sort of forgot about it," Gussie said. "And then once I began to see what Tony's program was doing for me, as well as knowing how furious he'd be if I had any"—she straightened her back as they sat side by side on the bench, and looked down at her slim, trousered legs—"it really didn't seem much of a hardship."

Mrs. Potter looked down at her own legs, which she might have considered fairly slim until she compared them with those of her old roommate. She poured the last of the drink in her glass back into the small jar, screwed the lid firmly shut, and smiled brightly.

14

Friday's dawn was gray, the skies lighted only by the white skirl of a seagull's wings overhead, the early morning quiet broken by his raucous cat-cry as he circled the town in search of a scavenger's breakfast.

Indoors, in the big kitchen at the rear of the white house, Gussie Van Vleeck and Genia Potter were sitting down to their breakfast. Privately, the latter decided that they might just as well have been standing up.

Earlier, as hostess and guest had met in the kitchen and shared an early pot of tea, Gussie had inquired (grudgingly, Mrs. Potter told her, your heart's clearly not in it) about breakfast preferences. She suggested several possibilities: bacon and French toast, apple pancakes, hot cereal with raisins. Mrs. Potter, resisting memories of Gussie's apple pancakes, which were made with sour cream, and rather like small, sugar-sprinkled omelets, had replied that she'd like exactly what Gussie regularly had for her own breakfast these days.

The glass of pale liquid now before her was the answer. Prettily set on a bright flowered Quimper plate, it also seemed to be the complete answer. She took a tentative swallow, and, as she had done in sampling Gussie's carrot juice the day before at lunch, she pronounced it delicious. It was at least drinkable.

"Carrots again, I'm sure," she said judiciously, "but some other flavors. Parsley? Watercress? Apple? Surely not *parsnip?*"

"You're a very good detective," Gussie told her. "You're right on everything but the apple. I tossed in a ripe Comice pear, the last of a Christmas gift box, and I thought the parsnip was a real inspiration. Like it?"

Absolutely inspired, Mrs. Potter assured her hastily, taking another swallow.

"Carrots to cleanse the liver," Gussie intoned, "and you ought to pay attention to that, Genia. Gin is really very hard on the liver. Celery for organic salts, and these are much better for you than table salt, although I forget why. Parsnips for fingernails—wonderful for that brittleness. Parsley and watercress for vitamin C—very potent, both of them. Green pepper for your skin and hair. The pear because it was ripe and needed to be used up. I have Tony's chart of all this on the wall in the pantry, just over the juice-extracting machine, so you can study it later and get all the special properties of things straight in your mind. The important thing is to know what you need, and that's what Tony is able to determine for each of us, and then of course to extract the fresh juices just before you drink them."

"Please show me how it's done, right after breakfast," Mrs. Potter said meekly, aware that "right after breakfast" would be any minute now. How long could it take to drink one glass of juice, no matter how complicated its flavors and chemical balance?

"We're running a risk with this, you know," Gussie told her. "What I need and what you need may be entirely different. I'm just going to have to persuade Tony to take you on as a client. Now come see the new pantry setup."

Mrs. Potter was impressed with the shining stainless steel extractor, the separate pantry refrigerator for storing special fruits and vegetables, the separate small sink that had been installed there. She was pleased to learn that the ivy-covered garden compost box profited from the fibrous residues. She then went upstairs to dress for the day, which she was told would include a walk downtown, Gussie's weekly visit to the hairdresser, and, of course, a first purchase of Portuguese bread to celebrate the official opening of the new bakeshop.

"I suppose you sent them flowers," she remarked later as they were walking down the street.

"Of course," Gussie answered, "although they may have to hang them from the ceiling in that tiny shop. I've become very fond of these two young people, through Teresa. It's hard to believe she's Mary's grandmother and yet certainly ten years younger than we are. Just got an earlier start in marriage and the family business, I guess. We'll leave the bakeshop for our last stop, on the way home."

The two were heading north on Federal Street from the paper store corner when a familiar figure emerged from the double doors of the post office. Arnold Sallanger, a black Astrakhan cap set jauntily above his generous nose, was stuffing mail into the pockets of his worn tweed topcoat. "Genia, you're looking *good!* Finest kind!" Arnold's brown eyes were bright behind horn-rimmed spectacles. He seized the ends of Mrs. Potter's long woolen scarf in a jovial pretense of pulling her face toward his own.

And feeling fit, she assured him. "You seem to be thriving on hard work yourself," she said. "At first I thought all your old patients were going to a new doctor—Count Ferencz, whom I met the first day I got back—but I'm glad to know you're still looking after all of us."

"I didn't do so well for our old friend Ozzie Wednesday night," he said, his eyes and mouth sobering. "Thought I'd stop in that evening to break the news about his secretary's death—poor kid, we were too late to save her after that severely allergic reaction—and I found the old ambulance-chaser dead of a heart attack. At least I'm calling it a heart attack for the records—it was that, of course, but I think the whole system was ready to go. We're going to miss him—the cribbage crowd, the Wharf Rats Club. To say nothing of losing a first-rate lawyer."

As he stepped aside to let them proceed, he spoke to Gussie. "Cocktail party still on for tomorrow?" he asked. "Hope you didn't cancel it on Ozzie's account. He wouldn't have liked that."

"What's that you're saying?" asked another man coming out of the post office and carrying a large padded mailing envelope. "Talking about Gussie's cocktail party?" Slightly testy, Victor Sandys acknowledged the presence of the two women with a brisk wave of his free hand. "Hi there, Genia, Gussie. Sorry I can't stay to chat now, but I'll see you both tomorrow. Galley proofs from my publisher just came and I can't spare a minute for you now."

"Isn't that great?" Gussie remarked as the two continued across the street toward the great white pillars of the Atheneum, the Nantucket library. "Victor must have a new book coming out, after all these years when we thought he'd given up writing. Should we have asked him what it's to be?"

"One never knows with authors," Mrs. Potter said. "I'm told there are some things you must never ask, like what they're working on now, or how many copies sold of their last book. I think that's considered as bad as asking a rancher how many cattle he has, which, in case you didn't know, is considered very bad manners in Arizona."

"He'll tell us tomorrow if he wants us to know," Gussie said. "Victor's not exactly modest about his achievements. I think one reason he's been grumpy and dull in the last few years was because he couldn't tell you what the critics failed to see in his last book anymore, it was so long ago. That, and being a little deaf, and too vain to get a hearing aid."

"Whatever it is, we'll each have to buy several copies and have him sign them and then figure out who to give them to," Mrs. Potter said. "I just hope I can figure out what it's about. As I recall, he's strong on flashbacks, so you never know which member of which generation is dreaming, or talking in his sleep, or engaged in an actual present-day ongoing orgy of some kind."

The two smiled in tolerant agreement. "I wonder who his publisher is?" Mrs. Potter continued. "Did you get a look at the mailing label? I did, although I had a feeling Victor didn't want me to see it, so maybe it's one of those vanity press places and he's had to pay to get it published. I think the name was Harlan, or something a little longer, anyway one I never heard of."

"I doubt very much that Victor could afford to pay to have a book published," Gussie told her, "although he looked pretty natty today, didn't he? That new brass-buttoned pea jacket coat and the plaid wool trousers? And that black Greek sailor's cap—wasn't that something? I'm sure he wears it hoping people will think Nat Benchley willed it to him."

"Or maybe he thinks he looks like William Buckley," Mrs. Potter offered. "Either way it probably makes him feel rather dashing."

They went up the broad wooden library steps. Gussie had several books to drop off and a stack of new mysteries reserved to pick up. Mrs. Potter exchanged affectionate greetings with the two librarians, longtime friends. Then, leaving, they found Leah studying the recent best-seller shelves in the center corridor. She quickly put back the book she had held in her hands. "Just trash," she assured them. "Just trash. Nothing you two would want to read. See you tomorrow at your house, Gussie. Cocktails at five?"

"I wish I knew what she was trying to keep us from seeing," Mrs. Potter said as they left. "From the pastel book jackets, I think our Leah was browsing in the section one might call Romance."

"The world's greatest widow? Don't be silly," Gussie told her good-naturedly. "Although, as I said yesterday, our dear bereaved Leah has certainly perked up, and it's a great relief that we don't have to hear much anymore about how absolutely wonderful her darling Fanwell was and what a positively idyllic life they had together. Maybe they did, for all I know, but as soon as anyone tells me she has a perfect marriage I'm immediately convinced it's nothing of the sort."

The hairdresser's small waterfront shop was only a few blocks away. As they entered, Helen Latham's voice filled the room, its midwestern accent harsh with emotion.

". . . simply walked out, after all these years," she was saying bitterly as the last rollers were put in her hair. "I don't know what got into them. The whole thing is insane!"

Seeing Gussie and Mrs. Potter, Helen turned in the chair. "Walter and Elna have quit," she told them, her tone almost challenging. "After twenty-eight years. Since we lived in Chicago. Can you believe it? I thought they were devoted to Lolly, at least."

Larry made comforting noises as he led her toward the dryer. Mrs. Potter and Gussie had no opportunity for questions or sympathy as Helen continued, even as the plastic dryer hood descended over her head. ". . . packed up and left just like that, and they refused to say why, or even discuss it. Finally I told them the next boat wasn't until morning, and even that didn't faze them. They just said several incomprehensible things, which couldn't be considered *reasons* by anybody in their right mind, and then they walked out. *Period.*"

Larry, muscular, his forearms tattooed, his chest hairy at the opening of his blue sport shirt (the husbands' name for him had been Hairy Larry, Mrs. Potter remembered, a double play on words), beckoned Gussie to the chair. "Wonder where they spent the night?" he said. "Maybe in the steamship waiting room. I've known a few people to get away with that."

Mrs. Potter remembered two faraway bundled figures, each carrying heavy suitcases, seen as at the far end of the telescope from the cupola window.

Gussie discouraged further discussion of Helen's domestic problems with a quick question about a slight trim. Just a tiny bit taken off. She showed him exactly where. A lift of her eyebrow in the mirror told Mrs. Potter, now seated behind her in a cushioned wicker chair and about to open a magazine, that the two of them would take up the subject later.

Mrs. Potter, surprised but not exactly shaken by the news that Walter and Elna had given notice, now found herself even more unmoved by spring fashions in the pages of *Éclat*. Dee has a more interesting life selling island real estate, she thought, than making decisions about photographers and models and all these crazy, unwearable clothes.

Her eyes wandered to Helen's lightship basket, close to her feet as she sat reading *The Hospital Manager*, a periodical she had obviously brought with her, and making quick, decisive notes in a small looseleaf notebook.

Helen's strong jaw and high forehead, slightly out of scale above her match-thin body, were accentuated by the plastic helmet of the dryer encapsulating her rollered head. Helen's basket was dark with age and old varnish, the color of old saddle leather, as was her own, and Gussie's, now on the floor beside the shampoo chair. Each had a different carving of ivory on its teakwood lid, beneath the rigid, swinging handle. Gussie's was a spouting whale; her own, a flight of seagulls, each a kind of armorial bearing instantly recognizable to its owner and her friends. Helen's had an ivory panel nearly covering the large oval lid, its scrimshaw design a carefully etched drawing of the front of her house.

It's a silly kind of snobbery, Mrs. Potter thought, that the older one's lightship baskets are (and eventually everyone collected several shapes and sizes), the better they and their owners are regarded socially. I wonder if people *do* things to make new baskets look old. I wonder how many basket makers and ivory carvers there are on the island now. I wonder what the early artisans—industrious early sailors with long stretches at sea, including those on duty on the lightship *Nantucket* during her years on Nantucket Sound—would think about present-day basket idolatry.

She remembered how shocked she had been at the price when Lew had bought her first one, more, she told him, than she'd ever paid for five summer straw handbags. Now, with the prices of authentically Nantucket-woven baskets and Nantucket scrimshaw what they had become, she wondered that anyone could afford one at all.

Maybe they weren't so expensive, after all, even at today's prices. That first gift from Lew was still going strong, with an occasional repair to the carefully crafted rattan hinges or to the hasp, which was secured by an ivory pin, and it had outlasted a dozen ordinary summer handbags. And there was always the fun of recognizing a fellow Nantucketer by smiling at each other's similar baskets, swinging from suntanned arms on other islands, from Captiva to Catalina, Maui to Mykonos, Bermuda, Eleuthera, St. Croix.

Old baskets, old money, she thought again. We all want to pretend we were born having both.

Yet she knew that Helen's basket and her beautiful brick house came from Lester's success in making watch bracelets and graduation rings; that Mary Lynne and Bo Heidecker's affluence had its origin, as had her own and Lew's on a lesser scale, in modest beginnings; that Dee probably got a commission for *selling* lightship baskets by bringing buyers to basket makers.

Gussie's money (she was not sure whether Gussie or Helen might have more) was both old and new, she continued to muse, coming from her family and also from two successful and hardworking husbands. Mittie's old money was slipping away, it seemed, with only the great hilltop house on the south rim of the harbor left to show for it, and the family's old house on Main Street. It was reassuring to believe that old family was far more important than money in Mittie's heritage.

She couldn't remember where and how Fanwell Carpenter had come into his comfortable Nantucket retirement. Probably by inheritance, she thought. Fanny never seemed very bright, although he was pleasant enough, sometimes even a little too much so. And Beth—nobody ever thought of money one way or the other about the Higginsons, only that there seemed to be enough not to worry about it.

The scent of a bowl of flowering narcissus on the small table beside her now seemed heavy and cloying in the overwarm, moist room, where Helen sat, her note-making discontinued, a helmeted astronaut from an alien planet glaring angrily into space. Gussie was now upright, her towel-wrapped head ready for Larry's clever scissors. All this thinking about baskets and money was footless, and her stomach was complaining irritably about its failure to receive a decent breakfast. Mrs. Potter began again to think about the two deaths on Wednesday and her growing, painful suspicions. Each time these dark thoughts had surfaced, she had denied them. And yet last evening, in certain, intuitive recognition, she had known how her old friend Ozzie and his secretary had died. She had known, even as she tried to hide her shock, when Gussie had said, so amiably, "Name your poison."

It suddenly seemed imperative that she should take some kind of action. Where could she learn something about death by poison? And could she do so without creating a storm of official inquiry? Her intuition, she told herself severely, might well be, and not for the first time, slightly off the mark.

The source of knowledge was only a few blocks away. The Atheneum, of course.

And what was she going to say to her good friends behind the librarians' desk?

"It occurs to me that two people on the island might have been poisoned, day before yesterday, and I need a little help on this." A fine start that would be. "Of course, I haven't any proof they *were* poisoned, and no idea at all of why anyone should have wanted to do them in . . ."

But she did know why. It had to be someone about whom the two might have had dangerous and damaging information. Someone who believed that what the two knew, or had, could threaten a career or a love affair or a life. Maybe even something just as crass as a big deal of some kind. Again, none of this could she speak aloud anywhere, let alone within the hushed walls of the Atheneum.

It wasn't even a suspicion she wanted to share with Gussie, and she hoped she was wrong in believing in the momentary shocked agreement of their raised eyebrows the evening before at the mention of poison. The reason for this reluctance was, she knew, Gussie's interest in Tony. She did not like what she had learned of him so far, from Dee, but it was not fair to him or to Gussie to suggest that he might have killed two people because of a long-ago tragedy, for which he might have been only indirectly responsible.

The Atheneum was out, unless she had more knowledge of

what to look up and could find it for herself in the card files. Suddenly she thought of Beth, who had spent all day yesterday at the science library. Beth must already share her suspicion of poison and must already know what she herself scarcely knew how to begin looking up.

"I'm going to take a walk," she said to Gussie as Larry unwrapped her wet head and flourished his scissors. "I might just go up to Beth's to see what she's up to, but I'll be back before you're finished, in time to go with you to the bakeshop."

The Higginson house on India Street appeared deceptively small. Its architecture was traditional Nantucket, two stories high in front, sloping to one, with a series of additions, in the back. The front door was at one side, and the house itself fronted directly on the street. A narrow brick-paved path led back along one side, with a winter-mulched edging of perennials. This led, as Mrs. Potter well remembered, past the old garden-shed addition to Beth's sunny herb garden behind the house.

There was no garage, and Beth's sturdy yellow four-wheel Scout was parked in front, its two left wheels up on the low sidewalk as an accepted and customary courtesy to other drivers on the one-way street.

Mrs. Potter knocked gently, then with increasing insistence. The deep bark of a large dog was her only answer. The drawn curtains of the front window twitched, the curious nudging of Samson's nose, she presumed, remembering his name.

His calm, unworried bark sounded more like "good morning" than "get out." The fact that Beth's car was there meant simply that she was out walking, as was her habit. Her own feeling of unease was only that of simple hunger. She had probably been secretly hopeful of the hospitable midmorning snack she knew Beth would have urged if she had been at home.

In spite of these reassurances to herself, she was still troubled as she returned to the beauty shop with a detour that took her partway around Brant Point, surveying the blank shutters of the big houses there, houses that in June would again be open to sun and summer laughter, as they had been for many years. She walked past now-deserted sandy beaches where golden children in bright trunks would dig and wade and learn to swim.

Later, as she and the newly coiffed Gussie headed toward the new shop called The Portuguese Bread Man, she knew there was no way in the world she was going to be able to resist tearing off crusty chunks of that fresh bread. She'd have to eat some right on the street as they walked home. What was there about making up your mind that you were about to start on a diet that made you so absolutely ravenously *starving*?

Her appetite was momentarily stayed by another silent question. Certainly it could not have been *Beth* behind her own drawn front-window curtains, deciding not to answer the knock of an old friend? She told herself again, sensibly, that Beth was only out walking and that they would at any moment meet her on the street somewhere on their way home. They did not, and after that she and Gussie were totally occupied with preparations for Saturday's tea party.

15

"There!" Gussie exclaimed with pleasure as she lighted the tall lemon-yellow candles in the branched silver candelabra. "That'll knock 'em dead!"

"If they don't die of shock finding they've come for tea instead of cocktails," Mrs. Potter added, trying to sound jocular and wishing she felt more in a party mood. Some way she'd have to get Beth aside for a minute later to get an inkling of why she'd gone to the science library and what she'd learned there. At the very least she could arrange for a time to see her alone, with the excuse of begging a sight of her house and new dog.

She tried to find reassurance, as well as pleasure, in the scene before her now.

The long oval mahogany table in Gussie's dining room was covered with a full-length tablecloth of embroidered white organdy. Its centerpiece of long-stemmed anemones—their counterparts to be known as ranunculus when they would appear later in Gussie's spring garden—had arrived from the florist ready-arranged but had been deftly and speedily separated by Gussie's quick fingers, then rearranged to her satisfaction in a great open basin of silver with scrolled and curving legs. The flowers' spring colors were echoed in fainter tints by Mrs. Potter's drugstore bonbons in silver compotes. A round silver tray was covered with thin slices of the hitherto neglected holiday fruitcake, and its twin offered the orange and cranberry breads Mrs. Potter and her hostess had baked on the preceding afternoon. There were clear shining glass plates bearing the thinnest of tea sandwiches, circles, triangles, diamonds, and rolled ones sporting flirtatious sprigs of emerald-green watercress, all of these still under cover of damp linen napkins, awaiting their debut.

At one end of the table was the large, comfortable armed dining chair (could it be that her cousin Theo, then Jules, and then Gordon had all successively occupied that same host's chair at dinner?) where Mrs. Potter prepared to seat herself as Gussie went to greet the first party arrivals. Before her was a gargantuan silver tray bearing the tools of the tea pourer's trade.

Mrs. Potter checked hastily to be sure that everything was in order. Teresa would bring in the silver pot of the strongly brewed tea essence, and she knew there was more in the kitchen, being kept warm to appear when it was needed. A spirit lamp burned beneath a shining handsome kettle, where freshly boiling water would be kept as near to that temperature as possible, this also to be kept replenished from the kitchen. There was a bowl of cube sugar with silver tongs (Mrs. Potter knew she would find herself using her fingers as the party went on), a silver jug of milk, a small plate of thinly sliced quarters of lemon, some of these with a whole clove imbedded, and a generous silver slop bowl for the lukewarm dregs of teacups returning for a second filling.

At the left of the tray were a dozen of Gussie's best Royal Doulton teacups and thin saucers, neatly stacked, and a stack of small matching plates. A pile of embroidered organdy napkins followed, and an array of teaspoons set out by Teresa with mathematical precision. On the sideboard were more teacups and saucers in different patterns of china.

Gussie was on her way to the front hall, where sprays of golden forsythia now bloomed in the big Chinese vase. Mrs.

Potter took her seat in the big armchair. Teresa brought in the tea essence and whisked the damp napkins from the tops of the sandwich plates. They were ready. Everything was ready. Tea would be served that day, in the big white house, to some thirty guests, all but one of whom would be coming in the certain, unthinking belief that they had been invited to cocktails.

Now Gussie was greeting the first arrival, pointing the way to the hallway benches and chairs for leaving his coat, escorting him to the dining room. Mrs. Potter knew that from now on, guests would simply be shooed toward the room where she was ensconced, coming in from the front hall through the big open double doors from the library. She knew that after receiving tea and telling her it was nice to have her back, most of them would eventually drift into the two similarly connecting front and back parlors on the other side of the house. She waited to see who would be first. She wished she could quell this feeling of growing unease.

"Well! Well . . . I must *say!*" Ted Frobisher proclaimed slowly as he made an uncertain passage to where Mrs. Potter was sitting. "We're having *tea!* Gussie, I can't tell you what a delightful surprise this is! Mother used to have tea parties like this! Genia, my dear, you're looking lovely today in that yellow dress. *Tea!* I can't get over it . . . I couldn't be happier!"

Ted's delight seemed totally genuine. He may have imbibed whatever was his usual quantity of vodka by this time of day, but as he bent to kiss Mrs. Potter's cheek, his bearing changed from that of middle-aged alcoholic vacuity to that of a happy young man. "No sugar, thank you, Genia," he said with obvious satisfaction. "My dear, is that Earl Grey tea I smell? If it is, I'll skip the milk. Just middling strong, thanks. And do I see cucumber sandwiches?"

By now Gussie was back in the big front hall and Mrs. Potter heard more arrivals, more greetings, more invitations to leave your coat here, anyplace, more announcements that Genia was in the dining room, where she'd be *so* pleased to see them.

Ted's apparent pleasure in the party was a help, and Mrs.

Potter's spirits lifted briefly as she affectionately was wel-
comed back to the island by a succession of friends. Still, she
found herself watching them, old and new, with even greater
than usual intentness. She could not completely push to the
back of her mind her uneasy fears about Ozzie's and Edie's
deaths, nor her inner certainty that Beth's library research
had to do with poisons. She could not shake the growing
feeling that someone among the party guests knew more
about all this than she did. She knew she was making an inner
recording of who arrived and what happened, at the same
time she was greeting and being greeted, being embraced
and embracing.

Mary Lynne arrived, her newly svelte figure smoothly encased in violet wool, her magnolia throat encircled with
pearls. The pearls at the open neck of Helen's heavy white
satin blouse, above her skirt of dark green velvet, were
smaller but, as Mrs. Potter realized, undoubtedly real,
whereas it seemed likely that Mary Lynne's, like her own
similar strand in the jewelry case upstairs, were certainly not.
Helen's daughter, in the tan wool dress she undoubtedly
wore for her Saturday at the science library and carrying the
same shapeless tan shoulder bag, was predictably plump,
pale, bespectacled, trailing her mother. A newly vivacious
Leah arrived in a black velvet pantsuit, white ruffles showing
at the neck, her earrings as green as her eyes, her silver hair
now appearing even a little more emphatically platinum.

Victor Sandys was resplendent in what appeared a new
and fashionable costume—a black velvet blazer over plaid
tartan trousers (a different tartan from the day before, Mrs.
Potter noticed), wearing shining new patent leather slippers
with a flat grosgrain bow. Arnold Sallanger's gray flannels
were baggy, his tweed jacket bore elbow patches of worn
leather, but his brown eyes were bright behind the rimmed
spectacles, and he smelled antiseptically clean. Dee's flat
dark hat and great earrings were as dashing as ever above the
white flash of her smile, and her high-necked, long-sleeved
fine wool knit dress, the color of mushrooms, was not only
timeless but clearly infinitely adaptable. Mittie wore a fine

creamy cashmere turtleneck sweater, equally timeless, with a long skirt of plaid wool in huge blocks of black and white—a skirt Mrs. Potter thought looked vaguely familiar, although of course much much smaller than any Mittie might have worn before. Beneath it Mrs. Potter glimpsed the trim toes of Mittie's tassel-tied black Belgian flat pumps. George Enderbridge arrived at the same time in a neat headmasterly suit of gray tweed, made more casual by his well-polished loafers and slightly more dashing by the striped ascot at his throat. All of the women had lightship baskets over their arms, some round, some oval, some small, some large, but all different in their ivory-decorated lids.

Interspersed among these old friends, mingling with them all in easy familiarity, were other islanders Mrs. Potter knew and remembered with fondness. The new couple Gussie had mentioned were not so new after all—they had met on her last Nantucket visit. There were those she had known for many years—couples, singles, some now retired, various academics, artists, and writers now making the island their home, and a few people connected with present-day island business, including the owner of the dress shop from which Mrs. Potter knew she could happily choose her wardrobe for the rest of her days. And, inevitably, there were more widows—bright, independent, attractive women who had chosen to come to Nantucket, or to remain there, now that their husbands were gone and their children grown.

In spite of these happy distractions, Mrs. Potter found herself tense and watchful. Beth, usually the first guest at a party, quick to see how she might be of help, was very late today, she thought.

Meantime, Ted Frobisher's initial reaction to the unexpected drama of the tea table, and his unconcealed enjoyment of the party as it progressed, were the most surprising, and to Mrs. Potter the most gratifying, response of the hour that followed.

Ted stood back politely between each round of newly arriving guests, then stepped forward to kiss each cheek or shake each hand. His smile was happy and his offers of assistance were eager and endearing as he pointed out the various sandwiches. He rejoiced over the arrival of the hot cheese puffs as Teresa brought them in fresh from the oven, and he spoke again his compliments for Gussie's special parsley sandwich filling as well as the blackly rich one with the olives. He offered to take people's cups back to Mrs. Potter for refills, as she was busy saying hello and being kissed. He brought the tray of second-best teacups from the sideboard when they were needed.

He inquired with a politely lifted eyebrow if Mrs. Potter needed Teresa to bring more boiling water. As the guests recircled the table and the room grew more crowded, he deftly shepherded those on the outer rim back out through the hall and into the parlor with freshly filled teacups.

"I don't know when I've had such a good time!" he said, beaming. His impeccably cut navy flannel blazer showed a discreet flash of its foulard-patterned lining at its back vent as he whirled back to the tea table, triumphant from a skillful maneuver of guests from dining room to parlor. The layout of the house, including the return shortcut by way of the back hall, was as familiar to him as to most of the guests. His step was quick and precise, his cheeks were pink in faint reflection of the crimson stripe of his neatly folded ascot.

It interested Mrs. Potter to observe that Lolly Latham was being a willing but slightly awkward aide at the tea table as well, taking cups and plates back to the kitchen as they were abandoned on the sideboard. Beth's undoubtedly right, she thought. We've underestimated Lolly, even considered her a bit slow-witted when she may be merely shy. Perhaps she's coming out of it at last.

Ted's unexpected boyish delight and his unassuming ease at the tea table were mildly contagious. None of Gussie's well-mannered guests showed any sign of obvious surprise to find the guest of honor pouring tea, and none inquired the way to the bar. All accepted a teacup with some expression of pleasure. The women nibbled token sandwiches, the men not a great many more. The party was decorous, too well brought up to show surprise. Everyone asked about Mrs.

Potter's health and that of her offspring. Everyone smiled. And smiled and smiled.

To everyone but Ted, she thought, this is a very dull party, and for myself I can't get over the dreadful feeling that something is wrong somewhere. Yet one good thing about it —Les Girls are able to observe their no-drinking diets, although so far Count Ferencz hasn't arrived to award any gold stars. Beside that, she told herself, there are people here who will enjoy their later dinners more than if they had drunk several cocktails and eaten too many hors d'oeuvres. There are people who will later rejoice that they did not talk too much, did not tell a dubious joke or betray an indiscreet confidence. There are people who will sleep better, wake up happier. But there are people here, maybe all of them except Ted (and that included herself), who would have found this party more festive with, say, at least one small glass of sherry in hand, deplorable as she knew this to be.

Then there was sudden excitement in the front hallway, out of her vision beyond the library door; the atmosphere was charged with new tension as Tony Ferencz strode into the dining room. Gussie, following, watched his progress with smiling eyes.

As he bowed and kissed Mrs. Potter's hand as she sat at the tea table, she felt again the hidden challenge of their earlier meeting. She was aware of the heightened vivacity of the women in the room. Count Ferencz made his sweeping rounds, kissing each hand, bowing his tall head courteously to Ted and the few men, who now, she noticed, began to slide away toward the parlor side of the house.

The count declined tea, but he stood for a moment at Mrs. Potter's side, saying that he hoped Gussie's dear Eugénie was having a happy return to the island, saying that he regretted that he had, of necessity, had to be away during the first few days of her visit. His gray eyes held hers briefly, then those in turn, with slow regard, of each of the women around the tea table. Leah and Helen, who had previously taken tea and then moved to the parlors, now returned.

Gussie, flushed and happy, spoke from the library doorway. "Peter's going to be here any minute, Tony says," she announced, "and Beth just came in at last. I asked her to take your place at the table, Genia, to let you circulate for a bit."

Mrs. Potter peered questioningly into the pot in front of her.

"Need some more? Let me get it," Beth offered quickly as she came into the dining room. Mrs. Potter saw that her usually rosy face was pale, despite the Christmas red of her wool suit, and that her eyes were underlined with purple shadows. "I see Teresa's busy at the moment . . ." Beth's gaze followed Teresa's measured progress with a white birch log for the library fire, her wood basket making evident her intent to continue to the twin marble fireplaces of the parlors. "I'll find it, Gussie, don't bother. I know my way around your kitchen."

From the front door, now unattended, came a genial shout. "Hey, guys! Anybody home around here?" the voice inquired loudly and unnecessarily to a houseful of amiably twittering guests. "Potter, wherever you are, come see what I brought to your tea party!"

Gussie's dash to the front door was followed by a press of others, Mrs. Potter among them. Peter Benson stood in the open doorway, bringing with him a rush of cold fresh air from the north.

"Look what I brung you," he repeated, this time to Gussie. "Just what every tea party needs at this stage of the game. A barrel of oysters and a keg of beer!"

Under the streetlight in front of the house was a long station wagon with SCRIMSHAW INN lettered on its sleek, wood-patterned side. There was a flash of bright smile from the driver's seat, and in back, Jadine, her well-blonded curls bobbing, waved vigorously.

"Okay, you two drive around to the side and unload at the kitchen porch door," Peter called to them. "Anybody in the kitchen to let them in?" he asked Gussie, almost in the same breath. "Don't look so scared. This part of the party is all under control. You don't have to do a thing except relax and have fun. We're going to have *frogs!*"

The word was repeated, blankly, by those of the guests nearest the front door, as Peter swept into the hall, exuberantly hugging each one in turn, men and women alike.

"I suppose you mean frogs' legs, Peter," someone said doubtfully. "Didn't we have those at the Scrim not long ago, dear?" the man asked his wife, whose smile did not quite cancel out the slight shudder glimpsed in her eye blink.

"Did he say frogs?" Victor Sandys queried with an unconcealed grimace. "I can't stand the little beasts. What's come over Benson, playing a schoolboy trick like bringing frogs to a party?"

"Do we *play* frogs, or hunt them, or eat them, or what?" Gussie asked. "I don't know what you're up to, Peter, or what oysters or beer have to do with it, but let's all go to the kitchen and let Jadine and your friend in, and maybe we'll all find out."

Those in the hallway crowded through the library and dining room to the kitchen, following Peter and Gussie. Those in the dining room who had not yet heard Peter's frog announcement, yet sensing the excitement, were following closely. Ted and Mrs. Potter alone remained at the tea table, where Beth was about to seat herself in the big armchair.

"At least you can pour yourself a cup of tea, even if the party seems to be deserting you," Mrs. Potter said. "I'm sure they'll all be back in a minute."

"Half a second," Beth said apologetically. "I left my basket in the kitchen when I got the fresh tea and I want my diet sweetener pills. After that, I think Ted looks as if he'd take a second cup with me." (Second, nothing, Mrs. Potter thought. This will be Ted's fourth cup at the very least. The man's not a lush, he's a tea hound.)

Slipping back through the press in the kitchen doorway, Beth seated herself. Making a visible effort to look up at Ted with a smile, she opened the lid of the basket on her lap, but her attention was centered on Ted and the teapot. Mrs. Potter stood idly watching as Beth poured a little of the dark amber tea essence into the thin china cup and was reaching carefully for the pot holding the hot water to dilute it. Seeing herself no longer needed, she decided to move toward the kitchen door with the rest, where Victor Sandys was bringing up the rear.

She looked back to see Ted, bending over beside Beth to await his fresh cup, waver visibly in his balance.

Only Mrs. Potter, in the back of the throng bound for the kitchen, seemed to hear Ted's voice—thin, high-pitched, a whisper that came to her ears with the vehemence of a scream.

"Beth Higginson, that's *poison* in your basket! That's *cyanide!* Don't touch it! You'll poison us all if that gets into the teapot!"

Still holding the partly filled cup with her left hand, Beth peered uncertainly into the opened lightship basket on her lap. With plump, tentative fingers she reached her right hand toward its contents.

With this, and as Mrs. Potter hurried back to his side, Ted's second thin screech was almost incoherent with fright. "Don't touch that!" he repeated. "That's deadly poison, Beth! I know what I'm talking about!"

Beth's right hand obediently flipped shut the lid of her basket, but Ted, now nearly hysterical, seemed to misinterpret her movement. "We'll all be poisoned!" His screak of warning was now nearly inaudible, but with a wild, spasmodic gesture he knocked the fragile cup from Beth's now-quivering left hand, spilling its contents across the expanse of embroidered white organdy. The teapot followed, dousing the spirit lamp, spilling the tea kettle, drenching cloth and table.

Confused, no one quite having heard Ted's words, but aware of some kind of accident, the party now crowded back into the dining room. Everyone reached for plates, compotes, candelabra, centerpiece, intent upon rescue. The flood of tea and hot water was an instant threat to both the polished wood of the table and the soft patterns in the oriental rug beneath it.

Teresa appeared with an armful of soft cloths and towels, dispensing these to waiting hands, Dee's among them. Mary

Lynne quite calmly rearranged a few toppled anemones in the silver basin, now relocated on the sideboard. Helen dropped quickly to her knees, raising the hem of her velvet skirt to avoid tea stains, mopping at minor flooding on the far side of the rug and motioning to Lolly, standing uncertainly on the sidelines, to help her. Mittie hurried in and out of the kitchen carrying teacups and plates with George Enderbridge helping her, their obvious aim that of clearing the decks so that a thorough mop-up could be accomplished.

Meanwhile, Gussie was wadding the sodden length of tablecloth into a large plastic basin Teresa had brought and assuring everyone that there was nothing, absolutely nothing, to be concerned about, that a little excitement was just what this party wanted.

Leah's bracelets were jingling nervously. Victor Sandys was eating hot cheese puffs as he carried their silver dish to the kitchen, and glaring at Arnold Sallanger, who had momentarily blocked his way coming out. Count Valerian Mikai Alexander Antonescu Ferencz stood impassively in the wide doorway to the library, removing himself from the hubbub of the kitchen passage, a swordsman at repose.

Still in the big chair at the end of the tea table, Beth sat motionless, dabbing ineffectually with her fingertips at the dark wetness on the front of her red suit.

"Are you all right?" Mrs. Potter asked, handing her a clean towel. "I don't think tea stains wool if you blot it right away and then sponge it with water."

Beth did not reply, but raised her plump hands toward her face, fingertips together, head bowed.

"Are you all right?" Mrs. Potter asked again. "I think Ted just lost his balance when we all came rushing into the room, but see—he's all right now, aren't you, Ted?"

Ted was now seated in one of the side chairs by the dining room window. He beckoned Mrs. Potter close to him, away from Beth and away from the others busy with the cleanup. "Beth might have poisoned us all," he said, his voice low. "You look for yourself at what's in her basket. She's got cyanide—an old blue bottle, skull and crossbones, you look and see. I had to spill things, Genia, much as I hated to make such a mess. *Cyanide*, Genia. We'd all have been dead." He was almost babbling now, in his whispered effort to convince her.

Oh, dear, he's been drinking all afternoon and I didn't know it, she thought with dismay. All this time I thought he was as sober as I've ever seen him, having as much fun as he probably used to at his mother's parties when he was the adored and dashing young son. He's been drinking all afternoon, probably sneaking a nip every time he went through the back hall.

"Look, everything's fine," she assured him kindly as he sat, still immobile, in his chair, and then she repeated the same words to Beth, equally motionless, seated in the center of the room. "Nothing's hurt and you heard Gussie say that a little excitement was just what this party needed. Come on, Bethie, let's go across into the downstairs washroom and sponge off your red skirt. Then we'll all go in the kitchen and see what new surprise Peter's got for us."

She guided a shaking Beth across the back hall, wondering where Ted had his cache of vodka. "We all know Ted's been drinking too much for years," she said, in an attempt at reassurance. "I'm afraid it's caught up with him today. Whatever did he see that set him off?"

Beth was mute, her small plump hands firmly clenched on the rigid handle of her basket.

"There now," Mrs. Potter continued, "that won't show if we blot it again with a dry towel. Put on a dab of lipstick and you'll be fine."

Beth nodded uncertainly, her hands still on the basket handle. "I'll be with you in a minute," she said. "You go ahead."

As she awaited Beth in the kitchen, she saw that Peter and his staff of two had taken over. Peter introduced the man who was opening oysters with professional speed at an improvised bar at the kitchen sink. "Jimmy's the one who cooks about half the good stuff at the Scrim that you give me credit for," he said, grinning.

He pointed at the wooden barrel placed in a shallow galvanized tub on the floor at Jimmy's side, where a white plastic trash can next to it was already filling with shells. "Bluepoints from Maryland," Peter said. "I had them flown in. Now, all of you, if you want to practice your French, talk to Jimmy the way Tony does—although his English is fine."

"As long as I don't have to read it," Jimmy said, smiling broadly. "If you want to write me a letter, do it in French *s'il vous plaît.*"

At the other end of the kitchen Jadine was setting out glasses, unpacking thick amber tumblers of water-glass size from a large carton, and a second set, equally heavy, of much smaller ones.

Mrs. Potter looked for Beth and hurried back into the now empty dining room. Both Beth and Ted, she saw, had apparently slipped away. Ted, she assumed, had left in befuddled alcoholic shame and confusion. Beth, who had not really looked well anyway, was in probable discomfort in her damp wool skirt, and possibly in some embarrassment over whatever Ted had seen in her basket and had so wildly declared to be a bottle of cyanide.

Sighing for them both, she returned to the kitchen to find that Peter had commandeered the long heavy sideboard there. He was setting out an array of paper napkins, wooden picks, bowls of oyster crackers, bowls of something red, smaller bowls of something white. From the pockets of his rumpled tweed jacket he produced bottles of Tabasco sauce. From a carton he extracted square, black-labeled bottles declaring themselves the product of a man named Jack Daniel. In the center he placed a wooden keg with a spigot.

"All right, guys, who's going to be the first for a frog?" Peter demanded, then answered himself. "Our hostess, of course. Berner, I mean Van Vleeck, step right up and show us what a brave kid you are. Come on, everybody, gather around and watch Gussie meet a frog. You too, Potter, come on closer, Carpenter, watch a frog meet Gussie."

Gussie gazed helplessly at Mrs. Potter, then imploringly toward the tall, aloof figure in the doorway. "Tony, rescue me," she begged. "Something tells me I'm going to like this, and I'll be *sorry!*"

Tony's face was expressionless, but he seemed to be displaying a certain icy tolerance, which Mrs. Potter interpreted as refusal to intervene.

"Oh, go ahead, Gussie," Arnold Sallanger urged. "Peter isn't going to play any tricks that will hurt you, and after all, it's your party."

Mrs. Potter knew her hostess well enough to realize that this reminder would ensure her taking up the challenge. It was indeed Gussie's party, and the two of them had given enough parties, separately and together, through their hospitable years to know that this one was being a dud. Its only real satisfaction so far had been that of giving pleasure to Ted Frobisher, and now apparently that was spurious. The other guests had had more fun in the helter-skelter of rescuing the table and the rug from the spilled tea than they'd had in the hour before. They were having more fun right now, crowding around to see what Peter Benson had thought of for their amusement. She knew what Gussie would do.

"That's a good kid," Peter praised her. "Now, first go down to your breakfast table and get two glasses from Jadine—one big one, one little one. Next stop, Jimmy at the oyster bar at the other end of the room. Eyes on Jimmy, now, everybody!"

A plump raw oyster, cool, opalescent, slid from its opened shell into Gussie's larger glass, and Jimmy smiled, with a flash of white teeth and gold fillings.

"Now come here to Uncle Peter" was the next command. "Here we go. A little Jack Daniel's in the small glass, next—not a lot, just a swallow, not even a half ounce. Now watch closely, while Uncle Peter makes a frog!" Taking the larger glass with the oyster in it, Peter held it under the spigot of the keg and filled it halfway with cold, foaming, pale golden beer.

"And now," he continued, "step right up and watch the little lady take on a frog! Bottoms up with the little glass, Van Vleeck!" Gussie closed her eyes and complied, and an audible shudder ran through those of Les Girls most closely surrounding her, all of them looking hastily at Tony Ferencz in the doorway to see his reaction.

Without giving her time to catch her breath, Peter continued his instructions. "Now, a nice cool sip of the beer. Good, huh? Have another sip," he urged.

He faced his audience. "And what has our fearless hostess had so far? Right! A good old-fashioned boilermaker, that's what. However admirable as that may be, it is not a frog."

"Face the nice people," he told Gussie. "Take another good swig of that beer. Fine. You're all ready now. Lift your glass, hold back your head just a little, open that lovely throat, and—whoops!—down goes the frog!"

Gussie's smile was immediate and triumphant. "That is absolutely delicious, Peter!" she assured him. "That was the best oyster—the best *frog*—I ever had! I adore oysters, and the taste is perfect in beer. In fact even the first sips of beer were marvelous with the salty flavor of the oyster coming through. Genia, you're going to adore this!"

While Mrs. Potter felt sure that she would, the party quickly divided into three camps. There were those who *knew* they were going to love frogs. There were those, like Leah and Helen, who announced that no one could ever persuade them to try one. And there were a few, like Arnold Sallanger, who were skeptical but curious enough to try.

"Anybody who prefers his oyster on the half shell, without the beer, report to Jimmy," Peter directed, "and then here for picks and cocktail sauce. You can mix your own the way you like it, right on the oyster with a dab of chili sauce, a little horseradish, and a drop of hot sauce. Or you can squeeze on a little plain lemon juice. Lemon wedges here, crackers on the side. Now everybody, it's frog time!"

It was a tribute to Peter's infectious good humor that even the few guests who were not oyster lovers seemed to enjoy watching the frog consumption by those who were. A few gentlemanly or ladylike boilermakers were taken on the side, Mrs. Potter noted, watching Mittie screen herself from Tony's sight as she and George Enderbridge edged to the far end of the room. A great many oysters were taken straight from the half shell as Jimmy continued to lay them open with skillful twists of his knife.

Gussie had moved propitiatingly to Tony's side in the doorway, Mrs. Potter noticed, bringing him an opened oyster balanced on a paper napkin, with a pick and a lemon wedge. She did not see whether he accepted it, for at that point she went again to look for Beth and Ted. A quick tour showed her that the two gold-and-white parlors were as empty as the dining room and library.

As she returned, she saw that Leah and Helen Latham, with Lolly at her side, were now with Tony in the doorway, and that none of that small group appeared to be eating or drinking. Later she noticed that Mittie, after her apparent side trip into boilermaker country, was standing with them, looking slightly flushed and guilty, partially shielding her mouth with a napkin as she talked, in an evident attempt to deflect the rich aromas of bourbon and beer.

By now Mrs. Potter was ready for a second frog, which proved to be even better, she decided, than the first. Jimmy was singing softly in calypso rhythm, as if to himself, as he continued to open oysters. Jadine was bouncing with enjoyment as she kept her table supplied with clean glasses and, Mrs. Potter suspected, herself supplied with an occasional sip of beer. Peter was cajoling, praising, encouraging, reaching out to embrace everyone in the room. Gussie was laughing and talking (not eating or drinking), moving about with a hostess's watchful eye to be sure no one was neglected or left alone. Teresa moved back and forth from the pantry with freshly filled plates of tea sandwiches, which were now disappearing rapidly.

The party was picking up in tempo, but the scene with Ted and Beth still weighed upon Mrs. Potter's mind. She looked about for Tony Ferencz, to see what part he might be taking in this.

"Tony just said good night," Gussie whispered to her in passing, as if in answer to her question. "Helen has a headache, so he's seeing her and Lolly home, and Leah thought she'd slip away at the same time."

As Gussie spoke, sounds from the piano in the back parlor moved the party, most of them with glasses in hand, from the kitchen. Peter had taken over there now, and he was playing music that drew them like a magnet—the songs with which they had embellished their youthful dreams, explained away their hurts, celebrated their occasional joys and triumphs, certain that each one contained its message of truth. They came as Peter played "Sophisticated Lady." Dee, her brimmed hat still perfectly straight, her white teeth and gold earrings gleaming in the firelight of the marble fireplace, sat at his side on the needlepoint-covered piano bench.

They sang. "It's a treat to beat your feet on the Mississippi mud," Victor Sandys proclaimed, in an offkey, thumping bass. "*Sweeet* and lovely, sweeter than flowers in May," warbled Mittie's clear, true soprano. "When your heart's on fire, you must realize, smoke gets in your eyes," responded George Enderbridge, his striped ascot slightly askew.

"I've got you under my skin," declared an impromptu quartet, of which Arnold Sallanger was the loudest member, in dubious harmony. "All aboard the Chattanooga choo-choo," Mary Lynne sang, beating time with a snapping thumb and forefinger.

Teresa came in with a tray of filled coffee cups and the platters of sweet sandwiches, which disappeared as quickly as had those of cucumber and cress with the beer.

When they all left, Gussie and Mrs. Potter stood in the front doorway as departing guests headed toward their parked cars on the cobblestone street, or on foot toward their nearby homes, all still singing in ragged unison.

"If I could *beee* with you one hour tonight, if I were *freee* to do the things I might," they sang, going home into the chill of the January night.

Mrs. Potter hoped that Ted had managed to get home safely and that Beth was tucked in, warm and comfortable and getting over the cold she must be coming down with, or whatever had made her look so pale and hollow-eyed. In spite of Peter's valiant attempts at introducing gaiety, the tea party had left its guest of honor feeling increasingly disturbed.

16

Next morning, the prayers of the congregation were invoked on behalf of Oscar Hamill deBevereaux. Mrs. Potter renewed her vow to re-create in needlepoint the five Tiffany stained-glass panels above the altar, together making a scene of Nantucket wild flowers and sky and a meandering, rush-bordered stream, if it took the rest of her days—or rather, of all future television evenings. The final hymn was sung and she and her old roommate knelt again in last brief memory of their friend, whose body was now returned to its native soil on another island.

The rector's words were brief, saying that the town's long-time leading attorney and trusted friend had been a member of the parish since 1959. His body would rest in the family plot in Southampton, where he had been asked to be buried beside the grave of his wife, Alice Chalmers deBevereaux ("Sunny," Gussie mouthed in unneeded explanation), who had died in 1958, and that of his daughter Martha, who had died in 1957. ("Marthé," Gussie whispered. "She was thirteen.")

"I didn't see Beth," she remarked as they left the church, after shaking hands with the new rector and explaining their inability to remain for after-church coffee in what Mrs. Potter still called the church basement, now renamed in what seemed to her a very British fashion, the Undercroft.

"Maybe she came at eight," Mrs. Potter offered as they hurried down the steps, waving and smiling but not pausing to talk with other departing parishioners. "I didn't see Ted, either. They both slipped away yesterday after the tea spill. I'm sure we'll see them both at Peter's picnic in an hour or so."

Last night's party cleanup, they now agreed, had been a breeze. Jadine and Jimmy, at Peter's direction, had removed all vestiges of the frogs from the kitchen—the trash can full of oyster shells, the restaurant glasses, bottles, even the leftover chili sauce. Only a yeasty scent of beer remained after they left in the restaurant's station wagon.

Teresa had all of the silver washed during the time of the singing, some of it flannel-wrapped and stored away, other pieces polished and shining behind the glass fronts of the china cupboard in the dining room. She had done a quick tour with the vacuum. She had neatly repackaged the last of the sliced fruitcake, which Gussie insisted she take home with her, along with a nearly full box of leftover bonbons and the last of Beth's burnt sugar almonds. "So I won't be tempted," Mrs. Potter had told Gussie. "I know what you're doing."

Teresa had left, laden not only with the party's bonus of treats but also with the damp bundle of the organdy tablecloth. "I'll soak it again all night, and then give it a little bleach if I have to," she remarked as she went out.

"I mentioned temptation," Mrs. Potter said, after she had gone. "I don't think we had such a sinful evening, from the standpoint of calories, as you may think, Gussie. I know you feel bad because Tony left early, before the singing began, and you may be worried that you've wrecked your diet and he'll never forgive you. But let's figure this out." Finding her crewel needlework bag, still at the side of one of the kitchen's easy chairs, and retrieving the yellow pad she had used earlier for making the tea party lists, she had jotted some figures.

"Peter said the bourbon part of the frog was less than a half ounce, right? Just a sip. That means less than fifty calories, certainly. How many frogs did you have? Well, I'll tell you I had three, the first one with bourbon and the other two with just beer. So that's fifty for Jack Daniel's. Three oysters . . . certainly both of us have dieted enough times to remember how many calories in an oyster, Gussie?"

"Oysters, four to six medium, seventy calories," Gussie recited.

"That means thirty-five calories for the oyster part. And beer?"

"Beer, twelve ounces, one hundred and seventy calories," Gussie intoned. "That's regular, not light. I know the whole thing by heart, after all these years, from apples to zucchini."

"I'm sure I didn't have more than four ounces of beer with each oyster," Mrs. Potter said. "It's hard to be exact with a bluepoint in the bottom of the glass. Suppose I had just that, twelve ounces of beer in three frogs."

"Add it up," Gussie said, with very little show of interest.

"All right, bourbon fifty; oysters, let's say fifty; beer, maybe two hundred to be on the generous side. That makes three hundred calories, which sounds like a lot until you stop to think that was my whole *dinner.*"

"Not even a cucumber sandwich?" Gussie asked doubtfully. "Not one of those lovely little watercress rollups you had so much fun making? Not even a slice of your very own grandmother's special orange bread when you were having coffee later in the parlor? I know with my own eyes I saw you eat at least one bluepoint just on the half shell."

"All right, I forgot. I had *two,* without anything but lemon. They're such a treat! I was only counting the frogs," Mrs. Potter replied, then, pondering, continued. "You know, to be honest, although I did have a cucumber sandwich, I actually don't think I had *any* of those other things. Shall we say I had a five-hundred-calorie dinner? I don't think that's too bad."

And, she thought now, remembering this Saturday night after-party conversation, I doubt that anyone at the party has wakened this Sunday morning with a headache or a remorseful stomach. There had been a lot of laughing and singing, but she felt sure that no one's sum total of frogs had added up to more than very mild inebriation (Peter had removed the Jack Daniel's, she noticed, when he went to the piano) and a fairly modest supper.

At that point, Saturday evening, Gussie had sighed and they had gone on to other talk of the just-finished party, although Mrs. Potter could see that she was still troubled. Gussie had wanted her tea party to be a tribute to the person who was clearly beginning to take an important place in her life—Tony Ferencz. Now, although she couldn't help being pleased that for most of the guests the party had turned into a resounding success, Gussie was undoubtedly reflecting that Tony had gone home in stiff and disapproving formality.

It had been, therefore, a relief to them both when the telephone rang and Gussie could return with good news. "He wanted me to know he understood the social pressures I was under, as hostess this evening," Gussie said, a new lilt in her voice. "He thought I looked marvelous—*do* I look marvelous, Genia?—and he has already forgiven Peter for what he calls 'his schoolboy prank.' And he's eager to see both of us again tomorrow at Peter's beach shack picnic."

Mrs. Potter had earlier decided not to mention Ted's unspeakable behavior. In fact, she scarcely wanted to think about it herself—an old friend of ordinarily impeccable manners, now so far gone in alcoholism as to create such a nightmarish scene at the tea table. How lucky it was, she thought, that only she and Beth had been witness to his sudden wild flight from reality.

Yet, behind Ted's accusations, drunken fantasies though they might be, there were troubling coincidences. There had been her own sudden guess that poison might have caused both Edie's and Ozzie's deaths. There was the possibility that poisons had been the subject of Beth's library research. And the idea of poison must have been somewhere in Ted's mind if he could imagine skull and crossbones on a blue bottle in Beth's lightship basket. Whatever the basket had contained, she wished that Beth had shown it to her.

At the end of the party, she could not bring herself to speak of any of this to Gussie, who by then was in such good spirits. Instead, she joined her in a quick tour of the house. They discovered a few last cups and saucers Teresa had missed. They rejoiced that the dining room tabletop and the soft blues and greens of the rug seemed undamaged by the tea spill.

Later, they even recalled a few more old songs. At Gussie's insistence, Teresa had left the washing of the teacups and plates. The two remembered long-forgotten lyrics and tunes as they took pleasure in washing and drying the fragile china, and Mrs. Potter felt the evening's unease finally dissipating.

"I'd like to get you on a slow boat to China," they chanted. Then, as they at last and somewhat wearily ascended the stairway to their bedrooms, it was "I get a kick out of you . . . Mere alcohol doesn't thrill me at all . . ."

Now on Sunday morning, hurrying the short distance home from church to change into warm clothes for Peter's picnic, they repeated their concern about Beth. "She really looked dreadful yesterday," Gussie said. "Those great circles under her eyes! Of course she was trying to be cheerful, being Beth, getting more tea and then taking your place at the table, but she just wasn't herself. And it wasn't like her to come so late."

They tried to cheer themselves again with the thought that they'd be seeing her again shortly, when perhaps they could find out what was the trouble.

As she changed from church clothes to the warm wool pants and sweater of the first morning's walk in the snow, Mrs. Potter felt thinner. I'm thinner in just three days, she told herself, with sudden elation. But I'm not going to stand in front of that hall mirror beside Gussie again until I feel a lot thinner than *this*.

She considered their regimen since that first morning. Breakfast, after the one of cranberry muffins with a then cheerful Beth, had been only a freshly expressed glass of vegetable juices, an improbable mélange newly invented by Gussie each morning, purporting to follow Tony's prescription for her special needs. Lunches continued to be a piece of fruit and a bit of cheese, or cottage cheese on salad greens. After the second day she had declined the glass of wine and the slice of Portuguese bread Gussie had offered. She was determined to eat exactly what her hostess did, and to keep up with her in the daily exercise session.

Cocktail time each day was leisurely. They drank soda water with ice and a slice of lime or a twist of lemon peel as they listened to the evening news before dinner. She found she was beginning to enjoy it.

She reviewed the dinner menus. The first night had been Gussie's Eggs Florentine-Benedict—a poached egg on chopped cooked spinach on a base of artichoke bottoms, hot and nicely seasoned. Thursday had brought a small broiled slice of beef filet, a small baked potato with chopped chives, innocent of butter or sour cream, and a salad of greens with a splash of Gussie's homemade tarragon vinegar. Friday the portion of fish was a little more generous—Nantucket plaice, lightly broiled. With it had been fresh broccoli, cooked quickly to remain green and slightly crisp, with lime wedges to go with both. There had been no salt on the table. Desserts had been a few sections of tangerine on a plate with a small bunch of cold green grapes; a handful of winter-shipped strawberries, *au naturel;* a halved pink grapefruit, prettily notched.

It wasn't being too bad, she told herself. And that waistband *had* been a little tight. Today, to her surprise, she found herself hoping Peter's picnic lunch wouldn't be so good as to undo the whole thing. Dear Peter. She needn't worry. Whatever it was, it would be perfect.

17

As they drove to the south shore, Mrs. Potter remarked that this was her first look at the island other than coming down on the plane on Wednesday, when she had seen the island as a whole from above—a rough triangle fourteen miles across and no more than six deep, thirty miles off the New England coast. This was her first time to renew acquaintance with moors and beaches and open sky, now empty, deserted, bleakly beautiful, so different from summertime's tranquil green and blue, gold and white.

Today's drive was a short one to the south shore, taking them past a narrow pond where a few dark duck-shapes moved among the bordering reeds. As they approached the shore front and before they reached the former end of the paved town road, they were halted by an imposing wooden barricade. Gussie, unsurprised, swung sharply to the right on a new gravel road. Ahead, fully ten yards beyond the barricade, Mrs. Potter could see grassy, clearly abandoned tracks of the old lane she remembered leading to Peter's beach house. "I hadn't realized how much erosion there has been on this shore!" she exclaimed. "The end of the town road must have washed away a lot more since I was here last."

"People keep telling me Nantucket will be all under water in another hundred years, or maybe I mean centuries," Gussie replied, in an unworried tone. "I think it just erodes one place and builds back up someplace else. Anyway, all the places that could be dangerous are blocked off. Nobody could possibly miss all the blockades and warning signs. The old road that used to branch off to the left here to Surfside is gone, of course, at least abandoned and I suppose mostly washed out. But that's no problem—you can get *there* directly from town on the next paved road. Luckily this new branch road the town put in to go to Peter's is now far enough back from the water to be good for years. They hope.

"Another day we'll do the full tour of the island," she continued as they drove down the new road. "Maybe we might even take a picnic lunch to eat on the bench down next to the pond. Wouldn't that be fun if it isn't too cold?"

As they approached Peter's small house, perched on the edge of the dunes, they could hear the crash of surf beyond the fringe of beach grasses in front. They smelled salt in the winter air, mingled with the fragrance of woodsmoke.

Gussie parked behind the house (spoken of as a shack only as one might refer to a favorite horse as a nag), finding a place among a half-dozen other cars there. As the two followed the sandy path to the doorway, they were joined by Arnold Sallanger, who had driven the road across the winter-bleached, but yet unfrozen, moors just behind them.

Peter was waiting for them at the open door, his stout sweatered arms wide in welcome, urging them in by the fire, saying that they could hear the sea from inside where they'd be warm, that there would be time for a beach walk later.

They entered a room occupied with chattering and ostensibly convivial luncheon companions. It took only a moment to see that the talk and conviviality were taking place in two completely different groups, each ignoring the existence of the other.

On their ocean side was a long window, its glass slightly frosted by the etching of blowing sands. Outside, the brief rise of sandy dune was topped with coarse tufts of dark dune grass, below a sky filled with scudding clouds.

Opposite was a large open cobblestone fireplace, its blazing logs giving welcome heat, and beyond that a door leading into what Mrs. Potter remembered as a small bedroom and bath.

Between sea and fire were two facing sofas—really banquettes, Mrs. Potter thought—each long enough to seat four or five people comfortably. Between them was a huge pine table of coffee-table height, sturdy enough to serve as a bench. As bench it was being used now, by people with backs to each other in a way that divided the room into two corridors.

In the first, it was easy to see that Tony, Count Ferencz, was the magnet. As he rose to kiss Gussie's hand and her own, and to brush Gussie's cheeks lightly with his lips, and as he continued to keep Gussie's hand, Mrs. Potter saw that Helen and Mary Lynne were sitting at his side. Mittie and Leah sat facing him, perched girlishly on the low center table, their hands around their knees.

In the second corridor, a flat-brimmed hat and flashing earrings, above a heavy turtleneck sweater and trousers of pale heather beige, declared that Dee, Countess Ferencz, was holding her own court. Rising from their places beside her on the second banquette were George Enderbridge, his dry, smooth cheeks rosy from the fire, and Victor Sandys, wearing a new white Irish fisherman's sweater, mighty with cables and popcorn-stitch bumps. His wool trousers were what Mrs. Potter knew to be the third tartan plaid she had seen him wear since their first meeting on the post office steps Friday morning. He was wearing glossy new leather boots, she noted later when he stretched them out before him to be admired on the tabletop.

As she greeted them all, Mrs. Potter again found herself an observer as well as a guest. Again guest of honor, she reminded herself. She must try to be good company even though, as yesterday, she was inwardly troubled. Until she could talk with Beth, she had nothing on which to base these now recurring misgivings. Meantime, she could not keep from watching and wondering, although for what, she would have found it impossible to say.

Peter, not part of either group, was now busy providing drinks, with Lolly Latham apparently helping him, or at least on her feet and awkwardly apart from the two corridors. It was typically thoughtful of Peter, Mrs. Potter thought, to have included her in this party, as Gussie had done in her tea invitation, a generous impulse on the part of both of them, since she was seldom included in her mother's social life.

There was more room in Dee's camp than in Tony's, and Mrs. Potter joined her there beside the other two men, as did Arnold Sallanger, without hesitation. Gussie first went to be with Peter at the far end of the room, the area that served as kitchen and bar, before returning to perch on the back of the banquette above Tony's well-tailored shoulder. "Peter's wonderful, as always," she called across to Mrs. Potter. "Wouldn't you know? Exactly the right drinks for everybody."

Dee, Victor, and George had large heavy beakers before them, holding what Mrs. Potter and Arnold rightly assumed to be Bloody Marys, and undoubtedly Peter's special mix of highly seasoned tomato juice and an equal measure of chilled clam broth. Arnold answered Peter's question by saying that's what he'd have too, and Mrs. Potter began to say that's what she'd like too, only as Peter knew, she'd like hers with gin, if it was handy, rather than vodka.

At that moment Gussie spoke again, calling across from her perch on the sofa back. "Peter's brought freshly made vegetable juices from his big extractor at the Scrim," she said. "He's got a wonderful new mix I'm going to try for you tomorrow, Genia. Carrot, of course, and then yellow turnip—that's rutabaga—and parsley—*remember*, Genia, parsley for your *liver?*—and all kinds of native Nantucket herbs he's been gathering. Tell me again, Peter, what has it got?"

"Calamus root, for one thing," Peter said. "The old settlers used to make candy with it. It grows along one side of First Bridge on the Madaket road. You have to be careful not to get the root of the wild flag, though, because that's supposedly poisonous, and it grows on the *other* side of the bridge. The special taste comes from ground holly. The berries are dry now and that's the time to gather them . . ."

"Gaultheria procumbens," Mrs. Potter heard Lolly whisper.

". . . when they have a very nice wintergreen taste," Peter continued. "But remember, guys, Tony's head guru around here. All I do is basically what he wants you to do—drink lots of fresh juices of all kinds. Only I try to make it a little fun. Give me a hand, will you, Lolly?"

Tony inclined his head by way of thanks, and Gussie's smile was proud.

Surprising herself, remembering her diet, Mrs. Potter made a choice. "I'd love some juice, too," she said. Across the table she saw Tony's questioning glance and Gussie's nod of approval.

Everyone was now listening to Peter's story about the casting for the next little-theater play—his attempt to pull both groups of his guests together, Mrs. Potter thought. Chancing to look beyond the shoulders of those facing her, she saw Lolly at the kitchen counter. She was quickly pouring one of the juice glasses half full of vodka before adding the pale vegetable juice.

Before Mrs. Potter could believe her eyes, Lolly had rather clumsily brought the tray of filled glasses, a plump forefinger and thumb almost casually encircling the noticeably paler glass, the one Mrs. Potter knew to be mostly vodka. She watched as Lolly made her rounds with the tray until only the pale glass remained, still awkwardly but definitely within her grasp. She continued to watch, from the corner of her eye, as Lolly, in her baggy jeans and too large gray sweater, standing apart from the others, sipped from it steadily, with no visible reaction. Her own first thought was relief that Lolly's drink had not been her own. Rutabaga juice and native plants were about all she could manage.

The two groups again divided as Peter finished his story. Conversation on Dee's side of the table ranged from the frogs and old songs of the evening before to the question of Victor's new book, which he refused to discuss. "I may have said galley proofs," he said flatly, "but you may be thinking of a new edition. I'm sure you all remember my *Backwards into Night?* Remember what the *Times* said? 'A new major talent in the world of fiction.' And you remember the book club review, the one calling it a true breakthrough in the exploration of the subconscious?"

Those beside him agreed dutifully. "I still think you've got a new one up your sleeve and you're planning to surprise us," Gussie told him, again speaking across the no-man's-land of the big coffee table. "See if you can pry it out of him, Genia."

The subject turned to Beth's health.

"I hope you're keeping an eye on her, Arnold," George Enderbridge said earnestly.

"If it were any of the rest of the women here," Dee said darkly, only half under her breath, "I'd know who to blame." She stared coldly across the table at her ex-husband, who gave no sign of hearing her.

In the opposing camp surrounding him, Mrs. Potter overheard similar expressions of concern about Beth. "Did you *see* those circles under her eyes?" Mary Lynne was asking.

"Even Lolly spoke about it," Helen Latham said, "and you know she never notices anything."

Gussie spoke up quickly, obviously distressed to hear Helen's daughter belittled to her face. "Lolly, you were terrific at my tea party yesterday," she said, turning to where Lolly stood woodenly by the big window, holding her empty glass. "Genia said you were dear helping out in the dining room with the guests, just as Ted was."

Lolly flushed unbecomingly, although she did not seem visibly affected by the ʼlarge amount of liquor she had downed so quickly. She looks just like her father, Mrs. Potter thought, seeing her face blank and expressionless in the cold light from the ocean. Maybe I was right about her slipping away to her room with a handful of cookies or a fistful of candy bars, only instead it may be a retreat into her own world with a surreptitious drink.

"It's getting quite late," Dee said, on her side of the table.

"Do you think Beth's forgotten? She says she's so forgetful these days. And where's Ted? He's always on time."

Peter rejoined them to answer the second question. Ted had phoned him before breakfast. Had a spur-of-the-moment decision to take the early plane and visit his mother in Wellesley, and said to tell everyone how sorry he was to miss the lunch party.

"Ted must have been drunk as a skunk yesterday, knocking over a teapot like that," Victor said loudly. "Heard him shrieking like a banshee after he did it. Served him right if he scalded himself."

Mrs. Potter's first impulse was to deny this. "He didn't *seem* tipsy," she said. "He was handing around cups and whirling back and forth between the tea table and the parlor and never missing a step. He drank gallons of tea, and he never seemed to be away long enough to have anything else."

"Drank a lot, you say?" Victor asked. "Probably nipping all afternoon in the back hall. I wouldn't put it past him."

Mrs. Potter sighed, in unhappy, reluctant, unspoken agreement. Ted had to have been drunk. At least she had been the only one to hear his wild accusation of Beth. The words *cyanide* and *poison* had not reached the kitchen.

"The phone here is on disconnect for the winter," Peter interjected, "or we could check on Beth. She probably got started planning a new garden layout and didn't notice the time. We'll go ahead with lunch and I expect she'll come dashing in any minute now, wearing some wonderful crazy new hat."

Brushing aside offers of help, Peter quickly cleared the big low table and placed two old arrowback pine chairs at either end, thus converting it into a luncheon table for twelve. He whisked away the empty glasses and brought a big clean ashtray to replace the one already overflowing in front of Victor Sandys. At each place on the bare, waxed pine, he set a heavy cranberry-glass goblet with a folded homespun napkin and a soup spoon thrust lightly inside, and a large flowered pottery plate. In the center of the table he placed a huge revolving tray of the same satiny pine as the tabletop.

"Lazy Susan lunch," he announced happily. "Everybody can reach, and everything's on picks to eat by hand, so you can choose your own menu. Just start in and keep it turning while I fill the glasses and then bring the stew."

Mrs. Potter observed that the goblets on Dee's side of the table were filled from a carafe of white wine; those on Tony's side from a pitcher of iced tea.

The revolving tray bore a varied feast. There were cheeses —Muenster, Edam, and Brie—with accompanying Swedish flatbread. There were neat small chunks of fresh fruits— apple and pineapple on small spears, strawberries and small clusters of black Ribier grapes providing their own handles. Raw vegetables flourished—radishes with tiny plumes of green leaf, crisp cauliflorets, sticks of crisp celery and carrot and green pepper. Chilled shrimp, flavored with the fennel broth in which they had been cooked and cooled, arrived wrapped in green snow-pea pods. And above all this was Peter, urging and inviting, as he brought and placed on each flowered plate a small hot tureen of creamy fragrance.

"Nantucket bay scallop stew," he told her as he set the first bowl in front of Mrs. Potter. "Dig in while it's hot. You'll never find bay scallops like the ones we get here, Potter, and I couldn't think of anything you might like better for your welcome-home lunch."

Mrs. Potter agreed. Each small scallop, no kin either in size or flavor to those she knew elsewhere, was plump and succulent, the size and color of a small white marble. The judicious amount of creamy elixir surrounding them repeated their flavor without obvious distractions, although Mrs. Potter remembered that Peter added a dash of both celery salt and garlic salt to the butter in which he briefly simmered his scallops before bathing them in hot milk and cream. The result was a dish in which tiny, perfect, tender scallops swam gladly in a small creamy sea, with a coral crest of paprika-dusted melting butter.

Mrs. Potter felt sure that the scallop stew on Tony's side of the table was less creamy, and that the basket of toasted

Portuguese bread there was also unbuttered. She would ask Gussie later.

Her enjoyment of lunch was not impaired by an occasional glance at Tony Ferencz, sitting opposite her. Conversation seemed more lively, and eating less concentrated, on that side, while beside her, Dee, George, Arnold, and Victor were primarily occupied with the food in front of them. I can see why Gussie and all of them are quite mad about the man, she thought, meanwhile beaming her compliments to Peter on the perfection of the scallops. Tony Ferencz really *is* a marvelous-looking man, and the fact that he remains slightly aloof and appears to play no favorites may be part of his undeniable appeal.

To keep from staring, she turned to Victor, suggesting that they turn the lazy Susan to bring the prosciutto and melon around again, just to clear their palates, so to speak. Busy eating, he did not hear. She turned it herself, whereupon he speared several of these colorful morsels in quick succession and then spread a generous slice of Brie on his toasted bread.

The two men were in striking contrast—the count tall, spare, elegant, his gray eyes piercing and direct, his smile an infrequent compliment; Victor, rather soft and pudgy, his shape and age accented by his youthful new finery, his skin slightly wattled, smelling strongly of tobacco smoke, and much more interested in himself and his meal than in the company of the women (herself and Dee) on either side of him.

She thought briefly about man-watching, something she might have discussed with Dee or Gussie with shared amusement, but which she ordinarily would not have admitted. We all do it, she thought, only not quite as often or as openly as men look at women. We probably assess their looks just as appraisingly, and sometimes as appreciatively, although we —at least women of my generation—do it very, very discreetly.

Peter, and her own sense of party manners, recalled her from these momentary mental wanderings. To her surprise, she found that she was honest in telling him that she really couldn't eat another spoonful of his bay scallop stew, magnificent as it was, and she hoped he'd permit her to skip the dessert.

"No problem, Potter," he assured her. "Dessert is going to be this: everybody into coats and scarves and caps and gloves and out for a walk on the beach!"

Amid general enthusiastic agreement, only Helen demurred. Seated firmly on the banquette, she thrust forth her thin legs to show dark city pumps. Helen's feet, like her hands, seemed too large for such brittle stems. "I'll stay by the fire," she told Peter decisively, "and Tony isn't dressed to walk in the sand, either." She pointed to his elegant English-made shoes. "You all go and we'll get along fine without you for a bit. Lolly, for heaven's sake, *you* go! After all that lunch, you need a workout if anybody does."

Leah offered to stay to keep the two company (she had left with them from the tea party the evening before, Mrs. Potter remembered), but Helen waved this aside, pointing out Leah's warm checked wool pants, her heavy green sweater, and her walking shoes. Leah, somewhat pettish in defeat, rose reluctantly to join the others, as did Victor, looking doubtfully at his shiny new boots.

In the fresh clear winter air of the beach, long, crested waves were breaking as they came from the open sea at the south. The sky was capricious in its refusal to stay long with either sunshine or clouds. The party, trying to find the narrow stretch of firm sand between high and low tidelines, gradually strung out in groups of two and three, and Mrs. Potter found herself bringing up the rear with Peter.

As they walked along in wordless enjoyment of the beach and surf, Mrs. Potter looked up, at one point, to see the crumbling end of the old paved road almost overhead, its ragged ends ready to break off, as they had done before, onto the sand ten feet below. She paused to study the fragility of the sandy turf, bound together only with a network of thick, fine grass roots, of which the island's surface was composed. She shivered at its vulnerability to the onslaught of the tides and thundering storms.

Peter had walked on without appearing to notice her brief halt, and she hurried to catch up, suddenly aware that his shoulders were slumping and that he looked tired.

Thrusting her arm through his, she smiled up at him. "You always make things such fun," she told him, "and your menu today was inspired, just as your frogs and your music were at the end of the party last night. You're the one who ought to be the diet expert. I'm sure you know as much about it as Tony does, and you know how to make people happy at the same time."

Peter managed a wry grin. "A working stiff like me? I started out as a short-order cook at a greasy spoon back in a little town in Indiana, Potter. None of that glamour stuff for me. Besides, just look at me, and then look at that guy."

"I think you look absolutely great," she told him, sliding her hand into his pocket for a friendly, reassuring squeeze. She was surprised to meet a cold, tight fist, or so it seemed until it relaxed, a welcoming paw, to clasp her own gloved fingers. "You get my vote any day."

"They all wanted to stay by the fire with him," Peter said, his grin now wider, seeming less forced. "Helen won. Helen almost always wins, but *all* the guys wanted to be with him."

"I didn't. I wanted to walk on the beach with you," she said as Peter gently withdrew his hand, looked at his watch, and with a shout summoned the others.

"Oley oley oats in freeee . . ." he called, his voice raising in a genial howl against the wind. *"Oley oley oats in free!"* Turning to Mrs. Potter, he began to laugh. "Thanks, old dear, for the kind words," he told her. "But don't get the idea I'm competing with Tony. All I want is to see my guys well and happy."

A few minutes later, as they all were leaving for town, Jimmy and Jadine pulled into the parking area in the big station wagon. They'll take over the cleanup, Mrs. Potter thought, waving to them, as they had done after the tea party frogs.

"Put the shutters back up, Jimmy, after you drain the

plumbing, the way I showed you," she heard Peter say, "and be sure to leave the key in the usual place."

Laughing, he turned to face the others. "Yep, same place you all keep yours if you've got a shack anywhere. Find a loose shingle at the side of the door where you can wedge it in, then hope you can remember which shingle and which side when you come back."

He put his hand on the car door handle. "I'll pull out first," he apologized. "I've got to get back to the kitchen in town now, guys—I'm a working stiff, remember, Potter? And Jimmy, you two try to finish up by four. I've got to get ready for a silver anniversary dinner tonight, but Tony says he'll drive the wagon and come back for you, so listen for his honk and be ready."

18

She and Gussie settled down for a quiet afternoon of reading and letter writing and the promise of an early bedtime after the two parties.

It had not been reassuring to hear Beth's dull, listless answer when, after several tries, Mrs. Potter reached her by phone.

"Just a little under the weather," Beth told her. "I'll see you tomorrow at lunch."

With that she had to let things stand for the moment, although she was now decidedly worried. *Why* had Beth resisted opening her basket? It would have been so easy then to prove that Ted was mistaken in his hysterical outburst about a bottle of poison. Besides that, there was the whole frightening business of poisons and possible murders, which must have some connection with Beth's day at the science library. Well, she was simply not going to believe that Beth—cheerful, loving Beth, whom she had known for thirty years—could be involved in any of this, except in a totally innocent and explainable way. Without much success, she tried to think what these innocent and explainable ways might be.

Later, as she and Gussie sat with a tray supper between

them in front of the library fire, she was temporarily distracted from these troubling thoughts by the reminder of another deep concern. Gussie's romantic interest in Tony Ferencz was growing. So were her own secret doubts about him.

"I've been writing my Sunday letters to Marilyn and Scott," Gussie said. "They met Tony at the time of Gordon's funeral, and of course when they were here at Christmas, but I wanted to tell them more about him. I can only hint to them about the foundation, naturally. . . ."

"What foundation?" Mrs. Potter inquired quickly. "You used the word before, but you didn't explain what you were talking about."

"Forget I mentioned it," Gussie replied. "Tony will announce it in his own good time, when he finds the right place for it and has all his financing and staff arrangements complete. Really, I wasn't writing the children so much about that as just to prepare them for, well, knowing how important he's becoming to *me*."

"Oh, Gussie, stop it!" Mrs. Potter said. "You promised me you'd not rush into another marriage, the way you married Gordon. You don't really know anything about Tony except that you—and most of the rest of Les Girls—find him charming. Glamorous. Handsome. And that his diets make you nice and thin and pleased with yourselves."

"At least that's pretty good for starters," Gussie said, exploding in sudden laughter.

"You know it isn't enough, Mary Augusta Baines," Mrs. Potter replied. "That's all just surface, and I don't think you or any of the others have the slightest idea of what he's really like as a person. Besides, what's all the rush?"

"Well," Gussie temporized, her laughter subsiding, "I'm not getting any younger, for one thing. . . ."

"Not good enough," Mrs. Potter told her. "Actually, I even wonder why you'd consider marrying a fourth time at all. Being a widow isn't the end of life, you know, except if you practice suttee or puttee or whatever it is. Lots of people manage to live alone and to feel happy and useful."

Gussie was now serious. "That may be all right for you and all those lots of other people you're talking about. Maybe I just happen to think of marriage as my career. I'm not awfully involved in good works, except for small things like Meals on Wheels and the garden club. Nothing big, like Helen's jobs. I love my home and my garden. I like having a man to cook for and dress for. Honestly, Genia, I don't see how you can really enjoy giving dinner parties alone, or going to them by yourself, that is, supposing anyone asks you by yourself."

"So it's really a matter of wanting a man around the house," Mrs. Potter said. "Fair enough. But please, Gussie, be sure you've got a good one this time, like Theo or Jules, and take your time before you start thinking wedding bells.

"Besides," she added, "I'm not sure I can find another green horsehair picture hat."

19

Monday was the regular lunching day of Les Girls. Today, the day after Peter's beach picnic, they were back on schedule.

"I don't know when we started to go to the Scrim instead of meeting at people's houses," Gussie said as the two walked briskly toward the small inn. "It's easier, of course, and the place has sort of become our club. Peter knows what we like, and it's always so comfortable there."

It used to be fun, Mrs. Potter reminded her, when they each put a sandwich in their baskets and took turns being hostess at home. Sherry or Dubonnet first, she reminisced, then dessert and coffee later, while they all caught up on the week's island news.

"Maybe it was the dessert part that finally got to be too much," Gussie said. "Not the trouble of making it as much as the fact that none of us except Beth eats dessert anymore, except maybe a little fruit."

"One day at your house," Mrs. Potter said, "you served Bride's Pudding. Remember that old recipe? And you said, 'Oh, it's just air and *love*' and we all ate it knowing very well that it was mostly whipped cream and fresh coconut under that heavenly sauce of fresh raspberries. And then—was it

Mittie?—anyway someone said when you urged second serv-
ings that no, she wouldn't but she *could* have finished the
whole enormous mold of it by herself? Funny the things one
remembers about food."

Mrs. Potter, feeling definitely thinner in spite of her few
transgressions at yesterday's picnic lunch, decided she would
at least *read* that old recipe in Gussie's cookbook. Maybe she
could trust herself to make it when she got back to the ranch,
she said, first making sure she invited enough people to eat
the whole thing at one dinner party, with no chance of
leftovers.

"Oh, I suppose it's in most old cookbooks," Gussie said, "or
something like it. I could recite it to you right now. You soften
two envelopes of plain gelatin in a half cup of water—okay?
You whip six egg whites to a froth with a pinch of salt, then
beat in—let's see—three-fourths cup of sugar. When it holds
a peak, you mix in the gelatin, slowly, to be sure it's mixed
well, along with a teaspoonful of vanilla. The last step is to
whip a pint of heavy cream and fold that in. And that's all
there is to it."

"How about the fresh coconut?" Mrs. Potter asked.

"Don't be silly," Gussie responded. "Brides don't grate
coconut. What you do is to butter a springform cake pan and
pat it with most of a can of flaked coconut. After you fill the
pan with the egg-white mixture, you sprinkle the rest of the
can on top."

"And the fresh raspberry sauce I remember so well?" Mrs.
Potter continued.

"Just plain thawed frozen berries," Gussie told her. "You
unmold the pudding when it's chilled firm—give it at least
four or five hours—on a big round chop plate and you dribble
part of a couple of packages of raspberries over the top and
pour the rest around the sides."

Mrs. Potter, hungry for lunch after their breakfast of fresh
vegetable juices and tea, listened with attention. She'd get
Gussie to recite it again when they got home, and write it
down.

Mary Lynne joined them from the opposite direction as

they came to the discreet weathered sign of the Scrimshaw Inn. Her thoughts seemed also of food—specifically of Peter's Sunday lunch. "The best meals I've eaten in my life," she declared, "were always at somebody's coffee table, either here or back home. Don't you love it when there's lots of wonderful food, like Peter's yesterday, and everything seems so easy and relaxed? And don't you think even Tony loved it?" Gussie nodded, but her smile seemed strained.

Mrs. Potter to date had not observed Tony eating or drinking very much of anything at all, but she did not mention this. And whether or not he loved the picnic, at least he had been the center of his small adoring circle yesterday. It seemed surprising to her that her friends should be so dependent upon his approval. What he's doing for them with his diet and treatments should be enough, she thought, without their expecting him to love them all, too.

Leah and Helen were already at the round table for eight in the sunny window, again, as they had been the previous Wednesday, the only luncheon guests as yet in the room at their chosen early hour of noon. A wood fire crackled as usual in the small fireplace. The pink holiday poinsettias glowed as before in their leafy setting of house plants beside the salad bar and the tiny hydroponic garden of herbs. Jadine was bustling in purposefully with a tray laden with salad greens, and Peter Benson was blowing kisses of welcome from the half-open kitchen door. Tony Ferencz was not in the dining room. It would be nice to be with old friends today without the tension his presence created.

Dee and Mittie arrived and the lunch table held only one vacant chair. "We may just as well have our juice before Beth comes," Helen announced, denying any possibility of opposition. "She won't want any, anyway."

The door to the private dining room was closed today, and there were no sounds of merriment. To cover the sudden silence as they all thought of Edie Rosborough's death, they began talk of choices for a new lawyer to handle their affairs. Mittie wondered if they knew the new young lawyer, Jonathan Silverstein. "After all, he's Harvard," she said.

They spoke of the instant and crazy success of the Pied Piper fragrance of the new bakeshop. They spoke of frogs and the comments they'd heard from other guests at Gussie's tea party. Frog lovers, predictably, included only those who liked beer, bourbon (neat), and oysters (raw).

There was unanimous agreement that the excitement of the tea spill and the consequent flurry of mop-up operations had really turned the tide of the party. Mrs. Potter speculated privately on how to stage a minor disaster for any future party at the ranch that had got off to a chilly start.

"Nobody heard what Ted was squealing about," Leah remarked, "but he must be all right, if he flew off-island to visit his mother yesterday. Let's hope we see Beth looking more like herself today when she gets here."

They had almost decided to proceed to the salad bar for their luncheon choices when Beth came into the room. Her face was white and drawn, she was hatless, without a coat, her curly white hair tousled, the purple shadows under her eyes alarming.

Peter, who had taken his place at the miniature herb garden, scissors in hand, rushed to meet her. "Hey, guy, you missed my picnic yesterday," he told her, one arm around her shoulders in an affectionate, forgiving squeeze.

Beth appeared not to hear him. Pushing aside his embrace, and without glancing at the friends awaiting her arrival, she went to the salad bar. She peered for a long minute at the hydroponic tank and the various herbs growing there, then, even more closely, at the display of color and greenery in the ornamental plants behind and around the salad table.

Without a word she turned, her body sagging, her face gray and expressionless, and walked slowly out of the dining room. As they heard the heavy old front door of the inn close, Mrs. Potter and Gussie rose to their feet.

"We'll catch her," Gussie told the others at the table. "Go ahead with lunch. Genia, grab your coat!"

Beth seemed to be walking blindly on the narrow brick sidewalk, almost grazing an old horsehead hitching post, stumbling, slowing, then rushing on in the direction of her own house.

"Where's your coat?" Gussie demanded as they caught up with her. "It's raw in this wind, Bethie. Here, take mine and we'll all huddle together and get back to the Scrim."

Mrs. Potter looked carefully at Beth's face and the unfocused stare in her eyes. "Look, we'll make a cape of both our coats, *so,*" she said, "with Beth in the middle, and we'll all go to her house. *Now.*"

Samson's hollow bark greeted them as they opened the door of the house on India Street, and his agitation was frantic as they entered. "Down, Samson, *good dog,*" Mrs. Potter said, hoping to calm him. Then as they saw the disarray confronting them, the two women swung into action.

"Genia, you put Samson on leash and take him out for a minute," Gussie directed. "After that I expect he may be ready for his dinner."

The tact of this remark seemed lost on Beth. It was apparent that Samson had not been walked and that he had not been fed.

"I'll just make us all a cup of tea and a sandwich," Gussie continued as she gathered up a cold mug, half filled with coffee, a thin milky film congealing on its surface, ignoring the crusty ring it left on the old pine of the table. Quickly she cleared crumpled papers from the chairs and floor. She turned off lamps, opening chintz curtains to let in the winter sunshine.

"Come on, Beth," she said gently, "come show me what we three can rustle up for lunch. And it's cold in here. Where's the thermostat? I'll turn up the heat."

Docile but unhelpful, Beth allowed herself to be led to her own kitchen, where the disorder was less apparent, except for long gashes, claw marks, clearly new, on the soft pine of the frame of the back door, showing Samson's earlier panicked attempts to get out.

"Soup," Gussie decided after a quick look at the kitchen stores, as Mrs. Potter and Samson returned. "Soup for us, and Samson's dinner—I found cans for both in the pantry."

Samson's voracious hunger was quickly appeased and he settled himself amiably enough on a rug in the corner. Beth took a few listless spoonfuls of hot soup, then appeared to lose interest.

"I mixed cream of tomato and green pea and added a little curry powder," Gussie said, hoping to tempt her. "Come on now, Beth. See, Genia's eating hers and it's *good*. Now a bite of cracker—that's fine. And a little more soup, while it's hot."

Finally able to coax Beth to eat, they were less successful in persuading her to talk. Mrs. Potter put a sympathetic arm around her plump shoulders. "What's the trouble, Bethie?" she asked again, as they both had done before.

The three sat in silence for several minutes before Beth began to speak. "I'm a murderess," she told them slowly, her voice low and unemphatic. "I poisoned Ozzie deBevereaux, and before that I poisoned his secretary. And Ted Frobisher thought I was going to poison him and a lot of other people at Gussie's party, and he knocked over his cup of tea and the teapot to keep me from doing it."

Gussie's eyes widened, at first in horror, then in complete disbelief. Beth munched another cracker.

"You couldn't have murdered *anybody,*" Gussie told her. "Edie Rosborough died of an allergic reaction. Don't you *remember?* And Ozzie died of a heart attack. Arnold said so."

As a clinching argument, Gussie assured her that Ted was *fine.* (He had drunk too much at the party, Mrs. Potter added, and said crazy things, but he'd recovered. He'd even flown off-island to visit his mother.) "You didn't poison anybody, Bethie," Gussie told her over and over, "you couldn't have."

Mrs. Potter again put her arm around Beth's now shaking shoulders. "Just talk to us about it," she implored. "We know you're sad about Ozzie and Edie Rosborough. We all are, but *you* didn't have anything to do with their dying." No matter how things look, she told herself.

Beth slowly ate another cracker before she spoke, and her voice was thick and mechanical. "The last proof was at the Scrim today," she said, "although I knew, of course, what it had to be. You both know what dumb cane is, don't you?"

"Yes, dieffenbachia," Gussie replied promptly. "Everybody has a plant or two around, I suppose. It's a popular house plant, easy to raise."

"Do you really know why its common name is *dumb cane?*" Beth persisted. "Because that's what it *does,* that's why. There are little needles of a crystalline stuff in it, and worse than that, a kind of enzyme in the leaves that causes swelling in the tongue and gullet. And it can *kill* people that way, just as it—just as *I*—killed that poor girl, Edie. You'll find my notes about it on the table in the living room." Her voice was clearer now, and almost matter-of-fact.

Gussie hastily retrieved the crumpled papers she had gathered earlier and had crammed into a chintz-covered wastebasket. Smoothing them uncertainly, she found one with the heading *Dieffenbachia* written in Beth's neat round script.

" '*D. sequine (Jacq.) Schott,*' " she read. "That's just a kind of shorthand for the botanical description, Genia. Here's what Beth wrote down after that. 'Poisoning: severe burning in the throat and mouth caused to some extent by numerous needle-like crystals (raphides) of calcium oxalate, but primarily by a protein (enzyme) aspargine.' And then she wrote down her source—*Human Poisoning from Native and Cultivated Plants,* second edition, James W. Hardin and Jay M. Arena, M.D."

"I found another one," Mrs. Potter said. " 'Members of the arum family grown as house plants include pothos, window leaf *(Monstera* sp.), elephant's ear, caladium and dumbcane. Poisonous properties. Swelling of mouth, tongue and throat may interfere with speech, swallowing and breathing. In severe cases can cause death by choking.' After that she wrote 'Plants that Poison, Ervin M. Schmutz and Lucretia Breasdale Hamilton.' "

Gussie searched through the crumpled papers. Beth halted her. "There's only one more on that murder," she said. "Find the one from the book *Deadly Harvest.*"

"Here it is, by John M. Kingsbury," Gussie said. " 'Some think practical jokes with these plants are funny but the truth is that more than one person has lost his life when tissues about the back of the tongue swelled up and blocked breathing as a result of taking a mouthful.' "

Beth ate another cracker. Samson snored on his rug.

"You think Edie died from eating dumb cane," Mrs. Potter said slowly, "and you seem to think you were responsible. Then how did it happen, and why?"

"They all came back for second plates of salad," Beth said dully. "You remember, Peter asked me to cut some of the herbs for a while? He had to go to the kitchen and Count Ferencz had gone away someplace." She paused, methodically crunching another cracker.

Prompted by Gussie's *"and then?"* she continued. "One of Peter's flowering begonias needed pinching back, and it was a variety I wanted a cutting from," she said slowly. "I don't think I took one—at least I didn't have it when I got home. What I did, and you can't escape the truth of it, no matter how you try . . ."

Mrs. Potter's arm tightened around Beth's shoulders, which began again to tremble.

Beth swallowed. When she went on, her voice was again measured and monotonous. "What I did was to cut a leaf of dieffenbachia instead. It's perfectly clear. I snipped up a green leaf of *dumb cane* over Edie Rosborough's salad, and she died."

Before either Gussie or Mrs. Potter could speak, she continued. "I had to look today to be sure," she said. "And there it was, as plain as day, the place where I cut the leaf from the plant.

"And now I suppose you want to know how I murdered Ozzie?" she asked calmly. "I took him foxglove leaves, thinking they were comfrey. Just see my notes on foxglove there someplace."

"We'll read them later," Mrs. Potter said. "We know foxglove contains digitalis."

"See Mr. Kingsbury again," Beth insisted. "He says it's a poisonous glycoside, that it's used to strengthen the beat of a weakened heart, but in larger amounts it can be fatal. Especially for someone who isn't already used to taking a little of it in regular doses in medicine." She pointed toward the remaining papers. "Now look for the one from *The Poison Trail*. The author's named William Boos. I've got them all memorized.

"So that's how I killed Ozzie," she said, rising to her feet and shaking herself free of Mrs. Potter's arm. "I didn't know it until Thursday morning when I went over there from your house, Gussie, and after I brought home what I thought were my dried comfrey leaves. As soon as I opened the jar, I saw I hadn't filled it with comfrey at all. I don't remember doing it, but I'd taken him foxglove leaves, still half green, as mine are, growing along the side path by the house.

"That's when I went right to the science library. I vaguely knew foxglove was poisonous, but I didn't know how it worked or how deadly it could be."

Gussie and Mrs. Potter were silent as Beth continued. "Once I'd read enough to know I'd poisoned Ozzie, it was only natural to wonder about the girl's death, too," she said. "And I told you what a help Lolly was, once she knew what I was looking for."

Gussie and Mrs. Potter looked at each other. Could Beth Higginson, however unintentionally, have caused *two* poisoning deaths? It was all the more implausible that the two, the same day, should have been caused by the most ordinary, commonplace plants of house and garden.

"There's got to be another explanation," Mrs. Potter finally told her. "Besides, you know there's no way in the world you could or would have poisoned Ted."

"That part's the worst," Beth said, her voice still a monotone. "When I opened my basket for my sweetener pills, Ted and I both saw what I had there. He knew it was cyanide the second he saw it—he's got an old potting shed, too."

Mrs. Potter stared at her uncomprehendingly.

"You don't have one," Beth explained tiredly. "Lots of people here do. When we bought this house, all the old tools and garden supplies had been left behind, for who knows how many years."

Mrs. Potter quietly removed the basket of crackers from

the table, even as Beth was reaching, unseeing, for another. In its place she set a glass of milk.

Beth took a sip, then set it aside decisively. "You thought Ted was drunk," she said, with no show of emotion. "But I saw the bottle, too. It wasn't any hallucination."

"Cyanide!" Gussie was incredulous. "You had *cyanide* here in your house?"

"People used it all the time in the old days," Beth answered easily. "Prussic acid, that's what we're talking about, hydrogen cyanide. An insecticidal fumigant, it says on the label. Ted said he used to have some, too, in that old corner of his basement. You probably have a bottle, too, Gussie, out in the garage or wherever the old garden stuff at your house was left behind when you bought the place."

For the first time, Beth almost smiled. "How I got my prussic acid—cyanide, Ted called it, same thing—from my house to your tea party is rather a blank to me," she said sweetly. "But I did, because it was there in my basket."

She now beamed more confidently. "Ted knew, of course, when *he* saw it. That's why he upset things and made such a mess. Ted wasn't going to let me poison any more people."

"Can you show us the bottle now?" Mrs. Potter asked gently.

"Here it is, in the corner cupboard," Beth said, now quite cheerful. "Naturally I couldn't let anyone at the party see it— it would have frightened them."

She took it down from the shelf. "It was empty, you know, but of course Ted didn't know that," she said, in tones of offering a reasonable explanation. "Jim checked it years ago, in case one of the grandchildren found it. He just wanted to keep it as a curiosity. When I got home, I made *sure* it was safe. I scrubbed it inside and out until the label came off." She smiled. "It's really quite a pretty old bottle, don't you think? Don't be afraid to touch it—it's clean."

"Is that the canister up there in the cupboard, too?" Mrs. Potter continued.

Beth lifted it down and set it on the table. "The foxglove leaves went out in the trash," Beth said, "and I washed it very carefully, too, so it's perfectly all right to use again if you need it for anything."

Mrs. Potter looked at the sparkling blue glass on the table, next to the clean tea canister. "How did you happen to take the old bottle to Gussie's party, anyway?" she asked in a casual tone.

Beth's face clouded, and the deep circles under her eyes seemed even darker. "That's one of three things I can't remember," she answered slowly. "One is how I could have happened to cut up dieffenbachia leaves on Edie's salad. Two is how I took a great wad of half-green foxglove leaves to Ozzie when I meant to fill the canister with dried comfrey. And three is why *ever* would I have put that dusty old bottle in my basket when I got ready for the party. I can't even remember taking it down from the shelf, although I think I remember seeing it out there in the shed not long ago."

Beth abruptly sat down on the braided kitchen rug and put her arms around her knees. "Those are the three things I can't remember, no matter how hard I try. Even when I finally get to sleep at night, I wake up every few minutes trying to *make* myself remember."

Samson pushed his nose against Beth's cheek, nudging her for attention, but she pushed him away without appearing to notice. "Anyway, I've decided what to do," she said dully. "I'm going to tell everybody and make a public confession. Don't you think that would be best?"

Gussie was at the telephone, casting a quick eye down Beth's list of numbers on the living room desk.

"Mr. Laurence Higginson," she said. "Please tell him I'm a friend of his mother's, Augusta Van Vleeck, calling from Nantucket."

There was a pause. "Yes, Laurence, I *do* understand that it's the middle of a busy day and you have an important client you're about to take to lunch—you'd like to call me back later? Forget about later, Laurence. Your mother needs you. Yes, right *now*. Yes, charter, by all means, and hold the plane to go back. Just get here, and Mrs. Potter and I will hold the fort until you come."

By the time her son arrived, Gussie and Mrs. Potter had persuaded Beth in and out of a warm bath and into suitable travel clothes. They packed a bag for her with a warm woolen robe and slippers, several pairs of bright winter pants and sweaters, underthings, a neatly polished pair of penny loafers, and her toiletries. They had called another number on Beth's telephone pad and the veterinarian's assistant from the animal hospital was on his way to collect Samson.

"Glad to keep him, Mrs. Van Vleeck," he had said. "Mrs. Higginson brings him out often, and Samson's a doll. Finest kind. Just let us know when she wants him back."

Beth, now oddly calm and untroubled, left with her son. Reassured by his promise to telephone as soon as the family doctor had been consulted, Gussie and Mrs. Potter gathered up Beth's crumpled notes, turned the thermostat down to fifty, and went home to Main Street in the early dusk of the January afternoon.

"We'd better call Helen. She'll want to be the one to let the others know," Gussie said as they reached her door.

"Only that Beth is ill and going to spend a few days in Providence," Mrs. Potter added quickly.

The three had already agreed that no one else would learn of Beth's self-accusations or erratic behavior. Arnold Sallanger had held Edie's death to be an allergic reaction, which indeed it was. He had declared Ozzie's death to have been caused by a heart attack, which it was. To hint at intentional use of poisonous plants in the two deaths could only make things worse for Beth now.

20

"But suppose Beth is *right?*" Mrs. Potter asked wearily, stretching her legs in the direction of the last embers in the library fireplace. "About *everything?* It's one last thought, Gussie."

"What do you mean, suppose Beth is right?" Gussie asked, yawning. "We've sat here talking about Beth and worrying about her ever since she and Laurence took off for Providence. It's almost midnight. We've both probably done more square inches of needlepoint tonight than in the last two months, and the one thing we've agonized about is that dear, happy, feet-on-the-ground Beth has gone off her rocker. She's *not* right. She's about as wrong as anybody could be."

Mrs. Potter nodded in reluctant partial agreement. "She's off the tracks," she said. "She's been neglecting her dog, forgetting to eat or sleep. She sounds crazy as a hoot owl. She says she's poisoned two people and that only Ted Frobisher, our favorite island alcoholic, saved her from poisoning him and maybe everybody else at your tea party Saturday. Using an *empty* bottle that *used* to hold cyanide."

"We've been over this too many times," Gussie said. "Time for bed. Come on, now—I'm not used to these late hours."

"Neither am I," replied her guest, "but just you sit down again one more minute. I asked you this—suppose Beth is *right?* Suppose Ozzie and Edie Rosborough both *were* poisoned. While you're at it, you can even suppose somebody *was* trying to poison somebody else right here in your own dining room Saturday." She paused. "Or was at least trying to make it look that way."

"The part about cyanide still seems like pure hysteria," Gussie said doubtfully.

"Shared hysteria, then," Mrs. Potter reminded her. "I told you what Ted was screaming. You all couldn't hear him in the kitchen—even Tony was out there then. I was bringing up the rear and no one else but me heard him, except Victor, and he didn't get it, of course."

Gussie yawned again as Mrs. Potter repeated the story of Ted's accusations. "Well, Beth couldn't have done a better job of getting rid of the evidence if she'd been as guilty as she says she is," she said. "We don't even know for sure if what she took Ozzie was comfrey or foxglove. Same thing with the cyanide. If the bottle was empty, why did she wash it out?"

"What if somebody was trying to make Beth believe she was crazy?" Mrs. Potter asked.

"That's terrible," Gussie said. "Why would anyone do that to Beth Higginson?" She sat down again abruptly and stared at the fast-graying embers.

"Let's turn the whole thing around," Mrs. Potter said, trying to summon new vigor. "We both know, and we've said over and over this evening until we're both half asleep, that Beth would scarcely swat a fly, let alone kill another human being. Even if an assassin with a drawn dagger came to her door, she'd invite him in for a good lunch and try to reform him with kindness and cookies." As she spoke, she, too, found that she was yawning and the library was growing chilly.

"If you want to turn it around, we'll do it in the morning," Gussie announced. "I'm going to bed."

When Mrs. Potter awoke, as usual with the first light of day, she found she had carried her needlework in its big crewelpatterned linen bag with her to the guest room. Reaching out a nightgowned arm, she pulled from it a lined yellow pad.

She pulled the soft coverlet over her shoulders. The ballpoint scribbled, half under the silky down puff, writing the question she had put to Gussie last night before they were both too sleepy to think. *Suppose Beth is right? About everything?*

Suppose, first of all, that Edie had not died from an unexpected allergy to one of the herbs at the salad bar but, as Beth insisted, by a chopped leaf of dieffenbachia, dumb cane?

Still possible accident, she wrote, remembering the press of young women around the salad bar and the banked ornamental plants behind and around it.

Who had scissors? Officially, only Peter Benson and Tony Ferencz, but actually, Beth and most of the others of their lunch party. None of these, all knowledgeable of plants and herbs, could have been likely to make such a wild and weird mistake.

It was possible that one of the softball league might have been playing a trick on the team captain without realizing its possible serious effect. She decided to reserve judgment on this entry, the question *Practical joke?*

She'd go on to Ozzie and come back to his secretary and the dumb cane later.

Ozzie's heart attack really murder? her pen inquired next. It could have been, she answered herself. Beth's notes on digitalis, which she and Gussie had studied in the library last night, made it clear that the drug might have acted in a way not only simulating a heart attack but actually causing one.

Mrs. Potter paused and peered back over her few notes, still trying to keep her arms and shoulders warm in the chill air of the bedroom.

There it was. She was going to believe that Beth was right. Oscar deBevereaux and Edie Rosborough had been poisoned. (Not by Beth, her mind cried, not by *Beth.)* She would believe that there had been a poison bottle in Beth's basket at the tea party, that both Beth and Ted had seen it, and that Beth believed it had been empty.

And that, for the moment, was *all* she would believe.

She slid out of bed and opened her bedroom door. "Gussie," she called down the long upstairs hall, "are you up? Yes, please, *get* up! I'm going to the kitchen to put on the kettle for tea and you and I are going to talk about Beth's story in a whole new light."

Gussie's initial reaction was skeptical. "We don't know *what* to believe," she said. "Beth just isn't making sense."

"I think she is," Mrs. Potter said. "Look at it this way. Suppose everything Beth told us yesterday is true, except for her being the one to be poisoning people. And while you're granting that possibility, don't forget which two people died."

Gussie was thoughtful. "A man and woman who were trusted with the affairs of nearly everyone on the island. At least of all of *us,*" she said at last. "Two people who might have had highly confidential information someone either wanted to get, or couldn't afford to have revealed."

"You might as well squeeze us some kind of breakfast," Mrs. Potter said as they looked at each other with dismay. "Maybe one of your concoctions will help us figure out what's behind all of this."

As Gussie started toward the pantry, Mrs. Potter offered a dark comment. "I'll bet I could find foxglove leaves in your garden right now, if I went out and started poking around there, or in practically any garden in Nantucket."

The whirring of the juice extractor kept Gussie from hearing the ring of the telephone, and Mrs. Potter rose to answer it.

"That was Paula, calling from Providence," she reported as the two women sat again at the breakfast table, glasses of pinkish juice before them. "Paula—Laurence's wife. I remember her slightly, but I really never got all of the Higginsons straight in my mind, daughters and daughters-in-law."

"Neither did Beth, sometimes," Gussie said. "I wish I could laugh about that now."

The family doctor had come to the house as soon as Laurence got his mother home yesterday, Paula had reported.

He said she was totally exhausted, that she had not been eating or sleeping. The doctor was concerned that she was deeply troubled by something she refused to talk to him (or even to her, Paula) about, and he seemed worried at the depth and suddenness of her apparent depression. He wants her in the hospital for a few days of rest and proper diet and observation, Paula said. She'd let them know as soon as there was anything more to report.

Mrs. Potter found it reassuring that Laurence was not using the words *poison* or *murder*, apparently not even to his wife. Arnold Sallanger had signed two unassailable death warrants. Nothing was going to disturb that official position, and no matter what confessions Beth might offer now, it was vital that they be considered delusions.

"I'd like to talk with Ted," she said. "Since apparently he did see a poison bottle, I've been wronging him in my mind. I thought he was using his perfect party manners, pretending to enjoy the party as a cover-up for spiking his own tea with vodka all afternoon. If he *wasn't* having a drunken fantasy, he may be able to shed some light on all this. I'll try to call him at his mother's, if I can find her number.

"Let's see—I remember he's Tedley, not Edward," she went on. "Tedley Tennant Frobisher, and as I recall he was a Two or a Three, which means his mother may well be a Mrs. of the same name. I'll try that 555-1212 information number."

A Frobisher, T. T., Jr. (not Mrs., of course—cautious widows do not thus expose themselves), was listed at what sounded a likely Boston suburban address, and Mrs. Potter dialed the number.

The conversation was no help at all, she told Gussie when she had finished. Very proper Boston voice, elderly, but also very strong. Used to getting her own way, brisk about cutting off questions. Ted *is* there (she had said "my son is unable to speak with you now") and she wasn't receptive to taking a message. To further quote her, they're leaving by plane at noon for the West Coast and from there on a cruise ship to Hawaii. Her son's accounts will be handled through the Boston brokerage firm he represents on the island. And that was that.

"She may be just covering up for him if he's gone on a bender," Gussie said. "Anyway, what you wanted to know is certainly nothing you could ask a Boston *grande dame*. 'Did your son thwart a mass murder at my friend Mrs. Van Vleeck's tea party here on Nantucket last Saturday?' Or how about 'At the very least, Mrs. Frobisher, did he see a bottle of prussic acid, which might or might not have been empty, in the open handbag of the guest who was pouring tea?'"

"Let's take a walk," Mrs. Potter suggested, "and think about something else for a while."

The two were just above Monument Corner, the old memorial to the island's sailors and soldiers, when Gussie stopped short. "The hospital!" she remembered suddenly. "I'm due there at ten. What time is it now?"

"Lots of time," Mrs. Potter assured her. "It's not even nine."

Gussie was on edge. "I almost forgot it, thinking about Beth," she said. "Helen asked me to report on the volunteer food-delivery program, and I've got to put together my notes. Do you mind if I rush back? You know what a demon she is at organization. You go on by yourself, and I'll be back for lunch."

Mrs. Potter continued walking slowly, thinking of how to proceed with the inquiries she knew she must make. Her feet slowed, and she, too, reversed her direction. Perusal of the old stones of the graveyard could wait, much as she enjoyed that occasional ritual walk, peering at dates and rejoicing in quirky Nantucket names and epitaphs.

As she turned back, her thoughts went again to Beth. Beth would have awakened this morning in a Providence hospital room, "under observation." That certainly was going to be no fun, racked with her self-torturing sense of guilt. She thought of Ted, off to Hawaii, undergoing maternal observation of a not dissimilar nature.

She thought again, with recurring shock, that if Beth and Ted were right, there had to be a *real* poisoner abroad on this small, beautiful island she loved so well. Beth and Ted seemed safe for the moment. But who was not? And what protection could there be? *Find out who it is,* her mind informed her. That's the only safety there can be.

The first thing she would do would be to write down her notes on Dee's story about the three beautiful people on Long Island. Then she'd try to have a good lunch ready for Gussie when she got back from her meeting. They were both on edge, she thought, from all this dieting. She would write on her yellow pad, and then she would cook something.

She wanted to talk again later with Dee, Countess Ferencz, but this would be another conversation she could not easily share with her old roommate. She wanted to talk with everyone she knew to have been a law client of Ozzie's, and she would have to start with the people she knew best, Les Girls.

There was Mittie, facing the first financial problems of her hitherto secure and sheltered life. There was Helen, rich, independent, but even she had apparently used Ozzie to prepare her tax returns. There was Mary Lynne, bravely widowed and newly rich. There was Leah, emerging from several years of plaintive bereavement.

There was even Peter Benson, the favorite restaurateur of the group. At the moment she did not let herself list the names of their favorite hairdresser, their doctor, their newly prosperous resident author, their boyish little retired clergyman and schoolmaster.

She might find some clue to the two unexpected deaths of the previous week. For Gussie's sake, she hoped to find reassurance about Tony Ferencz. For Beth's sake, she had to find out who was guilty.

21

"I just looked over your yellow pad, and I don't think it means a thing," Gussie said, after she had returned from the hospital and she and Mrs. Potter were sitting at lunch. "Anyway, thanks for having lunch ready. The soup tastes wonderful—how'd you make it?"

Mrs. Potter hesitated. She had not intended Gussie to see what she had written about Dee's story of the deBevereaux tragedy and Tony's part in it. She'd stick to talk about the soup. "There was that nice fresh bunch of leeks in the refrigerator," she began, and then halted. To say that she had not exactly looked forward to a next-day breakfast of raw juice of leek did not seem quite tactful.

Gussie finished her sentence. "And you were afraid you'd have to drink it in juice," she said. "Honestly, Genia, you should know me better than that."

Remembering what had seemed a raw breakfast borscht, with beets and cabbage, Mrs. Potter was not so sure. At any rate, she had made a low-calorie leek and potato soup that did seem comforting on a January day, and a welcome change from cottage cheese and raw apple slices.

"It isn't as fattening as it tastes," she explained meekly. "I sliced and minced all the tender parts of the leeks after I washed out all the sand, and I cooked them down gently in butter, to start with. Except I used exactly one teaspoon of butter, instead of the three or four tablespoons one might use. When they were wilted, I put in a small potato, peeled and diced rather fine, and an undiluted can of chicken broth. When the vegetables were simmered soft, I added a cup of milk. Skim milk, honestly, Gussie. I didn't purée it in the blender—I hope you like it this way."

Privately she was thinking that part of her enjoyment of their lunch was in the hot and slightly chunky substance of the soup, and the chewing of the slice of unbuttered toasted Portuguese bread she had served with it.

"All right, I expect it's not a bad diet lunch," Gussie said, "although I can't remember how many calories leeks have, can you? What I want to get back to is what you wrote on your yellow pad. Dee says Tony was negligent in the death of Ozzie's child. She implied that he was *criminally* negligent. I think Dee has reasons of her own to be vindictive about Tony. Besides, the story seems quite vague to me, and it's really ancient history."

Mrs. Potter tried to explain that Dee had seemed to be trying to be fair. "She said Tony might not have realized what he was doing to the child," she said carefully. "She even seemed to feel she herself was partly to blame by helping her new husband launch his career with favorable publicity in *Éclat.*"

Mrs. Potter did not mention Dee's saying that the name of Countess Ferencz had been useful in advancing her own magazine career. No one, not even the dear friend sitting across from her at the lunch table today, would ever hear from her lips the name Dora Stell Grumbley.

"Besides, what if Ozzie *did* think Tony had been responsible for the death of his daughter?" Gussie asked practically. "What if he *was* enraged by having Tony turn up here on the island, after all these years? What could he do now that he didn't do then?"

"Ozzie could have said, 'This man is a charlatan,' " Mrs.

Potter replied. "He could have said, 'This man's carelessness killed my daughter.'"

"That was *years* ago," Gussie said heatedly. "Even if you grant that Tony might have been negligent then, as a young man just starting out in practice, any revelations of Ozzie's now wouldn't seem very important. Genia, be honest. Would they?"

Mrs. Potter was briefly silent and Gussie continued her defense. "And, I ask you, why should Ozzie just last week suddenly seem such a dreadful threat to Tony? After all, he's been on the island ever since the first of last summer. The idea that Ozzie and his secretary might have been poisoned all this time later, to keep them from talking about an old tragedy, seems crazy."

Mrs. Potter sighed. "All right," she said wearily. "It doesn't make much sense. Nothing makes sense. Except two people died and Beth Higginson believes that she poisoned them."

"Don't forget she put a bottle of poison in her bag before she came to my party," Gussie said, still defensive. "Only she says it was empty. I say it again—Beth has just slipped a cog and that's all there is to it, sad as it may be."

Mrs. Potter was silent. When she spoke, it was with an amiable question. "Why don't I amble down street and buy some more Portuguese bread?" she asked. "You probably have more letters to write or something, and need a little time to yourself. I'll be back in time to exercise by four, and I promise *not* to eat a ginger ice-cream cone."

22

"I'll use the excuse of seeing if she wants a loaf of Portuguese bread too," Mrs. Potter decided as she approached Mittie's door after lunch. Not that she needed an excuse. Les Girls popped into each other's houses easily and often, just to say hello. The difference now was that the doors were locked.

Bundled to the ears in a bright pink turtleneck sweater, Mittie answered the old-fashioned doorbell. She was delighted to see Genia. No, no, she was not about to go out. Actually, she was in the midst of preparing a stew for herself and Dee for dinner later, and if Genia would come in and sit in the kitchen rocker, she'd be able to keep an eye on the browning lamb.

The old kitchen—a cook's kitchen, Mrs. Potter thought, arranged for the probable series of Irish cooks and maids who had accompanied Mittie's parents every summer to the island—was slightly warmer than the chilly front hall and dining room through which Mittie had led her. The temperature of the adjoining side parlors, she felt sure, was even lower. Like most kitchens whose former occupants have been old-school servants, it was large, colorless, and uncognizant of labor-saving devices. It was separated from the dining room by an equally bleak and inconvenient butler's pantry, its walls lined to the ceiling with glass-doored cabinets. Inside, Mrs. Potter knew without even looking, were good but mismatched sets of china and slightly dusty unused glassware, the pullout drawers below crammed with yellowing table linens.

The big commercial-size gas range, at which bountiful meals had been prepared for several generations of Mittie's family, was cold and slightly rusted. Mittie's lamb riblets were browning in a pot over a small electric hot plate.

"It's the *flavor* of lamb that counts," Mittie told her earnestly, "to bless the potatoes and onions and carrots, as old Reba used to say. Of course, she'd cube a whole leg of lamb for what she considered a proper stew for the family. For the two of us, I decided to try these riblet things. No sense in having a lot of leftovers. I'm going to add a diced parsnip, too, the way Reba used to."

"Gussie gives me parsnip juice along with other rather surprising things for breakfast," Mrs. Potter told her. "I suppose you're a juice addict, too, since Tony Ferencz came to the island."

"Tony's wonderful," Mittie assured her. "I don't have a juice extractor, but I'm sure it's a great idea."

Mrs. Potter, comparing the cost of the small bony bits in the pot with that of good stewing lamb, could very well guess why there was no expensive new machine in the old kitchen. She did notice, however, a small portable electric sewing machine on a table in the corner, and beside it, a strip of black-and-white-plaid wool. It *had* been a skirt she remembered, then, at the tea party, altered to fit Mittie's new waistline.

"The next step in Tony's program is supposed to be my skin," Mittie went on, "but I can't talk about it now. He doesn't like to have us talk about what he's doing."

"I hear mention of a foundation or clinic of some kind," Mrs. Potter said quickly. "Tell me about it."

"Oh, that's a secret, too. The Ferencz Institute of Beauty and Longevity," Mittie replied solemnly. "A temporary residence center. He likes the slogan I suggested: 'For people who want to enjoy long life, happily and beautifully.' Don't you really like that, Genia? Wouldn't you want to come to a place like that?"

"It suggests quite an institution," Mrs. Potter said, suppressing immediate distaste for the idea. "I suppose that means a staff and a facility of some kind other than where he is now, as I understand it, in that small bedroom suite upstairs at the Scrimshaw Inn."

Oh, no, it would be something quite comfortable, Mittie assured her, and very exclusive. Rooms for no more than six or eight guests. "Now, promise you won't tell," she went on, "but he thinks Nantucket is the perfect place for it, one that would attract exactly the clientele he'd like to serve."

"Good heavens, *where?*" Mrs. Potter asked, in secret and immediate fear that Gussie's beautiful house would suggest itself as an ideal setting.

"It's out of the question here in the Historic District," Mittie went on, as if in answer, "otherwise I'd love to turn over this house for it, as I expect Leah might with hers. All of us have houses big enough to be turned into quite nice residential centers. For either Leah or me, it might be rather nice to have some kind of foundation take over the taxes and overhead."

"Not Mary Lynne?" Mrs. Potter asked.

"Mary Lynne's coming into quite a lot of money," Mittie said hesitantly, "and not just insurance, although that seemed whopping to me. Bo's company—oil and gas and coal and things—was bought right after Bo died last summer by a big conglomerate of some kind. She's going to rake in scads and scads. He was the chief stockholder, she said, even though he was pretty much retired."

"I suppose Ozzie handled Bo's affairs, as he did everyone else's?" Mrs. Potter inquired.

"Mary Lynne just found out this morning she's going to be in the same boat with the rest of us, with everything doled out by a trust—with all of us but Gussie and Helen, that is," Mittie said. "Until today I guess she thought she could do as she liked with the money. Naturally, she'd have counted on Ozzie's help. He was there at the Wauwinet House the day Bo died. First I thought that must have been a comfort to her, but, on the other hand, the way I heard it from Peter, he really wasn't much help. Tony tried to revive him, you know, and Peter told everybody not to pay any attention to what Ozzie was saying that day."

Mrs. Potter was mystified, not sure she was following all this. "Was Tony sailing with Bo and Mary Lynne?" she asked. "I thought she brought the boat by herself. I didn't know Tony was there, or that Ozzie was."

Everyone was there, Mittie told her. Well, she herself had not been, and of course Peter had been busy in the summer season at the Scrimshaw. But Tony, most providentially, had been there when Mary Lynne beached the boat. He was having lunch there with Helen, as a matter of fact, and Ozzie had also been there, with Edie along, looking over some property with Dee and a client.

"I'll miss Ozzie, in a way," Mittie said, going back to her own concerns. "I had been furious with him lately because as my trust officer he absolutely refused to let me dispose of the Shimmo place the way I wanted to, but in the end I really had to admit he was right. The place would be perfect for Tony for the foundation, but there's no way I can afford to give it to him. He couldn't possibly buy the place himself—naturally he has everything invested in research and equipment. Just please forget I said anything at all about it. He'd be furious if he knew."

"That beautiful big house and all that land of yours must be tremendously valuable now," Mrs. Potter said. "What does it have—four or five acres right on the harbor? And, good heavens, how many bedrooms?"

"Six," Mittie said. "That is, with bathrooms. There are a couple of odd rooms that could be used to make suites, and then there are the servants' rooms—three and a bath over the garage. I always wished Daddy and Mummy had made it a little smaller when they had it built for our wedding present, but it would have been perfect for Tony."

Mittie was busy now peeling potatoes and scraping carrots to go into the stew with the few bony lamb bits. "Whatever I do with the place," she continued, "at least I don't have to feel guilty about the children. They couldn't possibly afford to keep it up, and besides they want to bring up their families in what they call 'a different life-style.' Can you imagine that, Genia? Whatever kind of life-style could compare to the kind of summers they had growing up here on the island?"

Mrs. Potter agreed that Mittie's children and the others of their generation, her own included, had been almost the last to enjoy long carefree teen-age summers and conventional long family vacations. Their successors had elected summer jobs, often the lowliest, or cross-country travel by motorcycle or bus, or youth hostels abroad. They had eagerly and gladly shed the restrictions of the parental roof, of madras jackets and Top-Siders, of chaperoned junior dances at the Yacht Club. There was something to be said on both sides.

"I don't like all this talk about money," Mittie said, busy now with the parsnip, her young eyes sad in the tanned, deeply lined small face. "There always used to be enough not to have to think about it, and now all that seems to be left is just two hunks of real estate. There's the Shimmo house, which I can't afford to run and can't afford to give away and the children can't and won't even consider. And there's this old house of Mummy and Daddy's, which needs so much work I can't even let myself *think* about the plumbing and wiring and insulating and painting. I found out how much all those things cost when I had the old carriage house made into an apartment, even though I did all the landscaping and planting myself. Heaven knows how much one of the regular landscape firms would have charged me for that part of it."

Mittie's voice sounded shaky, and Mrs. Potter felt sudden guilt at her trespass on the private dignity of an old friend. "I'll bring you a loaf of Portuguese bread to go with your stew when I get back from town," she said quickly. "It smells delicious already and I know how grateful Dee must be to share your company and your cooking. Don't bother to let me out. I know the way."

She turned back in an apologetic afterthought. "I just read an old mystery novel about garden poisons," she said. "You know all about gardens—I suppose nobody could have cyanide, prussic acid, these days?"

Mittie remembered that the old gardener at home had things he'd never let the children touch. For herself, she believed in clearing out old garden leftovers, just as she'd throw out an old prescription in her medicine cabinet. She doubted very much that anyone would be so foolish as to keep any old illegal poisons around nowadays, or that they'd be very effective anyway. She was too much a professional to have any such thing herself.

Across the street at Helen's, the borders of boxwood and yew, the careful plantings of holly and cotoneaster, were in perfect winter order. Helen was just leaving the porticoed entry of the house, giving the heavy doorknob a quick check to be sure it was locked.

Mrs. Potter quickly disclaimed any intent of coming to call, saying only that she hoped to stop by someday soon to admire the new garden room. This, a separate building with a small greenhouse now joining it to the main house, had been created within a carefully preserved outer shell. This once had been a small barn, as Mrs. Potter remembered it—a tool shed, in all likelihood, with room for a carriage and for horses to enter from the small street at the back of the property.

"Have a quick look now," Helen urged. "I've a few minutes before I'm due downtown to see Ozzie deBevereaux's nephew. He's here to distribute our files to everybody who was a client of Ozzie's, as I'm sure Gussie knows. Mine all seem to be in order—I hope hers are."

As she spoke, she led Mrs. Potter across the paved brick walk of the small side garden, and taking a ring of keys from her basket, she unlocked the deep blue painted door.

"Did I tell you there's going to be a magazine feature about this?" she asked. "And one of the Boston papers wants to do a piece about 'the queen of Nantucket society,' if you can imagine anything so ridiculous. They even spoke of doing a profile about my executive talent. I told them to wait awhile on that one."

Before she could ask what Helen meant by that, Mrs. Potter was led into the garden room. The air was warm and moist. Bow windows, small-paned, were filled with flowering plants under special garden lighting. Shrubs like small trees grew in great tubs of oriental ceramic design on a floor of turquoise tiles. White wicker furniture, deeply cushioned in blues and greens, offered an invitation to sit and admire. Still, Mrs. Potter knew she must insist she'd return for that another day.

"I don't see how you manage to keep this so perfectly tended," she said. "When I come back, you must tell me."

Helen's earlier glow of pride dimmed slightly. "Of course, Walter and Elna did most of it," she admitted. "Lolly can take over now, more or less, until I find new help. Certainly she ought to be able to manage the meals. TV dinners are fine as far as I'm concerned."

The thought of Walter and Elna seemed painful. "Can you believe their just walking out like that? After all these years? Everything seemed perfectly normal last Thursday afternoon—I think Lolly had just come home from her job—and then without a word of warning, they just up and *quit.*"

"They must have had a reason," Mrs. Potter said. It seemed suddenly important to her to find out what it was. "This couldn't have been an easy decision for them."

"They sounded absolutely crazy," Helen said. " 'We won't spend another night in a house doomed to self-destruction.' That's what Walter said, in that preacher voice of his." She shrugged. "Well, you know how simpleminded and superstitious colored help can be. I suppose something about Lester's death, all those years ago, set them off, although I can't imagine what it could have been."

Mrs. Potter remonstrated. *"Colored help!* You're talking about two people who have devoted themselves to you and your house and have looked after Lolly for nearly thirty years! The term in itself sounds insulting to most people, although it may not seem so to you. It's *certainly* insulting to say they're ignorant and superstitious!"

Helen held her ground. "What would *you* call that kind of reason for quitting without notice?"

"They always seemed warmhearted and dependable," Mrs. Potter insisted. "I think you're overreacting to the shock of having them quit, and saying things you don't really mean."

Helen did not retreat. "You talk about *insulting!* Elna kept ranting on about how I'd better keep a watch on the booze. *That* was *insulting!* I ask you, Genia, did you ever know me to be a heavy drinker? I insisted we keep a supply of liquor on hand for guests and parties—it was up to Walter to be sure there was an adequate supply—but even before Tony came, I never drank anything by myself at home, the way you do. And Lolly can't stand the stuff—she never even has a glass of wine."

Mrs. Potter did not intend to defend the before-dinner drink that had been her custom before she took up Gussie's diet. She certainly wasn't going to reveal that Lolly had a taste for vodka, if not for wine. Instead she tried again to speak up for Walter and Elna. "I don't know what they were talking about," she said, "but Lolly must know. She knew them better than anyone else."

"Oh, *Lolly.*" Helen dismissed any possible opinion her daughter might have had. "She hadn't any idea. All I can tell you is that they marched in to see me, bags all packed, gave their notice, then walked right out the front door and out of the house," Helen said bitterly. "And I have a suspicion they walked right into a job in New York the next day with summer people I know, which is the last straw. You don't suppose Gussie could spare Teresa for me until I find a new couple, do you?" She looked at the watch on her impossibly thin wrist.

Mrs. Potter declined to answer, quickly repeating instead that she'd be back for a proper viewing of the room another day when they both had more time. How little Helen seems to notice Lolly, she thought. It never occurred to her that Elna's warning about the liquor referred to anyone but herself. And she seems to have ignored whatever Lolly might have known or thought about Walter and Elna's leaving.

"Let's walk together down Main Street," she said as Helen checked the lock on the garden room door. "I'm on my way to see how the new little bakeshop is doing and to pick up a few loaves of Portuguese bread for Gussie and me, and for Mittie and Mary Lynne. Want some?"

"*Bread?* Heavens, no!" Helen said, as if the word itself were unfamiliar to her. "But I do know about the new business Klaus Muller's son has started. We knew his parents in St. Louis before Mrs. Muller died. *Excellent* firm. There was a time when I considered a joint venture—Latham and Muller—but Lester just couldn't be pushed into any kind of expansion. Along with the watchbands, which were all he cared about, we made college rings and fraternity pins, and the Mullers had a furniture subsidiary that made college chairs. You know, the kind with an emblem decal, the ones everybody buys at their fifth reunion?"

Mrs. Potter smiled, and Helen continued, her voice suddenly shaking with vehemence. "I could have made a tremendous thing out of Latham Jewelry and the Muller chair division. I don't know how many other ideas I had that Lester refused to consider. I ran the business for a while, you know, after his death, but the old board of directors was equally impossible, and I finally decided to sell out and move here to stay."

Perhaps here was a clue as to why Lester Latham had taken his own life. Mrs. Potter had wondered in the past why that plump, serious, bespectacled little man could have killed himself, and in such a violent manner. He had seemed such a quiet, passionless person to have been under such obviously unbearable pressures. How hard it must be for his daughter, she thought again, to have that memory and also to realize how much like him she had always looked to be, even as a pale, plump, unsmiling baby.

"For someone as competent and knowledgeable as you are," Mrs. Potter said, "I expect all you need from a lawyer is what Lew used to call having them sprinkle holy water on your tax returns." They continued to walk down Main Street. "I suppose you used Ozzie to do that for you?"

"He could be useful," Helen said carelessly. "He put his name on my returns, and he registered the name for me for the Latham Foundation, but that's something any lawyer can do in his sleep as long as nobody else has it."

Mrs. Potter tried to collect her wits. Helen setting up something called the Latham Foundation? For *Tony?* Not the Ferencz Institute, or whatever Mittie had called it?

The appearance of Victor Sandys, coming out of the clothing store on their right, forestalled further questions. "Murray's are having January sales," he explained, justifying his armload of packages.

Noting the new fur-lined storm coat he was wearing, one overlooked garment tag still sewn to a sleeve, the new porkpie tweed hat, the rich cashmere muffler, and the discreet gleam of new heavy walking brogues, it was clear that not all of Victor's purchases were those boxed and cradled in his protective arms.

"Victor must have sold a book again at last, after all these years," Helen remarked as the two women proceeded down the street, leaving Victor to transfer his bundles into what looked to be a new car parked around the corner. "I think he's blowing his advance royalties, and if that car is his, he's doing better for himself than he ever has before, for as long as I've known him."

Helen's good-bye was lost in the small throng of shoppers in line in front of the bakeshop. Mrs. Potter waved as she left, then took her place behind the others, surrounded with the heady perfume of baking bread.

"If it's like this in January, what'll it be when the summer people get here?" a stout woman was saying. Her companion seemed unperturbed. "Don't shove," she admonished someone behind her. "I can see the counter and there's plenty today."

A third speaker joined. "If I didn't know different, I'd say Manny was back. That bread's some good, as good as Manny ever made—and they say it's a young Kraut who's the new baker, somewhere out there in the back of the store. Hard to figure out where there'd be room for it."

The stout woman answered. "All I know is he's baking right this minute. You can smell it. Probably the only way they can keep the little place aired out is to have the ventilator right out on the street."

As the line grew shorter, there was a break in the press of afternoon bread-buyers, and Mrs. Potter finally found herself in the shop and for the moment the only customer.

"Mary, it's a smash hit!" she said. "Congratulations, both to you and to Hans! Mrs. Van Vleeck and I think his bread is just as wonderful as your Uncle Manny's, and this merchandising idea of yours is a winner."

Mary Rezendes was glowing, her pale biscuit-colored skin faintly moist with excitement and the heat of the small room. "It's such fun I can't tell you!" she said. "Every night we call Uncle Manny in Fort Lauderdale, and he can't *believe* how much bread we're selling now. Hans says if our present sales continue, even at a slightly slower pace once the original novelty wears off, we can do even a little better than break even for the next few months, which was all we had hoped for. Then, with the Daffodil Festival in April, we're going to begin real off-island promotion, and by summer Hans is convinced we'll be big business! Isn't it fantastic?"

Remembering Gussie's promise that they would learn to make Portuguese bread, and Hans's assurance that he would be their teacher, Mrs. Potter again sent her compliments to the baker, whose work had been done hours earlier and at least eight blocks away. "We'll give you time to get all this going," she told Mary, "before we take you up on those lessons. We'll wait until things settle down a bit for you."

And for me, too, she thought. "For now," she said, "you'd better give me six loaves. Two each, one sliced and one not, in three separate bags, if that's not a nuisance." She looked at her watch. There would be time to take one bag to Mary Lynne with the hope of finding her home for a quick visit, then to deliver another as promised to Mittie's door, although not time to buy a new colored leotard. She'd have to exercise in the old balbriggan pajamas another day.

As the crusty round loaves went into bags, she was able to voice a question, even though it was one she had intended to dismiss. "You know chemistry, Mary," she said. "I've read old mystery novels about cyanide being used in greenhouses once upon a time. I don't suppose you'd know anything about it?"

"Well, Uncle Manny's older brother used to be a gardener on the island, years ago," Mary said, "and I'm sure he told me potassium cyanide was used fairly commonly then. Of course, it was tricky to handle and you had to know what you were doing."

"I suppose it's illegal now?" Mrs. Potter asked. "I mean, it really *is* deadly poison, isn't it?"

Mary made an effort to speak as a Radcliffe honors graduate. "Oh, yes, it's deadly," she said. "The Food and Drug people outlawed it for general use years ago. I remember it's used commercially in electroplating metals and in photography, but I'm sure only with the strictest kind of controls."

Another customer entered the shop before Mrs. Potter could ask Mary Rezendes about old containers and how long old poisons remained lethal. She wondered, as she left the shop, how many dangerous and now illegal substances might be in her own garden cupboard at the ranch. DDT—could there be any of that left, on the back of a shelf? And what was it they had once used to sprinkle the gravel of the parking area to kill the hardy desert weeds? She had a sinking feeling that its other name might be Agent Orange. What was the only thing really effective against the Arizona ant colonies that made great barren circles around their central burrows, big enough to be seen from a plane thousands of feet in the air? That stuff was also a killer for the ferocious small red ants whose bites could be a stab of fire under your pants leg, just above your boot top. *Chlordane*, that's what it was. She knew there was still some of that around, even though they could no longer buy it. Was dieldrin off or on the approved list? Malathion? Her own shelves would not date back to days of prussic acid, but they still might hold a threat she hadn't ever really worried about.

Her reflections had led her down Orange Street to Mary Lynne's handsomely columned white house, another well-preserved mansion from the island's whaling past.

A quick yapping of small dogs responded to her rap on the brass knocker. Mary Lynne's surprised greeting, "Why, *hello* there, Genia!" as she answered the door, carried powerfully, unmistakably, almost overwhelmingly, a breath of chocolate and peanuts.

23

We all go off our diets once in a while, Mrs. Potter thought as she presented her gift of Portuguese bread, aware of Mary Lynne's split second of delay before her invitation to come in. It's a fact of life. No matter how well we're doing, we slip now and again—possibly because of an unresolved problem, anger, anxiety, sometimes it seems out of pure perversity.

If Mary Lynne was eating what she thought—the Goo Goo Clusters of her Tennessee youth—she was probably reacting to temporary stress, perhaps the responsibility of the new island tradition of the spring Daffodil Festival.

Once at Mary Lynne's urging in the past, Mrs. Potter had eaten a Goo Goo, a mound of chocolate, peanuts, caramel, and marshmallow apparently beloved by all who grew up south of the Mason-Dixon Line. She calculated the depth of Mary Lynne's probable remorse tomorrow, as she followed her into the high-ceilinged parlor, noting again how much weight she had lost and how lightly she moved.

To keep herself at this slim weight, Mary Lynne, a woman of medium height, not given to active sports, was likely to have a maintenance calorie limit, to be generous, of not more than fifteen hundred calories. It wouldn't take many Goo Goos to blow that sky-high.

Mary Lynne led her to a curved Victorian love seat, and as she did so, Mrs. Potter noticed that by a slight nudge of the toe she had at the same time pushed a flat box, lying on the floor, under the skirt of a yellow damask-covered wing chair.

Two small dogs, yapping rather crossly, rushed back and forth across the room, first glaring at her with unconcealed dislike, then back to sniff, questioningly, at the base of the yellow chair.

"You'll have to forgive my babies," Mary Lynne said quickly, picking up a small multicolored dog under each arm. "You haven't learned your party manners yet, have you, lambies? Mother's going to put you in your pretty bedroom now, and we'll have us a good little romp later. 'Scuse me a minute, Genia, honey? Incidentally, whatever happened to that beautiful Weimaraner of yours?"

Mrs. Potter was able only to murmur, "He's dead now," in a tone that invited no further inquiry.

"I remember he had such a nice name," Mary Lynne continued, still holding a dog under each arm. "This little girl is Sen-Sen, but I haven't got the right name yet for brother."

"Sen-Sen?" Mrs. Potter asked. "You mean that pinhead-size dark stuff—licoricish and peppery—the bad boys used to chew to cover up the smell of cigarettes on their breath?"

"Or moonshine," Mary Lynne said wisely. "I think it sounds so oriental, don't you? And spicy and lively? Just like her. But I can't get the absolutely perfect right name for my boy. You and Gussie put your minds to it and help me think of one."

As Mary Lynne left with the small dogs, still noisy in their excitement, Mrs. Potter noticed that her toe gave a second small nudge to the box, with which it disappeared completely from sight beneath the skirted chair.

The absolutely perfect name for little brother is obvious, she decided, but this is not the time to suggest it. I'm glad Mary Lynne didn't mention it, and even more grateful that she didn't offer me any. She was not sure whether the idea of a binge with Goo Goos was terribly funny or totally revolting.

When Mary Lynne rejoined her a few seconds later, sharp complaints continued from the two little dogs somewhere in the back of the house.

Ignoring them, Mrs. Potter issued a reassuring bulletin, as she had done with Helen over the phone the evening before. Beth was slightly under the weather, she said, but everyone felt sure that after a few days with Laurence and Paula in Providence, she soon would be fine again. As soon as she could, she began in a roundabout way to approach the subject of Mittie's casual allusion earlier in the afternoon. She wanted to know about Tony's being on the scene when Bo died.

"Everyone's so proud of you, Mary Lynne," she began.

"You mean the festival?" Mary Lynne asked. "You know just as well as you're sitting here on my love seat, Genia Potter, that there's no way in the world I could run that whole great big whoop-te-do by myself if every single soul on the island wasn't helping me with it, night and day."

"I'm very sure not only that you could run the whole show very competently," Mrs. Potter replied, "but that you're actually doing so, in spite of all this modesty. Come on, Mary Lynne, don't play helpless southern belle with me. We've known each other too long."

Mary Lynne's wide smile pursed into a small grimace, the gesture of a child caught in an innocent prank.

"I wasn't thinking of the festival," Mrs. Potter continued. "I know it will be a huge success again this year and that you know exactly what you're doing, as you always do. I hope to be back for it. What I'm talking about is how you managed as you did in the sailboat when Bo was taken ill. Forgive me if it's painful to talk about it, but ever since Gussie called to tell me last summer—was it August?—I've been marveling at how you were able to handle that big sloop alone and get back for help."

"You don't want to hear that old story again, Genia," Mary Lynne protested. "Honest to gracious goodness, everybody's made too much of it. Bo had his attack when we were sailing, that's what happened, when we were way up the harbor on the Coatue side, past the Five Fingers and just off Coskata. He was the one that was wonderful, not me."

"Gussie said all the other boats were out of hailing distance," Mrs. Potter went on. "To think that the harbor was full of boats, as it would have been at that time of year, but none of them close enough to hear you call for help." She was suddenly aware of how really awful it must have been.

"It was just plain the worst thing that ever happened in my whole entire life," Mary Lynne replied. "There was Bo sailing along, merry as a Tennessee cricket, saying how glad he was to get me to go out sailing with him, which, honestly Genia, I tried to get out of whenever I could. I'm not used to boats and usually I'm scared out of my mind and sick as a pup. But that day was bright and calm and he talked me into it."

"And then he was suddenly taken ill?" Mrs. Potter asked, shaken. She had come to find out how Tony Ferencz and Ozzie deBevereaux were involved in the rescue, but she knew that until now she had not fully understood Mary Lynne's ordeal.

"I'm not much of a saltwater sailor myself," she went on. "I grew up with canoes and rowboats and outboards, and some of us had small sailboats, but here I didn't go out in our old Indian alone. The children did, but I know it meant using both arms and legs, right down to both big toes, to do it. It was like yours, I think—twenty-two feet, wood hull, Marconi rigged, with a centerboard? Anyway, the three of them were all such good sailors and so were their friends that usually all I had to do was enjoy myself and remember to duck when someone called 'Ready about, *hard alee!*' That, and to bring the sandwiches and Cokes. I'm sure I couldn't have taken over and sailed it all by myself as you did."

"Yes, an Indian," Mary Lynne said vaguely. "I gave it to the Yacht Club later and I don't know what happened to it. Anyway, it had a little triangle sail in front—that's called the jib, Genia—and a big triangle sail with a long stick across the bottom, and that stick is the boom."

"Yes, I know," Mrs. Potter said.

"And I knew about the centerboard," Mary Lynne continued. "Bo pulled it up in shallow water that day, near shore, and then let it down again as soon as we were back where the water was deeper. He'd explained all this to me before, too, but honestly, I never paid a bit of attention. I just thought about other things and said, 'Oh, I *see.*' That day I was just riding along, and for the first time in my life, honest-to-goodness almost enjoying it."

"Tell me what happened," Mrs. Potter urged, wondering how she might have acted in Mary Lynne's place.

As Mary Lynne spoke, she could visualize the far reaches of the harbor in summer, dancing blue in the sun, dotted with sails, and she heard Mary Lynne's story as if it were taking place before her eyes.

The big man, laughing and talking, at ease in his boat in the late morning sun, suddenly felt a pain in his neck and shoulder.

"Come back and sit by me," he asked his wife in a strained voice. "See if you can steer for a bit. I'll tell you what to do."

He showed her how to pick a spot on the horizon and tried to explain how to hold the boat steady on course for it. "That's it," he said. "The Wauwinet House. It's big enough to see."

The pain increased. "That's good," he encouraged her. "Just hold her steady."

Then without speaking again he fell forward on his face, lying heavy and motionless on coiled lines and damp floorboards, dislocating a plastic bailing bucket, which rolled forward slowly, making a dull clatter.

The woman dropped her grasp of the tiller and dropped to his side, but found herself unable to lift him or even to squeeze herself into the space directly beside his bulk and the centerboard. He did not answer when she spoke to him, her cries and entreaties increasing, unheeded.

A flat paddle lay at her side, and she seized it and began to wave it aloft, shouting now for help to other sails in the distance. No one saw her or heard her.

The breeze freshened and the big sail, now swinging free, threatened to knock her off her feet. She crawled back to the tiller, beneath the wildly careening boom, trying frantically to remember what she had been doing before, when she had been told to keep her eye on the big hotel across the harbor.

Now the sloop regained headway and the swinging boom was no longer a danger as long as she held her course with the following wind. The man in the bottom of the boat was silent and motionless.

The wind changed slightly and with a sickening thud the heavy boom now swung to the other side. She was only just able to duck as it passed her head. The boat seemed to be moving faster now in the water, and she desperately wished she knew how to make it slow down so that she could go back to the motionless figure, facedown, just beyond her feet.

At last the beach of the summer hotel was ahead. The boat approached it rapidly, head on, until the woman heard and felt its rough scraping on the sandy bottom in the shallow water. Again the boom went wild. The woman knew the boat would overturn, until she remembered how she had been shown to raise the centerboard. Then, at last, she saw too how to release the line to lower the straining, threatening sail.

Mary Lynne took a deep breath, as if in an effort to regain her calm, and again the rich smell of chocolate and peanuts came across the space between her chair and the Victorian settee.

"Sorry if I seem upset," Mary Lynne apologized. "Of course, I get stirred up remembering all this again, but besides that I had some news this morning that makes a difference in my future plans. And beside *that,* I had an important appointment canceled for four o'clock, and that's what's really bothering me at the moment."

"What happened when you came ashore on the beach?" Mrs. Potter asked. Now she must concentrate on the information she had come for.

"The boat just coasted right up on the sand," Mary Lynne concluded her story, "and I started screaming for help. And you won't believe it, but Tony Ferencz was the first one out of the hotel, and everyone said how providential that was, with his medical knowledge, so that if anything *could* have been done for Bo, there wouldn't have been any delay. But of course he was already gone. I'm sure he died instantly."

"He was dead, then, by the time you came ashore," Mrs. Potter repeated sadly. "You know how sorry we all were, Mary Lynne. I've written you several times and I want to say it again now. But until today I hadn't really been able to imagine what a terrible ordeal you'd gone through."

Mary Lynne's voice took on a touch of indignation. "Ozzie deBevereaux was there, too. He and that secretary of his came rushing down from the veranda, and he was worse than no help at all. He just kept hopping up and down and saying, 'Get that man away from him!' and 'Call a doctor, Edie!' and trying to push in beside Tony. As if *he* knew anything about it!

"The comforting part about that," she continued, "was that somebody told Peter later on that Ozzie had been yelling at Tony, practically accusing him of not knowing what to do for Bo, and Peter was wonderful. He told everybody he didn't know what Ozzie must have been thinking of."

The old clock ticking on the mantel showed three forty-five. "Gussie's expecting me," Mrs. Potter said reluctantly. "She's a stickler for exercise time. I hope you enjoy the Portuguese bread, but give it away if it's any threat to that diet of yours. You really look beautiful at that weight, and you're a great advertisement for Tony, just as Gussie is."

Mary Lynne sounded uncertain. "I've been hoping Tony's program and treatments could help a lot more people in the future," she said as Mrs. Potter reached the door. "I thought it would be simply marvelous if we all could help him set up a world-famous center for beauty and rejuvenation here on the island. He plans to call it 'Daffodil House'! Isn't that perfect?"

Mary Lynne's brush of cheeks, saying good-bye, was scented with chocolate and peanuts, and Mrs. Potter left wondering whether it might have been the awareness of trust limitations on spending, the cancellation of the four o'clock appointment, or a combination of both, that had been the reason she had gone off her diet.

One more brief encounter, this by chance, was to provide speculation for even more yellow-pad notes later on. As Mrs. Potter hurried across her shortcut path to the church parking lot and came out on Fair Street, she found Leah leaving the church.

"I wish we could chat a minute," Mrs. Potter said, "but I've got to get home. May I stop in for a cup of tea someday soon? I'd love to have a visit, just the two of us."

Leah seemed flushed and in some way embarrassed.

"I don't mean to be a nuisance," Mrs. Potter said easily. "Just give me a ring some day."

Leah was quick to insist her eagerness for just such a chat, but she still seemed ill at ease. In what seemed an irrepressible burst of confidence, she explained that she, too, was in a hurry.

"Tony's expecting me at the Scrim at four," she said. "He just called and said he had found himself free, and that he's going to begin a new series of treatments for me. Don't you say a word about this to Gussie or anybody, will you? He'd be furious if he knew I even mentioned it."

Leah's retreating back as she hurried down the street looked very young. She was wearing leather boots to the knee, and above these her pleated wool skirt swung as jauntily as a teen-ager's below her dark reefer.

She looks and sounds like a woman on her way to a lovers' tryst instead of an appointment with a diet doctor, Mrs. Potter found herself thinking. Leah—the world's greatest widow? Leah, with new green sparkle in her eyes and a swing in her step?

Since she was thinking of him, it came as only a small surprise to have Gussie speaking of Tony when she returned to the house.

"I asked him to join us for dinner, just the three of us," Gussie was saying. "You know I'm dying to have you two know each other better, and I certainly don't want you to go on believing bad things about him just because of a dubious story about Ozzie deBevereaux's daughter all those years ago."

"What time is he coming?" Mrs. Potter asked, tired after her afternoon rounds, thinking that if she was going to exercise a half hour every day, she'd rather do it in the morning than at four in the afternoon, and wondering if she really wanted to see Tony Ferencz this evening.

"Oh, he's *not,*" Gussie said, with obvious disappointment. "I said I *asked* him. But he's tied up with a business appointment this afternoon at four and he felt it might go on into the evening, so we made it for tomorrow night instead."

"That's fine," Mrs. Potter said, with what she hoped was not obvious relief. "You and I were up too late last night worrying about Beth. Let's make this Health Night, shall we, and go to bed early? I challenge you to one game of cribbage after dinner. Loser runs the dishwasher and turns off the lights."

She knew she couldn't wait to get back to those yellow pages, and there was nothing in today's notes that she could possibly share with Gussie.

One of these, she knew, would have to do with Tony's possibly prolonged business appointment. She now knew that he was, in various ways, playing the field, although Helen and Gussie appeared to hold top priority. This made him seem less and less a suitable candidate for Gussie's fourth husband.

Another note, even more serious, would be how she could make sure Tony had not withheld lifesaving emergency treatment from Bo, even though Peter, who must have known Ozzie very well, had assured everyone that Ozzie's apparent suspicions were not to be taken seriously.

She wanted to write down Walter's doom-filled reason for leaving and Elna's parting admonition about liquor, with an added note of how little Helen knew about her daughter.

She wanted to ponder whether anyone would murder a

trust officer for refusal to let her give away property that represented her only security.

It seemed a lot to think about until she reminded herself of Beth.

24

At breakfast the next morning—fresh juice of celery and carrot, with the usual handful of parsley added, and today for a special fillip, raw turnip, its small crest of top leaves included—Gussie returned to the subject of Beth's sudden deep depression and alarmingly erratic behavior.

"I'm going to call Paula and Laurence as soon as I think they'll be up," she said. "Certainly seven thirty can't be too early. They have young children and Laurence is a hardworking lawyer. He probably gets to his office by nine."

The report was brief. Beth was still resting quietly at the hospital and the doctor preferred that she not have visitors for a few more days. Whether that sounded bad or good, it was hard to tell.

Listening, Mrs. Potter sipped a second cup of breakfast tea, which she found restorative while her system absorbed the calcium Gussie assured her the turnip juice was pouring into her teeth and bones.

"I think we should go to the science library this afternoon and check Beth's notes on poisonous plants," Gussie said, Beth still on her mind.

"There are probably a lot of others," Mrs. Potter prophesied soberly.

Earlier she had reexamined the crumpled pages of Beth's notes. "These look pretty detailed and complete once you get them all laid out," she said. "Still, you're probably right about more research. If it suits your morning plans, I think I'll go out for a bit now." She headed for the back hall coatrack. "Be back to go to the library with you later. I'll have lunch out before then and give you a rest."

"Fine," Gussie called back cheerfully from the library. "Ozzie's nephew is on the island to distribute his clients' files, and he's coming with mine at eleven. Meantime I'll organize things for dinner when Tony comes tonight. Don't forget your diet, and I expect a full report on everything you eat and drink. Shall we count on doing the library about two thirty?"

Arnold Sallanger first, Mrs. Potter decided as she started out into the January sunshine, only slightly muted by a fine white film overhead between island and sky. He used to have morning office hours after his hospital rounds. If Jenny Spicer is still his office nurse and receptionist, maybe she'll squeeze me in for a quick few minutes with him, just to say hello.

A very pregnant young woman was coming out of the small neat brick building, whose doorway plaque was engraved in script with the name *A. R. Sallanger, M.D.*

"Mrs. Potter!" Jenny greeted her with affectionate surprise as she entered the small waiting room. Jenny's hug and kiss were warming, and Mrs. Potter thought how much this happy, energetic little woman, no longer young, contributed to Arnold Sallanger's practice of medicine. Maybe some people only need that hug and kiss to feel better, she thought, and maybe Arnold is the one doctor in the world with enough humor and humility to admit the possibility.

"Doctor's still at the hospital," Jenny told her. "Seems to be baby season. I'm trying to persuade him to bring in a partner, a young OB. This day-and-night stuff is too much at his age. Not that he's *old*," she amended hastily, "any more than I am. But all these new young Navy wives on the island are keeping him busier than one man ought to be."

"He'd have enough to do just looking after all his old patients, I'd imagine," Mrs. Potter said. "Although the ranks are getting thinner, like losing Ozzie deBevereaux last week. Ab Leland and Fan Carpenter died before I left, but there was Gordon Van Vleeck last fall. Not to mention Bo Heidecker last August. He was a patient too, wasn't he?"

The waiting room was unoccupied and Jenny moved about as she spoke, rotating the bowl of flowering narcissus on her desk against the sun, plucking off a dead leaf or two from the plants on the front windowsill, reaching up with a practiced finger to test the moisture of the hanging pot of Swedish ivy.

"That was a hard one for Mrs. Heidecker," she remarked. "I suppose you know the story of how he died out in the sailboat."

Mrs. Potter nodded. "Awful for her," she agreed, "particularly if his heart attack was as unexpected as Mr. deBevereaux's. Or had he had warnings?"

"Oh, he'd been a patient of Doctor's for quite a time for it," Jenny said, debating whether to snap off a flowering red geranium head, still colorful but beginning to shed a few petals, like great drops of blood, on the waiting room carpet. She snapped it. "The reason he retired when he did was a first heart attack back in Tennessee—I thought you'd have known. None of my business to mention it, but I still think if he hadn't taken up smoking again, and hadn't put on so much weight, he might never have had that second one out in the boat."

Jenny had provided part of the information Mrs. Potter was seeking. Bo's fatal heart attack was not unexpected. Her brief, unhappy suspicions on that score seemed groundless. "I suppose he died instantly, then," she said, "the way most people say they want to go, doing something they really love, as he loved sailing."

"Nobody knows if it was *instant*," Jenny said, striving for professional accuracy. "Doctor thought so. That new Count Tony, whatever his name is, administered CPR, so they said, but it was apparently way too late. The funny thing was that Mr. deBevereaux asked me that same thing, the next day, and so did Peter Benson, the man who owns the Scrimshaw. All I could tell them was that a half hour later, when they got him in town to the hospital, the general agreement was he'd been dead maybe an hour."

So both Ozzie and Peter had been suspicious of Tony, just as she, instinctively, had been when she found out he'd been the first one to reach Bo's body in the sailboat. It was a relief to find that the three of them had been wrong about this, chiefly because Mary Lynne need not face the added sorrow of thinking something might have been done to save his life.

After a few exchanged inquiries about each other's families, Mrs. Potter left, saying she'd try to schedule a checkup for herself while she was on the island. I think I'll lose a few more pounds before I do, she decided. I don't want Jenny Spicer, much as I love her, looking up old records until I'm sure the scale won't show any added pounds since my last visit.

She walked briskly, rehearsing notes for the yellow pad when she got home. A quick stop to see Larry, the hairdresser, had to be next on her list. Disliking herself for the subterfuge, she would use the pretext of consulting him about having her hair cut.

Fortunately the only customer in the small shop was an elderly woman Mrs. Potter knew to be deaf, asleep under the dryer. Predictably, Larry recommended a new hairstyle. Mrs. Potter studied the illustrations he showed her in a glossy trade publication, and actually looked with some interest as Larry unpinned her hair, tousled and lifted it, showed her—almost convincingly—that she could look younger and better if he took her in charge.

"I'll have to think about it a little longer," she told him. "All my friends look so much better these days. I'm sure you deserve a lot of the credit, but of course it all seems to have begun when Count Ferencz came to the island."

Larry apparently had no reservations about Tony. "The man is great," he said. "All my rich widows—excuse me, all my best clients—look better. Better hair, better figures. I think he gives them vitamin shots."

He brushed Mrs. Potter's hair into an approximation of cotton candy of a flavor she could not define. An anemic taffy, she decided. "All my regulars are eating out of his hand," he went on. "Even the Latham girl, not that she ever comes here to the shop, seems to be gone on him, the way I saw her looking at him on Main Street the other day. Not that he'd bother with *her*."

Mrs. Potter was torn between the wish to learn more from Larry and the embarrassed realization that she had stooped to exchanging gossip with her friends' hairdresser.

"You like the man?" she asked. "What do people around town think of him?"

"Maybe there's a few who aren't so keen on him," Larry admitted. "I'm told Peter Benson might be having some second thoughts about him, but he's too good a guy to turn the man out—that's the way I've got it figured out. Personally I think he ought to cash in on that private beauty hotel everybody's talking about, with a resident plastic surgeon and the works. He could do the kitchen. And wouldn't it be something if yours truly was the official hairdresser? Put in a word for me if you get a chance, will you?"

The arrival of a young woman with two children for haircuts provided a chance for Mrs. Potter to escape without committing herself to having one herself, and she promised to let Larry know what she decided.

It was a little early, she thought, for lunch, but perhaps all the better time to catch Peter before the influx of other luncheon guests at the Scrimshaw. Jadine was lighting a freshly laid fire when she arrived, and the room was, as always, warm and welcoming.

It *is* like a club, she thought. Peter is the one who ought to be setting up an exclusive, expensive diet-resort hotel for rich widows, a place with wonderful food, artfully planned and skillfully cooked for trimming off a few pounds, with an exercise program geared for fun and relaxation as well as figure-molding. A good hairdresser, of course, and whatever other amenities seemed necessary in the pursuit of health and beauty without setting impossible goals. With Peter to run it, it would be a place where his "guys"—she knew all his guests would be his "guys"—would have fun, feel better, maybe even live longer.

"Afraid I haven't got the salad bar set up yet," Jadine informed her, "and it's too late for breakfast, but what can I get you? Mr. B.'s already sent out the luncheon menu, so look it over and maybe you'll see something you'd like there, if it's ready yet. Or, how about a cocktail while I finish the salad setup?"

Mrs. Potter hesitated. If she ordered a glass of white wine, she'd have to confess it to Gussie. I'll be shot for a sheep, she decided, or a goat. Whatever. "Yes, a martini please, Jadine. Bombay gin on the rocks, very little vermouth, and a twist of lemon. Mr. Benson knows how I like them, if he's in the bar pantry, and if he is, Jadine, and he's not too busy, will you ask him if he has time to come out for a minute?"

Peter himself brought the drink. "Naughty, naughty, Potter," he admonished her. "Sneaking one behind Gussie's back, are you?" They laughed together with the ease of old friends as she told him, quite happily, that that was just what she was doing and that she had already composed her speech of contrition.

"Sit down a minute, Peter?" she asked. "If you have time?"

The square, tweedy figure took the chair beside her own. "Let's have it, Potter," he said. "You've got something on your mind. Tell Uncle Peter all about it, if you can do it in"— he looked at the watch on his wrist—"in exactly five minutes. I'm timing a pan of fish timbales for lunch, to be served with a spoonful of lobster Newburg. Very simple, but they'll be nice."

"I'll come right to the point," Mrs. Potter told him. "I think Gussie is falling for this Count Tony Ferencz of yours, and I can't bear to think of her having another unhappy marriage after the several quite miserable years she had with Gordon. So I'm playing father of the bride, or whatever you'd call it. I'd like to learn something more about the man, besides the fact that he's handsome and sexy as all get out and that all my friends think he's God's gift to Nantucket."

"Good question," Peter said, his voice sober and quiet, all hint of laughter gone. "He's staying at the inn for the winter, so I guess you think he's here under my sponsorship. Actually he's not my guest and I'm not going to tell you who the bills go to. When he came to the island last summer, I hadn't seen him for twenty years. He stayed with various friends as a houseguest through the summer, I think, and for August, as I recall, he was staying with some people you'd probably know in one of the houses out at Wauwinet."

(So Tony *did* have a reason to be there, Mrs. Potter thought. His being the first to reach the sailboat was natural enough.)

"How did you come to know him?" Mrs. Potter asked.

"Oh, I was learning the restaurant business then," Peter explained, "in New York. I was sort of a rotating apprentice at what was a rather fashionable place in the East Sixties. It folded up since—I don't think I had anything to do with *that* —but at the time it was drawing pretty classy trade, and part of the owner's secret was that Count Tony Ferencz was plugging the place with his society clients, people who had just taken him up as a health and beauty authority. No doubt but that Tony was well paid for what he did for the place. Anyway, I got to know him then and we remembered each other right away when he turned up here last summer."

Mrs. Potter decided to be direct. "Is he heré, then, as a drawing card for the Scrimshaw, Peter?" she asked. "You're doing too well here to need anything like that. It doesn't sound like you, Peter, if you want me to be honest about it."

Peter's response seemed uncomfortable. "Of course I don't need Tony Ferencz or anybody else to show me how to run this place, Potter. I know as much about diet and health and nutrition as he does, and a heck of a lot more about making it taste good. But he showed up, and all the guys fell for him— Latham, Carpenter, Heidecker, even your dear Gussie—and one thing led to another. . . ." Peter's friendly face clouded. "Anyway, he's here for the winter, and he sees a few clients in his rooms upstairs. He seems to feel pretty much at home at the Scrim, but I don't really feel I know him, even now."

"You're being evasive, Peter. What I want is your honest opinion of Tony as a person. Is he good enough for Gussie?"

It seemed obvious that Peter was speaking against his will. "There may be a few things I don't like," he admitted slowly. "There were some questions about how and when Heidecker's husband died, and personally I didn't much like the thought that he was treating Gordon Van Vleeck last fall. But nobody seems to take these seriously."

He hesitated, and then his ready smile prompted her own. "He may be as terrific as the guys think he is. You're a better one to decide about that than I am, Potter."

"Everybody says he's going to set up an exclusive private diet clinic here on the island. What about that?" Mrs. Potter persisted.

"Yeah, I heard that story too, including hair by Larry of Nantucket and food by yours truly at the Scrimshaw. I don't know what's going on, Potter, any more than you do, and probably a darned sight less."

Peter looked at the watch on his square muscular wrist. "Hey, I've got to get back to my timbales. Tell Jadine what you want and I'll fix it for you."

Mrs. Potter nodded. As she had suspected, Peter shared her doubts about his friend but was too honest and loyal to say more. She bent to inhale a cold, gin-fragrant whiff of her drink. "One more quick question," she said as Peter rose to leave for the kitchen. "Do you know where Tony was between the time you first knew him in New York and when he turned up here on the island?"

"Oh, sure." Peter's reply was easy. "His mother, Eva, ran a health spa of some kind in Europe and he was there working with her until she had a run-in with the authorities over something—some kind of tricky stuff. Nothing he's using now, I'm sure."

The martini was as good as Mrs. Potter remembered, realizing with amusement that she was enjoying it as a past and bygone treat, although she had actually been on the island only a week.

So Tony had been in Europe, improving his knowledge of diet and health at his mother's establishment. Had someone mentioned Romania? Was that the yogurt place, where people lived practically forever? Or the glandular injection clinic? Was the "tricky stuff" that supposedly magic but illegal drug with the wonderful name—what was it?—*Gerovital?* Other vague recollections of miracle cures and treatments, from half-read pages in *Vogue* and *Harper's Bazaar* and *Éclat,* came to mind as Mrs. Potter sipped her martini.

Jadine appeared at her side.

"Lunch?" Mrs. Potter responded, roused from her conjectures. "Oh, yes, *lunch.* I'll have the fish timbale with lobster sauce if it's ready, Jadine. I might as well make my confession a good one."

25

"*Everything's* poisonous," Gussie whispered, although she and Mrs. Potter were the only occupants of the long table, and for the moment the only visitors in the science library, which in summer would have been crowded with bird watchers, wild-flower fanciers, and other nature lovers of all ages, studying Nantucket flora and fauna. Today, watching them with little apparent interest, Lolly Latham leaned on the desk at the end of the room, occasionally dropping a pencil or rustling through a wastebasket.

"Shh, it's not that bad," Mrs. Potter whispered back. "Show me your list."

Gussie slid her yellow pad across the table, one of the two Mrs. Potter had brought along for their note-taking. "Nice innocent little lily of the valley. How do you like that?"

Mrs. Potter read the notes. "Leaves, roots, flowers, and fruits contain cardiac glycoside . . . symptoms loss of appetite, irregular heartbeat, nausea . . . hallucinations . . . heart failure."

"Awful," she murmured, pushing back Gussie's pad. "At least you say it's not as potent as some other plants in the family and that it tastes worse. I suppose that's something to cheer for."

Gussie was already immersed in another page. "Listen to this!" she whispered. "Delphinium seeds! Fatal if eaten in large quantities! When I think of all the delphiniums I've planted from seeds—tiny little dark things—you could bake them on a poppy-seed roll and not notice the difference."

Mrs. Potter felt an inner chill thinking of minced dumbcane leaves atop a green salad and remembering the look of agonized bafflement in a girl's eyes as her throat closed, cutting off her last breath, with the sounds of "Happy Birthday" fading away.

The two women again bent closely over their books, a shared small stack Lolly had piled haphazardly in front of them. They had long passed checking the sources of Beth's crumpled notes about dieffenbachia and foxglove. *"Digitalis purpurea,"* Gussie had written earlier. "She had it all straight."

"Poisonous common houseplants," Mrs. Potter now said, half under her breath, writing rapidly. "Daffodil, rhubarb, holly, Jerusalem cherry, English ivy. Mistletoe! How's that for a dual-purpose Christmas trim—kiss or kill, whichever suits your fancy."

"Nerium oleander," Gussie reported. "Leah has some, houseplants about eighteen inches tall, and they bloomed indoors for her all last spring and summer. And here's *ranunculus*—the flowers we had on our tea table Saturday! But no, I guess they just might give you dermatitis. . . ."

She was silent again, then leaned across the table. "Did you ever see Erica Wilson's crewel design called 'Woody Nightshade'? It was gorgeous the way she worked it, with purple leaves and yellow flowers and red berries. Here it's called climbing nightshade—even more poisonous than deadly nightshade, which we've all read about in old mystery novels."

Lolly approached the table. "Are you finding what you want? When you're ready, I can bring you what we have on poisonous mushrooms." She paused as the two, sighing, shook their heads and Gussie looked at her watch.

Mrs. Potter motioned Lolly to sit at her side. "I know Mrs. Higginson was here last week," she said earnestly, "and she seemed terribly upset and worried afterward. She said you were so very kind and helpful to her, so I'm sure you remember. Can you tell us about what happened that day? Last Thursday, wasn't it, Gussie?"

Lolly sat silent, twisting her fingers. "The day after your friend Edie died," Mrs. Potter said gently. "You remember— Mrs. Higginson said you walked home with her at the end of the afternoon."

"I guess maybe I did," Lolly said. "She was pretty nervous."

"And I think you even got her to talking about her own garden, just to get her calmed down," Mrs. Potter said. Lolly smiled uncertainly.

"Did she tell you why she was looking up plant poisons?" Mrs. Potter persisted.

"Not exactly," Lolly admitted. "I think she already knew all the answers. Mrs. Higginson knows a lot about herbs and garden plants. All I did was get out the books for her, the way I did for you and Mrs. Van Vleeck today."

"You realized how upset she was," Mrs. Potter said, kindly but decisively. "You walked her home and you even made tea for her. Tell us what she said, everything you can remember."

Lolly seemed even more uncertain and alarmed. "I *told* her she never meant to kill Edie and Mr. deBevereaux," she blurted suddenly. "I *told* her those two plants, the *Dieffenbachia J. Schott* and the *Digitalis purpurea,* probably wouldn't do anything more than make people sick for overnight. I *told* her I knew she hadn't meant to hurt them. It was like about a thousand to one, I told her so. You saw all the figures about how few people ever *died* from them. I told her it had to be just a horrible, horrible accident that they *died.*" Lolly's voice, lowered in spite of their being the only ones in the library, was now almost a whisper.

"I *told* her I knew it was just a horrible, horrible accident. I knew she never meant to kill Edie and Mr. deBevereaux."

Mrs. Potter turned to Gussie and began to stack the books on the table before them. "Thanks, Lolly, for all your help," she said as they gathered their notes to leave.

"Everything's poisonous," Gussie repeated mournfully as they were walking home in the early dusk. "Everything in your house or your garden is just sitting there *waiting* to do you in."

"It isn't that bad, and you know it," Mrs. Potter said. "Lots of plants contain poisonous substances, but honestly, Gussie, how many people actually ever *eat* them? I just read that castor beans are deadly, five beans for a child, eight for an adult. And yet Grandpa Andrews always planted a great row of them the whole west length of the barn, just because they were big and showy and easy to grow, and a background for Grandmother's hollyhocks. Nobody ever told Will and me they were poisonous. I'm sure nobody *knew* it, or Grandpa wouldn't have had them on the place."

"Did you ever eat a castor bean?" Gussie asked practically.

Mrs. Potter said that apparently it had never occurred to her or her brother to do so, and that in any case the very word *castor* would have evoked instant revulsion. "I can't drink grape juice to this day," she said, "because that's the way we had to take castor oil, supposedly disguised in the stuff." No, they would never have willingly eaten a castor bean, although she clearly remembered the high, rough plants, taller than sunflowers, and the hairy, tough seedpods that contained such deadly poison, unknown to them or their garden-loving grandmother.

"Remember our oleander hedges at the ranch?" she asked as they continued walking toward home.

Gussie nodded. *"Poisonous.* 'A single leaf may kill within twenty-four hours. Nausea, stomach pains, weakness, abnormal heartbeat, and coma.' I put that in my notes."

Yet, Mrs. Potter continued, while everybody says it's poisonous to both humans and animals, she had never known a single soul, or heard of a single horse or cow, who had actually even nibbled a leaf or blossom.

"A real killer here on Nantucket might be green hellebore, and you might mistake that for early skunk cabbage," Gussie said. "But who'd eat *that?*"

"People do eat pokeweed greens around here in the spring," Mrs. Potter said. "Maybe you should worry about that—shallow breathing, paralysis, spasms, convulsions—but that comes from the root, not the greens. I never pull wild flowers up by the roots, of course, but when I think of the *times* I've cut pokeweed to use for a flower arrangement once the berries are purple, late summer . . ."

"Nicotiana—I always grow that for the evening fragrance," Gussie said. "Potent alkaloid, vomiting, slow pulse, respiratory failure. It's too much!"

All the way home Mrs. Potter had considered telling Gussie that she knew who had poisoned Edie and Ozzie. She decided it was only fair to wait for further and incontrovertible proof.

The intensity in Lolly's voice when she said, "It was just a horrible accident," had told her two things. Edie and Ozzie were not supposed to have died. And Lolly Latham, for whatever reason or by whatever accident, had been the one to administer the dumb cane and foxglove.

Accidental poisonings do happen, part of her mind was telling her. Maybe with some frequency, in spite of her own perhaps unusually fortunate experience to the contrary. Nevertheless, the afternoon's research seemed to show that it would be a gamble, at best, to plan to murder someone that way. A premeditated killing—that is, if the perpetrator had any degree of sophistication in such matters—would employ something more certain, like a knife or a gun or a hypodermic injection.

If only Tony were not coming to dinner, she thought. Right now, for Gussie's sake, she must put all this out of her mind for a few hours. After that, she could decide what to do about it.

It was a relief, once they were home, to find there was no

time for exercise, and to sink into a warm and fragrant bath in the long old-fashioned tub. It was even a relief to know she must hurry to dress as she put on what Gussie had told her to wear—a deep-green wool dinner dress, long-sleeved and high-necked, its color a good background for her best but not-quite-emerald earrings. Still thinking of Lolly, she caught a quick look at herself in the long hall mirror before going down, and decided that she might look a little slimmer than a week ago.

Not that any such thought was related to Tony Ferencz, she told herself as he came across the parlor from where he was standing with Gussie in front of the fire, to bow lightly and kiss her hand. The challenge was there and unmistakable, but she knew her own inner response to be cool. This is not the man for me, she told herself, even if he seems to be for Gussie.

And for Helen and Leah and Mittie and Mary Lynne. Apparently he was the man for all of Les Girls except for Dee, and even Dee had succumbed to his undeniable appeal when she had married him, even if as much for reasons of ambition as of romance for them both. His taut lean body, his steady gray eyes, his slight accent, even the deep dome of his forehead, were all part of it.

More than any of these physical attributes there was the exhilarating flattery of his attention. If only just for the moment, she thought, he makes you feel you're the only woman in the room, in the world. That's his secret. You're *Eve*.

"Tony's never seen the town at night from the cupola," Gussie was saying. "We've decided to make a quick trip up to see the view and then come back to have our Perrier here by the fire. Grab a sweater or jacket, Genia, as we go up—it will be chilly up there, remember."

Tony was solicitous in wrapping Gussie's shoulders in a warm handwoven stole before they ascended the wide hall stairway. The radiance of her smile as he did so, looking directly into her eyes, made Mrs. Potter hope he really might be as wonderful as Gussie thought.

Any disquieting suspicions, she reminded herself as they

went up the second, narrower stairway, and the third one to the cupola, are, except for Dee's derogatory remarks and a few vague and unproven hints, entirely in my own mind. Also I must remember what I realized earlier. Plant poisons would not be the choice of a man who knows as much about both herbs and plants as Tony Ferencz must have learned in his years as a diet authority. The chances are much too heavily weighted on the side of their not being fatal. A killer *kills*. If Tony were a killer, he wouldn't administer something likely only to make someone sick for a few hours.

The lighted moon of the South Tower clock came to meet them through the windows; the town twinkled its lights on the streets below. "Your mirador," Tony said to Gussie, moving from one windowed side of the small room to the other. "Watchtower for a princess. I correct myself—watchtower for a great queen." Again his gray eyes fixed Gussie's.

She separated herself from his gaze with obvious effort, with the excuse that she just remembered something in the kitchen. Knowing the planned menu—the small roasting chickens in the oven, timed to be ready later, and the dessert of chilled lemon soufflé ("with fresh strawberries," Gussie had remarked when they came back from the library. "At least *they're* not poisonous"), Mrs. Potter could only assume that some other dish required attention. Probably the freshest of vegetables available on the island earlier in the day.

As she left, saying she'd rejoin them in the parlor, but not to hurry, Mrs. Potter realized that Gussie was giving her a first opportunity to be with Tony alone, a chance to get to know him. "Don't rush," she instructed them. "Let Genia point out the sights to you, Tony."

Mrs. Potter forced herself to smile at the tall man beside her. "You've been on Nantucket for months, and you must know where everything is. Let's just stand here and *look* for a few minutes and I'll spare you the guidebook routine, not that I'm very good at it."

"I'm sure you are very good at whatever you are doing,"

Tony assured her levelly. "What I am *not* sure of is what you are doing these days has to do with *me.*"

The man is more intelligent and perceptive than I knew, Mrs. Potter thought. She decided to be as forthright as he appeared.

"All right, I want to learn everything I can about you," she said, "everything that tells me what kind of person you are. Gussie is one of my dearest friends and we've been part of each other's lives for forty years. I've seen her through three marriages . . ."

"Please go on," Tony said, gravely courteous and attentive.

"The third time was to a man you must have known—Gordon Van Vleeck," she continued.

Again Tony nodded politely. "A sad thing he died, then? Maybe so, maybe not."

Mrs. Potter turned toward the view of the harbor light. "Gussie's a very special person and she deserves to be happy. Gordon was—well, frankly, the cowboys on the ranch would have said he was no kiss for Christmas."

Mrs. Potter caught the glint of a brief smile as again Tony inclined his head in affirmation. "From what I saw and heard of the man, he wasn't worth a damn," he said. "I might have helped him with some vitamin injections, but he wouldn't let me get near him. Still, that's not your concern now. What you're wondering and questioning people about is if I'm the right man to succeed him."

"Yes," Mrs. Potter said.

"You want me to tell you if I would make a good husband for our dear friend?" he continued. "If I say yes, you can assume I am lying. If I say no, that also may be a lie. I fear, Eugénie, darling, there is no way I can help you decide. Am I what your cowboys would call a 'kiss for Christmas'?" His sudden laughter was unexpected.

She found herself laughing as well. "Let's go down and join Gussie, shall we?" For the evening, she told herself, she would forget her misgivings.

Again he appeared to read her mind. "But you will begin again tomorrow to ask the questions, am I right? No matter. I will try to defend myself." His smile now was as disarming as his unexpected laughter had been. "Now will you show me the town from the rooftop before we go below?" he asked, indicating the ladder-steep steps to the roof walk. "Let me put my jacket over that light sweater, *so* . . ."

His gray eyes were now holding her own.

Mrs. Potter very well understood her own impulse to yield, to be wrapped in the folds of lovely navy French wool with the sterling silver buttons, to admire the swordsman's shoulders and lean torso in the impeccably fitted white shirt with its tiny monogram above the right cuff. Perhaps her interest in Tony Ferencz was not as cool as she had thought.

She also understood the tremor of fear that followed this first primitive impulse of attraction to the man whose jacket was gently but insistently enfolding her.

"Let's go up and look at the town together," Tony repeated quietly. "If I come up directly behind you, I can reach past to open the skylight when we get to the top."

Mrs. Potter put a foot on the first step of the ladder-like stairs.

"It is not so cold, and we will just stay for a moment." Tony's hand covered her own, now on the rope handrail. "Let's laugh together again, Eugénie. Your laugh is lovely."

Mrs. Potter remained motionless, ready to take the next upward step. Then she pictured the open platform at the top of the steep stairway, five stories above the street.

Tony's hand restrained her momentarily, but turning, she slipped past him quickly to regain the neutral ground of the broader open stairway leading down to the lower floors. With an effort she hoped was imperceptible, she slid neatly out of the jacket.

"I think it's too cold and blowy for the roof walk now," she said. "Let's go down and join Gussie in the parlor." She hoped he did not see that she was shaking and that he had been unaware of the sudden panic of her retreat.

Over Perrier in the parlor, and later at the long mahogany table in the dining room, conversation was remarkably sprightly. To Mrs. Potter, Count Ferencz was friendly and courteous. His attention centered on Gussie, who seemed happily impervious to any undercurrents.

Trying to take her cue from Tony's apparent failure to see her descent from the ladder as the terror-struck flight it had been, Mrs. Potter endeavored throughout dinner, as casually as she could, to learn more of his background. Ordinarily one could establish a certain fund of information by knowing about former schools, about possible mutual friends, about places and times of mutual interest. These delicate thrusts were parried with grace and sometimes wit. Schooling? A boarding school in Switzerland, one she'd not be likely to know, run by crazy monks. He was reminded of a funny story about one of them. University? Heidelberg, naturally. Mrs. Potter did not know what *naturally* implied. The only person connected with the place she could think of was the Student Prince, and she couldn't even claim to have known Nelson Eddy.

Mutual friends? Tony's stories were amusing, affectionate, occasionally deftly malicious, but they all involved people Mrs. Potter did not know, other than to know *of.* Princess Grace, Maria Callas, various wives of Greek shipping magnates or of Middle East rulers rich in oil and power. All had one thing in common, beside the fact that Mrs. Potter had never encountered any of them except in the pages of the press: They were all dead. She would never hear what stories *they* might have told in turn about the charming Count Ferencz who knew so much about health and beauty.

In vain she tried to think of someone living whom she might know and with whom Tony would claim acquaintance.

Never before, she realized, had she dined with a man she was afraid of, even though her fears might be groundless in the light of what she now knew about the poison deaths. She was making dinner table conversation with a man she had— at least momentarily—thought capable of pushing her over the low parapet of the roof walk to what would have been her certain death on the cobblestones below.

26

"I *knew* you'd like Tony," Gussie was saying the next morning. "You just needed a little time alone with him to realize I'm right—he's a wonderful man!"

Mrs. Potter had wakened much earlier with a shattering sense of remorse. Gussie's words now were of no help. I as much as accused the man, at least in my own mind, of trying to murder me, she had told herself. He's too courteous to show it, but he must have found me unforgivably insulting. Only the ease and urbanity of his dinner table conversation made it seem that he misunderstood (or chose to ignore) the hint of accusation in her flight from the cupola.

She forced herself to be honest about her fears. Was it that she was afraid, not of Tony but of her own feelings about him? Like Gussie and the others, was she beginning to find him all too compellingly attractive?

Mrs. Potter wrenched her thoughts away from Tony Ferencz and the cupola.

She tried to summon a mental picture of Beth in the Providence hospital. Was there a psychiatric ward? Were Laurence and Paula allowed to visit her? Her imaginings showed a quiet woman, her white curly hair beginning to show the need for Larry's skillful shaping and trimming, a woman possibly heavily sedated, burdened with baseless guilt.

There was no doubt in her mind now that Lolly was guilty, however much the girl might tell herself it was all a horrible accident. And no matter what had been the reason for the two poisoning deaths, she would never be able to forgive Lolly for what she had done with the old poison bottle.

She knew, from seeing the furtive drink Lolly had poured for herself at the beach shack picnic, that Lolly was clever in disguising her actions. She could have been just as clever in putting the blue bottle in Beth's basket at the party. No one ever really noticed what Lolly was doing. The unbelievable part was Lolly's quick, dark cunning in seeing the possibilities of the old bottle in the first place.

In spite of herself, her thoughts went back to Tony. There was no escaping one fact, no matter what Lolly had done. None of this had happened before Tony came to Nantucket. She heard Dee's words again in her mind. *You'll all be sorry.*

Now, as she and Gussie drank their morning juices, Gussie was still speaking happily of her pleasure in the threesome dinner party the evening before.

"Did I tell you what Tony's decided as the name for the clinic?" she asked. "He told me just before he went home. It's so perfect you'll have to agree there's no possible other choice. It's going to be Eve, Nantucket. Just that—for his mother, of course. Don't you love it? And he thinks now he might be in business by July at the latest, although that's all he'd tell me about the details."

Mrs. Potter was shaken. The man reads my mind, she thought. Or maybe I read his. In all honesty, she had to agree that the name might be a good one, and certainly better than some of the others she'd been hearing. Eve, Nantucket would probably be a tremendous success, wherever on the island and with whosoever's money Tony was going to get it set up in time for the Nantucket summer season.

Gussie continued her breakfast chatter. Helen had just called, she reported, and asked her to take one of the new volunteers along on her weekly Meals on Wheels rounds today—one of the nice new widows on the island who had been among the tea party guests. So Genia could beg off, if she liked, or tag along.

Mrs. Potter elected to beg off. She needed time to think, and she said she would take a walk instead, and then have lunch ready when Gussie got back.

It was late morning when she returned from a long, fast walk, first to the Jetties to smell the salt air and watch the gulls and eventually to climb the winding stone-paved path to the Cliff Road. Delaying, she made a detour on her way back to Main Street, providing an excuse to send postcards later to the children, reminding them that they, too, had once been on Easy Street.

On her way home she passed the paper store. Its windows were blazoned with posters. A NEW ROMANCE BY VICKI SANDS! EVEN BETTER THAN *Midnight Love!* EVEN SPICIER THAN *Secret Wife!*

There was a blown-up jacket cover showing a young woman in a bikini, unaccountably depicted in a field of spring flowers, a shadowy male figure striding toward her out of the woods in the background. DON'T MISS *Ravished!* VICKI SANDS'S LATEST ROMANCE WILL MELT YOUR VERY BONES WHEN YOU ENTER YOUR OWN PRIVATE WORLD, *Ravished!*

At least one question, although not on her list, was answered. Victor Sandys was raking it in as Vicki Sands. She wished that all of her answers were that simple. At least it would amuse Gussie to tell her about it. What was that old song they used to consider so naughty, and used to chant so cheerfully and innocently? "Violate me in violet time," they would sing, with mock leers, "in the vilest manner you know." Gussie might remember the rest of the words—she could not, at the moment.

Then before she returned to the house, she found herself walking with George Enderbridge. George's route, she observed, often seemed to be from the church, then up Main Street, past Gussie's, in the direction of Mittie's house.

She remembered that George was a clergyman as well as a

retired headmaster. "I need some help," she said impulsively. "Have you ever known a murderer?"

George seemed unsurprised, and his answer was definite. "Never one who really thought he was," he said with conviction. "When I was starting out in the church, in a pretty seamy Boston neighborhood, I knew a few people who caused deaths, and they were, in fact, judged guilty of murder. None of them seemed to think he or she was a murderer, or admitted starting out with that intent."

George teetered back and forth on his heels, considering the question. "The courts said they were murderers. They just thought they'd figured it wrong. They wanted to get even by hurting someone, but *not that much*. They thought they'd get someone out of the action temporarily, but *not for keeps*. All of them, now that I think about it, were honestly surprised once they saw that someone actually died."

He looked mildly disappointed when Mrs. Potter thanked him and asked nothing further. Then, with a vague smile, apparently feeling that he had performed his priestly office, and, as always, accepting of the foibles of his friends and parishioners, he went on up the street.

At lunch in the kitchen, somewhat later, Mrs. Potter's only mention of her morning's encounters was that of the bone-dissolving secret world of *Ravished*, by Vicki Sands.

"We'll have a new Barbara Cartland in our midst!" Gussie exclaimed. "Victor will dress like a peacock, not that he hasn't begun to already, and he'll give interviews to adoring young reporters as he lolls about in bed until noon, and he may even get a hearing aid and start to be fun again, after all these years of moping."

She tasted her soup. "This is *good!*" she proclaimed. "*Sopa de ajo!* The last time I had it was with Jules in Mexico years ago. Marvelous for a winter day on Nantucket!"

Mrs. Potter's hasty lunch inspiration had been garlic soup, slightly altered from the original Mexican recipe (not that she remembered this exactly) to fit limitations of time and calories. With no time to simmer a rich beef broth, she had begun with two bouillon cubes and two cups of water in a shallow skillet. With the flat blade of a heavy knife, she whacked four fat garlic cloves into instant shedding of their papery skins, whacked them soundly again into total submission, then finished them with brisk, brief chopping. Garlic soup was not for the fainthearted.

As the minced garlic simmered in the broth, she reminded herself to look up on Tony's chart in the pantry what garlic was good for. Everything, probably—old folklore claimed miracles for it. The chart would probably just say that it reactivated the spleen, or something equally uninteresting.

The Mexican recipe called for a generous amount of shredded Gruyère or Swiss cheese. She found neither in Gussie's refrigerator, but in their stead she measured out a careful half-cup of shredded low-fat mozzarella—far less than the expected quantity, she was sure.

Just before she called Gussie to the table for lunch, she very gently slid two eggs into the simmering broth, and at the same time put two slices of Portuguese bread in the toaster. When the eggs were softly poached, she transferred each, with the hot broth, into a heavy heated pottery soup bowl, and divided the shredded cheese over them. Each bowl was quickly topped with a round of the toasted bread, virtuously uncheesed and unbuttered.

The two smiled happily at each other as they savored each spoonful—the texture of the long strands of melting cheese, the firm egg white, the richness released by the soft-cooked egg yolk, the broth-soaked goodness of the firm toasted bread, the heady aroma of garlic.

"Let's see how this adds up," Mrs. Potter said, reaching for a fresh yellow pad, one of which was by now to be found at hand in the kitchen and the library as well as on her bedside table in the guest room upstairs. "Broth, hardly enough to count, six calories apiece for bouillon cubes, I think. Garlic— did you ever see a calorie chart listing garlic? Let's say a little less than a half of a small onion, which is fifty. Let's say twenty, shall we—ten apiece? Cheese, a quarter-cup each, maybe three-quarters of an ounce. Oh, let's make it an ounce and say a hundred calories."

"Large egg, eighty calories," Gussie added. "I'd say seventy-five for that slice of Portuguese toast. I get a total of two hundred and seventy-one, do you?"

"My feeling is that we could divide a Temple orange for dessert," Mrs. Potter offered, "and still feel reasonably holy."

"We'll reek of garlic for the rest of the day," Gussie said comfortably. "I'm glad Tony's not coming for dinner tonight. He called, did I tell you?"

Not only had he phoned with thanks for a delightful evening, but he wanted Gussie to know how happy he was to have begun to know her dear Eugénie. "In fact," Gussie said, "since he seemed so receptive and I knew you wanted to get your own diet program, I made a date for you to see him this afternoon at the Scrim. Aren't you pleased?"

27

I'm going to dress just as I would for an afternoon walk, Mrs. Potter told herself. Ordinarily if she had a doctor's appointment, she'd make sure to wear a dress she could slip out of easily without disarranging her hair. And, she thought guiltily, a rather pretty slip underneath, preferably of a nice color other than white, so she'd feel more in command of the situation once she undressed.

Today, she reminded herself, her visit to Tony Ferencz was not an appointment with a doctor, and she had no intention of undressing, for any reason at all. She would dress for a blustery afternoon, and in so doing would encase herself in as many hard-to-take-off garments as possible.

Over underclothes, she put on a blue jersey turtleneck pullover, and added a pair of ribbed wool knee socks over her usual sleek panty hose. She put on zippered wool pants, gratified to see there was no slight crosswise wrinkle below the waistband in the back, the telltale sign of their being too tight. She added a leather belt with an intricate buckle, ordinarily a little bothersome in its fastening. Over all of this she put on a heavy ribbed sweater, its dark blue matching the trousers. And as an afterthought, she further enclosed her already swathed neck with a firmly tied blue-and-white silk scarf. She put her wool-stockinged feet into sturdy walking shoes and knotted the laces.

On her head she pulled down a firm white wool beret. And, as she left the house, she added her well-zipped, buttoned, and belted storm coat.

As if the garlic soup were not enough protection, she thought. The man is not going to try to seduce you. Still, one might as well present as many defenses as possible, and he might have had garlic for lunch as well.

The day, although blowy, did not justify such warm armor, she found, as she walked to the Scrimshaw in the early afternoon. The ground was still unfrozen to her footsteps as she crossed a bit of soft turf. The only chill she felt was an inner one, the memory of the previous evening.

Today she would be seeing Tony in one of the two small upstairs suites at the Scrimshaw. Peter would possibly be in the other, his own quarters, next door. Jadine and Jimmy, maybe even very late luncheon guests, would be below in the kitchen and dining room. And yet again today she admitted to herself the combination of fear and fascination she had felt from the first time she met Tony Ferencz. She fought an impulse to turn and flee as she went up the small stairway. Each stair tread showed a hooked rug pattern of a different island motif—a sailboat, a windmill, a bicycle, a sea gull, a spouting whale.

Tony was standing at the open door of his sitting room. "Naughty Eugénie," he said as he took both of her gloved hands. "You have now decided I did not intend to push you off the roof? And that I may not be such a big bad wolf, after all? Let's forget all that nonsense and concentrate on you."

The small room was almost too full of crewel-covered chairs. There was a well polished Governor Winthrop desk of near museum distinction, a long pine settee, a number of cushioned footstools. The pine floor planks, gleaming with age and wax, were nearly covered with more hooked rugs, like that of the stairway runner, in soft faded colors and primitive island designs. It was the coziest and least threatening situation Mrs. Potter could imagine, and it was also very warm.

She allowed Tony to take her heavy coat, and seated herself, choosing a wing chair that appeared to be well barricaded with candlestand pine tables and footstools.

"It seems I'm here as a client," she said, with a new rush of courage and determination. "You've worked wonders with all of my friends, and I'm sure I'd be foolish if I didn't see what you could do for me."

Tony looked at her appraisingly. "Naturally, your own special diet first," he murmured. "Of course. We shall have to see just what it is that your system needs."

In answer to what must have been a momentary flash of panic in her face, Tony continued, his voice quiet and matter-of-fact, his gaze drifting past her to the window, then back to the small fire on the hearth. "There will be tests for this later, naturally, and laboratory reports from my staff, but nothing of the sort today. In fact, there will be no general examination of any kind today."

Mrs. Potter relaxed slightly.

"I have found, however, that my clinical experience permits me to make many valid preliminary findings based on a superficial examination of the hands." Tony's voice was entirely professional now, and impersonal. Without moving from his own wing chair opposite, he leaned forward and stretched out a long arm and a finely shaped long-fingered hand. "First, the left," he instructed her, his voice casual and yet authoritative.

There was nothing alarming about his touch. Actually, Mrs. Potter thought, as she felt his fingers moving her own finger joints, pressing and testing the cushions of her palm, and as she saw him studying the texture of her fingernails and the skin over her knuckles, this is really quite interesting.

Her right hand followed, and the examination seemed partly gentle massage as Tony's hands manipulated her own. It felt good—in no way a threat, no suggestion of intimacy.

Briefly she winced as he probed the base of her index finger. "A little arthritic condition there," he told her gravely. "Possibly you write a great deal? We shall take this into account."

The otherwise agreeable hand-examination ended, almost to her regret, and Tony, with slow courtesy, returned her extended hands to the arms of her chair.

With the toe of a well-made English boot, he now pushed a low footstool into place at her feet. "And now the feet," he said quietly. "There is no need to undress—only to remove the heavy shoes."

In the warmth of the small room it was good to be free of her walking shoes and the thick woolen knee socks. Mrs. Potter reminded herself comfortably that she was encased in nylon from toe tip to waist, and over that by a pair of well-secured woolen trousers.

Tony's fingers gently probed and moved each toe within the nylon-stockinged foot, moved heel and ankle, stroked each area of sole and instep. His touch seemed increasingly more insistent, more deeply pleasurable.

Again to her regret, the manipulation of her feet was over and Tony was handing her woolen socks and walking shoes, again with the same grave courtesy. She put them back on, almost reluctantly.

"Now it is only the hair of the head," he said. "Please to remain seated as you are." As he spoke, he circled candle-stands and footstools to a position behind her wing chair. Gently, carefully, he removed the white wool beret.

The touch was impersonal, in no way intrusive, and yet again infinitely agreeable. Tony's fingers lifted the hair gently from the nape of her neck and ran lightly beneath the over-tight, now over-warm layers of scarf and sweaters at the base of her throat.

Mrs. Potter could not restrain a tiny sigh of pleasure as she loosened the scarf. Here, she thought, was a man who could really know what you meant when you asked would he please scratch your back. She moved her shoulders slightly, in frank enjoyment, against the crewel-worked back of her chair, as Tony's fingers explored lightly in a circle about the base of her throat.

She closed her eyes. From a height above her head and behind her, she heard (later, she was not sure she had heard —or, to her private, half-embarrassed amusement, if she had imagined—words that might have come from a Vicki Sands novel), "Naughty Eugénie. We shall have to punish you a little, I think, before we make you beautiful."

There was a brisk rap at the sitting room door.

"Yes?" Tony asked, his fingers gently following the shape of Mrs. Potter's skull.

"Just me" was the response from the hallway as Peter Benson, smiling, half apologetic, pushed open the door. "Thought you'd like to know Carpenter's downstairs, Tony, old boy, and Latham's on the house phone. Says your line must be off the hook—she's been trying to get you."

Mrs. Potter stretched easily in the wing chair as Tony excused himself, then started upright in total disbelief. She had come here to find reasons for her mistrust of Tony Ferencz. She had remained to find herself beginning to accept him as what Gussie and the others thought him to be—an authority skilled in diagnosis and therapy and in matters that would eventually relate to her diet, her health, perhaps to her looking younger and living longer.

She shook herself. Nobody looks better and lives longer because they enjoy having their hands and feet massaged, she told herself severely, or because it feels good to have the back of the neck stroked so lightly. And if Tony has diet secrets, other than eating fresh foods in variety, other than eating less and drinking less, which we all know anyway, I haven't yet discovered what they are.

However, Larry had spoken of vitamin injections, and others had hinted at special treatments. This had to be Tony's secret—vitamins, or some other kind of chemical or hormonal medication. And Peter, bless him, had given her time to break Tony's almost hypnotic spell, time to look for some real evidence. He had been telling her, as clearly as he could, that he no longer trusted Tony.

Quickly she crossed the room and lowered the front of the old Winthrop desk. There, in the multiple pigeonholes across its back, were ten—perhaps twenty—syringes of various sizes, filed in neat order. In the center drawer her hasty fingers found sterile packets of hypodermic needles. She remembered the secret, false-bottom drawer that every such desk has. In it was a box of ampoules labeled in a language she was unable to recognize.

The door to the room closed again briskly before she was able to restore the hidden drawer.

"So," Tony Ferencz was saying, "at last you think you have found bad things to use against me with your beloved Gussie?"

With courage born of knowing that Peter Benson was below and within call, Mrs. Potter managed to regain her beret, to retrieve her coat, and to leave with what she later assured herself was dignity, although dignity in haste. She nearly tripped over the sailboat stair tread as she reached the bottom of the narrow stairway and rushed out into the slightly salty breeze of the small winding street.

28

"March is supposed to be trumpery season around here, not January," Gussie said as she looked up from reading Mrs. Potter's yellow-pad notes, from which only the mention of Lolly Latham had been removed. Her voice was indignant.

Local folklore held that Nantucketers, imprisoned on the island through a long winter of limited company and ingrown interests, would enliven the drab days before spring by inventing gossip about their neighbors. "Trumpery season" had been its designation as far back as anyone Mrs. Potter knew could remember.

"I didn't say any of those things about Tony were *true,*" Mrs. Potter defended herself, "and they're only for my private speculation. I don't *publish* them, and I just decided to let you see them, since I wanted you to know what I've been worrying about."

"They're still hateful," Gussie said. "Honestly, Genia, you're going too far. And you'll feel terrible when I tell you this—Tony called just before you got back. He said you'd had a delightful first consultation and he's already planning his program for you. I don't know *what* he thought when you rushed off. He and Peter must have decided you were batty, running down the stairs like that. And *I* can't imagine why you went out bundled up that way, just to walk to the Scrim."

Gussie grimaced at Mrs. Potter's notes, to which she had made hasty additions after her return from seeing Tony. In them, she had summed up how Tony Ferencz might be served by his present Nantucket followers. A diet clinic, whatever it was to be called, required more than adulation. There was money, first and foremost. A suitable location. Impeccable references. Dignified promotion in the world of potential clients. Skillful management. Money. More money.

"First you suspected Tony of poisoning Ozzie and his secretary because of that old story of Dee's about Ozzie's daughter," Gussie told her. "Now you're trying to prove he's a fortune hunter, trying to get all of us to support his clinic. To top that off, you seem to think he might have pushed you off my roof walk, and as a last straw you seem to think he was threatening you some way this afternoon in his office."

Mrs. Potter was silent as Gussie continued her diatribe. "Genia, use your head! You poked into his desk and found— what? A drawerful of vitamin preparations and the hypodermic syringes for injecting them. Perfectly innocent. Too bad you can't read Romanian."

Although these notes of Mrs. Potter's had not included Lolly's name, there were other questions Gussie had not seen before. Was Bo Heidecker dead when Mary Lynne beached the boat, and if not, was everything possible done to resuscitate him? Did Ozzie have suspicions about this?

Mrs. Potter now admitted she had already pursued that as far as she could. However, it meant something that Peter shared these doubts about Bo's death, and so did his intimation that Tony had given medication to Gordon Van Vleeck.

Gussie was suddenly furious. "Of course Tony met Gordon," she said, "but Gordon hated Tony the first time he set eyes on him. He was positively rude, and he refused to talk with him about any treatment at all."

As Mrs. Potter recalled, Gordon Van Vleeck had been rude to almost everyone at one time or another, including his wife.

"It's *monstrous* to hint that Tony had anything to do with

Gordon's death, any more than he had with Bo's heart attack on the boat," Gussie said. "Gordon's emphysema was too far advanced for help, and he refused to give up smoking. Arnold Sallanger would tell you that, Genia, if you weren't so intent on proving Tony is going around murdering people. You might as well think Mary Lynne murdered Bo for his money."

"Women *do* kill their husbands," Mrs. Potter reminded her, suddenly thinking of pale, plump, serious Lester Latham and the demands of an ambitious, possibly overpowering wife.

Gussie was now quiet and thoughtful. "How do you know I didn't kill Gordon myself, then?" she asked. "He really was rather a pain in the neck, Genia, although I've never admitted this to anyone before."

Mrs. Potter declined to consider the idea.

"How do you know if I challenged Jules Berner to some kind of crazy stunt that caused *his* heart attack?" Gussie persisted. "For that matter and for all you know, it might have been my gun that shot your own cousin Theo in the woods all those years ago."

This was getting a bit out of hand, Mrs. Potter realized. "For heaven's sake," she said quickly, "for all you know I strangled Lew Potter in his sleep! There were certainly times when I felt like it!"

"Okay. For all we know Mittie bashed in Ab Leland's head with one of his tennis trophies," Gussie said, her voice slightly tremulous with both laughter and tears. "Or Leah maybe decided she'd had quite enough of dear sainted Fanwell."

Mrs. Potter realized that, while tensions were eased, both she and Gussie were overwrought. "I think we're both hungry," she said. "That *sopa de ajo* was a long time ago. Let's have a glass of carrot juice, and then I challenge you to a game of cribbage."

"I suppose you'll say it's for the championship of North and South Dakota," Gussie said with resignation. "You always offer a medal for that one when you're feeling lucky."

As she brought out the juice and Mrs. Potter set up the

cribbage board, Gussie spoke of her morning. "I forgot to tell you about Ozzie's New York nephew. He brought my files from the office, the way they do when there's no partner to take over. Helen called to ask about it while you were at the Scrim. You know how she thinks none of us can take care of things without a little help from her. Her files were complete, and so were Mittie's and Leah's and Mary Lynne's. She hadn't checked with Dee yet."

"That's nice," Mrs. Potter said. "Now, do you want to try for the championship of North Dakota first, or South, or shoot the works for the two together?"

That Gussie won the double two-state trophy (invisible and imaginary) may have been due to Mrs. Potter's thoughts of Dee. There was another story she wanted to know, and as soon as she could she persuaded Gussie to curl up with a book before dinner.

"I'm going to look in on Dee for a minute," she said. "After the miles I have to drive in Arizona to see someone, it's a marvel to be able to walk a couple of blocks to make a call. I'll be back in time to help with dinner."

Lights shone from every window of the carriage house apartment as she arrived there a few minutes later. (Mittie pays the light bills, she told herself. She might have to chivy Dee again about this, as she had the other day.)

Dee, as she had been before, seemed glad to see her. "I can give you a glass of champagne!" she said, with hospitable satisfaction. "I'm just looking over what seems to be a solid contract for the property I was showing on Thursday—remember? The buyers sent over a bottle to celebrate the purchase before they flew off-island. To thank me, they said, for finding them such a bargain—only four ninety-five."

Mrs. Potter repeated the numbers rather blankly.

"The sellers were asking five twenty-five," Dee told her, "but even I had to tell them that was a bit high. Anything over five hundred seems hard to move at this time of year."

Mrs. Potter gulped mentally, realizing that "five hundred" meant five hundred thousand dollars, and at the same time trying to guess what the commission on this might be for

Dee. "That's wonderful," she said. "You'll be buying one of those half-million-dollar houses for yourself soon, at that rate."

Dee's back was toward her as she took glasses from an almost empty cupboard in the small kitchen, and as she deftly opened the wine. She did not answer, other than to put glasses and the bottle on a tray and to lead the way to the living room, where a fire burned comfortably beneath Ab Leland's picture of a four-masted schooner in a blue and unthreatening sea.

Mrs. Potter toasted Dee's current sale and her continuing success in island real estate. "We're all very proud of you," she said honestly. "You've made a wonderful second career for yourself after leaving the magazine business."

Dee's gaze was penetrating, but she made no reply to the implication that she must be doing well financially.

However, Mrs. Potter had not come to pursue Mittie's problem, that of her need of money while Dee stayed on as a nonpaying guest. She had come for only one reason, to learn more about Tony Ferencz. Dee was far too intelligent for indirect approach.

"I told you I was concerned about Gussie," she said, "and the more I learn about Tony, the less I think he's the man for her."

Dee sipped her wine and looked at the fire.

"The first day I was back on the island, you said everyone at the lunch table would be sorry they knew him," Mrs. Potter continued. "Then the next day, when I asked you, you told me the story of what happened to Ozzie deBevereaux's daughter, and I was appalled. But I told myself that people do make mistakes in life, and then can be sorry and perhaps even very much better afterward."

Still Dee was silent. Then, seeing that her glass was empty, she rose quickly to fill Mrs. Potter's only partially empty one and to refill her own.

"There had to be more on your mind than a teen-ager's falling for a diet fad, even though it proved fatal for her and tragic for her parents," Mrs. Potter said. "There had to be more about Tony that only you know, to make you speak out as strongly as you did that day at lunch."

"I told you about Dora Stell Grumbley, for Gussie's sake," Dee said reluctantly.

"And you know I'll never repeat it," Mrs. Potter replied.

"I know," Dee replied, "and I also know you've found out that Tony is a bit of a shit, as our English cousins would say. He's not above making love to some of his ladies to get their adoring support, and Peter even thinks he may be using some illegal drug injections from his mother's old clinic in Europe. I doubt it. I think he's too smart for that. He probably just lets them believe he's got secret stuff so miraculous the Food and Drug is afraid to approve it."

Be that as it may, Mrs. Potter decided. Now it was her turn simply to be silent and nod, and to realize that this was very good champagne.

"If I didn't trust you, or if I weren't so fond of Gussie, I'd never tell you," Dee continued as she rose to leave the room. Returning quickly, she put a silver-framed photograph on Mrs. Potter's lap.

The picture, that of a handsome dark-haired boy—perhaps fourteen, Mrs. Potter thought—held her in shocked disbelief as she saw the intensity in the wide gray eyes. "Your son?" she asked incredulously. "Yours and Tony's?"

"Mikai will be twenty-eight next month," Dee told her. "He looks younger, of course. Mikey—that's what they call him at Fieldstone Hall—is never going to grow up. He's beautiful, yes. He's gentle, most of the time, and he's quiet. In fact he never spoke at all until he was nearly twelve. But Mikai is in most ways a four-year-old. He's subject to a four-year-old's tantrums and rages, in a body as strong as a man's, and there's no way he can live anyplace except in a very carefully controlled and guarded environment."

Mrs. Potter's impulse was to embrace Dee in shared sorrow, but her friend's bearing rejected any show of sympathy.

"He's been everyplace," Dee continued, almost cold in her dignity. "He's had the best doctors, the best diagnosis, the best treatment money could buy. At least I don't have to bear the pain of knowing he could have been helped. He's had the best."

"And you've had the anguish and expense of all these years of doctors and special hospitals," Mrs. Potter said slowly.

"The magazine salary, good as it was, couldn't pay for it," Dee said. "I did double stints for a long time, keeping on with my job there and at the same time cranking out those awful romance novels Leah reads. You know—imperious but virginal young woman carried off by hypnotically fascinating, experienced older man. And then he turns out to really love her and they get married and everything is hunky-dory. I could do it in my sleep, and for a while I think I did, trying to run a good fashion magazine daytimes and making enough on the side writing romances every night."

She poured another glass of wine for them both and added another log to the fire. "Finally I broke down myself," she said, "and Peter Benson, bless him, loaned me his beach shack as a place to stay here on the island while I was getting myself together again. He's the only person I ever trusted enough to tell him the story about Mikai, until today. I'd known Peter from his restaurant days in New York, and by then he'd come here and started up the Scrimshaw."

"And eventually you got into selling real estate, and that's where things stand now," Mrs. Potter continued the story for her. "Is Mikai all right? I mean, is he in a place you're satisfied with?"

"Fieldstone Hall is perfect," Dee said, "if anyone can use that word for what has to be a completely unnatural world. The place is beautiful, it's safe, and Mikai is happy there."

"And it costs a small fortune every month," Mrs. Potter said soberly. Selling real estate was a chancy business at best, she thought, in spite of an occasional big windfall of commissions. Only by rigid economies and by using her wits in every way to earn extra money could Dee have paid all the years of such bills.

"Why isn't Tony taking his share of this?" she asked suddenly. "There's no doubt whose son he is. Clearly his age says he was born during your marriage—"

Dee interrupted. "Two months before I filed for divorce. Mikai is Tony's and my son. Tony refused to share any part of the responsibility, and when we learned that Mikai could never be normal, he took off for Europe, just to escape."

Mrs. Potter was puzzled. Weren't there legal ways of insisting on child-support payments, especially in a case like this?

"I told you Tony Ferencz was a bastard," Dee said, her voice icy. "What he threatened then was a countersuit so unbelievably messy, although a complete lie, I decided to take care of Mikai on my own."

She shrugged, an indication of the end of the discussion. "It was only a couple of weeks ago, when things were again pretty tight for me, that I thought I might do something about it. Tony was on the island, and he seemed on the way to making a good thing out of it here. So I asked Ozzie what he thought, and he insisted I get all the necessary documents together for him. Marriage license, Mikai's birth certificate, doctors' reports, hospital receipts over the years, the whole thing. He thought we should start an action now, although I told both him and Peter I'd probably never go through with it."

Mrs. Potter's sympathy and concern were real. "I suppose you got all that stuff back from Ozzie's nephew when he was returning clients' files," she said. "You can turn it all over to another lawyer if you decide to, later on."

"That's the odd thing," Dee said. "All the copies of old real estate contracts were there in my file, ever since I came to the island. The papers on Mikai were missing." She paused. "Maybe it's just as well if they've been destroyed. Tony would have weaseled out some way, or else would have made up such a scandal I'd lose more than I gained."

Mrs. Potter was silent. Here was the one thing she knew that could destroy Tony's plans for a diet clinic, his Eve, Nantucket. None of her friends, she knew, no matter what the degree of their infatuation or involvement, would lend support to a man who had abandoned his wife and mentally disturbed child, and who refused to take any responsibility for his care.

Dee followed her thoughts. "Now you know what I mean about Tony," she said, "and how he's capable of using people. He worked on Leah first, I think, before he found out that the Shrine, being in the Historic District, couldn't be used for the clinic he wants to start. He still probably has hopes she'll sell it and give him the money instead.

"He gave up on Mittie when Ozzie put his foot down on her giving him the Shimmo house, but then he played Mary Lynne along, hoping she'd buy it for him with all her new money. Then it turns out that's all controlled by a trust officer, too.

"The game for him now is where it really has been from the beginning, between Gussie and Helen, because they can be the most help to him. They're equally rich, I suppose. I think he intends to use them both, but if anything, Helen may have the edge. She could be wonderful help to him in getting the clinic established and managing the place, raising money, that sort of thing, and he'd get all of that besides her money. Gussie's charm and warm heart wouldn't weigh very heavily in that decision.

"Knowing Tony, I think he'll try to get Helen's money and Gussie's, too, but he hasn't the slightest intention of marrying either of them, I can promise you that. He knows he's much too attractive just as he is to all the other rich widows who'll be flocking to Nantucket for an expensive stay later on. Then he'll put them on diets anybody could get in a book, give them some placebo injections, get them to exercise, and look into their eyes and kiss their hands.

"Can't you see it? What Tony has to sell is *Tony*, not any magic diet program. Tony the man—the handsome aristocrat, slightly aloof, yet attentive enough to persuade any of the ladies she's the one he secretly prefers above all the rest.

"He's not going to marry any of them," Dee concluded. "He'd lose his best, maybe his only, asset—the challenge and chance of a grand romance."

At the risk of appearing sentimental, Mrs. Potter kissed Dee good-bye as she left the carriage house.

Then, as she went down the outdoor stairway, she thought

of Mikai's story, now not in relation to her sympathy and admiration for Dee, but as the crucial bit of evidence that would have killed Tony's plans for Eve, Nantucket.

Who most wanted it to succeed? Presumably the whole island would be delighted with it. Prestigious, exclusive, nonpolluting, it would bring a few carefully screened rich women at a time to the island. Some of them might return as future residents and contributors to the good life there. In any case, all of them would add considerably to the island economy during their stay.

Everyone she knew seemed to want Tony's diet center. Even Larry, hoping to be the official hairdresser; perhaps, in spite of his professed doubts, even Peter, to display his skills in the kitchen. Helen might want it most fiercely, as an outlet for her executive talent and ambition, to run what she had called the "Latham Foundation," with Tony as her star attraction.

There wasn't anybody, as far as she could see, who did not want it, and thus no one was above suspicion in the removal of Dee's papers from her files. But there was no one, she felt sure, who had a better reason to want them than Tony himself, although he might have used someone else to clear the way for him to get them.

As she reached the corner of Main Street, instead of turning toward Gussie's house, Mrs. Potter made an abrupt left and headed toward the science library. By the streetlight in the winter dusk, she peered at her watch. With luck, she'd be there by closing time, to walk Lolly home.

29

Under the next streetlight she recognized the scurrying, plump figure in the tan raincoat and round brimmed hat, the shapeless tan plastic bag dangling from one shoulder. Lolly was already on her way home. At that moment Mrs. Potter had an even better idea for her intended conversation.

"Come to the Scrim with me for a cup of tea, Lolly," she urged in a friendly invitation, fighting her own reluctance to go back where she might encounter Tony again. At least in the dining room Peter would be nearby at this time of day.

"Yes, please, this is important," she said kindly. "What you and I have to talk about we can do privately there, just the two of us, or we can go to your house and discuss it as a threesome with your mother. Which would you rather?" Lolly's face was expressionless, her nod of acceptance scarcely more than the blink of her eyes under the hat brim. Mrs. Potter took her gently by the arm as they turned back toward the small inn.

There, she chose a small table by the wall next to the fire, the length of the room between it and the big round table in the bay window, Les Girls' usual table, where Peter was serving cocktails and chatting with a group that looked to be businessmen from off-island, and one woman, whose blond head was facing the window.

"Just tea, please, Jadine," she said to the waitress, at the same time waving to Peter in a way calculated to tell him to stay where he was and that she wanted to be alone with Lolly. "I think it's too near dinner to have anything with it. *No*, change that, please. I think we'll have some of whatever's sweet. The little cinnamon rolls, Jadine, cookies, cake, whatever." Something told her Lolly would be able to talk more easily if there was food before them.

They sat quietly, Lolly apparently staring at the fireplace behind Mrs. Potter's shoulder, until Jadine reappeared.

When the tea and tiny cinnamon rolls were set before them, Jadine remained, poking ineffectually at the fire, which was clearly refusing to burn. "Green wood," she muttered.

"Never mind," Mrs. Potter told her, turning to look. "It'll catch. Just give it time." She didn't want Jadine or anyone else to hear the words she had already framed in her mind.

"I know the whole thing, Lolly," she began, after Jadine had given the logs a few resentful jabs and retired, still muttering. "Don't pretend you don't know what I'm talking about. I know how your friend Edie and Mr. deBevereaux died."

Lolly stared into her teacup, then reached slowly, almost absently, for a cinnamon roll.

"I know you didn't really plan to poison them, Lolly. You just knew a little about what those plants would do, reading about them at the library. You thought you could make both of them sick for a few hours, long enough for you to get Edie's keys"—she suddenly remembered Lolly's offer to take Edie's things to the hospital—"and long enough for you to get something from the office that night."

Lolly shook her head in a definite negative, but her eyes were downcast as she spread butter on another bit of the sweet roll.

Mrs. Potter took a quick guess. "*You* didn't go to the office? You gave the keys to someone else?"

Lolly's eyes were those of a stubborn child, now apparently fixed on the smoldering logs behind Mrs. Potter's shoulder.

"You were terribly surprised and shocked and sorry when both those two people died, weren't you, Lolly? You had been so sure they would just be a little upset for the rest of the day and evening."

Then, for the first time, Lolly spoke. "It was an accident, a horrible accident," she said thickly, repeating her earlier words.

"Then the next day Mrs. Higginson came to the library, first for a while in the morning, then back in the afternoon," Mrs. Potter went on. "You could see how distressed she was, and you knew she was looking up the possible effects of the same two poisonous plants you'd given to Mr. deBevereaux and Edie. You knew she believed the whole thing was her fault because she was the one to take the comfrey to him."

Her voice was suddenly colder. "You figured out that switch in a hurry, it seems to me, just as soon as you heard her say, right here in this dining room, that she was going to take him the comfrey tea. It must have seemed so easy to you. You knew his door would be unlocked. You knew you could slip in and put foxglove leaves in Mrs. Higginson's jar instead, and that he'd never know the difference."

Lolly's pale face remained blank, and she continued to chew, buttering still another cinnamon roll.

"I think you were even quicker to see how you could make sure she would blame herself for what you had done. You went home with her and—"

Lolly interrupted. "I only went home with her because I felt sorry for her," she said defensively. "Honestly. I didn't intend for her to be blamed and I didn't want her to feel bad."

"But you took that old cyanide bottle when she showed you her potting shed, Lolly. It's quite clear you planned to make sure everyone thought she was a poisoner. You planned it all very cleverly, Lolly, and you had to do it all very quickly. Mrs. Higginson was right when she said we had underestimated you all these years."

For the first time, Lolly swallowed hard and her voice was clear and certain. "Not for her," she said, "not for *her*. It was for me."

Mrs. Potter sat silent for a long minute. "You took the cyanide bottle from the shelf to kill *yourself*," she said at last.

Slow tears rolled down Lolly's cheeks. "She was my friend. She was my friend. And I killed her."

Mrs. Potter was suddenly near to tears herself. "But why, Lolly, *why?* Who asked you to get Edie's keys?"

Lolly ignored the question. "I knew about cyanide because it was used in my father's business, back in Chicago," she said. "I knew it wouldn't take but a little. I told them I deserved to die, but then they showed me the bottle was completely empty, rinsed and clean. They said God would punish me in his own way and his own time."

Mrs. Potter again paused. "That was Walter and Elna, of course. You told them what you'd done, and that you wanted to kill yourself?" she asked doubtfully.

"Then they said they were leaving, and they packed and walked right out of the house," Lolly said. Mrs. Potter remembered two faraway figures with heavy suitcases, seen from the cupola, walking down Main Street in the early January dusk.

"They said they'd done the best they could bringing me up, but they couldn't stay in a house with a second suicide," Lolly went on, her voice now bitter. "They said they had a job waiting for them in New York anytime they wanted to quit. They said they'd always been afraid I'd kill myself, just like my father."

Incredibly, Lolly poured herself another cup of tea from her small pot, added sugar, and drank it almost greedily. "I couldn't take the poison because the bottle was empty, and I couldn't shoot myself. I wouldn't know where to find a gun or how to load it or how to shoot it. If I had, I'd have killed myself that way in spite of them."

Mrs. Potter now remembered the raincoat-clad figure glimpsed leaving Helen's front door shortly after she had seen the couple with the suitcases headed in the opposite direction.

"You went out after they left," she told Lolly. "Where did you go, and who was it who asked you to get those keys?" There was no answer, and she added still other questions. "When did you get the idea of putting the empty poison bottle in Mrs. Higginson's basket at the tea party? Or did someone else think of that?"

Concentrating on Lolly's face and her own questions, Mrs. Potter had only vaguely noticed that other people were moving about the dining room, none of them intrusively near. She had not seen that Jimmy had come in from the kitchen and was studying the smoking logs in the fireplace. Hearing him now, she turned to see what he was doing.

He smiled at her broadly, showing his flash of gold teeth. With her mind focused on Lolly, it took her an instant to see that he held in one narrow fine-boned hand a can of charcoal lighter fluid.

"Oh, no! Jimmy, *no!* That's not the way you do it!" she shouted. "Jimmy, *no!*"

Her warning was too late. Jimmy had directed a jet stream of the clear liquid at the smoldering wood. There was a flash that reached out in a long, flaming tongue from the hearth, the tongue of a dragon. Jimmy clutched his hands over his eyes, screaming in sudden pain.

Peter and Jadine came running from the kitchen, drawn instantly by Jimmy's agonized cries. Seemingly at the same moment, Tony materialized from the hallway door with Helen, one thin hand resting regally on his bent forearm. The blond woman detached herself from the group at the round table in the window, and one of the men joined her in the shocked and curious circle.

Mrs. Potter looked down in disbelief at the right arm of her sweater. Several inch-wide circles of wool and of the pullover beneath it had completely disappeared. All she could see were gray patches of what must be her scorched flesh beneath. The smell of burnt wool and her own skin reminded her of something, she thought in detachment as she looked up, in equal disbelief, to see that the woman and man were Leah and Victor Sandys. Then hot, red pain pierced her arm and shoulder.

Still sitting at the table, she heard Peter's reassuring voice and felt herself doused with a pitcher of ice water. "Hang in there, Potter," he said firmly. "We're seeing to Jimmy first. Tony, you put these wet napkins on his eyes. Sopping, lots of water. Jadine, call the ambulance for him, and then get Dr. Sallanger here for Mrs. Potter. Helen, you take a look. I don't think her burns are serious."

As Mrs. Potter lowered her head to keep from fainting, she remembered what the smell made her think of. Burning feathers. You burn feathers to *keep* people from fainting, she thought. I'm not going to faint. I'm going to hear Lolly's answers.

A tuneless humming was the first sound she recognized, then, as she felt cool, rounded surgical scissors cutting away the sodden sleeve of her sweater and the turtleneck jersey beneath it. "Let's have a look," Arnold Sallanger was saying, interrupting his own humming, the apparently unconscious accompaniment to his examination.

"Not too bad," she heard him say. "Peter, Genia has you to thank for quick action. Flooding with cold water was the best thing you could have done."

He bent closer to Mrs. Potter, now sitting upright again, but now in a chair in the center of the room. "I'll get you fixed up, kid, and then take you home to Gussie's. You'll be fine in a few days. Just a little discomfort until then."

Arnold resumed his humming as he wrapped her arm loosely with sterile bandages, assuring her that that was all he was going to do, since although the skin was blistered, its protective surface was unbroken.

"I hate doctors who say things like 'a little discomfort,'" Mrs. Potter told him. "Tell me you know it hurts like blue blazes, or I'll call you at three A.M. and scream in your telephone."

"Do that, and all I'll tell you is to take another two of these," he said, putting a small packet in her lightship basket.

"If you keep on screaming, I'll tell Gussie to stick pins in you wherever it *doesn't* hurt."

She managed a forced grin. "Thanks, Peter, for the good first aid," she said. "I'll let Arnold drive me home now. Call me when you have news of Jimmy from the emergency room, and Peter—did you see what happened to Lolly?"

Jadine was the one to answer. Lolly hadn't been splashed by the burning lighter fluid, she said, but she just sort of disappeared somewhere along the line.

"Well, you know Lolly," Peter said. "Probably scared to death, and nobody noticed what she was doing. I'll check with Helen and let you know about her, too, at the same time I call with the report on Jimmy. Poor devil, I don't know what he thought he was doing, trying to coax that fire with lighter fluid. I guess they don't have the stuff where he comes from."

Jadine interrupted. "The count drove the station wagon to the hospital, right behind the ambulance, the way you asked him to," she reported. "I don't know what good that will do. No matter how friendly he tries to act when he comes in the kitchen, that man doesn't give a hoot in hell about any of *us.*"

The sound of Arnold Sallanger's car horn in front of the inn announced that he had pulled up to take Mrs. Potter home. Peter helped her to the curb, with Jadine on the other side, both of them careful not to touch her right arm.

Gussie was equally and gratifyingly solicitous when Arnold delivered her at the side kitchen door of the big house on Main Street. "Peter called me," she said, "and he feels terrible about all this—your being burned, and especially about Jimmy. He feels so responsible for anything that happens at the Scrim. Oh, yes, and he said that as far as he knows, Lolly went home. I think he said Tony drove her, or maybe just saw her leave with her mother. Seems Helen had her station wagon there, too."

It was later, when Arnold had repeated to Gussie how many pain pills Mrs. Potter should have, and how often, and that he'd be in to take a look at her before his hospital rounds in the morning, that Mrs. Potter reminded Gussie that they should call Helen.

She had not yet told Gussie more than that she had visited Dee at the carriage house, and nothing of the story of Mikai and Tony's abandonment of his son. She had mentioned only briefly her own sudden impulse to take Lolly to tea at the Scrim once she had met her on her way home from the library, but nothing of the interrupted questioning there.

Gussie, she noticed, listened to this brief recital with her head lowered, but her clear blue eyes raised and her eyebrows arched, unmistakable signs that she knew she was not hearing the whole story. She'd have to tell Gussie the whole thing soon, but at the moment her pain—*slight discomfort*, she raged inwardly, all doctors are alike!—gave her reason to postpone these long expositions.

"Call Helen, will you?" she repeated, shifting her arm awkwardly as she sat in one of the easy chairs, now pulled well away from Gussie's kitchen hearth. "Just ask her if Lolly's home. That's all I want to know."

Gussie returned from the phone and Mrs. Potter knew from her face that she would be expected to produce further explanations later. Helen says Lolly called from a friend's house, Gussie reported. Said she was staying overnight so the two of them could go to the Cape tomorrow on their day off and take in the January sales in Hyannis. She sounded pleased that Lolly had another new friend. Helen apparently hadn't got the name.

Or bothered to ask, Mrs. Potter thought, suddenly disturbed, and at the same time realizing that she did not feel quite well. Gussie moved quickly, telling her she was going to bed immediately. As she helped her up the stairs, Mrs. Potter kept saying, rather irritably, that her legs were all right. It was just the slight discomfort in her right arm. Being burned, even a small blister from an unprotected kettle lid, always made her feel scratchy and cross, and she took some pleasure in resenting Arnold Sallanger. *Doctors!*

The next morning, Friday, she let Gussie bring her breakfast in bed, although she was impatient to be up. Outside her windows she could see that a soft blanket of snow had fallen in the night, much like that of her first morning back on the island, happy and unworried. She got up to peer down at footprints on the sidewalk below as she drank her tea, somewhat clumsily, with her left hand.

As soon as she could, she called Peter. Jimmy's vision was still in doubt, he told her, and he'd insisted that they fly him to Boston. He had wanted to go along himself, but it was hard to leave on a busy Friday. He was glad to hear the news of Lolly's weekend plans, when Mrs. Potter told him what Helen had reported.

"That's just what the poor kid needs," he said, "and I'm glad she's got another friend—one of the softball girls, I expect. They all seemed awfully nice and friendly to her that day they were all together. I'll try to find out who it is, and let you know, since you're worried about her. Anyway, this much is good news, and I'm encouraged. Maybe she'll be all right, after all. I was afraid she might be cracking up, the way her father did."

Arnold arrived a short time later and said she was healing nicely. With his help, her loose, floating wool caftan slid down, a bit awkwardly, over her burned arm and his fresh wrappings.

As soon as he had left, she pulled on wool trousers beneath it, and put on her wool knee socks and shoes.

"You promised me a drive all over the island," she reminded Gussie, who met her coming down the front stairs. "It's a beautiful day, the sun's out and it's stopped snowing. Let's go for a long drive. Helen's alone, and she might like to go along, or how about some of the others?"

"Four is enough in my little car," Gussie said, "and I guess we could manage if you sit up front with me where you won't get bumped. I'll see who's free today and wants an island bus tour."

As Gussie went to the phone, Mrs. Potter reviewed what she had learned in three quick calls of her own, after speaking to Peter and before Arnold arrived.

First, Lolly had yet not come to work at the library, but it was not her day off and they were still expecting her, although with no concern. Apparently she often took a day off and since she was a volunteer, and apparently not particularly needed at that, no one thought much of it. The only number they could suggest to call was that of Helen's house, which Mrs. Potter already knew.

Second and third, and not exactly to her surprise, no one seemed to remember whether Lolly Latham, or anyone answering her description, had been on any plane to Hyannis, either last evening or this morning. No one seemed to remember if she had been on the morning boat to Woods Hole. Lolly, Mrs. Potter thought, was, of all people, designed to disappear in a crowd.

She reported these calls to Gussie, elaborating on the fruitless minutes with the steamship ticket agent. "In fact, he didn't even know who she was," Mrs. Potter said, "until I told him it was Mrs. Latham's daughter. Then he said, 'Oh, *her*, yeah, *red brick!*' He insisted he didn't know any daughter."

Gussie pondered this briefly. "You know who is always the guilty one in mystery stories?" she asked. "The one person you never suspect, because they're exactly like Lolly. No one ever notices what they're doing. You're looking for a poisoner, Genia, we both are, so we can get Beth to realize she isn't one. I just got it—it's Lolly! And now all we have to do is figure out how and why. Just remember who told you. And now let's go for your drive. Mittie and Mary Lynne are coming along, but you're company. You get to say where."

30

It had been a long cold walk to the south shore. Luckily she had dressed warmly in the morning before she went to work, and luckily there was enough light in the sky, as the mist-circled moon appeared, to find her way on the road beside the pond. She was pleased with herself for thinking to snatch the remaining cinnamon rolls from the table, cramming them into her shoulder bag, when she had been told she must go, and where. There had not been time for more than a few words.

Luckily, too, she was now able, after a little fumbling, to find Peter's key, just where she remembered. Peter had been so nice about asking her to his lunch party last Sunday. She would be safe in Peter's house, safe from all the questions and from her own fears.

She remembered the two long facing sofas. Groping, she made her way to the farther one, the one facing the door. The cushions were soft, but the room, in the silent, lifeless chill of a closed house, seemed even colder than it had been outside.

As soon as she had rested, she found the matches and candle she remembered on the long rough mantel. She could not risk a fire. Its smoke would be a certain signal of her presence there if anyone should be watching. The light of the candle seemed safe behind the shutters. She found blankets, a deep drawer full, smelling of lavender.

She arranged these carefully on the sofa she had chosen. Perhaps she should not risk even the light of the candle any longer. She felt for the cold, sticky rolls in her shoulder bag. That would be her dinner.

Nibbling slowly, licking her fingers carefully, she settled herself under the lavender fragrance, wondering how it was possible for the cushions beneath her and the wool piled on top of her to be so cold.

Eventually she slept.

Cracks of light around the shuttered windows told her it was morning, and she could hear the muffled sound of the surf. Friday morning, she thought. It seemed she had been in this cold, dark shuttered room much longer. All of her life, she told herself, half in sorrow, half in self-contempt.

Cautiously, she went to the door. A light drift of snow had come in under the outer storm door. Carefully she swung it open, just a quarter of the way. The beach world outside was softly snow-covered. She was safe, just as she'd been told she would be. She went back to her blankets.

Later, hungry and thirsty, she again risked the light of the candle.

The water was turned off at the sink, of course, as she knew it would be. She found an empty coffee can to use as a chamberpot, then decided instead to use the toilet in the small bath off the little darkened bedroom, pleased with herself at thinking to add antifreeze from the plastic gallon container she found there.

Returning to the cupboards, she knew there was no chance of soft drinks or canned foods left to freeze and explode in a winter-closed house. She found crackers in a covered tin, small ones with seeds on them. Her hands groped, in the flickering light, and found the bottle she was looking for. Ah, vodka, and more bottles behind it.

The answer was there to her cold and hunger and her fear, as it had been to all of her problems as long as she could remember. Was I really only ten when I found out it made me forget, she wondered? Vodka, rum, whisky, gin—anything I could find and that no one might miss.

It had been only in later years she had known they were keeping her well supplied. No one ever questioned depleting stores, full bottles becoming empty ones. There were always, miraculously, new bottles in their places in the liquor closet off the kitchen, and nobody ever said a word. Nobody ever called her a wicked girl about *that.* Only about the cyanide when they thought she was going to kill herself.

She found a glass, and with the bottle in hand made her way back to the nest of blankets on the sofa. There were more bottles in the cupboard. She was safe.

Warmed by the first drink, she began to reproach herself. It had seemed such a simple thing she'd been asked to do. She *never* had thought that Edie and Mr. deBevereaux were going to be quiet forever, instead of just for a few hours. She hadn't *ever* thought that could happen.

She should never have repeated the story Edie had told her. Never. That's what started the whole thing.

Pouring into the glass in the near darkness was difficult. She would have to drink straight from the bottle. Much easier.

She should never have told *anybody* what Edie had said about that poor sick little boy, growing up all alone, no father to look after him. She knew just how that little boy must feel. If she hadn't told, nobody would have asked her to get those keys, and then none of this would have happened.

The drink made her feel a little better. After all, she had done it only with the promise that the little boy would be helped. She squinted at the faint line of daylight around the windows, thinking she was not so sure about that promise now. It bothered her that the poison bottle had been taken away from her, ever so gently, being told it was for her own good. Putting it in Mrs. Higginson's basket was awful. She was glad she hadn't done *that,* anyway. In fact, she hadn't really thought about that part of it until today, trying to answer all those questions.

She should have known not to tell anybody about *anything*.

She should have known from the start, back when she was ten. She should have known that some day it was going to happen to her, too.

31

At midmorning, with Gussie at the wheel of her small four-wheel-drive car, a twin of the one Mrs. Potter drove in Maine, the four women began a tour of Mrs. Potter's favorite spots on the island. She had not found it necessary to explain that these were chosen for a reason other than past affection and happy memories, and in fact the memories returned, at times so vividly she had to remind herself what she was actually looking for on the drive. She had dressed for a long day in the wool caftan, with trousers and heavy socks and shoes beneath, and wrapped overall in one of Gussie's soft handloomed stoles of richly colored wool. She had tucked the packet of Arnold's pain pills into her basket. What the others might consider a winter's day outing was for her, the day after the flash fire at the Scrimshaw Inn, an entirely serious quest.

The feathery snow in the night, they all exclaimed, had again transformed old delights into new ones. The hillside oriental carpet of fall in its rich colors on all sides of Altar Rock was now almost majestic in winter white, dignified to the point of small mountainhood.

Mrs. Potter, in the first of the unplanned jolts of memory,

thought of Benjie, serious and intent as a ten-year-old, searching for arrowheads there on sunny summer afternoons. As a joke, she had told him that all of the stones up there looked like arrowheads. Pick up one anywhere, she told him, and *call* it an arrowhead! Leaning over in the gravelly path of the road by the car, she had blindly picked up a stone, felt its odd smoothness to her fingers, looked at the pattern of its chipped surface, then held it up for her son's inspection. They had both gasped in disbelieving laughter. She fingered the arrowhead now, still in the bottom of her lightship basket, where she had kept it all these years as a treasure of serendipity.

Their old summer house on 'Sacacha Pond, beyond which lay the open ocean to the east, now gray and flat on a winter morning, was shuttered, quiet, looking larger than Mrs. Potter remembered, the hedges certainly better trimmed. No footprints led to its front door or small barn, and so far in the drive she had seen none leading to any other closed summer dwelling, as well as she could see from the road. Here she thought of Louisa on warm summer evenings at the piano—the weathered old grand piano, its finish crazed by years of neglect and sun. Louisa had surprised them by painting it a rich Venetian red, displaying her artistic skills even more than her less certain musical ones.

The beach at Quidnet was deserted, the only tracks in the snow covering the dunes being those of the gulls and winter seabirds. She thought of small Emily, a sprite in minuscule red bathing trunks; of Emily a few summers later, or so it seemed, in the midst of a throng of chattering teen-agers; and so few years after that, a serene young woman in white coming down the aisle on Lew's arm at the church.

"Could we manage the road into the Hidden Forest?" she asked Gussie. Skeletal trees, vast silences, dark marshes, surrounded them there. Mrs. Potter now thought about how many secret and hidden places there were on the island, not all so foreboding as this one, but places, unseen and off the beaten track, on tiny rutted roads or game trails. She thought about how much of Nantucket was still wild, uninhabited in winter or summer except by wild creatures, and how easy it would be to disappear there.

They drove to the Haulover, that narrow sandy spit of land separating harbor from ocean above Wauwinet, and there they ate the apples and cheese Gussie had brought for an early lunch, with a vacuum bottle of hot spiced cranberry punch. Mrs. Potter surreptitiously swallowed one of Arnold's pills.

All the while as Mrs. Potter looked and remembered and thought about wild places, and while they were having their car picnic, the others had been talking and laughing and producing their own summer memories. Those of the present spot, they all suddenly realized, were ones of sorrow, rather than laughter, for Mary Lynne.

"I know you all are trying every bit as hard as you can to talk about other things and not remind me of Bo," Mary Lynne told them as they finished the punch. "Just be easy about it. I'm all right. We both knew it was coming someday, and I'll always have the comfort of knowing he died doing the thing he loved best—sailing that old Indian."

They agreed, when Gussie asked them, that the long slow drive on north to Great Light would be better attempted another time and at an earlier hour. There were no car tracks ahead in the light snow and the only life they saw in that direction was a great snowy owl rising from a dune beyond the few deserted beach houses, plus the tracks of hundreds of small scampering creatures on the sand near the water. Gussie drove cautiously as she turned. There were soft patches in the yet unfrozen sand where even this rugged small car might have foundered if she had got off the narrow road, its course now blurred with the snow.

They drove to the top of what Mrs. Potter had always called "the painted hill" on their way back to town along the upper road, another high spot at which Mrs. Potter got out to stretch her legs and to look out over the pale, deserted winter calm of the harbor. Here, all of them saw it in summer blue, an ever-shifting pattern of sailboats on its surface. They thought of summer swimming and picnics and mosquito bites across the harbor on the outer arm of Coatue across the harbor, and Gussie spoke of the day Jules had swum over and back. "Of course, Scott rowed along beside him," she said, "with me in the boat. He was such a tiger." Her voice was wistful.

They drove west of town, past Dionis and then around the shores of Long Pond, briefly disturbing a resident colony of winter ducks, and Mittie told them about her favorite haunts for bird-watching there. "Ab was as enthusiastic about birding as I am," she said, "but he was a passionate duck hunter, too. That may sound like a contradiction, but he didn't think so. He gave as much to Ducks Unlimited as he spent on his guns, and if I told you, you wouldn't believe what those English guns of his cost." Her voice, too, was slightly wistful.

They viewed the many-angled houses that had been built at Madaket, rising high against the horizon, and they drove on to see where the '48 hurricane had created Esther Island out of what had once been a narrow westerly arm of Nantucket itself. They all were able to remember where they had been at the time of the storm.

On the way back to town they made a quick jog to the south shore, pausing as Mittie spoke of how much of the island had eroded there, in some places in great crumbling chunks, places where old roads had disappeared into the ocean.

Peter's beach shack was part of the tour. Shuttered, as they knew it would be against the drive of blowing sands, it was, like every other deserted place they had visited, devoid of all prints except those of birds and small mammals and the occasional sharp prints of the island deer.

In late afternoon, just as the early January dark was descending, they returned to the white house on Orange Street, where Mary Lynne gave them tea, to the accompaniment of continuing, suspicious barking from the back of the house.

Outside, the snow had nearly disappeared, as it had the day of Mrs. Potter's first village walk, melting in the unseasonably warm early winter weather. It would be cold, they all agreed, if you were walking in the wind, and probably frigid inside all the closed summer houses, but there had not yet been a really hard freeze. That, Mittie reminded them, would create its own problems in gardening. "As long as it's nice for Daffodil Festival weekend," Mary Lynne said, "it can do anything it wants to in the way of weather now. Shall I bring out little Sen-Sen and her brother now, to show you how cunning they are?"

Gussie looked at Mrs. Potter. "This girl is going to bed," she announced. "Come on, Mittie, grab your coat, if you're coming with us as far as my house. I knew I shouldn't have taken her out today, or kept her out so long."

Before Mrs. Potter drifted off to an uneasy sleep in the guest room bed under its crewel-embroidered canopy, she could think of many, *so* many, *too* many places a frightened person could hide on Nantucket, and of how easy it would be to disappear there just by stepping a few feet away from the road. There was the elephant's graveyard—a dumping ground of old cars on a blind road not far from the airport, visible only by air or to a determined explorer of back ways. Lolly might be cowering there in an abandoned auto chassis, minus its wheels.

There were places in the deep pine woods, the scene of some of their best summer picnics, when the sun was hot and the depths of the small forest were cool. Only light snow would have drifted to the soft needle-covered carpet there, and Lolly might be burrowing like an animal to find warmth.

Wherever she was, Lolly was hiding. Mrs. Potter knew that now. She was hiding not only from her, Mrs. Potter, her inquisitor, but—and far more dangerous for Lolly—from whoever had asked her to get Ozzie's office keys.

32

Mrs. Potter, ignoring the discomfort of her bandaged arm, propped the note on the breakfast table. *Borrowing the car,* she had scribbled. *Thanks. Back soon.*

She had awakened long before daylight, hearing briefly a spatter of rain on the windows, and had dressed quietly in the same loose warm clothes of the day before. As she left the house now, she was counting on Gussie's assumption that she was making a return sunrise pilgrimage to the old house on the pond, or perhaps to visit another of the places there had not been time for yesterday. Gussie had deplored the omission of 'Sconset, with its summer contrast of tiny, rose-covered dollhouses with large-scale grand estates. She had not known how carefully Mrs. Potter had eliminated those areas impossible to check on a brief, part-day driving tour.

Now the sweep of the wiper blade, turned on for a moment to wipe away soft morning mist, marked a wider arc of the compass than the pattern that had awakened Mrs. Potter from a troubled sleep. She now headed, in answer to its message, not to the east, as she was sure Gussie would guess, but back to the south shore.

The suddenly recalled pattern in her mind that had

shocked her into wakefulness was the arc a storm door would make in soft snow, pushing aside an unassuming, gentle white curve on a wooden doorstep unmarked by footprints.

She rebuked herself. If Arnold's pain pills had been less potent, she should have been aware of it yesterday afternoon. What she knew now, and should have seen then, was that the outer door of Peter's beach shack had been opened. It had been opened just wide enough for a look outside, after the snowfall and by someone from inside the small house behind the dunes.

As she drove to the shore, the roads now bare, her headlights still needed, she thought of what she must say. She knew it was Lolly who was there in the house. Lolly had run away from her questioning, probably more in dread of having her mother know about the poisoning deaths than in fear of the law.

Helen must be told now, of course. Between the three of them, mother and daughter and herself, they would figure out the best thing to do. Helen must be made to understand that Lolly had acted out of blind devotion to Tony, the one person who could have persuaded her to get those office keys. Helen would see at once that Tony needed the incriminating documents from Ozzie's office, to protect his grand scheme for a world-famous clinic.

They could, she and Helen, at least arrange for Lolly's proper defense.

It was hard to drive with the encumbrance of the stole, and Mrs. Potter's right arm was stiff and sore. It was awkward to shift gears on Gussie's small car. She drove slowly and carefully, glancing toward the east to see the first light of the sun. As she neared the head of the pond, she slowed almost to a stop, nearly stalling the motor. What, she asked herself in sudden shock, what if the lighter fluid explosion had not been an accident after all? Not just the result of Jimmy's using an unfamiliar product, labeled in a language he did not read? What if someone had put the spray can in Jimmy's hands, or even casually suggested it, as a guest of the inn might do?

What if it had been an intentional diversion, seen to be vital at that very moment, to interrupt her questioning of Lolly?

This presumed a degree of evil equal to that of putting the empty poison bottle in Beth's basket. Two gentle and innocent people, Beth and Jimmy, had been cruelly used and deeply hurt.

She drove on slowly. She had to persuade Lolly to return and confess. Even more important, she had to get Lolly's final, certain confirmation of who it was who was capable of this greater evil.

She turned onto the new stretch of road to Peter's house and pulled into the small parking area in back. A long, shiny station wagon was there before her. She was not the first to find Lolly's hiding place.

It could be Helen, she thought, in an irrational burst of hope. Then—Helen? There to rescue the daughter whose whereabouts she apparently hadn't troubled to learn? Not likely. She sat motionless in the car, her eyes fixed on the bare doorstep.

As she sat there, the terror returned. This was the terror she had felt in the cupola, thinking of the open roof walk overhead, five stories above the cobblestones. This was what she felt when she opened the Winthrop desk with its menacing array of hypodermic syringes and needles. If not Helen, it must be Tony, driving the Scrimshaw station wagon. Tony Ferencz had arrived before her, threatening Lolly, perhaps expecting her own arrival, waiting for her, to settle all scores.

She was shaking now from fright and indecision. Then she thought of Lolly, alone and afraid. She might not be too late. Some way the two of them together would escape.

As she forced herself to leave the car, the only sounds were those of the surf on the beach in front of the dune grasses and the harsh cry of a gull overhead in the growing light of the sky.

She took a long breath, approached the step, and pulled open the outer door. "Lolly?" she called loudly as she rapped vigorously on the closed door inside it, still not sure she had courage to open it. "Lolly, are you there?"

At the same moment as she began to turn the doorknob, she heard two quick clicks, then the sharp, sudden, heart-stopping bark of exploding gunpowder, a shock of sound that held her feet on the doorstep as it registered, not in her mind but in the pit of her stomach.

The door swung inward.

Even before her eyes could accept the sight, she was halted by a smell in the air, a smell that took her instantly to lessons on a half-forgotten rifle range, to times of shooting skeet with Lew, the smell of a just fired gun.

Then, in the faint light from the open door, she saw Lolly Latham, her shattered skull bleeding, her cracked and bloody spectacles askew on what was left of her face, her body sliding slowly, slowly, sidewise against the cushions, held partly upright by the wrapping of blankets around her.

There was a small movement in the darkness behind the banquette, and she froze in her terror. Then she recognized the familiar stocky figure. As Peter spoke, the terror lifted. Whatever had happened, whatever the evidence of her eyes, she would have the comfort of Peter's presence, and he of hers.

"We're too late, Potter," he said slowly. "Seems we both figured out where she might have run to hide, and I got here only just before you did. Then I turned my back for a minute and—I expect you heard the gunshot, even from outside the door. I couldn't move fast enough to get it away from her."

"Peter, oh, *Peter*. I'm so glad it's you!" Mrs. Potter was nearly incoherent in her relief. "I was sure it was Tony, and when I heard the gun I thought he'd killed Lolly. What has happened is ghastly beyond belief, but at least I know *he* isn't the one standing where you are, holding the gun and in-tending to shoot me next."

Peter remained where he was, behind the long sofa. "You're all right," he said briefly. "Tony isn't here."

"It's too late, isn't it?" she asked. "There isn't anything at all we could do now?" A glance at Lolly's face was her an-swer.

"Did she bring the gun here to shoot herself? When did

you guess where she was? What did she say when you got here? How did she get here from the Scrimshaw?" Mrs. Potter, freed from her terror, could not restrain the almost hysterical flow of her questions.

"I thought she was asleep when I came in. When I turned my back to see about getting some light in here, she shot herself. That's all I know." Peter remained motionless behind the banquette, and his voice was unsteady. Mrs. Potter remained, still unable to move, on the doorstep.

"The poor kid was always afraid she'd do this, you know," Peter went on, his voice now stronger and more confident. "I guess she never got over her father's killing himself this way."

"Where's the gun?" Mrs. Potter asked, unwilling to step into the room. As she spoke, she saw the dull gleam of metal. "You've got it!"

More slowly now, she added another question. "How could *you* have the gun, Peter?"

Even as she spoke, she knew. Even as Peter was saying that he'd taken the gun from Lolly's fingers, Mrs. Potter knew who had brought the gun to the beach shack and who had fired it.

"Peter, oh, no. Not you, Peter, *not you.*" She was almost whispering. "It couldn't be you. You didn't have any *reason.*"

Peter stepped forward slightly and his face was visible in the light from around the shuttered windows, the same light that had showed the cold gleam of the gun. "Why did you have to show up now?" he asked, his voice low and despairing. "Everything would have been all right if you'd got here an hour later, or if I hadn't decided to let her have a day here by herself, so she'd get good and drunk and knock herself out. I didn't want to have her *look* at me."

Mrs. Potter was unable to speak, unable to move.

"Everything would have been all right," he went on. "First everybody would have said, *'Poor Lolly, just like her father.'* And then, later on, you'd have figured out Tony shot her, and told all the guys, and even if you couldn't prove it, their beloved Count Tony Ferencz would have had to leave the island."

The undisguised hatred in Peter's voice as he spoke the name provided all the answer Mrs. Potter needed. He did have a reason, then, a reason that had set in motion all of the strange and terrible events of the past ten days.

"You hated Tony," she said wonderingly. "You were determined to get rid of him. You were jealous, you thought he was taking your place with the others as the center of your little world."

"It's my world. It's my island!" Peter spoke defiantly now, although he did not move from his position in the half darkness. "Nantucket's *my* island. I built up the kind of place at the Scrimshaw that everybody loves. The first money I made there went into this shack. Nantucket's *my* turf. And then Tony showed up."

"But people still loved you, Peter. You hadn't lost your friends."

"Oh, *no?*" His reply was scornful. "How do you think I felt, Potter, seeing them fall for that phony? He was just a piece of cardboard. They were falling all over themselves trying to set up the kind of place for him I'd been planning and working for all my life. My Nantucket year-round resort inn. Supposedly for health and beauty, because that's what the guys want, for losing a few pounds, sure, but *fun. My* place. *My* guys."

Mrs. Potter, still in the doorway, saw a montage of hasty pictures in her mind, all of Peter. Of Peter teasing, amusing, and surprising them. Of Peter's picnics and little dinners, of Peter's frogs and of groups clustered around a piano, of Peter providing good food and music and laughter. She could only now glimpse the unknown, unsuspected Peter who demanded undivided adoration in return. He could not share his island. He could not share his guys.

"None of what happened was my fault," he went on fiercely. "How could I know Lolly would be dumb enough to *kill* those two, just to get the keys? All I needed were those old papers about that crazy kid of Dee's and I could have got

Tony off the island for good. Nobody would have got hurt at all if she hadn't been so *goddamned* dumb."

Mrs. Potter did not interrupt as he poured out his resentments. "Dee wasn't going to do anything. She told me so. I had to have those papers in my own hands, not stuck away in some old cubbyhole file at Ozzie's office."

He gestured contemptuously toward the slumped body on the banquette in front of him, and again Mrs. Potter could see the metal of the gun, the smooth indentations of its chamber catching a glimmer of light. "She felt sorry for the poor crazy kid after Edie told her the story, and she spilled it out to me. I told her we might be able to help him, if she could just get me the keys for a couple of hours. Then the first thing I knew she'd killed two people and come running to me telling me how sorry she was and how she didn't mean to do it."

Mrs. Potter, too, stared at Lolly's body, closer to the light than Peter's face. It was no longer visibly bleeding.

"What the *hell* did I get myself into?" Peter's voice rose, a shout of bewilderment and anger. "What the *hell* went wrong? I didn't ask for any of this mess!" He was now almost screaming.

Mrs. Potter summoned courage for another question of her own. "Could you have saved Edie's life that day she was choking?" she asked.

"Oh, my *God!* I didn't even know then what Lolly had *done!*" Peter raged. "Do you think I'd have let her pull a crazy stunt like that at the *inn?*"

Still accusatorial, he returned to the subject of Tony. "I spent all summer trying to make them see he was no good. For a while, after you got back, I thought you'd take the bait and think he'd killed Heidecker's husband, or maybe that he was using dangerous drugs. I almost had you scared enough with that one."

Mrs. Potter was again briefly silent, realizing how her suspicions of Tony had been fed. When she spoke, she regretted her words as soon as they were uttered. "You can't blame Lolly for what you did with the cyanide bottle," she said flatly. "You knew what that would do to Beth. And what about Jimmy? How badly is he burned? How do you feel about *that?* What are your guys going to think of you now?"

"They aren't going to know. You aren't going to tell them." The rage in Peter's voice was cold now, as he stepped forward toward where Mrs. Potter still stood, framed in the doorway against the pale January dawn.

Almost without thought, she slammed shut the door she was holding. As she did, she heard the heavy sound of Peter falling. She shuddered at the thought of blood-slippery pine floorboards, but she had time to regain the seat and key of Gussie's small car.

She spun into a quick reverse turn. Almost before she was on the new road leading to the pavement, and then to town and safety, she heard the roar of the heavy car taking off behind her.

There was no way to outdistance its menace. She even knew exactly at what bend, once she was on the main road, Peter would overtake her at the head of the pond. She knew exactly at what spot he could force her car from the road into the ditch, and at what point she would again see the dull gleam of the gun.

There was no escape for either of them. Peter had shot Lolly, and now he would have to shoot her as well.

At the end of the new road from Peter's shack, she did not hesitate. Instead of following its well-defined turn left onto the road that would lead past the pond and to town, she drove straight ahead, the gas pedal pushed to the floor, across the old intersection, long since blocked off to traffic.

As she hurtled across the ragged pavement edge, already pierced with growth of rough beach grasses, she could see the abrupt ten-foot drop on her right, with the sand of the beach below and the white line of the surf just beyond. The small car faltered on the edge of the drop. She felt the ground give way beneath the right rear wheel, but speed and momentum carried her forward, and she found herself back on the long-abandoned shorefront track she remembered.

Behind her, the heavy station wagon had taken heed of her barely averted plunge onto the beach below the cliffside.

Laboring, it was making its own track a few feet farther from the edge. Thus slowed, it remained behind her.

So far, she had gambled successfully on finding and using the old road tracks. It would be only a moment before the car behind would find them too. Ahead, just ahead, had to be the particular stretch she remembered so well. It had to be there still if she was to win.

She shifted into four-wheel drive, forcing herself to accept the painful slowing of speed and aware that now the big car behind her was closing the gap between them. Then, although not as near as she had hoped, she saw the short stretch she had gambled to find—there where she had once, years ago, been entrapped in the old blue convertible, stuck for hours in the hot sun waiting for a tow truck from town.

With a long breath she gripped the wheel and drove Gussie's car into what she knew was deep, soft sand.

Her wheels spun and began to dig in. She forced herself to accept a snail's pace. The station wagon behind was closing in fast, and she could imagine Peter's face, distorted in rage and frustration, judging the distance before his attack. Thinking of his square hand on his recently fired gun, she knew that if she failed he would shoot her here. She would die alongside a deserted Nantucket beach road, and he would be convinced that she was a part of the things that had gone wrong in his life, wrong beyond his intent or his comprehension.

There was one last gamble, that she could manage to get through the sand and the heavier car could not. If they both were stuck there, she would be an easy target for Peter's .38.

The small car groaned, halted, then pulled slowly forward to firm ground. It was not until then that Mrs. Potter allowed herself a clear look in the mirror at the left of her car door.

The station wagon was no longer the pursuer, but a prisoner. She watched, as she increased the short distance between them, to see the familiar stocky figure step out of the stalled station wagon, now up to its hubcaps in the sand.

She was still near enough to hear Peter's last wordless scream of rage, like that of a wounded animal. She heard the single gunshot, which she knew, this time, was not intended for her.

To regain the traveled road ahead, Mrs. Potter had to crash through the back of a wooden barrier, one she knew must carry on its other side warnings of erosion and danger, an old sign declaring the road long closed. That was easy—a crash of weathered white-painted splinters. Past small boarded-up cottages, she turned abruptly left, again on a paved town road, to safety.

Her memory of Nantucket back roads had not failed her. Now, shaking as she drove, Mrs. Potter had to make herself remember where the police headquarters building was. The only time she had ever been there was when Benjie at sixteen got his first speeding ticket.

After she left the small building, Mrs. Potter, still several blocks short of Gussie's house, pulled to the side of a small street, alone in early morning quiet and for the first time again aware of the pain in her right arm and shoulder. Tears streamed down her face as, for a moment blinded, she wept helplessly. Poor little Lolly. Poor Peter, who in his rage to be loved, didn't know what the *hell* he had got himself into, or what kind of hell he had made of his life.

33

"Tony?" Gussie asked brightly. "Didn't you all know? He's gone to Palm Springs. Really a much more suitable place for his diet center than here on Nantucket—don't you all agree? None of us was really rich enough for him."

"I told you he was a bastard," Dee said in Mrs. Potter's right ear. "He'd have figured out a way to look good even if Peter had managed to expose him with those papers of mine. I say good riddance, and I'm certainly not going to file suit against him now. I never intended to, in spite of Ozzie's urging."

In answer to Gussie, Mary Lynne nodded emphatically. "Those old Chattanooga skinflint lawyers wouldn't listen to my buying Mittie's house for him, anyway, as I guess you all know," she said. "They've got everything tied up tight as a crocus sack, and I'm just plain going to have to get down on my knees to them for every red cent Bo Heidecker left me." She sounded totally unconcerned. "Now let me tell you about another new idea for the Daffodil Festival."

It was Monday, the last Monday in January, a little more than two weeks after Lolly's death and Peter's. No one at Gussie's house, where Les Girls were meeting for lunch, each bearing a sandwich in her lightship basket as they had in years past, had needed to speak of this today. Their shared knowledge and sorrow had been talked out. At least for the moment, they were bravely pretending that Les Girls, as a weekly institution, would some way go on, in spite of their grief. And perhaps, Mrs. Potter thought, it would. Women their age had learned to be both strong and resilient.

Today's news was that Beth would be back with them soon. Laurence and Paula said she was fine again. Awfully thin, for her, but beginning to get a little appetite back. One of the granddaughters is coming with her to stay for a while, they said, the one who wants to study astronomy and has got a temporary job at the science library.

There was a moment of silence. *Poor Lolly* was unspoken.

"The news about Helen is about as good as we could hope for," Leah offered next. "You all know, I expect, that she's gone off somewhere in New Jersey to study hospital administration, to make a career of it. I don't think she'll be back on the island, but at least she's going to try to make a new life for herself."

There was another long moment of silence. None of them could yet bear to speak of Peter. The pain was too raw. Each of them felt that she had in some way contributed to his destruction. "We took him for granted," Gussie had said in private mourning with Mrs. Potter. "We should have seen how jealous he was of Tony, before it was too late."

They knew that Jimmy's sight would be somewhat impaired, but they had arranged for his care and for a new job on the island when he returned, as a helper to Hans Muller in the bakery. Jadine was already at work part time behind the counter at The Portuguese Bread Man, in her free time from her training as a bank teller, having announced that she was ready for a new line of work.

All of them had agreed that they had been spared, not the sorrow of Lolly's death and Peter's, but the indignity of the public ordeal of the murder trial that would have resulted if Peter had lived.

"The island would have been so crowded with reporters

and cameramen it would have sunk under water," Mary Lynne said. "We wouldn't have been able to walk across the street without being interviewed, and heaven only knows what would have been said about us. We were the ones who were there when Edie died. We were the ones who knew Ozzie best, we were the friends of Lolly's mother, and Peter's regulars at the Scrim. We'd have been massacred."

Mrs. Potter privately agreed with this. A trial would have resulted in a public caricaturing of her friends. She felt sure that they would have been shown as shallow, useless, incredibly frivolous women, with their fashionably thin bodies and their big Nantucket houses. They would have been pictured as rich, idle, and useless, with no acknowledgment of their contributions to the life of the island, their hours of hard work in the community, their generosity of spirit and money, their genuine concern for others.

Dee, perhaps even more aware of all this than Mrs. Potter was, insisted on a complete change of subject. "About Mittie's house," she said, "there's no more problem about its being sold, even if Mary Lynne can't buy it and wouldn't want to now if she could. I know the name may sound a bit alarming, but a very nice man, a Mr. Ali Akbar, just signed the sales contract this morning. Wonderful price—highest ever paid for anything on the island!"

"I'm delighted, of course," Mittie said. "Daddy would never let us be intolerant about nationalities. However, I don't intend to spend any part of the money fixing up the old house on Main Street." Turning squarely to face Dee, she spoke with youthful insouciance. "Since Dee's going to be rolling in money with the commission, she's going to find a place of her own . . ."

Dee's hat brim nodded agreement, and Mrs. Potter felt a quick hope that the sum would assure Mikai—Mikey—a good many years, perhaps *enough* years, at Fieldstone Hall.

Mittie had not finished. ". . . so I'm moving into the carriage house apartment and furnishing it with all my favorite pieces of Mummy's, and moving all Ab's ducks and stuff into the old house, to help that sell, too, as soon as Dee finds

THE NANTUCKET DIET MURDERS271

another rich buyer. Now comes the nicest part. With the money, George is going to help me set up my own landscaping and garden service business, with our own greenhouses, as soon as we find the right location on the island. George has a wonderful business head, naturally, after all those years running his school. And we've decided on a church wedding in September, as soon as we get the business well started."

Mrs. Potter thought wildly that Mittie was about to ask them all to be bridesmaids, in chiffon and maline. Clearly, Gussie had the same flight of fancy. They grinned at each other companionably, sure that this, at least, would not happen.

Mittie still had not finished. ". . . Before that, next week, as a matter of fact, I'm going to Boston for a few weeks. When I come back, I expect you all to say I look wonderfully *rested*, the thing people say when they know someone's had a face-lift. That's another part of Tony's program for me I couldn't afford before."

Mrs. Potter controlled an inward shudder. She had once, hoping to counteract the effects of the Arizona sun, consulted a plastic surgeon herself, about what her friends assured her was a comparatively simple operation. When she found out what it actually entailed, she had left his office in horror. Horror compounded later, she recalled, by his bill just for describing the procedure. Still, this was Mittie's business, and those clear young eyes belonged in a younger-looking face.

"I think we should drink a toast to George and Mittie," Gussie said. "I squeezed fresh juice for us, but how about a glass of white wine first? I'll be right back."

"Let's toast me a little bit, while we're at it," Leah said. "I've got a job too, more or less. Victor's *such* a fine writer—you all know that—and he's selling his new novels as fast as I can think up the plots for him. The movie people were even here talking with us—remember, at the Scrim, the day of the fire, Genia? We may even have a new slogan. 'Victor Sandys, the man who put *man* in romance!' Don't you *love* it? And he won't have to be Vicki Sands anymore."

Mrs. Potter thought of Peter's description of Tony as a

cardboard man. He had never been anything but that, even to Gussie. Just a cardboard figure in a romantic novel.

"Speaking of diets," she said, although they were not and it was only the thought of Tony that made her bring it up, "I lost eight pounds this month, with all this Nantucket dieting. I think I should be toasted too, particularly since I figure roughly that I've lost eight pounds every two years for the last forty years, then spent the next two gaining it back again. That comes out to one thousand, six hundred pounds—right, Gussie? I have lost more than three-quarters of a ton, and I expect to round that out to a full two thousand if I live that long, which I fully intend to do. Aren't you proud of me?"

"Not of your arithmetic," Gussie told her. "Get out your yellow pad. You always *were* shaky on zeroes."

Dee spoke up suddenly. "You know who are the best diet authorities in the country?" she asked. *"Us! We* are! We got in on the whole thing at the start, when we were about twenty! I'm not sure calories were ever talked about before then— does anybody know? Our mothers and grandmothers didn't diet . . ."

"Maybe they were more concerned with having enough to eat," Leah said unexpectedly.

"Well, maybe," Dee conceded. "The thing is that *we're* the ones who have lived through the whole history of modern dieting. I've got to look that up—when the word began to mean eating to get thinner!" Her enthusiasm for the topic was mounting. "Remember the milk-and-banana diet? That's the first one I ever tried. Three bananas a day, and three glasses of skim milk. You alternate⌐ them, spaced out in six so-called meals through the day."

"How about the grapefruit diet?" Mittie asked quickly. "I can't remember what the actual meals were, but you ate a half grapefruit before each one, and that was supposed to do the trick."

"Remember the micro-macro thing?" Leah said. "We ate all we could hold of unsalted brown rice, and decided everything as to whether it was Yin or Yang."

"Remember the three-day one with cottage cheese and

sliced canned peaches for every meal?" Mary Lynne asked. "You got a toasted RyKrisp with it if you felt too awfully deprived. I could lose five pounds in those three days every time."

"The real crash was the airline pilots' diet," Gussie recalled. "I can't remember much about it except that it was a killer and you only had three or four hundred calories a day. That was for when you absolutely *had* to be ten pounds thinner by Saturday, to fit into something or other."

"Tiger milk!" Mrs. Potter exclaimed. "That was the forerunner of all the Metrecal things, only you mixed it up yourself. Instant dried milk and eggs and salad oil and whatever else I can't remember. It was drinkable, but a terrible bore. After a day or so you began to think you'd beg on the streets for something to *chew.*"

"Another one I used to fall for," Mary Lynne admitted, "was the one where if you were absolutely dying for one particular thing, like a hot fudge sundae, it was all right to have one. You just had a hot fudge sundae, nothing else, for one meal. After that supposedly you were calmed down enough to go back to the lettuce and carrot sticks."

"Remember the Drinking Man's Diet?" Gussie asked. "Genia and I thought that was a dandy for a while."

"Sort of like the Doctor's Quick Weight Loss, wasn't it, except with a martini before dinner?" Mrs. Potter said. "It was mostly proteins, which Lew thought was great for the cattle business and the ranch. Breakfast could be a big cheese omelet as long as you didn't have any toast with it; lunch could be all kinds of cold meats and mayonnaise and a handful of salted nuts; dinner, lots of steak and not much else. Maybe you got a little jaundiced after a week or so, but you could count on losing ten or twelve pounds in two weeks on that one."

"Until the next two weeks, when it started coming back pretty fast," Gussie recalled cheerfully. "My choice was the one with sherry and prunes—remember, Genia?"

"A glass of sherry with every meal," Mrs. Potter said, "including breakfast. I can't remember which meal was which—

one was six stewed prunes, one was two hard-boiled eggs, and one was a small steak. I suppose it didn't much matter."

"The Scarsdale Diet wasn't bad, do you think?" Leah asked. "One of the restaurants here on the island made quite a good thing of that for a while. It was really my favorite for a long while, although I certainly didn't like Dr. Tarnower."

"You know, I'm going to do an article on all this and see if *Éclat* will buy it," Dee said. "A sort of summing up of all the diets we've lived through—the works. While I'm at it, I might include everybody's favorite all-time diet tips."

"Mine would be simple," Gussie said. "Don't eat anything out of the package, and don't eat standing up. Put it on a plate, look at it, and then sit down to eat it nicely, if you're going to eat it at all."

"Always say you don't eat candy unless it's *white*," Leah offered. "That's almost foolproof. How often do you see divinity these days, anyway?"

Mrs. Potter interrupted. "That sort of contradicts another diet I just remembered," she said. "One of those calories-don't-count ones. You ate pretty much what you wanted to as long as you *didn't* eat anything white. Or anything that had any white ingredients—flour, sugar, milk, rice, bread, pasta. Remember that one?"

"I've learned to cut a sandwich in thirds, drugstore style," Mittie said, returning to the subject of diet tips. "You cut off one corner to make a triangle. Then you put your knife on the opposite corner and cut the rest in two. Plain halves never look like much, and four quarters look like four bites. This way you're convinced you've got a sandwich and a half."

Mary Lynne spoke soberly. "We've got to remember that we're going to slip once in a while. My advice is this—don't finish it, just because you started. The very minute you can stop gobbling, throw the stuff out, whatever it is, or drown it under cold water in the sink. You'll have to feel guilty about a few hundred little old calories, maybe, but not about *thousands*."

Mrs. Potter saw that Dee was looking at her expectantly. "The best thing I know is to brush my teeth three times a day, just as soon as I can after every meal," she said. "My dentist is very happy with me, and he says I'm probably saving myself some expensive periodontal work later on. It's the best safeguard I know against eating between meals—it simply makes it too much trouble."

She looked at Dee. "And what's yours?" she asked. "Although I can't believe you ever needed to diet."

"Don't be silly," Dee replied. "I learned mine the hard way, too, and a long time ago. It's just this: *Don't eat when you aren't hungry.* If you think you are, maybe you're just thirsty—*drink a glass of water.* Maybe you're just tired—*do something else,* like taking a walk if you've been working at your desk. You may just need to go to the bathroom—*go.* You might be putting off something you should be doing—*do it.* Just don't get mixed up, that's all I say, about what's sending you signals."

"That one's great," Gussie said. "Now, how about a glass of wine?"

As she passed the tray of filled glasses, she momentarily offered a new topic. "Did we tell you all that we finally showed up for our Portuguese bread lesson?" she asked. "You'll love it! There we were, Genia and I, on a couple of straight chairs in the middle of the big bakery kitchen. Standing up in front and obviously expecting us to take notes, was our young Harvard MBA."

"With a lecture on the action of yeast and gluten," Mrs. Potter added. "This came after we'd been shown all the giant commercial mixers and the big bake ovens and the cupboards with specially controlled humidity. For what he called 'proofing,' which is what we call letting the bread rise."

"We acted terribly interested, of course," Gussie continued, "since Hans had been nice enough to make time for us. I mostly just enjoyed watching Mary Rezendes. She sat in a chair beside where Hans was standing, and she kept beaming up at him and once in a while patting his hand."

"It was rather warm," Mrs. Potter went on, "and I found myself pressing my fingernails into my palms trying to keep from nodding."

"The only really interesting part was that Hans's father came in at the end," Gussie said. "He's here on a visit from St. Louis to look over the operations. I could see he's delighted with everything. In fact, he seemed to be fascinated by Nantucket, and I think he may be staying on for a bit."

Mrs. Potter was inwardly groaning at the thought of another wonderful man in Gussie's life. If Gussie became Mrs. Klaus Muller (it was possible—Helen had said he was a widower), she would become Hans Muller's stepmother. If Hans and Mary got married, she would be Mary's stepmother-in-law. Stepmother-in-law to her cleaning lady's granddaughter, and step-something to Manny, when he got back from his Fort Lauderdale condominium in the spring. Only Gussie could manage this social tangle gracefully. She would always bet on Gussie. And Teresa.

"That ends the chapter on learning to bake Portuguese bread," Mrs. Potter said, trying not to think about these complications. "There's one other piece of news. February is time to prune roses at the ranch. Gussie already knows—I'm leaving tomorrow on the early plane for Boston, and then to head west."

As she spoke, she thought of mountain valleys of pale winter topaz, of blue cloudless skies, of mountains holding violet shadows at sunset, of cold nights and dry, bright sunny days. She could hear the morning question of the Mexican doves in the tall pine trees around the ranch house. *Who cooks for you?* they'd be asking. *Who cooks for you?*

What Mrs. Potter did not know was that the Gulf Stream was bringing a Tuesday of fog, grounding all planes from the island. Gussie would be waving at the morning boat as it rounded Brant Point, and she would be scrabbling in her lighthouse basket for pennies.

JULES BERNER: GUSSIE'S SOUR CREAM APPLE PANCAKES

Peel and thinly slice **2 firm tart apples** and brown gently in **2 T. butter**. Whisk together **¼ c. milk**, **2 T. sour cream**, **¼ c. flour**, **¼ t. salt**, and **2 egg yolks**; fold in **2 egg whites**, stiffly beaten. Arrange a fourth of apple slices with **1 t. butter** on hot griddle or skillet at 375°, and cover with a fourth of the batter. Fry until golden, turn carefully. Sprinkle with **sugar** and keep warm until all are cooked. Serve with additional **sour cream**.

NANTUCKET CRANBERRY CUP PUDDINGS

Mix **1 c. sugar** with **2 c. flour** sifted with **2½ t. baking powder**. Stir in **⅔ c. milk**, **1 egg**, and **3 T. melted butter**, then **2 c. cranberries**. Fill 12 greased muffin cups, bake 20–25 min. at 350°. Serve hot (or reheated) with old-fashioned pudding sauce: Heat in double boiler **½ c. butter**, **¾ c. cream**, and **1 c. sugar**; add **brandy** to taste.

LEW POTTER: MOCHA WALNUT TORTE

Beat **6 egg whites** and **½ t. cream of tartar** to soft peaks, gradually beat in **½ c. sugar**; set aside. Combine **6 egg yolks**, **6 T. strong cold coffee**, and **1 t. vanilla**. Gradually add sifted dry ingredients: **1½ c. flour**, **½ t. salt**, **1 t. baking powder**, and **1 c. sugar**. Beat well. Gently fold into beaten whites, along with **1 c. broken walnuts**. Spoon into ungreased 10″ tube pan, bake 40–45 min. at 375°. Invert until cool, remove from pan. Slice in thirds crosswise, fill and frost with **2 c. cream**, whipped, flavored to taste with **chocolate syrup**.